Fox River Valley PLD
555 Barrington Ave., Dundee, IL 60118
www.frvpld.info
Renew online or call 847-590-8706

TWELVE DAYS

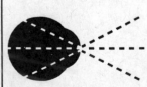

This Large Print Book carries the Seal of Approval of N.A.V.H.

TWELVE DAYS

ALEX BERENSON

WHEELER PUBLISHING

A part of Gale, Cengage Learning

GALE
CENGAGE Learning·

Farmington Hills, Mich • San Francisco • New York • Waterville, Maine
Meriden, Conn • Mason, Ohio • Chicago

GALE
CENGAGE Learning

LIBRARY OF CONGRESS CATALOGING-IN-PUBLICATION DATA

Berenson, Alex.
  Twelve days / Alex Berenson. — Large print edition.
    pages cm. – (Wheeler publishing large print hardcover)
    ISBN 978-1-4104-7506-0 (hardcover) — ISBN 1-4104-7506-9 (hardcover)
    1. United States. Central Intelligence Agency—Fiction. 2. Intelligence officers—Fiction. 3. Large type books. I. Title.
  PS3602.E75146T88 2015
  813'.6—dc22   2014047523

Published in 2015 by arrangement with G. P. Putnam's Sons, a member of Penguin Group (USA) LLC, a Penguin Random House Company

Printed in the United States of America
1 2 3 4 5 6 7 19 18 17 16 15

For Max Cohodes,
the baddest dude around

PROLOGUE:
TWELVE DAYS . . .

MUMBAI, INDIA

For as long as he could remember, Vikosh Jain had wanted to see India. His family's homeland for a hundred generations. The world's largest democracy. The birthplace of his religion.

While his friends moved out after college, he lived at home, paying off his loans and saving money for what he knew would be an epic adventure. The trip became an obsession. He mapped every train ride across the subcontinent, Mumbai to Delhi, Kashmir to Madras. Finally, when he'd saved the twelve thousand dollars he'd budgeted for a ten-week trip, he bought his ticket.

What a fool he'd been.

After a month, he couldn't wait to get home. He was sick of India. Sick *with* India, too. He'd stayed away from street food and drank only bottled water. Even so, he found himself glued to a toilet a week after he arrived. The cheekier travel websites called what had happened to him "the Delhi diet." It sounded like a joke, but by the time the doxycycline kicked in, he'd lost ten pounds. He could hardly walk a flight of stairs. His skin let him pass for local, but his gut was suburban New Jersey through and through.

Not just his gut. Coming here had taught him how American he really was. Every time he stepped into the streets, he was overwhelmed. By the dust coating his mouth. The shouting, honking, hawking crowds. The pushing and shoving and relentless begging. The way the men pawed women on buses and streetcars. He felt disconnected from all of them, even the ones who had money. Especially the ones who had money. He'd planned to spend a week with his father's family in Delhi, but he left after two days. He couldn't stand the way his aunt screeched at her maids and gardeners, like they weren't people at all.

Before the trip, his parents had warned him his expectations were unrealistic. When he emailed home to complain, long paragraphs of frustration, his father had answered in one sentence: *You need to accept it for what it is.* And after another long screed: *Don't you see? This is why we left.*

Even as Vik read those words, his stomach pulled a 720-degree spin, like a reckless snowboarder had taken up residence in his gut. He wondered what he'd eaten this time. He wasn't scheduled to fly home for another six weeks. But enough. Enough was enough. He clicked over to united.com and found that for only two hundred dollars he could change his flight. He could leave this very night. He tried to convince himself to stay, that he would be quitting, betraying his heritage. But India wasn't his country. Never had been. Never would be.

He reached for his credit card.

Now, after an endless taxi ride to Chhatrapati Shivaji International Airport, an hour-long wait to enter the terminal, three bag searches, two X-rays, and a barking immigration officer, Vik was almost free. He had maybe the worst seat on the plane, 45A, a window in the cabin's last row. So be it. He'd be close to the toilets.

Nick Cuse had captained nonstops to Mumbai and Delhi for two years. After twenty-eight years at Continental — and he would always think of CAL as his employer, never mind the merger or the name on the side of the jet — he could choose his runs. Most captains with his seniority preferred Hong

9

Kong or Tokyo, well-run airports that weren't surrounded by slums like the one in Mumbai. But Cuse had started as a Navy pilot, landing F-14s on carrier decks. He was keenly aware that every year commercial aircraft became more automated. Every year, pilots had less to do. He wanted to end his career as something other than a glorified bus driver. Mumbai was a lot of things, but it was rarely boring. Twice he'd had to abort landings for slum kids running across the runway, airport cops chasing them like a scene from a bad movie.

His co-pilot, Henry Franklin, was also ex-Navy, just young enough to have flown sorties in the first Gulf War. They'd shared the cockpit three days earlier, and Cuse was happy to have Franklin with him for the ride back. Ninety-nine times out of a hundred, a civilian with a week of training could have done what they were about to do. But the hundredth time defined the job. A good pilot felt a crisis coming before his instruments did, and defused it before it became serious enough to be a threat. Cuse had that sixth sense, and he saw it in Franklin. Though the guy was a bit sharp to the crew.

Now they sat side by side in the cockpit making final preflight checks, their relief crew sitting at the back of the cockpit. A flight this long required another captain and first officer. Their Boeing 777 was just about full, making weight and balance calculations easy. Two hundred sixty-one passengers, seventeen crew members. Two-seven-eight human souls traveling eight thousand miles, over the Hindu Kush, the Alps, the Atlantic. They would fly in darkness from takeoff to landing, the sun chasing them west, never catching them.

Every time you leave the earth, it's a miracle, Cuse's first instructor at Pensacola had told him. *You come back down, that's another. A miracle of human invention, human ingenuity, human cunning. Never forget that, no matter how routine it may seem. Always respect it.*

"Captain," Franklin said. "We're topped up." An eight-thousand-mile flight into the jet stream required the 777 to leave Mumbai with full tanks, forty-five thousand gallons of aviation-grade kerosene. The fuel itself weighed three hundred thousand pounds, accounting for almost half the jet's takeoff weight. They were carrying fuel to carry fuel, an inherent problem with long-range flights.

Cuse glanced at his watch, a platinum Rolex, his wife's present to him on the day they signed their divorce papers. Nine years later, he still didn't know why she'd given it to him. Or why he'd kept it. 11:36 p.m. Four minutes before scheduled departure. They'd leave on time. By Mumbai standards they had a good night to fly, seventy degrees, a breeze coming off the Indian Ocean to push away smog from trash fires and diesel-spewing minibuses. He looked over his displays one more time. Perfect.

Cuse liked to keep the cockpit door open as long as possible, a throwback to the days when pilots didn't regard every passenger as a potential terrorist. Now the purser poked his head inside. "Cabin ready for pushback, sir."

"Thank you, Carl. You can close the door."

"Yes, sir." The purser switched on the cockpit lock and pulled shut the door.

"Cockpit locked, Captain," Franklin said. In aviation lingo, he was the "pilot monitoring," with the job of talking to the tower and watching the instruments. Cuse was the "pilot flying," responsible for handling the plane.

"Thank you, Henry."

"Greetings, United Flight 49. I'm Carl Fisher, your purser. We've closed the cabin door and are making final preparations for our flight to Newark. At this point, United requires you to put your cell phone on airplane mode. To make the flight more relaxing for you and everyone around you, we don't allow in-flight calls. But you are free to use approved electronic devices once we've taken off. The captain has informed me that he's expecting our flight time to be sixteen hours. We do recommend that you keep your seat belt fastened for the duration of the flight in case we run into any rough air, as is common over the Himalayas . . ."

Vik thumbed in one last text to his mother — *On the plane, see you tomorrow* — and then turned off his phone. Even if his stomach settled down, he doubted he'd sleep. He was caught between the cabin wall and a chubby twenty-something woman wearing a Smith College sweatshirt and hemp pants. She smelled of onion chutney and positive thinking.

She caught him looking at her and extended a hand, exposing a dirty Livestrong bracelet. "We're going to be neighbors for sixteen hours, we should know each other's names. Jessica."

Vik awkwardly twisted his arm across the seat to shake. "Vik. Let me guess. Yoga retreat?"

"That obvious? How about you?"

"I came to visit family."

"That's so wonderful. Getting to see the place where you're from."

"Sure is." Despite himself, Vik liked this woman. He wished he could have seen the country through her eyes instead of his own.

It was 11:50 p.m. by Cuse's Rolex when he swung the jet onto 09/27. For years, the airport here had tried to operate a second, intersecting runway, a prescription for disaster. Complaints from pilots and its own controllers finally forced it to stop. Now 09/27 was the airport's sole runway. At this moment, it was empty, two miles of concrete that ran west toward the Indian Ocean.

"United Airlines four-nine heavy, you are cleared for takeoff on runway nine. Wind one-two-zero, ten knots." The air-traffic controllers here had call-center English, clear and precise.

"United forty-nine heavy, cleared for takeoff on nine." Franklin clicked off.

Like all new-generation jets, the 777-200 was fly-by-wire. Computers controlled its engines, wings, and flaps. But Boeing had designed the cockpit to preserve the comforting illusion that pilots physically handled the plane. Instead of dialing a knob or pushing a joystick, Cuse pushed the twin white throttle handles about halfway forward. The

14

response was immediate. The General Electric engines on the wings spooled up, sending a shiver through the airframe.

Cuse lifted his hand. "N1." For routine takeoffs, the 777 had an auto-throttle system for routine takeoffs, though he could override it at any time.

"N1." Franklin tapped instructions into a touch screen beside the throttle handles. "Done."

Cuse dropped the brakes and the three-hundred-fifty-ton jet rolled forward, at first slowly, then with an accelerating surge. They reached eighty knots and Franklin made the usual announcement: "Eighty knots. Throttle hold. Thrust normal. V1 is one-five-five."

At one hundred fifty-five knots, the 777 would reach what pilots called V1, the point at which safety rules dictated going ahead with takeoff even with a blown engine. Franklin spoke the figure as a formality. Both men knew it as well as their names.

"One-five-five," Cuse repeated, a secular *Amen.*

Cuse's gut and the instruments agreed: V1 would be no problem. The engines were running perfectly. Cuse felt as though he were wearing blinkers. The city, the terminal, even the traffic-control tower no longer existed. Only the runway before him and the metal skin that surrounded him.

The markers clipped by. They passed one hundred thirty knots, one forty, one fifty, nearly race-car speed, though the jet was so big and stable that Cuse wouldn't have known without the gauges to tell him —

"V1," Franklin said. And only a second later: "Rotate." Now the Triple-7 had reached one hundred sixty-five knots, about one hundred ninety miles an hour. As soon as Cuse pulled up its nose, the lift under its wings would send it soaring. Cuse felt himself tense and relax simultaneously, as he always did at this moment. Boeing's engineers and United's mechanics and everyone else had done all they could. The responsibility was his. He pulled back the yoke. The jet's nose rose and it leapt into the sky. *A miracle of human invention.*

"Positive rate," Franklin said.

"Gear up." Cuse pushed a button to retract the landing gear. They were gaining altitude smartly now, almost forty feet a second. In less than a minute, they would be higher than the world's tallest building. In five, they would be able to clear a good-size mountain range.

"United four-nine heavy, you are clear. Continue heading two-seven-zero —"

"Continue two-seven-zero," Franklin said.

"Good-bye," Cuse said. That last word was not strictly necessary, but he liked to include it as long as takeoff was copasetic, a single touch of humanity in the middle of the engineering, *good-bye, au revoir, adios amigos, but no worries, I'll be back.*

They topped four hundred feet and the city bloomed around them.

"Flaps," Franklin said.

"Flaps up. Climb power."

Vik pressed his nose against the window, looking down at the terminal's bright lights. He felt an unexpected regret. Maybe he should have stayed longer, given the place another chance. He might see it again. Once he married, had children, a trip like this one would be impossible. Unless he married a wannabe yogi like Jessica and got stuck taking trips to India for all eternity.

"I miss it already," she said, as if reading his mind.

"What's not to love?" He wondered if she knew he was being sarcastic.

Second by second, the jumbled neighborhoods around the airport came into view. At ground level, Mumbai hid its massive slums behind concrete walls and elevated highways. But from above, they were obvious, dark blotches in the electrical grid, the city's missing teeth. Some of the largest surrounded the airport. Vik had read a book about them. He imagined rows of rat-infested mud-brick huts, children and adults jumbled together on straw mattresses, trying to sleep, plotting their next dollar, their next meal. So much desperation, so much bad luck and trouble. They pushed on. But then, what else could they do?

Then, from the edge of the slum nearest the airport, Vik saw something he didn't expect.

Twin red streaks cutting through the night. Fireworks. Maybe someone down there had something to celebrate, for a change. But they didn't peter out like normal fireworks. They kept coming, arcing upward —

Not fireworks. *Missiles.*

Following a failed al-Qaeda effort to shoot down an Israeli passenger jet in Kenya in 2002, the Federal Aviation Administration had considered making American airlines retrofit their fleets with antimissile equipment. But installing thousands of jets with chaff and flare dispensers, along with radar systems to warn pilots of incoming missiles, would have been hugely expensive. Esti-

18

mates ranged from five to fifty billion dollars. Worse, the engineers who designed the countermeasures couldn't say if they would allow a passenger jet to escape. Passenger planes were far less maneuverable than fighter jets. Their engines gave off big, obvious heat signatures. And major airports were so congested that the systems might have caused jets to fire flares in each other's paths.

The seriousness of the threat was also unclear. Despite their reputation for being easy to use, surface-to-air missiles required substantial training. After a few months of memos, the FAA shelved the idea of a retrofit. And so American jets remained unprotected from surface-to-air attack.

From the cockpit, Cuse felt the missiles before he saw them. Something far below that didn't belong. He looked down, saw the streaks. They had just cleared the airport's western boundary. Unlike Vik Jain, he knew immediately what they were.

"Max power." He shoved the throttle forward and the turbines whined in response. "Nose down —" He dropped the yoke.

"Captain —"

Cuse ignored him, toggled Mumbai air-traffic control. "Mumbai tower, United four-nine heavy emergency. Two missiles —"

"Repeat, United —"

"SAMs." The tower couldn't help him now. He flicked off, snuck another look out the window. In the five seconds since he'd first spotted them, the missiles had closed half the gap with the jet. They had to be deep in the supersonic range, twelve hundred miles an hour or more. A mile every three seconds. Of course, the Boeing was moving, too, at three hundred miles an hour and accelerating. With a two-mile horizontal lead and a thousand feet of vertical. If the SAMs were Russian, they had a range of three to four miles. At three miles, the jet would probably escape.

At four, it wouldn't.

The world's deadliest math problem. Those beautiful deadly streaks would either reach him or not, and the worst part was he'd already played his only card. He couldn't outmaneuver the missiles, or hide from them. He could only try to outrun them.

In 45A, Vik had felt the surge of the engines. Then the plane leveled off, more than leveled off, started to drop. *They know. They'll do whatever they do to beat these things and we'll be fine.* But the missiles kept coming, closing the gap shockingly fast, homing in on the jet, arrows from the bow of the devil himself.

He grabbed Jessica's hand.

"Whoever you pray to, pray. *Pray.*"

"Hail Mary, full of grace, the Lord is with thee —" The words tumbled out of her. Vik just had time to be surprised. He'd expected a yogic chant. One of the streaks flared out, fell away.

But the other didn't.

The Russians referred to the missile as the Igla-S — *igla* being the Russian word for "needle." NATO called it the SA-24 Grinch. The Russian military had put it into service in 2004, updating the original Igla. They'd invested heavily in the redesign, knowing that man-portable surface-to-air missiles had a wide export market. Armies all over the world depended on them to neutralize close air support. A single SAM could take out a twenty-million-dollar fighter. The Russians more than doubled the size of the Igla's warhead. They improved its propellant to allow it to catch even the fastest supersonic fighter. They added a secondary guidance system.

And they lengthened its range. To six kilometers.

Twelve seconds after its launch, the Igla crashed into the Boeing's left engine. The warhead didn't explode right away. Its delayed fuse gave it time to burrow inside the casing of the turbine. A tenth of a second later, five and a half pounds of high explosive detonated.

In movies, missile strikes inevitably produced giant midair fireballs. But military jets had Kevlar-lined fuel tanks. In the real world, missiles destroyed fighters by shearing off their engines and wings, sending them crashing to earth.

This time, though, the Hollywood myth was accurate. The 777's fuel tanks weren't designed to survive a missile strike, and the plane carried far more fuel than a fighter jet. It was a flying bomb, fifty times as big as the one that had blown up the Alfred P. Murrah Federal Building in Oklahoma City.

The explosion started in the fuel tanks under the left wing and created a superheated cloud of burning kerosene that tore apart the cabin less than two seconds later. From Nick Cuse, in the cockpit, to Vikosh Jain, in the last row, all two hundred seventy-eight people on board were incinerated. The ones nearest the fuel tanks in the wings didn't die as much as *evaporate,* their physical existence denied.

Despite his immediate action, Cuse couldn't save his jet. Even so, he was a hero. By getting the Boeing offshore — barely — before the missile struck, he saved the city from the worst of the fireball. If the explosion had happened over the slums, hundreds of people would have burned to death. Instead, Mumbai's residents lifted their heads and watched as night turned to day. The tallest buildings were the worst damaged, so for once the rich suffered more than the poor.

The fireball lasted a full thirty seconds before fading, replaced with an unnatural blackness, a cloud of smoke that didn't dissipate until the morning. By then, the toll of the attack would be clear. Besides the two hundred seventy-eight people on the plane, two people on the ground died. One hundred sixty-five more suffered severe burns. Planes all over the world were grounded.

And the United States and Iran were much closer to war.

PART ONE

1

WASHINGTON, D.C.

The images were horrific. A man's legs, brown skin sloughed off, exposing the yellow-red meat underneath. A layer of jet fuel burning on top of the ocean, charring a chunk of bone. Worst of all, bits of a stuffed toy, blood smearing its white fur.

The first reports of an explosion in Mumbai showed up on Twitter ninety seconds after the jet was hit. A half hour later, 12:30 a.m. in India, 2 p.m. in Washington, the Associated Press and Reuters confirmed a plane crash. The Indian navy had sent ships to search the waters west of the city, Reuters said. Two hours later, a bleary-eyed spokesman for the Indian Ministry of Civil Aviation identified the jet as a United Airlines flight bound for Newark. "The situation is difficult. At this point, we cannot expect survivors."

Almost immediately, Reuters broke the

news that the jet's captain had reported missiles in the air seconds before the plane exploded. Then an Indian news agency reported that airport authorities had surveillance video that showed a missile striking the jet. By 8 p.m. Eastern, CNN and Fox and everyone else had the video. The anchors murmured somberly, *Disturbing, we want to warn you so you can have your children leave the room . . .*

The video was silent, not even a minute long. The camera was fixed and faced west from the airport's control tower. It didn't capture the actual launch. The missiles were already airborne when they entered the frame. From left to right, twin red streaks rose toward an invisible target. After five or six seconds, they faded, too far away for the camera to catch. But they hadn't stopped their chase. The proof came with the explosion, a white flash tearing open the night, resolving into a mushroom cloud. The shock wave hit seconds later, rattling the camera as the cloud in the distance grew.

HORROR IN THE SKIES, the crawl under the video said, and this time CNN wasn't exaggerating. India's navy would call off its search by morning. No one could have survived.

The inevitable next act would be assigning blame.

The video ended. CNN cut to a serious-looking man in a gray suit with a white shirt. *Fred Yount, Terrorism Analyst at RAND Institute* —

John Wells flicked off the screen before he had to hear Yount. A man squeezed a trigger in the dark. A few seconds later, almost three hundred people were dead. Whatever Yount had to say wouldn't change those bare facts.

Wells had quit the Central Intelligence Agency years before. But he'd never escaped the secret world. He knew now he never would. He felt like a swimmer fighting a whirlpool. He was strong enough to avoid being sucked down, but not to reach land. He could only tread water, knowing that one day his body would fail.

He was in his early forties, but his chin was still sturdy, his shoulders thick with muscle. Only the patches of gray hair at his temples and the permanent wariness in his brown eyes betrayed his age and his too-close acquaintance with the world's sins.

Now he lay back on his bed, stared at the ceiling. He was in room 319 in the Courtyard by Marriott at the Washington Navy Yard, a hotel favored by randy congressmen for its nearness to their offices. More than anything, Wells wanted to close his eyes. Sleep. But he had a plane to catch in less than four hours. He had arrived in the United States only the night before. Now he was going back the way he'd come, over the Atlantic, bound for London and Zurich. To meet with a man who didn't much want to see him. Then, maybe, to Mumbai.

Wells understood. He didn't want to see himself either. Not at the moment. He was carrying himself around like a rain-soaked cardboard box about to burst. Too many miles. And too much death. Wells blamed himself for the downing of the jet. A few days before, he'd discovered the truth about a plot to maneuver the United States into war with Iran. He'd nearly found a way to stop it. But his enemies had outplayed him.

He'd failed.

Wells turned out the bedside light. He closed his eyes, and for sixty seconds thought of the jet's passengers. Then he made himself forget them. Nothing else to do.

A light knock stirred him. The room door swung open. "Nice opsec." Ellis Shafer's gravelly, mumbly voice. The lights flicked on.

"If it came to that, I could kill you in my

sleep, Ellis."

"Hitting you hard?"

"I'm all right." Wells pushed himself up.

"Of course you are." Shafer sat on the bed next to Wells. "They probably didn't even know what hit them. Except the captain. Obviously."

"You should be a grief counselor."

"Should I tell you they're in heaven with seventy-two million virgins each?"

"Ellis —"

"Too soon?"

Wells had been raised Christian but converted to Islam more than a decade before, in the mountains of Pakistan. Shafer was a Jew who had declared his atheism at his bar mitzvah more than fifty years earlier. Unlike Wells, he still worked for the CIA. Barely. Until one of the new director's new men got around to dropping off a letter of resignation for him.

Over the years, Wells and Shafer had worked together on a half-dozen operations.

But they had never faced a mission as tricky as this one.

A few weeks before, Iran had begun a secret campaign against the United States. Assassins working for the Quds Force, the foreign intelligence unit of Iran's Revolutionary

Guard, killed a CIA station chief. Then the Guard smuggled radioactive material onto a Pakistani ship bound for Charleston, South Carolina. Fortunately, a rogue Guard colonel tipped the CIA to Iran's efforts, enabling the Navy to intercept the ship in the Atlantic.

Then the colonel gave the agency an even more disturbing piece of intel. He said Iran had moved three pounds of weapons-grade uranium to Istanbul. The uranium was ultimately destined for the United States, according to the colonel, who called himself Reza.

Wells and Shafer knew that the truth was very different. Iran had nothing to do with the killing of the station chief, or the smuggling. Reza wasn't a Revolutionary Guard colonel at all. He worked for a private group trying to trick the United States into attacking Iran. A billionaire casino mogul named Aaron Duberman had paid for the operation. Duberman hoped to stop Iran from building a nuclear weapon that it might use against Israel. Iran regularly threatened to annihilate the Jewish state, and a nuclear weapon would make the threat real. Even if Iran never used the bomb, its mere existence would give the country new freedom to launch terrorist attacks against Israel.

Since the fall of the Shah in 1979, the United States had stood firmly with Israel against Iran. Now the relationship between Washington and Tehran was warming. The White House had recently agreed to loosen economic sanctions against Iran. In turn, Tehran promised to stop work on its nuclear weapons program. But those promises in no way satisfied Duberman and the mysterious woman who was his chief lieutenant. They had decided to force the United States to act by fooling the White House into believing that Iran was trying to smuggle the pieces of a nuclear weapon onto American soil.

Wells and Shafer had unraveled the scheme in the last couple of weeks, after Wells tracked down Glenn Mason, an ex–CIA case officer who had betrayed the agency to work for Duberman. Senior CIA officials refused to consider that Mason might be involved, for a reason that at first seemed airtight. Mason had been reported dead in Thailand four years before, and the death report appeared genuine. Mason hadn't used his passport or bank accounts since. In reality, Wells discovered, Mason had undergone extensive plastic surgery, so he could travel without setting off facial-recognition software.

After chasing Mason across three conti-
nents, Wells finally found him in Istanbul.
But Mason turned the tables, capturing
Wells and imprisoning him in an abandoned
factory. Wells spent a week in captivity
before killing Mason and escaping. Wells assumed that the Turkish police would find
Mason's body at the factory, setting off an
investigation that would unravel the plot.

Instead, Duberman's mercenaries dis-
posed of Mason's body and cleaned up the
factory, leaving police with nothing to find.
Wells and Shafer had no other evidence to
prove that Duberman was involved.

Meanwhile, the plot was close to success.

Tests conducted by the Department of
Energy had shown that the weapons-grade
uranium the CIA found in Istanbul didn't
come from any known stockpile. The DOE
and CIA agreed that Iran was the only logi-
cal candidate to have produced it. Kilogram-
size chunks of highly enriched uranium
didn't exist in private hands. And Iran had
worked on nuclear weapons for decades,
doing everything possible to hide its efforts
from international inspectors. The United
States and Israel had repeatedly unearthed
hidden enrichment plants over the years.
But Iran was twice as big as Texas. No one

could say for sure that every plant had been found. In fact, Iranian exiles had told the CIA of rumors that the government had opened a new plant deep under central Tehran.

Despite his fears of starting another war in the Middle East, the President decided he had to accept the reality of the Iranian threat. In an Oval Office speech, he gave Iran two weeks to end its nuclear program or face an invasion. To support his threat, he ordered drones and stealth fighters to bomb Tehran's airport. Congressional leaders in both parties backed the President. Ironically, the earlier deal with Iran increased his credibility. A man who wanted an excuse to invade Iran wouldn't have spent years trying to end sanctions.

China and Russia protested the American attack on Tehran, but neither country offered any military aid to Iran. Afghanistan and Turkey, which had long-standing rivalries with Iran, agreed to allow the United States to use their territories as bases for American forces who might eventually invade. The rest of the world stayed on the sidelines. Most countries seemed to think the United States and Iran deserved each other. One was a fading empire that used its military too often, the other a dangerous theocracy that couldn't be trusted with nuclear weapons.

Iran responded furiously to the American threat. Its supreme leader, Ayatollah Ali Khamenei, gave a two-hour speech accusing the United States of lying to justify an invasion: *"Iran shall never open its legs to the filthy Zionist-controlled inspectors. Our people will gladly accept martyrdom. The Crusaders and the Jews will suffer the fury that they have unleashed . . ."*

Now someone had shot down an American plane. Iran was the obvious suspect. And the Islamic Republic had a history of terrorism against the United States.

Shafer turned on the television. CNN was replaying the explosion yet again.

"Think it was Duberman?"

"A couple hundred civilians wouldn't stop him, if he thought it would fuel the fire."

"On the other hand . . ." Shafer didn't have to finish the thought. The Iranian government might also have downed the jet. The fact that it was innocent of the nuclear plot made it *more* rather than less likely to lash out. From Iran's point of view, the United States had created fake evidence as an excuse for an invasion. Iran was not likely to wait for American troops to cross

36

its borders before it took revenge.

"We have any idea where Duberman is?" Wells said.

"Probably Hong Kong," Shafer said. "When not starting a war, he's got casinos to run. Those rich Chinese want to see the man who's taking their money."

Wells wondered if Duberman was cold-blooded enough to glad-hand wealthy gamblers while goading the United States into war. He'd never met the man. But the sheer boldness of Duberman's scheme suggested that the answer was yes. And Duberman was not just an ordinary billionaire, if such a creature existed. He was one of the richest men in the world, with a fortune of almost thirty billion dollars. He had mansions all over the world, a small fleet of private jets, his own island. He had spent $196 million on ads in the previous presidential election, making him the largest political donor ever. Some analysts believed that the President wouldn't have won without his help.

"You talk to Evan and Heather?" Shafer said. Wells's son and ex-wife.

"Yeah. They agreed to hang out a few more days. Though they aren't happy about it." "Hang out" translated into *stay in FBI protective custody.* Before Wells killed him, Mason had threatened Evan and Heather.

Wells didn't know if Mason had been serious, but he couldn't take the risk.

"Where are they?"

"Provo. Heather told me the biggest risk was death by boredom. And Evan says I'm going to get him kicked off the team. He just cracked the rotation and now this." Evan was a shooting guard on San Diego State's nationally ranked basketball team.

"We all have problems. You mention you killed five guys three days ago?"

"We had a nice conversation about it."

The room door banged open. Vinny Duto walked in. Strode in.

The former Director of Central Intelligence, Duto was now a Pennsylvania senator. He'd crash-landed in the Senate after the President pushed him out of the CIA. He was an old-school politician, unpolished and raw with power. No one would call him handsome. He had stubby fingers, a heavy Nixonian face. But his intensity had resonated with Pennsylvania's flinty voters. He had dominated the debates.

As DCI, Duto had saved Wells's life more than once. Now they were working together to stop Duberman. But Wells could barely stand Duto at the best of times. He saw Duto as the worst kind of Washington opportunist. And he knew that Duto pegged him as an adrenaline junkie who took unnecessary risks.

They were both right.

Duto offered Wells a thin-lipped smile. "Gentlemen. Hope I haven't interrupted anything." Duto liked to irritate Shafer by accusing him of having an old man's crush on Wells.

Wells felt the itching in the tips of his fingers that meant he was ready to fight. Three hundred people dead and Duto was cracking jokes. Wells knew exactly what Duto thought of the downed plane. Not a tragedy. A *moment.* One that might help his career if he played it right.

"Imagine you lost a donor on that plane," Wells said. "Then you could pretend to care."

"Life lessons from you, Johnny? Definition of irony."

"Boys. Already?" Shafer clapped his hands like a cheerleader trying to distract a drunken crowd from a blowout. "Same team here. Same team. We have bigger fish to fry, *n'est-ce pas?*"

Shafer's horrendous French broke the spell. "Did you just say *n'est-ce pas?*" Duto said.

"He did," Wells said.

"You two ready to be grown-ups?"

They both nodded.

"Then let's move on. Please tell us you have something CNN doesn't, Vinny."

The new CIA director, Scott Hebley, had tried to freeze Duto out. But Duto still had sources in the National Clandestine Service, the former Directorate of Operations.

"Video analysis says the missiles traveled at least five kilometers from launch, maybe six. Based on distance and speed, the betting is they're late-model Russian SAMs. Possibly SA-24s. Which only came into service in 2004. Unfortunately, they're pretty much untraceable. The Russians have sold them all over, including Libya. After Qaddafi went down in 2010, we had a report that both Iran and Hezbollah agents got their hands on a bunch."

"And could easily have moved them to India," Shafer said.

"The White House will see it that way for sure. At this point, I don't think we have any way to know whether this is Duberman pushing buttons or the Iranians firing across the bow."

"Anything on the ground?"

"The Indian security services have responded with their usual efficiency," Duto said.

Meaning none. In 2008, terrorists had attacked hotels, a synagogue, and the central train station in Mumbai. The police didn't respond in force for hours, allowing ten attackers to kill 166 people and wound hundreds more. "Good news is that the Bureau" — the FBI — "has a five-man forensic team permanently in Delhi. They've flown in, along with some of our guys. Bad news is that there are a bunch of slums around the airport. Very dark at that hour, no security cameras. It's just possible whoever did this was dumb enough to leave the firing tube on the ground. Otherwise." Duto raised a mock missile to his shoulder. "Drive in, pow-pow, drive out."

"Pow-pow," Wells said.

Shafer grunted at him: *You made your point, now lay off.*

"White House planning anything?"

"If they are, they're not telling me. But at the moment, I don't think so. They suspect Iran, but they've got no evidence. I think for us the best bet is to stay away from Mumbai, stick with the original plan."

That morning, before the attack, the men had met at Duto's office in Philadelphia and agreed that finding the real source of the Istanbul uranium was their only chance to stop the plot. They were caught in the

41

world's worst game of chicken-and-egg. With the President already having launched a drone strike against Iran, the CIA wasn't about to chase new theories. Especially one that accused the President's largest campaign donor of treason.

Wells, Shafer, and Duto would have to find their own proof. But they were stuck on their own. They couldn't have NSA crack open the servers at Duberman's casino company. They couldn't go to the CIA for surveillance or Special Operations Group help.

But if they could prove that someone other than Iran had supplied the uranium, then the President and CIA would at least have to consider their theory about Duberman. And no matter how careful Duberman and his operatives had been, the agency and NSA could unravel what he'd done if they focused on him.

Unfortunately, at the moment they had no idea who might have supplied the uranium. They faced the same blank wall that had led the agency to conclude that Iran had been the source. And they were short on time to find out. The President had given his speech, with its two-week deadline, almost three days earlier. They had less than twelve days left, if they were lucky.

Wells saw that Duto was right. Mumbai was a blind alley. Let the FBI and CIA work it. Their first plan was still their best option.

"Fine," Wells said. "Zurich it is." Zurich was home to Pierre Kowalski, an arms dealer, both friend and enemy to Wells over the years. Kowalski was dirty enough to know who might have been sitting on a stash of weapons-grade uranium. Wells could only hope he was clean enough to want to stop this war.

"You going tonight?"

"Through London."

"He know you're coming?"

"He knows."

"He gonna help?"

"He said he'd see me. Not sure he knows anything." *Must we do this?* Kowalski had asked when Wells called. To which Wells had said, *Yeah. We must.* And hung up before Kowalski could object.

"But he'll *see* you? How sweet."

Before Wells could swipe back, Shafer intervened. "You talk to Rudi, Vinny?" Ari Rudin, who had run the Mossad until two years before, when the Israeli Prime Minister forced him out.

"Yeah. He tried to tell me he was too sick to meet."

"Sick?"

"He has lung cancer. Been keeping it quiet. Told him I'd come to Tel Aviv. I'm not expecting much. I fly out tonight. Twenty-two-hour roundtrip for a ten-minute meeting." Duberman's wealth and his importance in Israel meant that the Mossad must have watched him over the years.

"Too bad you don't have lung cancer, too," Wells said. "You could make him meet you halfway."

"What about you, Ellis?" Duto said. "You going to look for the leak?"

The final thread. Duberman's team seemed to have a source inside Langley. Wells, Shafer, and Duto weren't sure whether the leaker knew the truth about the plot or had simply been fooled into giving up bits of information that Duberman could use. In any case, they saw the leaker as an opportunity as well as a threat. He was another potential avenue to Duberman. But they risked alerting Duberman to what they knew if they went after him.

"At this point, no. Ice is too thin. I'm just going to go into my office, keep my head down for a couple days. May try to talk to Ian Duffy. Mason's station chief in Hong Kong. He's back in D.C. now. Lobbying. Maybe he knows something about how

Mason connected with Duberman."

The move was a long shot at best, but all they had right now were long shots.

"So we go our separate ways," Duto said. "John, in terms of" — Duto made a pistol with his thumb and forefinger — "I know you've had difficulties getting hooked up." Without access to a diplomatic pouch, Wells had trouble getting weapons across borders. "Some places, I still have friends. Russia, for example."

Wells wasn't entirely sure why Duto was working so hard. Getting involved with this mess carried serious risk. Duto wouldn't bother unless he smelled a bigger payoff.

Then Wells realized. "You think this is your ticket, don't you?"

Duto must have expected the Senate seat would be his last stop. He had won his race as a conservative Democrat, a breed that rarely survived presidential primaries. But now he had a chance at the biggest prize of all. If he could prove that the President's largest donor was trying to lure the United States into war, he could demand whatever he wanted from the White House. A promotion to Secretary of State or Defense. Done. The President's endorsement in the next election? Absolutely.

Duto had used Wells and Shafer before.

But never for stakes this high. And Wells had never seen the con so early in the game.

"La, la, la," Wells said. Arabic. No, no, no.

Duto nodded. *"Nam."* Yes. "Unless you prefer the alternative."

He tapped his wrist. "Come on, you can ride with me to Dulles."

"I'll get there myself." Wells couldn't bear sharing a car with this man.

"As you wish." Duto walked out.

Wells and Shafer sat side by side on the edge of the bed.

"We can't," Wells said.

"Can't what?"

"He's not fit." Wells wasn't one hundred percent sure about much, but he was sure that Duto shouldn't be President. Part of him wanted to flip on the television and watch ESPN for the next eleven days. Let Duto solve this, if he could.

"You want another war, John? Me neither. Take a minute so you don't run into him in the elevator. Then go. You have a plane to catch."

Wells had nothing left to say. He went.

2
ELEVEN DAYS . . .

HONG KONG

The woman who called herself Salome had spent three hours running countersurveillance, MTR to taxi to Star Ferry and back to MTR, the Hong Kong subway. She reached the pickup spot, an alley behind a run-down Kowloon hotel, just as the gray Sprinter van arrived. She pulled open its cargo doors and stepped inside.

She was certain that she hadn't been followed. Wells had no way of knowing where she was. But she was furious with herself for what had happened in Istanbul four days before. She couldn't afford another mistake.

Now she squatted inside the van's cargo compartment, holding a cheap white nylon bag. Gleaming white urinals and dull plastic pipe surrounded her. Anyone who happened to check the van's license plate would find it was owned by HKMCA Plumbing PLC. The corporation was real enough, one of forty-five hundred subsidiaries of Duber-man's casino company. Thus the Sprinter had every reason to make its way through the tunnel that connected Kowloon and Hong Kong Island and fight through the island's congested avenues until it reached the narrow roads that led up the side of Victoria Peak. Its destination was Duberman's $200 million mansion. The house was one of just a handful of private homes on the upper slopes of the Peak, the eighteen-hundred-foot mountain that provided a lush green backdrop to Hong Kong's skyscrapers.

After fifty minutes, the van stopped. Through the wire mesh that split the cargo compartment from the front seats, Salome heard the driver lower his window and mumble in Chinese. A buzzer sounded. The van turned, rolled forward, stopped again. "Here," the driver said. Salome pushed aside a sink and hopped out the back.

She found herself in the center of a five-car garage, its concrete floor spotless. Around her: a yellow Lamborghini Aventador, a red Ferrari 288 GTO, a white Rolls-Royce Phantom, and an orange Porsche Carrera GT, a twin of the car that had killed the actor Paul Walker. All spit-shined each week so that they gleamed under the halogen lights that hung from the ceiling.

The cars were flawless, worth millions of dollars. They were protected by a fire-suppression system that could fill the garage with a nontoxic foam in twenty-five seconds. Yet as *vehicles* they were basically useless. Duberman drove them once a year at most. They didn't even have gasoline in their tanks. Gas was flammable and corrosive, and its impurities might leach out and damage their fuel lines since they were run so infrequently. They might as well have been gold bricks with rubber tires.

Still, they served a purpose. Duberman brought in his biggest 88 Gamma bettors to see them, along with his other collections in Las Vegas and Los Angeles. *Lose $2 million, you can sit in them. $5 million, start their engines. $10 million, maybe I'll let you drive one.* The whales coveted these invitations, though Salome couldn't imagine why. For the money they gambled away, they could have bought the cars themselves.

Duberman himself traveled in a four-ton gray Bentley sedan outfitted with armor plates and inch-thick windows that would stop anything up to a .50-caliber round. The security at his mansion was similarly over-the-top. The property was hidden from the street by a reinforced concrete wall ten feet high and three feet thick, built to survive a five-ton truck bomb. A mantrap ringed the inside of the wall. Five feet wide and fifteen deep, the trap was hidden under the narrow green lawn that Duberman's engineers had carved out of the mountain.

Duberman's security hadn't always been so oppressive. He'd added a lot of it since his wedding two years before. Salome supposed the additional protection made sense. His wife, Orli, was a celebrity in her own right, a Victoria's Secret supermodel. And they had two infant children, obvious kidnap targets. But Salome wondered sometimes if Duberman had added the extra security to make himself feel better about the risk he'd taken funding their operation. Though he surely knew that all the mantraps in the world wouldn't stop a Delta team.

The van pulled out. Salome was briefly alone with the cars. Then the house door opened to reveal Gideon Etra, Duberman's personal bodyguard.

"Salome."

Etra knew her real name. But both he and Duberman usually used her cover name, which she had borrowed from a famous biblical vixen. According to the Gospels of Matthew and Mark, Salome danced before her stepfather Herod so seductively that he

50

offered her whatever she wanted. She demanded the head of John the Baptist. Despite his misgivings, Herod gave it to her.

For a dance.

She had picked the name as her legend almost ironically. She was no one's courtesan. She could have been pretty, but she didn't want to be. She didn't wear makeup and left her brown hair in a boring shoulder-length cut. Though she had an athlete's body, trim and fit, she hid it behind neutral-colored suit sets. She wore a wedding ring, too, discreet white gold, though she had never married. The clothes and ring were the female version of camouflage, her way of making herself forgettable.

Nonetheless, she had grown to love her chosen name. Lately, as her plan moved ahead, she found herself wondering if it didn't carry its own biblical magic. A foolish thought, but one she couldn't shake.

"Gideon." She reached for the Ferrari's door. "Want to go for a ride?"

Etra blinked, then computed that she was joking and smiled. Humor wasn't his strong suit. He was in his early fifties, with close-cropped gray hair, an old-school bodyguard. He could have passed for one of Duberman's executives. He wore tailored gray suits and carried a Sig Sauer P238, an undercover officer's weapon meant for close-range use, easily hidden but short on stopping power.

Nonetheless, underestimating Etra was a mistake. His nickname was Chai-Chai, though only Duberman used it. Etra had earned it as a sniper for the IDF, the Israeli Defense Forces. The name was more than slightly ironic. In Hebrew, *chai* had two meanings. Eighteen, and life. Etra had finished Israel's 1982 war in Lebanon with thirty-six confirmed kills, more than any other IDF soldier.

"Any problems?"

"The plumbing and I had a fine time."

"That means no?"

"Not that I could see."

"What's in the bag?"

"Phones. Burners. For your boss. And a picture. For you."

She tossed him the bag. He unzipped it, pulled out a photo.

"Who's this?"

"His name's John Wells." She had taken it in Istanbul. The only smart decision she'd made about Wells. "He's not a friend."

"Can I share this with my team? Or is it just for me?"

"They can see it, but don't tell them who he is."

He opened the house door, and she followed him inside.

The house had been cantilevered over the mountainside, with floor-to-ceiling windows that looked out on the city. This view always awed Salome. Enormous skyscrapers soared from Hong Kong Island and the mainland, looming over a forest of smaller towers. Hovercrafts, ferries, fishing boats, and even a few antique Chinese junks churned across the roiling gray waters of Victoria Harbor. Cars, trucks, and motorcycles fought for space on the causeways. When the sun set, the city's neon would glow in the dark and the view would be even more spectacular.

"Boss's running late. Be here in a few minutes," Etra said.

"Few meaning five? Or an hour?"

Etra didn't answer. He treated even basic questions about Duberman as state secrets.

"You're so helpful, Gideon."

"Thank you."

She wasn't sure if he knew she was mocking him. She nodded at the city below. "You know, this is what we're trying to protect."

Out of necessity, a dozen mid-level functionaries at 88 Gamma had helped support Salome's operation. They were the lawyers who created shell companies that she used for safe houses and vehicles. The accountants who funneled money to the accounts that paid her mercenaries and hackers. Even the pilots who shuttled her from country to country.

But none had any idea what she was doing. She and Duberman had chosen employees whose evaluations showed that they followed orders unquestioningly. Inside 88 Gamma, Salome was known as an independent consultant who worked with the company on development projects in countries where it couldn't advertise its presence.

But she and Etra could speak honestly. He had known what they were doing as soon as Duberman agreed to fund her plans. The men spent nearly every hour together. And Salome didn't worry about Etra's loyalty. A decade before, Duberman had spent two million dollars on an experimental leukemia treatment for Etra's son Tal, a prototype gene therapy. The treatment, which no insurer would cover, saved the boy's life.

"Hong Kong is what we're trying to protect?" Etra parroted back to her. "Not too many Jews here."

Salome wondered if she should explain. Of course, a city of eight million Chinese wouldn't be at the top of the Iranian hit list. But like Tel Aviv and New York, Hong Kong stood as a monument to modern civilization. Iran's mullahs pretended that they hated Israel and the United States. Salome knew better. They hated freedom in all its forms. Religious, economic, sexual. They hated women. They hated *success*. They couldn't compete, so they threatened to lash out with the most destructive tools they could find. A few kilograms of dull yellow metal would tear a hole in this city, kill hundreds of thousands of people. Worst of all, the Iranians could never have invented a nuclear bomb on their own. But they had no shame about stealing the West's discoveries and using them against their creators.

"It's not just us. They hate all this."

"I don't care who else they hate. Or who else they love. They hate me, that's enough for me."

Etra's phone buzzed with a text message.

"He says fifteen minutes."

"But he's here, right? In the house? You're here, he's here."

"I guess."

Not exactly a definitive answer. "And what's keeping him? Casino business?" Of course, Duberman wouldn't poke his head out and tell her himself. Billionaires rarely explained. And never apologized.

A shrug.

"Gideon. You probably know him as well as anyone."

"Maybe."

"Ever met his friends?"

"Maybe."

"I mean, his real friends. People he grew up with."

Etra shook his head as if he couldn't believe she'd had the audacity to ask the question. And walked out holding her bag of phones, leaving Salome to consider what she knew about her boss.

Duberman's parents had arrived in the United States in 1946 and settled in Atlanta. After escaping the Holocaust, they dreamed no great American dreams. Or just one: to keep their heads down and survive. Nathan managed a rent-to-own store in Oak Knoll, a poor neighborhood southeast of downtown. Gisa taught kindergarten.

After five years, they had scrimped enough money for a down payment on a fourteen-hundred-square-foot house in the city's Midtown District. They quickly had three sons. Aaron was the youngest and by far the most ambitious. He attended the University of Georgia on a wrestling scholarship, majored in business, moved to Las Vegas to work for Hilton.

I was tired of the South, he'd told *Fortune* for a cover profile a decade before. *It had all this history that didn't have anything to do with me. I liked Vegas from the minute I saw it. Empty space, blue sky. It seemed like anything was possible.* He rose quickly at Hilton, but he didn't stay. *When you work for a company that has somebody else's name on the door, you know there's a limit to how high you can get.* At the tender age of twenty-six, he and two other junior Hilton executives struck out, buying a scrubby hotel-casino in Reno called The Sizzling Saloon.

Duberman had never fully explained how he came up with the eight hundred thousand dollars for his one-third share, though he hinted at the answer in *Fortune. I had friends. The kinds of friends that the Nevada Gaming Commission looked down on. But they were always decent to me. If I paid on time. Besides, what's the casino business without a little gamble?* So he began his march toward fortune.

He didn't get far at first. The Sizzling Saloon's blackjack tables were scorched with cigarette holes, its waitresses with stretch marks. After three years, his partners tired of the grind. They wanted to sell to the casino next door. Duberman refused. He bought them out instead.

Now I owned the place, but my friends owned me. Duberman had a streak of Donald Trump in him, a natural talent for self-promotion. He dropped Sizzling from the casino's name, calling it simply The Saloon: *Where the West Comes to Play.* He promised to take any bet. He put up billboards around Reno showing himself wearing a ten-gallon hat and holding a revolver in each hand. *Can You Out-Gun The Saloon-Keeper? Take Yer Best Shot!*

The fact that the Saloon-Keeper was a Jew from Atlanta was part of the joke. And Reno laughed. Within three years, the casino was the city's most profitable. Duberman branched out to Las Vegas, opening two more Saloons. They were miles from the Strip and catered to locals. They, too, were hits. He bought out his silent partners. *Finally, I had the money to say good-bye to my old friends. Not cheap, but money well spent.* He expanded to Iowa and Mississippi and took Saloon Gaming Inc. public. At thirty-seven, his fortune topped $100 million.

Then Saloon started to lose ground. Its casinos couldn't compete with the eye-catching attractions that its bigger competitors offered. Its Western theme seemed

58

dated and cheesy. Still, its customers were loyal. Duberman could have milked them for years. Instead, he changed Saloon's name to 88 Gamma. He mortgaged his fortune to redesign his casinos with a sci-fi theme. He installed oxygen bars, shark tanks, brushed aluminum tables, huge flat-panel screens dangling above the casino floor. He wanted to attract young Asians, who were often heavy gamblers. He succeeded wildly. By 2001, he was a billionaire.

Then Duberman made his biggest bet yet, a $2 billion casino in Macao. The only other casino mogul to invest in Macao at the time was Sheldon Adelson, who like Duberman was an outsider in the gambling industry. MGM and other, more established companies avoided the territory. It had a reputation as a lawless place dominated by Chinese gangs called triads. But Adelson and Duberman saw opportunity. *The big companies were afraid of the crime, the triads, the Chinese government,* Duberman told *Fortune. They were doing risk analysis, hiring consultants, blah blah blah. Me, I'm a simple guy. I didn't get an MBA from Harvard. I had a simple theory. I said, wait a minute, you're letting me build a casino across the border from a billion people who love gambling more than breathing? And who can't do it legally any-*

where else? Uhh, sounds okay to me.

It was. 88 Gamma Macao did not have an empty seat or slot machine for nine months after it opened. By then, Duberman had broken ground on an expansion that tripled its size. Two days before his fiftieth birthday, his fortune reached $10 billion, putting him in one of the world's most elite clubs. It now topped almost $30 billion.

For a while, Duberman's public profile grew with his fortune. He became the largest individual donor to Israel, a supporter of close ties between the United States and China. He gave cheeky interviews like the one with *Fortune.* But in the last couple of years, he had fallen almost silent, and cut back on his charitable spending.

Meanwhile, he had become the largest political donor in American history, putting up $196 million to help reelect the President. Investigative reporters had tried to tear down the veil of secrecy and expose why Duberman had spent so much. *What Does Aaron Want?* The most popular theory was that Duberman needed White House access to lobby for better relations between Washington and Beijing.

"He's worried if we make China mad, they retaliate, close the border with Macao," one analyst told *The New Yorker.* "His stock falls eighty percent overnight." Salome had laughed out loud when she'd read the article. *Them that know don't tell, and them that tell don't know . . .*

She'd met Duberman while she was working for Daniel Raban. He was a right-wing member of the Israeli parliament, the Knesset, who had won a silver medal in the pole vault. The achievement made Raban an instant hero in a country short on successful Olympians. He was a perfect television politician, tall and handsome, with an adoring wife and three young sons. Off camera, reality was less appealing. Raban was infamous for sexually harassing his female staffers. Inevitably, Israeli political journalists called him the Pole.

He had hit on Salome more times than she could count, always unsuccessfully. She put up with his antics because he served on the Knesset's Foreign Affairs and Defense Committee. Every member of the committee could pick one aide to sit in on classified briefings from the Mossad and the IDF. Raban had chosen Salome, giving her access she would otherwise have needed decades to achieve.

Plus, though she disliked him personally, she agreed with his politics. He had won his

Knesset seat with the slogan *Peace Last!*
The Palestinians and the Arab states had to
accept Israel's right to exist before negotiations on a permanent peace deal could
begin, he said. *Give up trying to kill us, we'll
talk. Peace Last!*

At the beginning of Raban's second term
in parliament, Duberman invited Raban to
a private lunch at his villa in Jerusalem. The
offer was not a surprise. Duberman visited
Israel regularly and cultivated young right-
wing politicians. Naturally, Salome came
along. She served as Raban's personal Wikipedia, memorizing the facts he couldn't be
bothered to learn.

Duberman recognized Raban as an empty
suit by the time his waiters had cleared away
their salads. He focused questions about
Israeli's strategy in the West Bank to Salome.
He seemed genuinely interested in her
answers. She liked him immediately. More
than liked. He wore his brown hair slightly
longer than was respectable for the chief
executive of a major company. Though he
was well past fifty, his eyes radiated enthusiasm and energy. His body was solid under
his suit, his hands thick and powerful.
Salome had never been attracted to older
men, but she found it easy to imagine those
hands around her. He was the most self-

assured man she had ever met.

His mind was equally appealing. He understood a truth that many Israelis still disliked discussing aloud. In the last sixty years, the Jews had carved a modern state from the desert. Israel could boast a strong economy, with first-rate hospitals, universities, and highways. It had a powerful army, free elections and media. Meanwhile, its Arab neighbors plunged deeper into tyranny and filth every year. In Iraq, the Shia and Sunni blew each other up as fast as they could. In Egypt, the elite lived like pharaohs while tens of millions of their subjects barely survived. The Saudis married their cousins and stoned women to death for adultery. And in Gaza and Lebanon and Jordan, the Palestinians bred like rats in their pathetic refugee camps. Like if they made themselves miserable enough, Israel would have to accommodate them.

Anyone who looked at the situation rationally could reach only one conclusion. Israel couldn't trust its Muslim neighbors. Not now, not ever. It would simply have to manage them, so that Jews could hold on to their birthright, the land they had settled three millennia before. The Bible was filled with myths. But the Zionist claim to Judea and Samaria was real. Jews had prayed on the Temple Mount a thousand years before Muhammad drew breath. When the Arabs drew maps that erased Israel, they weren't just spitting at Jews today but at *every* Jew who had ever lived.

Salome didn't say any of this at that first lunch. Neither did Duberman. He didn't have to. She knew he understood. He discussed the Palestinians with a certain briskness, like a warden dealing with an unruly cell block. When they were finished, he took her hands and promised to call the next time he came through Jerusalem.

"Don't know why you were trying so hard," Raban said after they left. "He likes them way prettier than you."

"You're only jealous because he saw you for what you are. A baboon in a suit."

"I should fire you."

"Who would keep you from embarrassing yourself?" They'd had this conversation before.

Over the next couple years, Salome saw Duberman whenever he came to Israel. They had breakfast at his villa, or he picked her up on his hour-long drives between Jerusalem and Tel Aviv. She wondered if they would become lovers. But when she suggested they meet for dinner instead of breakfast, he told her he was too busy. Even before he began dating Orli, Salome saw the truth of Raban's barb. Duberman preferred his women as conventionally gorgeous as his cars. She wanted to think less of him for his shallow taste, but in reality his unreachability only made him more attractive.

To make sure she didn't betray her feelings, she kept their meetings as academic as think-tank seminars. She briefed him on the secret operations and strategic analyses that the IDF and Mossad disclosed to Raban's committee. The information was classified, of course, but Salome never worried about telling him. Duberman believed in Israel as much as any *sabra.*

On the surface, Israel's position seemed stronger than ever. With jihadis focused on fighting the United States in Iraq and Afghanistan, Israel was enjoying a peaceful period. It had walled off its Palestinian enemies in Gaza and the West Bank. Its strike on a Syrian reactor in 2007 had left Bashar al-Assad with no hope of building a nuclear weapon.

Yet, quietly, it faced increasing danger from Iran. After the United States invaded Iraq, Iran's leaders had made the bomb their top priority. *The mullahs aren't fools.*

They can read a map. Armies of American soldiers to the west and east. I think mainly they want nukes to keep the Americans out. But once they get them, who knows what they'll do?

Salome worried that her focus on Iran might bore Duberman. She was wrong. Their moment of truth came over breakfast on a winter morning in Jerusalem, on the glassed-in patio of Duberman's villa. A faint dusting of snowflakes coated the Old City, frosting on a golden cake. Snow here was rare but not unprecedented. Jerusalem's hills rose a half mile above sea level, and winter winds from the north swept down cool air from the mountains around the Sea of Galilee.

In keeping with the weather, Duberman's chef had prepared bowls of oatmeal heaped with brown sugar and raisins. "Don't know where he found it," Duberman said.

Salome fluffed the oatmeal with her spoon. "I've never had it before."

"Never?"

"I've only been to the United States and Europe in the summer."

"Mount Hermon, skiing?"

"Not for me."

"I think you have to grow up with it."

Salome tasted the oatmeal, put down her spoon.

"You don't like it," he said.

"It tastes like paste." She had never much cared for polite fibs. "Anyway, I have a briefing in an hour. A new program they want to tell us about. Rumor is it's good."

"So why don't you look happy?"

"They're trying. But there are things they won't do."

"Such as."

"Attacking those European parasites who sell the Iranians their equipment."

Duberman's steward appeared to refill their coffee. "Leave us, please." The steward vanished. "Tell me."

"We've traced several. A machine tool factory outside Hamburg, a software company in Singapore that specializes in modeling fluid dynamics —"

"Fluid dynamics."

"To understand what's happening inside the warhead as the chain reaction takes over —"

"Wait, please. Understand who you're talking to. I run hotels. I don't even know what it means to enrich uranium."

So Salome explained. Uranium existed naturally in several different forms, called isotopes. When it came out of the earth, newly mined uranium ore consisted of 99.3 percent of the U-238 isotope, 0.7 percent U-235. U-235 could be used in a bomb. U-238 could not. The two kinds of uranium had to be separated. Nuclear scientists called the process enrichment.

"Like oil," Duberman said. "You can't run your car on crude oil, you have to refine it."

"Kind of. Anyway, during World War II, the United States figured out how." American scientists had come up with several ways to enrich uranium. One still in use today combined uranium with fluoride to make it a gas. Then the gas was injected into spinning tubes called centrifuges. The lighter molecules spun out against the centrifuge walls. The heavier molecules stuck to the center. Because U-235 was lighter than U-238, the gas against the wall held more U-235 than natural uranium did. The gas was vacuumed into another centrifuge, where the process was repeated. Slowly but surely, the amount of U-235 increased. Until, finally —

"You have enough of the good stuff. And boom."

"There are other steps, too, but yes. But the centrifuges need special parts. High-strength steel. Perfectly round bearings because they spin so fast. The fluorine gas is corrosive. All this takes advanced equipment that the Iranians can't make themselves. They have to buy it. Mainly from Europe."

"If we stopped the suppliers, would we stop the program?"

"Not necessarily stop it. But slow it down, sure."

"But isn't it illegal, what the suppliers are doing? Violating sanctions?"

"Yes. We've told the Germans, the French. And so have the Americans. But what we know isn't always the same as what we can prove. The Iranians are smart. They use front companies from China and Russia to buy the stuff. The Europeans say they can't be responsible for what happens if they sell equipment to a legitimate buyer in China and then that company sends it to Singapore and then to Dubai and then Iran. And the Chinese won't listen, they don't care."

"But these European companies *know*?"

"Oh yes. It's a very specialized business."

"The Mossad won't stop them?"

"They've said no to attacking the suppliers directly. They're worried what the Europeans will say. But they're making a mistake. Someone needs to hit these people."

"Someone."

"It wouldn't be that hard. They aren't government officials. No bodyguards or police looking after them."

Duberman pushed back from the table, scratching his chair against the tile floor. His villa sat atop one of Jerusalem's highest hills, with a view over the gold-encrusted Dome of the Rock and the Mount of Olives. The snow had stopped. The winter air was crystalline, the city's buildings etched against the gray sky. He stood, looked at the Old City, the narrow alleys where Jews and Muslims and Christians had fought and mingled for fifteen hundred years.

"Whatever I want, it's mine. Too much money to spend in ten lifetimes. No wife, no family." At this point, he hadn't met Orli. "Even if I did. One percent of what I have would be enough for my children and their children and their children, too. What do I do with a fortune like this?" He turned to her. "What is it you're saying? Clearly, now."

Until this moment Salome hadn't been sure herself. She'd been thinking out loud. Writing letters to the stars, as her high school boyfriend said. But the words came to her. She knew they were true. Her legs trembled under the table, but her voice was steady.

"For a few million dollars, we can do this."

"Men from the Mossad? The IDF?"

"Too easy to trace. And I don't think Tel Aviv" — where the Mossad was headquartered — "would approve."

"Where, then?"

"Men who kill for money aren't hard to find."

"Do you have specifics? Of how this might be done?"

"I have ideas."

"A budget? Employees?"

She saw he was putting the operation in the terms he understood best, a business plan.

She shook her head. The wrong answer.

"Then you're wasting my time. If you truly believe you can do this, the next time we meet, you'll have details. What it costs. How we do it without our friends in Tel Aviv catching on. I can move money wherever you need. Ten, twenty, even fifty million a year. But everything else, that's up to you. The logistics. How big a team. How we find them. What we tell them."

"I understand."

"No. You don't." His voice a lash. He'd never spoken to her this way before. Like she was an employee who'd disappointed him. "There's no timetable. You call me

71

when you're sure you can answer my questions, *all* my questions, and we'll meet. When you're ready. Not before."

"All right."

"Zev will see you out." Nothing more. He walked off, leaving her to watch her oatmeal turn to concrete.

Like the CIA, the Mossad ran espionage operations all over the world. The Israeli Defense Forces had the simpler but equally crucial task of stopping suicide bombers before they reached Jerusalem or Tel Aviv.

Spy services made elaborate, months-long efforts to recruit agents. The IDF used a simpler strategy. Like a big-city police department, it paid for tips. The Palestinian security services viciously punished anyone they caught collaborating with Israel. Even so, with the average Palestinian making less than two thousand dollars a year, rewards of a few hundred dollars attracted plenty of informants.

Salome had seen the strategy succeed firsthand. Israel had a military draft. After basic training, she joined the IDF's intelligence division. She learned surveillance and countersurveillance, how to find and recruit potential agents, interrogation techniques. Then she went to work as a junior intelligence officer, handling low-level Palestinian informants in the West Bank. She had come away after her two years of service feeling that for enough money, anyone could be bought.

Still, she had no illusions about her ability to handle an operation like the one she'd proposed to Duberman. She could hire the hackers and forgers she needed for communications and passports. Eastern Europe was full of those guys. Finding the trigger pullers would be much harder. She had told Duberman the truth. Plenty of men would kill for money. Unfortunately, they were mostly the wrong men: untrustworthy, uncontrollable, and potentially police informants. She couldn't risk scraping together a new team for every job. No, she needed eight or ten men with clean passports who could travel all over Europe and Asia. Mercenaries and paramilitaries. She couldn't find them herself, so she needed to find someone who could. He would make the hires and run the op on a day-to-day basis, serve as a screen between her and the team. Ideally, he would be American, ex-military or -CIA.

She knew there had to be CIA or Army officers who would bite on the deal she would offer. They were the men who'd come home from yearlong tours in Kabul to find that their wives had moved out. Who waited for noon so they could settle on the couch with a bottle of Smirnoff and a glass of ice. Who slept with their pistols under their pillows. Who would be desperate to try anything that might let them stop thinking about themselves.

Her man was one of those.

But how to find him? She couldn't exactly put out an ad: *Troubled former CIA officer needed to run assassination cell. Competitive salary, full benefits. Must be burned out, but not completely.*

It wasn't as if anyone kept a list of these men.

Then she realized she was wrong. Of course someone kept a list.

She told Raban he should investigate whether the Mossad was doing enough to manage its troubled case officers. At first, the idea bored him. Then she explained that the hearing wouldn't have to be classified. The chance for television exposure warmed him up immediately. *You think it's important, that's enough for me, sweetie.*

She knew that the committee would never hold such a hearing. No matter. She had Raban make an official request. Then she asked a friend at the IDF to put her in contact with the CIA. Not the National Clandestine Service or even the Directorate for Analysis. The human resources department. She told the good folks in HR that she and her boss wanted to reform the way the Mossad dealt with difficult officers. *These people, they've served us. They deserve our help, we can't just toss them aside like used tissues. I know some of them we can't reach, but at least we have to try.* She figured, correctly, that human resources managers didn't get much respect from their frontline cousins and would appreciate being taken seriously. *I hate to bother you with this, but our people are stonewalling me. I ask them for numbers, they just say these problems are rare. I ask how rare, they say internal matter. I ask how they respond, they say internal matter. Internal matter this, internal matter that, I'm so sick of hearing those two words. I'm hoping I might run some questions by you. Pick your brain, isn't that the English expression?* She had top-level Israeli security clearances. Anyway, she wasn't asking for the details of ongoing operations, just how the agency handled burned-out case officers. Three weeks later, she found herself in a conference room at Langley. *I'm interested in warning signs, how you intervened, when you realized cases might be hopeless. How much damage they did, how you contained it. I don't mean in just the obvious ways, blown operations or agents. I'm talking about more subtle problems, hits to station morale, lost management time. The stuff the frontline guys pretend doesn't matter, but in reality matters a lot.* She watched that last line score. A half-dozen heads nodded. And the horror stories began.

Obviously, I wouldn't want you to tell me names. But I would hope you would stick to the facts of their lives and careers. In other words, if someone was drummed out for being an alcoholic in Cairo, don't make him a heroin addict in Tokyo. The more accurate the information you give me, the better sense I can make of it.

And the easier it will be for me to find the man I need.

They provided even more information than she'd hoped. Whatever else it might be, the CIA was a bureaucracy. Everybody had a file. After two days, Salome had learned about dozens of troubled officers. One in particular stood out. A man who served with distinction in Baghdad, then transferred to Hong Kong and flushed his career away. Who lost millions of dollars gambling. Who rejected the agency's every effort to help and was ultimately forced out. *Millions of dollars? Weren't you concerned where the money was coming from? If he was selling secrets?* Of course, the CIA managers said. But the money turned out to be his own, an inheritance. His parents had died in a car accident. He'd received a large settlement. After a review of his career, the agency determined that he was not a security risk despite the gambling losses. There was no evidence that he had tried to contact the FSB, the Chinese, or any other foreign intelligence agency. Nor had he tried to hide his problems. They had been obvious from the start of his Hong Kong posting. And even if he'd wanted to betray his own agents, he hadn't had any to give up. In Hong Kong, he had hardly worked. In Baghdad, he had teamed with the military on operations against al-Qaeda in Iraq. But those missions had little ongoing intelligence value.

So the officer had been forced out, his security clearance pulled. He could never work for the agency again. But he hadn't been prosecuted. The CIA had even let him keep his pension.

So Iraq made him break down? The stress? The managers confessed they couldn't be sure. All along, the officer had refused to discuss his problems. *And where is he now?* Still in Hong Kong, they said. They had asked the station to monitor him. But its chief had insisted that anything other than an occasional look-in would be a waste of manpower. The consensus was that the officer would drink himself to death in a year. If he didn't put a bullet in his head even sooner.

Sounds like a tragic case. Exactly the sort of situation I'm hoping to prevent.

She met Duberman four days later at his villa in Jerusalem. No oatmeal this time, and no patio. He sat at an ornate gilded desk that looked like it belonged in Versailles. Spread across it were pictures of sharks, ugly beasts with squared-off heads. He held one up.

"What do you think?"

"I think that's why I never learned to surf."

"My casino manager wants to put in a new tank in Macao, drop in a couple of those. I'm not sure looking at them would make you want to throw down a thousand dollars on red." Duberman put down the photo. "So. You asked for the meeting, here I am."

She told him what she'd done. Normally, he was difficult to read. Not now. He started grinning right away. Five minutes in, he interrupted.

"You conned the CIA into giving you a list of its worst burnouts."

"You haven't heard the best part." She told him about the Hong Kong officer who had lost everything gambling in Macao. "I know there's no guarantee he played at 88 Gamma —"

"You said he lost millions?"

"That's what they told me."

"And he's American, not Chinese?"

"That was the impression they left. He had served in Baghdad."

Duberman reached for his phone. "Start the timer on your phone. It'll take me two minutes to get his name if he played with us. Five minutes if he did it somewhere else. Round-eye losers that size are rare."

He was wrong, barely. Three minutes passed before he hung up. "Glenn Mason."

"You sure?"

As an answer, he reached across the desk, put a finger to her lips. His touch was heavy, firm. A jolt of sexual energy coursed to her hips. She forced herself to lean back so that he was no longer touching her.

"Mason lost three million dollars with us.

Blackjack. Two and a half million of his own, a half million on a chit. Far as we can tell, he never played anywhere else. Ironic. We cut him off a few months ago. We have his address, but we haven't put any pressure on him because he's broke. They'll email me everything we have."

"Great." Her voice sounded breathy in her ears. She hoped he didn't notice.

"So now?"

She cleared her throat. Time to stop acting like a teenage girl who'd just been touched for the first time. "Now I quit Raban's office and start spending your money. A reliable source for passports. Anonymous email accounts. Phones. Pistols. Eastern European stuff. Won't take long."

"Why not talk to him first?"

"Because he'll have questions. He'll want proof that we're serious, and the more I do the more details I can give him."

"Will you tell him it's about Iran?"

"Yes. He'll figure that out anyway."

"But nothing about where the money's coming from."

"Of course no."

"If he says no?"

"We move on. I've got twenty possibilities. They won't all be as easy to find as he is, but they're all real."

"So nothing subtle."

"No. I'm just going to show up." The IDF philosophy. No mincing around. Make a direct approach, get a yes or no. The first betrayal was the toughest. Later on, people found reasons to keep getting paid. "From what they said, they're hardly even watching him. If he agrees, then everything else falls into place."

"Make sure he's not too broken."

"He spent years in Iraq. He's tougher than you think."

The next day she told Raban she was quitting to become an independent consultant to companies interested in making Middle Eastern investments. She hinted that Duberman was a client, but told him she couldn't be more specific because of a nondisclosure agreement. Raban said he understood.

After a couple weeks recruiting hackers in Eastern Europe, she flew to Hong Kong to recruit Mason. She knew he would agree as soon as he opened the door of his apartment and stared at her with his haggard, bloodshot eyes. As she'd predicted to Duberman, once she had Mason, everything else clicked. Within a few weeks, Mason traveled to Thailand to fake his own death.

Then he had plastic surgery so he could travel without worrying about tripping facial-recognition software. As soon as he recovered from the operations, he began recruiting. Over time, Mason's guys met her, but none learned her real name. And even Mason never figured out who was funding her.

While Mason recruited, Salome created the network of safe houses and vehicles and communications gear he needed. She became an expert at using anonymizing browser and email software, learned to judge a fake passport. The preparation was necessary. Still, she chafed at the wasted time. The Iranians were inching closer to a weapon. She knew because she still had access to the Mossad's analyses, thanks to Raban.

Every couple of months, she had lunch with him. She peeled his hands off her legs while he updated her on the Mossad and the IDF. He still thought of her more or less as one of his staffers. Staying connected to Raban helped in another way, too, by giving her an excuse to talk every so often to right-wing groups in Washington that supported Israel. Through them she could get invitations to the circuit of cocktail parties and conferences where CIA analysts and Pentagon lifers mingled with defense contractors and Middle Eastern lobbyists. She moved carefully, of course. She knew that she would set off alarms if she seemed too pushy. She kept her job description vague, a common practice at these gatherings, where business cards often had titles like *Principal* or *Managing Director/Services.* As she'd hoped, she became a familiar face. Even in an age of drones and metadata, informal networks mattered. She traded tidbits about Israel's fight against Hamas for tips about the European and Asian companies that were making hundreds of millions of dollars by helping Iran enrich uranium. Slowly, she built a hit list.

And a year after that snowy breakfast in Jerusalem, she gave Mason his first targets, two executives at a German metal company that was selling high-strength steel to Iran. Seventeen days later, he called her at her office in Zurich. The killings had gone off perfectly.

She had feared guilt might overtake her afterward. Instead, she felt the childish thrill of a bullied ten-year-old who had punched her tormentor and sent him gasping. *You thought we couldn't touch you, but you were wrong.* Her lack of empathy surprised her. *I suppose this is what it means to be evil,* she thought, but the word had no sting. She'd chosen these men to die, and their deaths had come.

Over the next year, Mason and his team kept killing.

Yet the Iranian program steamed ahead. Then Raban told her that the Mossad had pilfered the most recent American National Intelligence Estimate on Iran. The NIE reported that Iran remained determined to build a bomb and would complete one in two years, three at most.

Their work had failed. Tehran was too determined. Only obliterating Iran's nuclear facilities could stop its program.

In her twenties, Salome had fallen into a depression so deep that it seemed as if every cell in her mind was misfiring at once. Merely breathing became unbearably painful. The word *depression* didn't begin to describe how she felt. She had slid to the bottom of a crevasse five hundred meters deep, the kind that swallowed climbers on Everest. Not only could she not see the sun, she couldn't even be sure it existed.

She was at her lowest for only a few weeks, but the experience stamped her, changed her deep in her bones. To this day, she wasn't sure what had brought her down.

The experience forced her to face her own mind's fragility. Yet, paradoxically, it had given her a sense of invulnerability. She no longer feared the world. It couldn't hurt her as much as she could hurt herself.

Hearing about the NIE didn't instantly send her back down the hole. But it did make her remember what those days had been like, and to realize she was at risk. If this project failed, she'd lose everything. The Iranians would have the bomb, and she would know she had missed her chance to stop them.

She forced herself to retreat. To think. She still had Mason and his team. She needed a new way to use them. She drove east and south from Jerusalem into the desert, to the Dead Sea. The lowest point on earth, hundreds of feet below sea level. A depression, yes. Mountains on either side flanked the grandly named sea, in reality nothing more than a narrow salt-filled lake. Third-rate hotels clustered in a resort community midway down its shore, offering Dead Sea mudbaths and all-you-can-eat buffets, salmonella included. They catered to Russian immigrants and pensioners who didn't have the money to go anywhere else. Yet Salome felt strangely rejuvenated when she came to this ugly place. Maybe because of the sulfurous warmth. The fear that threatened her was *cold.*

On her third day, she watched Russian television, the foreign minister complaining about the White House. "The Americans think they can do whatever they like," he said. "They invade this country and that country. They pay no attention to national sovereignty. One day they will see the rest of the world does not jump to their drum."

They invade this country and that country . . .

Only the American military was powerful enough to destroy Iran's weapons program. But the White House didn't see the danger Iran posed. Or it feared another war in the Middle East too much to respond. Salome needed to force the United States to see the risk of allowing Iran to build a bomb. If the Iranians weren't yet ready to threaten America, she would threaten it for them. She would *foretell* the future, in order to prevent it.

She spent the next day figuring out realistic ways she might bait the United States. Then she flew halfway around the world to meet Mason in Indonesia. He told her she was insane.

Then he told her what she needed to do to succeed.

■ ■ ■ ■

She knew she'd have to tell Duberman face-to-face what she wanted. They rarely saw each other. The rest of his inner circle would notice if they spent too much time together. Anyway, he was married now. She had seen his wife Orli in magazines. She was Israeli, the daughter of Russian emigrants. In the photos, she was absurdly gorgeous, with long blond hair and hazel eyes. Salome hadn't been invited to the wedding. Hah.

Salome came to Duberman's mansion in Tel Aviv, catching a glimpse of Orli on her way to do whatever supermodels did in the morning. Pilates? A Botox refresher? Orli wore a long black T-shirt and yoga pants. She was as beautiful as her photos. Two men in suits waited at the front door, one large and one small. Her bodyguards. The muscle and the shooter. Salome felt the need to say something as she walked by.

"I work for your husband."

"Don't we all." Orli gave Salome the brilliant white smile that had sold a million Kias. Salome found herself unexpectedly charmed.

Duberman waited for her in his office. No hammerhead shark this time, no small talk.

The international version of CNN played on a television behind her. He muted it but left it on. Letting her know that her visit was an interruption.

"We have a problem." She told him about the National Intelligence Estimate. He listened with hands folded, eyes hooded. As if she were a casino manager explaining a $20 million loss.

"I'd say that's more than a problem," he said. "I'd say we're done."

"This makes it even more critical we don't give up."

"Then I hope you have a better idea."

"I do."

He reached for the remote control, turned the television off.

"The spies call this a false flag." She explained her plan, that they needed to make America attack Iran.

"Impossible," he said when she was finished. "Even if you could pull it off, which you can't — you know what she tells me, the last few times we talked?"

"She?"

Duberman looked vaguely irritated that Salome couldn't read his mind. "Donna." Meaning Donna Green, the National Security Advisor, as close to the President as anyone. "I've pushed her. I mean, carefully,

I don't want to make her mad. But she knows where I stand, and she knows I'm connected over here, so she half expects it. I say, Donna, you can't trust them, no matter how many cups of coffee you drink with them in Vienna. Even if they sign an agreement, it doesn't matter. She tells me, we don't want Iran to get a bomb either. And I say, tell me that they're not getting close. She says, maybe. I say, I know that means they *are* getting close. I say, the Israelis want you to get out your pen, draw some red lines. She says, it's great to hear from you. Next time you're in Washington, come by, let's meet in person. Do you understand?"

"Yes."

As if she hadn't spoken, he repeated the question. "Do you understand? They are not going to war with Iran."

"Unless we make them."

He laughed. A dry, asthmatic sound, the sound of someone trying to reason with a crazy person. "*Make* the United States go to war?"

"The uranium. If we can get that." What Mason had told her in Jakarta. *Get the HEU, they'll have to listen.*

"You have a source?"

"Not yet, but I will." Though Mason had also said that finding weapons-grade uranium would be impossible. Nothing on earth was guarded more closely.

"And our current guys, none would wonder about this change in strategy?"

"These men, you give them a mission, that's what they do. Long as they get paid. So —"

He reached into the desk, came out with a battered deck of cards. He shuffled them expertly, a perfect riff. Another new trick. Their backs were powder blue, with *H*s in white.

"These are almost forty years old, these cards. Hilton made new managers work the floor. To learn the business up close. There were no mechanical shufflers back then. So I learned." He flipped through the cards. "My boss back then, he liked to say, 'Your first loss is your best loss.' You understand? If it's not working, walk away."

"That's how you see this? A deal gone bad? A game? I guess I underestimated you."

She pushed her chair back and stood. She was conscious of the theatricality of the gesture, conscious, too, that her anger was real. The man across the desk from her had put up the cash, but she had done everything else.

"Sit down."

She didn't.

"Understand what you're proposing here. I'm an American citizen. This is treason. Punishable by death. And I'm not in the same place I was when we started."

Yeah, you married the best Barbie money could buy. I married Glenn Mason. Salome didn't say a word.

"Orli's pregnant."

Her stomach twisted. More proof that the life she'd imagined with Duberman had never existed anywhere but her mind. Strange to know his greatest secret and so little else about him.

"Congratulations." She choked out the word.

"Thank you. I'm trying not to think about the fact that I'll be in my seventies when they're teenagers. So this thing you're proposing —"

"It's a long shot. And if we get caught, yes. I understand. There's only one reason to do it, Aaron." She rarely permitted herself to use his name. "If we don't, Iran's going to get the bomb. And not just one. Sooner or later, they'll turn that city behind you into a pile of smoke. Maybe your kids will be there when it happens. You don't care about that, then there's nothing else I can say."

He shuffled once more and then shoved

the cards away.

"You know how leverage works, right?"

"No more business jargon. Please."

"Put up a dollar of your own, borrow nine, now you have ten dollars. Then you do something with it. Buy a stock, whatever. If what you buy goes up ten percent, to eleven dollars, you pay back the bank the nine dollars, keep two dollars. That's leverage. The investment only went up ten percent, but you doubled your money. But if what you buy goes down ten percent, you're wiped out. You multiply your gains and your losses. You get it?"

"You're saying this is leverage. The bank being the U.S. military." She wasn't sure, but she thought he was convincing himself, the way he had years before, putting the scheme in business terms, his native language.

He grinned. An odd expression. His face wasn't built for big smiles. "But that's it. The Pentagon *isn't* a bank. If they catch us, they won't sue us. They'll string us up."

She didn't know where he was going. Silence seemed to be her best choice.

"Do you believe?"

"Excuse me?"

He pointed at the ceiling in all apparent sincerity. "In God."

In truth, she didn't. Her depression had wiped out any belief she had in a universal power, much less an afterlife. Any God who allowed the mind to inflict such pain on itself was either nonexistent or impossibly cruel. She preferred the former. But she didn't think that answer would satisfy Duberman. "God? I guess so. I mean, maybe."

"That's no. If you have to think about it, it's no."

"No —"

"You don't have to spare my feelings. Me, I believe. Everything I've been given, how could I not? Funny, isn't it, we've never really talked religion before."

"There's a lot we don't know about each other."

"I guess." He turned away from her, to the window. "Out there, Tel Aviv, the gays, fine. They haven't been to temple in their whole lives. Then in Bnei Brak, these ultra-Orthodox with ten children, spending their day mumbling over the Torah." Duberman folded his hands together, rocked back and forth in his chair, imitating a Hasidic man praying. "Can't stand each other. Can't even talk to each other. But they're all Jews. The Nazis, they were right about that. We're a race. Not a religion. Not a culture. A race. Brothers in blood."

Salome thought of Orli, her long blond hair. Of Ethiopians and Chinese converts. But now was not the moment to argue.

"Germans, Iranians, Russians, two thousand years ago Romans, Egyptians then and now — all of them, they all want to stamp us out. Crush us. Nothing else in common, but they all hate Jews. The pogroms and the camps and the wars. All the way back to the Babylonians. We've always survived."

"Yes."

"You're sure this is the only way? Treason."

"I don't know any other."

"Then all right. If you can find that highly enriched uranium, we'll do it."

She felt as though she were watching them both from fifty thousand feet up. All of Tel Aviv below her, the sea to the west, the skyscrapers along the beach, and she and Duberman floating above, protecting them all without their knowing.

"What are you thinking?"

"That I wish we had a film crew here. Or at least a hidden camera. This moment ought to be recorded for posterity."

"Not sure that would be a great idea." He looked down at his desk in a way that let her know they were done, she was dismissed. Amazing that he could make a decision so momentous and then push her aside.

"You have an incredible ability to compartmentalize."

His nostrils flared in a silent laugh. "You want to stay for lunch, talk about your feelings? Go find the stuff."

She turned, walked to the door. She knew she shouldn't say anything to jeopardize her triumph, but she couldn't help herself.

"Whatever happened to, your first loss is your best loss?"

"Corporate crap. Never believed it. If I had, I would have walked away from The Sizzling Saloon. Don't you know anything about me? I like to gamble."

In the next months, she put the pieces together. She found an Iranian exile who could pass as a Revolutionary Guard colonel. And the only man in the world who had a private stash of weapons-grade uranium. She met Duberman in Hong Kong to tell him, get his final go-ahead. She saw that he was thrilled, and half terrified, too. She understood.

Her luck, or Duberman's God, or both, were on their side. Their new plan *worked*. Reza played his part as colonel perfectly. They gave the CIA enough evidence to make his story plausible. Only a few months after agreeing to discuss the end of sanctions, the United States and Iran were at the brink of war.

There was only one problem.

John Wells.

Wells tracked Mason to Istanbul. Mason and Salome played back, caught him there. Then Salome messed up. She let Mason convince her to hold Wells prisoner instead of killing him. Wells escaped, killed Mason and four of his men along the way. Salome had barely contained the aftermath. She knew Wells would keep coming. But did he know who she was? That Duberman was behind her?

She'd spoken to Duberman a few days before, to let him know that they had captured Wells and cleared the way for their final move — leading the CIA to the highly enriched uranium. She didn't want to discuss the new situation over the phone or email, even in code, even through anonymizing software. She flew to Hong Kong for a face-to-face chat.

Now, at last, she heard his confident steps coming toward the living room. Then the man himself. He wore a black turtleneck, dark gray pants, sleek black shoes. He looked like a cool college professor, one who was a little too old but could still fill an auditorium. In fact, the clothes were hand-tailored and cost as much as a car. He looked as he had when they'd met almost a decade ago. She figured he had a high-end anti-aging regimen going, testosterone and human growth hormone and whatever other potions doctors used to stop time. But even guessing at his tricks, knowing his vanity, she felt herself loosen in the usual places. He might be married to another woman, but he would never lose his hold on her.

The realization annoyed her.

"Aaron. Nice of you to make it."

"Congratulations." He came to her, wrapped his arms around her, and squeezed. He had never hugged her before. He smelled faintly of an aftershave almost medicinal in its harshness, simple and expensive. She wanted to cradle her head against his shoulder. Instead, she detached herself, stepped back.

"See if you still want to hug me after I give you the news."

"Soon enough. Meantime. Notice anything different?"

Now she did. On her last visit, the room's couches had been white leather over steel frames, a vaguely Nordic look. The frames were the same, but the leather was now red.

The change had probably cost fifty thousand dollars.

"You redecorated."

"Tinker Bell." Duberman's impolite name for his five-hundred-dollar-an-hour decorator. Every so often he said something like that, reminding her he was from a different generation. "He didn't ask. I should have fired him, but I feel a certain loyalty since he set me up with Orli."

Salome refrained from pointing out that putting a billionaire with a supermodel didn't exactly qualify as groundbreaking in the matchmaking department. For whatever reason, Duberman felt talkative today, not ready for business.

"You have to live it to understand, being this rich makes you the center of your own little solar system. Somebody buys my furniture, somebody drives. It's not just that somebody else gardens. Somebody else *hires* the gardeners. All I do is breathe and write checks. Though somebody else signs them, mostly."

"I'm having a hard time sympathizing."

"I feel sometimes like I'm not living my own life. This thing we've done, it's the only thing in the world that's really *mine*."

"And your kids."

"They're Orli's, really. They love me, but

if I vanished tomorrow she'd have a thousand men at her door. She'd pick a good one and it'd be like I was never there." Duberman looked vaguely embarrassed, as though he'd said more than he meant. She had never seen that expression on him before, and she didn't like it. Embarrassment didn't suit him.

"So you're telling me you decided to start a war because firing your decorator would have been too difficult."

"Exactly." He grinned. "Anyway. You didn't come halfway around the world because you have good news."

His library was a square room with books on every side, an old-school gentlemen's club. He flipped a light switch to expose a keypad. He tapped in a code. A section of books on the back wall slid into the floor, revealing a safe room.

"Does it connect to the Bat Cave, too?"

He led her in, closed the door. The room was a cube, ten feet on each side. Two narrow twin beds were pushed against the walls and a three-foot-high gray safe occupied the center. The place looked like an unfinished art installation, a parody of itself: *The Safe Room, a/k/a The Billionaire's Mind.*

She patted the safe. "Let me guess. Five

hundred thousand euros and a pistol."

"Why don't you tell me the problem." A statement, not a question. Now he was the one who was annoyed. So she explained how Wells had escaped, killed Mason and the others, fled Turkey.

"Now? Where is he?"

"Back in the U.S. I had a lawyer hire detectives to watch for him at airports all across the East Coast. Didn't say who he was, just that we were looking for him. One picked him up coming through Boston."

"So we have eyes on him?"

"No. Too dangerous. I let him go. I'd rather have guys on Ellis Shafer. That's his main contact inside the agency. Even so, it's tricky. These private detectives, the good ones won't touch anything that crosses wires with the CIA. It's one thing to look for a guy at an airport, but once they know Shafer works for the agency, only the low-rent ones will go near it."

"So Wells is loose."

A few minutes ago she'd thought they were friends. Now his voice was quiet. Icy. She wished he would shout at her. Anything but this. She waited.

"We're close on this," he said finally. "Especially after what those animals did in Mumbai —"

His words brought Salome back to the reports from India. She had focused so closely on Wells that she hadn't thought much about the downing of the jet. But Duberman was right. The war drums were beating.

"They must want a war," Duberman said.

"Want it or think it's inevitable." Most Iranian Muslims were part of the Shia branch of Islam. And the drive to martyrdom had been part of Shia culture from the very founding of the sect. The first Shia had believed Ali, the son-in-law of Muhammad, was his true heir. Other Muslims, calling themselves Sunnis, opposed Ali. At a battle near the Iraqi city of Karbala, the Sunnis killed Ali and slaughtered his men. They had dominated Islam ever since. Today, ninety percent of Muslims were Sunni.

But the Shia remained faithful to Ali. In fact, the name Shia meant "followers of Ali." Each year, hundreds of thousands of Shia made pilgrimages to Karbala to commemorate that first battle. Recently, Sunni terrorists had made a habit of attacking the pilgrims. No matter. They kept coming.

When Salome heard analysts say that Iran would never use a nuclear weapon against Tel Aviv because it knew that the Israelis would respond with a hundred bombs of

101

their own, she thought of those pilgrims shuffling along, unarmed, unprotected, awaiting their fates.

She pushed the pilgrims out of her mind. "So have you talked to Donna?" The National Security Advisor.

"Not since the uranium turned up. It's better if I don't get involved right now. They know I want them to attack. I can't seem like I'm celebrating. At this point, if I do call, it'll be directly to POTUS. And it'll be one time only. Best to keep that card tucked away in case of emergency. The question is, does your friend Wells know enough to make a case? And will anyone listen?"

"He and Shafer weren't getting anywhere with the agency. That's why Wells came to Istanbul by himself. Everything he did, he did on his own. As far as the CIA is concerned, Glenn Mason's been dead for years."

"You think Wells knows about me?"

Salome hesitated.

"Tell me the truth."

"I'm trying to think it through, Aaron. He found Mason, so he and Shafer must know about the money Mason lost in Macao. Whether they jumped to you, I don't know."

"Let's assume they have. What about anything Wells might have seen in Istanbul.

License plates? IDs? The factory?"

"We're safe on the factory. Paid for from an account that doesn't come anywhere near us. Wells did steal a laptop when he broke out, but all our computers have software on them that erases the hard drive if the wrong password is used or someone tries to copy it. Wipes it clean."

"You're confident in that."

"I've seen it happen."

"So what do you think we should do? About Wells."

The ultimate question. The reason she had flown more than ten thousand kilometers to see Duberman.

"I think he's too much of a risk. We have to neutralize him."

"You mean kill him."

"We already took him captive, and that blew up."

"He have a family?"

"A son and an ex-wife. But they're gone. Probably Wells has the FBI looking after them. Anyway, going after families usually causes more problems than it solves. The same with Duto and Shafer. A senator, a CIA officer, they're untouchable. But Wells, he takes chances. He'll come at us. We catch him —"

"Last time you caught him, he killed five of your guys. What makes you think you'll have better luck this time?"

"We'll be ready." She knew the answer sounded lame.

"As far as you know, Wells doesn't have anything more than he did last week."

"Unless he's put you and Mason together."

"So what, some dead CIA officer lost money at my casino. Millions of people do that every year. I never met the guy."

"But —"

He raised a hand to silence her. "As a rule, I don't like waiting. I want the other side reacting to me. But right now this war has its own momentum. We keep our heads down a few more days, the United States will attack. After that, John Wells can say whatever he wants."

"If you'd seen what he did in Istanbul."

"Then you should have killed him when you had the chance." He'd made up his mind, she saw. "Assuming you find him again, you watch him. You think he's getting close, we'll talk. Those phones you gave me are clean?"

She nodded. He opened the door and let them out of the ridiculous little panic room. Salome had a sudden premonition that she'd never see him again. She wanted to kiss him on the lips. Just once.

"Don't," Duberman said.

"What?"

"Don't go after him, Salome. I can see it in your eyes, that's what you're thinking."

In the living room he hugged her again, lightly this time, for show. Then he walked off to the family quarters of the house. Where he *lived.* Without a thought of her. She was alone, looking out over Hong Kong.

Why did she let him tell her what to do? She'd devoted her life to this project. Every hour, every day, for years. He hadn't done anything except reach into his bank accounts and give her orders. Yet somehow, he was the boss. She couldn't disobey him.

She would do what he said. She would watch Ellis Shafer. She would find John Wells and watch him. She wouldn't touch them, either of them.

Not yet.

3

ZURICH

The boxy Mercedes Geländewagen waited outside Zurich Airport's Terminal B, a police placard attached to its front windshield so it didn't have to circle like everyone else in the world. As Wells emerged from the terminal, an awesomely ugly man slid out of the SUV's back seat. Blond hair sprouted in random patches from his skull. His eyes were so small they didn't even qualify as beady. He wore a baggy nylon sweat suit that Wells knew concealed a snubnosed pistol.

Wells had met him once before. He was a Serb who went by the nickname Dragon. A bodyguard for Kowalski. Wells remembered him as skinnier, more feral, and even uglier. The years living in Zurich had softened him. Though Wells guessed that he still knew how to squeeze a trigger.

"Dragon."

The man smiled in surprise, touched a finger to his chest. "Goran now."

"You'll always be Dragon to me."

"You have weapon?"

Wells shook his head. "More's the pity."

Dragon pulled open the SUV's front passenger door, waved him in. The windows were cracked, but the Mercedes stank of stale Eastern European tobacco.

"Uncle Pierre know you smoke in here?" Wells said. No answer. "Bad for the leather."

The driver turned up the radio. Lousy German pop. Not that there was any other kind.

Wells closed his eyes and tried to rest. It was midafternoon in Switzerland, the winter sun disappearing behind the jagged snow-capped mountains west of the airport. Wells had slept a few hours over the Atlantic on the first leg of the trip, his overnight flight to London. Not nearly enough to make up for the sleep he'd lost in the last two weeks. Especially the nights he'd spent chained to a wall in Istanbul. Many Special Forces operatives used amphetamines to keep themselves awake during long missions. Wells had never tried speed, but the idea seemed especially tempting today. He felt dull and slow, gray around the edges.

Zurich was a city of bankers. Yet the global

financial crisis hadn't touched its wealth. Audis, BMWs, and Mercedeses filled the highway from the airport to the center of town. Farther east, in the wealthy neighborhood along the Zürichsee where Kowalski lived, the mansions gleamed, their walls not so much painted as polished.

Wells hadn't been to Zurich in years, yet he remembered the tiniest details of the place. The city had imprinted itself on him then because his emotions had been so high. On that trip he'd come intending to kill Kowalski. The arms dealer had tried to assassinate Wells, but his shooters had botched the job. Instead, they'd wounded Wells's fiancée, Jennifer Exley, a CIA officer. Exley, who was pregnant, had lost the baby. From her hospital bed, she begged Wells to stay with her, not seek revenge. Wells went to Zurich instead.

Ultimately, Kowalski bought back his life by giving up information that helped Wells stop a terrorist attack. They would never be friends, but they weren't exactly enemies. But Exley had never forgiven Wells for leaving her. She'd quit him and the agency both.

In the years since, Wells had met Anne, a New Hampshire cop. Now Anne had left him, too, rejecting his marriage proposal. The two women were very different. Exley was a brilliant blue-eyed pixie who judged herself more harshly than the world ever would. She had worked herself to the brink of exhaustion after 9-11 to punish herself for failing to foresee the attacks, even though no one else had either. Anne was tall, brown-eyed, athletic and strong, practical and cynical. Wells wasn't sure the two women would have liked each other. Yet they'd both reached the same conclusion about him. That he cared for his missions more than either of them. That he would rather die than leave the field.

He'd been weighed in the balance and found wanting.

And now Wells found himself aching for Exley as the big Mercedes rolled through Zurich's silent streets. Her absence centered on his shoulders, his upper back, where she had wrapped herself around him on their motorcycle rides. The fact that Kowalski was still in his life while Exley was gone seemed a cosmic joke.

Or maybe not. When she'd needed him most, he had left her. Not exactly proof they were soul mates. Maybe he had preserved his memories of Exley in amber, romanticized a love that would inevitably have faded. Even a child wouldn't have guaranteed anything. Wells had walked away from

109

a child and a wife once already.

He put aside these unpleasant speculations as the Mercedes pulled up outside Kowalski's red-brick mansion. He reached for his door, found it locked. Behind him, Dragon slid out, opened it from the outside.

"Step out, turn around, hands on the roof."

Wells did as he was told. Dragon frisked him thoroughly, an unapologetic and professional job. When he was done, he yelled something over his shoulder and the front door swung open. Pierre Kowalski. He'd gained weight since Wells last saw him. He had a ruddy complexion, two ample chins. He wore a blue polo shirt and folded his thick arms across his chest. His bulk came across as aristocratic. A European trick, one that fat Americans could rarely pull off.

Wells reminded himself to be friendly as he walked up the slate front steps. He needed a favor, and he was short on leverage and time.

"John Wells."

"Pierre." Wells extended a hand.

Kowalski took it in both of his. "You must be in trouble if you're being polite to me."

The mansion looked as Wells remembered,

its walls covered with nineteenth- and twentieth-century art. "You still have that thing in the other room?"

"*Romulus and Remus?* The AK and the RPG?"

"That's the one." The piece consisted of a rocket-propelled grenade launcher and an assault rifle preserved for eternity inside a clear plastic box, buffed in a way that made their murderous details hyperreal and beautiful.

"A few weeks ago, a Qatari tried to buy it from me. Seven million dollars. I said no. Probably my favorite piece. I'm surprised you remembered."

"It stuck with me. And the art history lesson."

"Oh yes. *The Physical Impossibility of Death in the Mind of Someone Living.* The tiger shark in the box."

"You told me it was at the Metropolitan Museum. I tried to see it once when I was in New York, but I couldn't find it."

"The man who owned it took it back. Never trust a hedge fund manager." Kowalski was as smooth as Wells remembered. His practiced finesse no doubt played well with the dictators who bought his weapons. He led Wells into the kitchen, more suitable for a restaurant, twin six-burner stoves and

111

Sub-Zero refrigerators, along with a fleet of copper pans hanging from the ceiling.

Kowalski nodded at the granite-topped island in the center of the room. "Sit, please. Would you like a drink? Something to eat?"

"Nein."

But Kowalski pulled two Heinekens from the nearest Sub-Zero. "If you change your mind." He popped them open and they sat catercorner on the island. Dragon lurked at the edge of the room.

"You look healthy, John."

The phony gentility suddenly irked Wells. Kowalski paid for this mansion and its art by selling weapons to third-world countries. At best, he encouraged poor governments to spend money they couldn't afford on helicopters and personnel carriers they didn't need. At worst, he spread untold misery in shabby little wars that rated five minutes a year on CNN.

"We're such good buddies, how come Dragon had to feel me up before I could see you?"

"Goran. He's respectable now." Kowalski sipped his beer. "You came all this way to reminisce. Or no?"

Wells had told him only that they needed to meet as soon as possible.

"It's about Iran."

"No surprise."

"You want the long version or the short?"

"I think the short might be safer. For both of us."

"Know anyone who might have been sitting on a hunk of HEU?"

"You think Iran is getting it from an outside source?" Kowalski shook his head. "No, not that. You think someone fooled the CIA. The Iranians are telling the truth, the HEU isn't theirs. Someone wants America to invade Iran. Mossad?"

"I thought you didn't want the whole story."

"It's impossible, John. Even the Mossad couldn't do it."

"My question is, if I came to you, said, Pierre, I need weapons-grade uranium, cost doesn't matter, but it's got to be enough to make someone sit up and notice, where would you send me?"

"The Democratic People's Republic of Korea." North Korea. "If you were crazy enough to go. But they would take your money and put a bullet in you."

"Plus they can't enrich to ninety-four percent."

"That's right."

"Where else?"

"Nowhere. Nowhere else."

Footsteps. Wells turned to see a tall blonde, high cheekbones and full lips. "Nadia," he said. Kowalski's girlfriend. She was a Ukrainian model, the most beautiful woman Wells had ever seen. He had met her on his previous trip. She'd kissed his cheek as he left, gently. Even in his rage over Exley, he had felt the pull of her beauty.

Now she looked at him blankly. Wells saw she didn't remember him. And something else, too. Her arms and legs were as slim as ever, but her belly swelled under a loose T-shirt. She was pregnant. "Congratulations."

She laid a hand on her stomach. "Thank you."

"Nadia, do you remember John Wells? You met years ago."

She looked at him, and he saw the realization in her face. "Yes. Of course." She smiled, but warily. Wells realized that he reminded her of a time when life hadn't been quite so certain.

"Nadia and I are married now," Kowalski said.

"Congratulations again." Married. And pregnant. Even the arms dealer and the model had moved on with their lives while Wells wasn't looking. "You're a lucky lady."

"I think so, yes." She came to Kowalski,

rubbed his cheek. "Just remember we have the banquet tonight. No snacks."

She floated off, beautiful as ever. Wells watched Kowalski watching her go.

"I love her," Kowalski said.

"You want me to applaud for your good taste?"

"You think she's easy to love because she's beautiful?"

An odd tack from Kowalski, considering he was the one who'd chosen her. Wells wasn't in the mood to pursue the argument. "North Korea aside, you have no idea where I might pick up a kilo of HEU?"

"I do not."

"You want me out of your happy home, give me *something,* Pierre. You can't find it for me, send me to someone who might. The dirtiest guy you know."

"When you say it like that, it's easy. Mikhail Buvchenko. Russian."

"I don't know that name."

"Spetsnaz, until he figured out he could make a lot more money in my business. He's in his mid-thirties, connections all up and down the Red Army."

"You've dealt with him."

"We've bumped into each other a few times. He'll sell to anyone. Assad, Burma, Congo. Places where the Kremlin has an interest but doesn't want to do business directly. You want chemical weapons, he can help. Even has a little private army."

"Army?"

"That's too strong. A battalion, say. Several hundred men. They were the first ones on the ground in Ukraine, a way for Putin to make a low-risk move, see how Europe and the U.S. would react."

"Or not react."

"Exactly."

"But if he's so connected to the Kremlin, would he deal HEU without their say-so?"

"I can't be sure, but I think his agreement with them is that he answers when they call. In return, they don't interfere with his other arrangements, as long as he doesn't do anything directly opposed to Russian interests."

"I'd like to meet him."

"Mistake. He's not so nice. And he won't come west. You'll have to go to Russia."

"Set it up, Pierre."

Kowalski drummed his fingers nervously against the granite countertop.

"Even if I vouch for you, I can't promise he won't kill you."

"If I didn't know better, I'd think you cared, Pierre." Wells found himself smiling. "You're afraid if you vouch for me and I kill

116

him, his mercenaries will be here five minutes later. Blowback."

"Maybe I care a little, too."

"Maybe you don't."

"Maybe I don't."

"I promise you, I'm not interested in him.
Compared to what's at stake, he's nobody."

"I wouldn't try that argument with him."

"Fair enough."

"I do this, we're even, John?"

"Sure." *Until the next time I need you.*

"It may take a couple days."

"Sooner is better." Though Wells didn't
mind getting at least one decent night's
sleep. But he couldn't wait here. And then,
suddenly, he knew his next stop. A city that
aside from its wealth was as unlike Zurich
as anywhere he could imagine.

4
TEN DAYS . . .

Room 219, Hart Senate Office Building.

Unlike the White House Situation Room or the Pentagon's Tactical Operations Center, 219 didn't show up often in movies. But everyone at the CIA knew its importance. The "room" was actually a suite of offices that housed the staff and hearing rooms of the Senate Select Committee on Intelligence. Unmarked frosted-glass doors hid 219's real front entrance, which was permanently guarded by Capitol police officers who shooed away tourists and other uninvited guests. Behind the second door, a corridor turned sharply right, a way to keep anyone in the foyer from glimpsing the offices inside, or the staffers who worked in them. At the end of the hall, a biometric lock secured access to the conference room where senators received briefings from the DCI and top intelligence officials. The hearings took place within a huge elevated vault, a larger version of the secure rooms that the CIA operated inside American embassies. The room was mounted on pillars so that technicians could easily sweep its steel walls for bugs. The steel itself blocked noise and electromagnetic signals from escaping. No one had ever managed to spy on the hearings. Information regularly leaked nonetheless, in the simplest possible way — from the committee's senators to reporters.

After all the security, the vault's interior usually disappointed visitors. It had the same furniture as any congressional hearing room, with wooden conference tables that looked decent from a distance, cheap up close. But the room had played host to plenty of fireworks over the years. During the 1980s, when some senators called for the CIA to be abolished over the Iran-Contra scandal, case officers called 219 as the Lion's Den. Since 9-11, the acrimony had faded for a while. Aside from libertarians like Rand Paul and liberals like Ron Wyden, Congress generally supported the War on Terror. But the recent revelation that the agency had spied on committee staff members as they prepared a report about CIA interrogation programs had again poisoned relations. And today, Brian Taylor feared the room might live up to its old nickname.

Taylor was deputy chief of base for Istanbul. (Technically, the CIA's station in Turkey was located in Ankara. By long-standing tradition, the CIA could have only one "station" in every country, so it referred to its office in Istanbul as a "base.") He had found the weapons-grade uranium that the United States accused Iran of producing. He was the only agency officer ever to meet Reza, the Revolutionary Guard colonel who had tipped the CIA to Iran's plans. Now Reza was in the wind, and the United States and Iran were close to war. And after initially rushing to support the President, members of Congress were expressing concerns about a military confrontation.

"This isn't Iraq. We know the uranium is real," an anonymous senator had told *The Washington Post* that morning. "But we need to know why the White House is so sure it's from Iran. Just like we need to know who blew up that jet. The hearings today and tomorrow will be critical."

A laundry list of top officials would testify at the hearing, including the DCI, Scott Hebley. But Taylor knew he would be the star witness. Without him, none of this

120

would have happened.

The agency understood the importance of his testimony. It had flown him and his boss, Martha Hunt, to Virginia three days before. Since then, Hebley's aides had rehearsed with him nonstop. Max Carcetti, Hebley's top lieutenant, played the committee's head, an Illinois senator named Laura Frommer. Carcetti cut Taylor off, jumped on inconsistencies in his answers. *You just told us that Colonel Reza claimed Iran had produced enough uranium for several nuclear weapons. Earlier you said ten. Which is it, Mr. Taylor?*

Hunt, the Istanbul chief of base, would attend the hearing but wasn't scheduled to testify. Part of Taylor wished she'd stayed in Turkey. She was slim and beautiful, her delicate blue eyes hiding her intelligence and toughness. For as long as they'd worked together, Taylor had had a hopeless crush on her.

But he and Hunt had worked side by side to find the uranium. Suddenly, his crush didn't feel so hopeless. On the charter home, they hadn't done anything as obvious as hold hands. But Hunt had slept beside him on the otherwise empty jet. Close enough for him to smell her perfume, something light and floral and faintly sweet. She'd settled in, with her head almost on his shoulder. Almost.

Still, Taylor knew that if he blew his testimony, she'd never forgive him. The night before the hearing, after a dinner of mushroom pizza at their Reston safe house, she walked Taylor through his testimony yet again. "Stick to the facts. They ask why you think Iran would do this now, that's above your pay grade. They ask about alternatives to an invasion —"

"That's above my pay grade."

After an hour, Taylor rebelled.

"Martha. Stop treating me like your idiot little brother."

"I am limiting your downside."

"And yours."

She stood, put her fingers to her lips, blew him a kiss. "See you in the morning."

"You have nightmares, you know where to find me."

"Night, Brian."

Taylor hardly slept that night. At 5 a.m., he gave up trying. He showered, shaved, dressed. He spent two hours trying not to drink too much coffee while he read over his reports and checked his email. They didn't have full access to Langley's classified feeds here, but they could port in through a virtual private network.

Not much had happened overnight. Reza was still missing, still hadn't touched the hundreds of thousands of dollars that the CIA had put in a Swiss account for him. No surprise there. Taylor didn't expect him to turn up. In India, the leads in Mumbai pointed to Hezbollah. But despite a lot of door-kicking, the Indian police had no suspects. Meanwhile, Israel reported that Iran had mobilized its "Widows Brigade," seven hundred female suicide bombers who would attack American soldiers if they crossed the border.

More proof that an invasion of Iran would make the wars in Iraq and Afghanistan look easy. Iran was larger, its army better trained. Most important, its people were far more unified than Afghanis or Iraqis. In those countries, the United States had fought factions. In Iran it would be at war with a nation.

Hunt emerged from her room at 7:30, showered and scrubbed. "You sleep?"

"I look that bad?"

"I'll put some foundation on you. Hide the circles —" She swept her hands under her eyes.

"Martha, I am not wearing makeup."

"It'll be subtle."

Much as he wanted to feel her fingertips

on his skin, he had to draw this line. "No one's expecting me to be minty fresh."

"Minty fresh? I don't suppose you want to go over your talking points one last time."

"If you weren't my boss, I'd tell you what I really want."

Three hours later, Taylor sat in the secure room at the heart of 219 as Senator Frommer and the rest of the select committee took their places on the dais before him. Frommer had asked for Taylor's testimony first, in place of the DCI, a not-so-subtle shot at the agency. *This hearing runs on our schedule, not yours.* She was in her early sixties, with a helmet of dyed black hair and a face whose wrinkles had been Botoxed into submission.

She's smart, Carcetti had told him. *And she trusts her instincts. She can afford to. She's in a safe seat and she's got no plans to run for President. They listen to her on that committee. Both parties. They like her. Keep her on your side, you'll sail through.* He didn't have to say what would happen if Taylor couldn't keep Frommer on his side.

Hunt sat beside Taylor at the witness table. Carcetti had wanted a lawyer, too. But Taylor insisted a lawyer would only make him nervous, and Carcetti finally agreed.

She's not much for ceremony, Madame Frommer, Carcetti had said. *At ten thirty sharp, she'll hit that gavel to get started and get to the point. That's one reason they like her.*

Sure enough, as senators were still settling themselves, Frommer tapped the gavel. "We will begin this hearing of the Select Committee. I am not sure I've ever been involved with a more important session. A few days ago, the President of the United States presented the American public with shocking news about Iran's nuclear intentions. The United States believed that Iran could be a partner for peace. But if the White House is correct, the Islamic Republic has secretly been preparing for war all along. Under such circumstances, I think we agree that the President has the right to defend our interests and keep Americans safe.

"Unfortunately, recent history compels us to treat presidential pronouncements about weapons of mass destruction with skepticism. Over the next two days, we will hear testimony from the DCI and other members of the intelligence community. But I want to begin by hearing from the CIA officer who found the uranium. We are in closed session. I am going to use your real name, sir, Brian Taylor. And your real title, deputy chief of base for Istanbul. Mr. Taylor, please stand and raise your right hand, so I may administer the oath."

Taylor stood, raised his hand. "I, Brian Taylor, do solemnly swear —"

For the next forty-four minutes, Taylor explained everything that had happened in Istanbul since the day when the first letter from Reza arrived on his desk. "Thank you for allowing me to testify," he said when he was done. "It's an honor. I'm happy to answer any questions."

He spoke mostly from memory, referring to his notes as little as possible. *Try not to read the whole time,* Carcetti had said. *Head up, so you can look the committee members in the eye. They like that.* Taylor wasn't so sure. He'd expected his statement would sway the senators, break the tension in the room. It seemed to have the opposite effect. He felt like a kid who had broken a window and been called into the principal's office. Only the faint hum of filtered air pumping through the vault's narrow vents broke the silence.

Frommer cleared her throat. "Mr. Taylor. We appreciate your coming before us. You do understand, the story you're telling is unusual." She drew out the last word. "Would you agree?"

Defer when you can, Carcetti had said. *She's the boss. Don't fight her. When in doubt, stretch out the at bat, get more information. And never cut her off. Never never. Senators don't like that.*

"I'm not sure exactly what you mean."

"I mean the way you handled Reza's recruitment and handling. The fact that he came to you. That you never learned his real name or position within the Quds Force. Have you ever had another agent like that?"

"No, ma'am — chairwoman."

"Senator, please. And the fact that the agency cannot find Reza despite a quote-unquote intense effort, that's also unusual."

"Yes."

"What do you make of these oddities, Mr. Taylor? I remind you that you are under oath."

If Frommer meant to intimidate him by mentioning that he was under oath, she succeeded. Taylor heard his pulse thumping in his skull, the blood surging through. The funny part was that he had told the truth. He believed in Reza. Even so, he felt like a kid caught in a riptide pulling him out to sea. If he kept calm, didn't fight the current, he'd be fine. But it was hard to keep calm with the water lunging into his nose. The next few minutes would be crucial. If he failed, the President might face a revolt on Capitol Hill.

"Mr. Taylor? Still with us?"

Taylor didn't know how long he'd been silent. Too long. Hunt leaned over, murmured in his ear, her breath warm against his skin, her perfume filling his nose. "You all right?"

Her words broke the spell. Or maybe her perfume. That fast, Taylor knew what to say. "Chairwoman Frommer. I'm sorry. I wanted to answer you as precisely as possible. You are correct that walk-ins are unusual. Most of the time, the agency makes the initial approach. That's the classic method. In our training at the Farm, we spend a lot of time practicing recruitments. And it's true that walk-ins can be double agents dangled by foreign services. I assume that's your paramount concern, that Reza is working for a foreign agency trying to fool us into attacking Iran."

"Yes."

"But walk-ins have been among the best assets in the CIA's history. They have unique advantages. They are often spies themselves, so they understand tradecraft and don't need hand-holding. They give up vital information quickly, because it is the very *importance* of the information that has caused them to approach us. Put another way, they're motivated. We don't have to play games with them. I hope that makes sense."

When you're answering, don't go on and on, Carcetti said. *Pause halfway through. Get them to buy in.*

"I suppose."

"I believe the man who called himself Reza was one of these ultra-high-value walk-ins. Do I wish I knew his name? Yes. That we had him under our protection, in a safe house somewhere? Yes. Would I prefer someone else had seen him? Of course. At least then I wouldn't be the only one in front of the firing squad."

Taylor thought he was close to breaking through. But Frommer merely shook her head.

"Mr. Taylor. If a firing squad is required, you won't be its only target. We're going to hear much more testimony today. And, of course, we will discuss next steps."

"That's above my pay grade."

Even as the words left his mouth Taylor knew he'd made a mistake. Frommer was in no mood for canned lines.

"You are correct. Far above. Let's focus

on the question that you are here to answer. Is the man who calls himself Reza who he claims to be? Is he real?"

Taylor's life had shrunk to the microphone in front of him. He reached for it, cupped it toward him. His hands weren't shaking. A small victory.

"Believe me, I understand what that question means for our country, Chairwoman. I've spent more hours than I can count thinking it through. And my answer is *yes*."

"Why?"

Because no one could be that good an actor. But Taylor knew Frommer didn't want pronouncements. She wanted specifics.

"Because the truth is that no one betrays his country without good reason. I saw Reza's motivations up close and they were real, believable, and specific. I've outlined them today and I discussed them in detail in my reports, which I know the agency has made available to you. Nor do I fault Reza for his desire to keep his real name secret. He mentioned Edward Snowden and Bradley Manning when I promised to protect him and his identity. I can't disagree with his assessment of our security flaws."

"Is that all?"

"It is not, ma'am. I believe a foreign agency would have presented someone

130

whose cover story didn't raise as many questions as Reza's. I repeatedly demanded more information from him. A would-be double agent would have answered at least some questions. Tried to ease my suspicions. His superiors would have insisted. Reza refused. He never gave me the impression that he was under anyone's control."

"So the holes in his story actually make him more plausible?"

"I know that's counterintuitive, but yes. He told me repeatedly that the intelligence he provided would speak for itself. And that has proven to be correct."

"Mr. Taylor, the agency sometimes uses the term *source capture,* does it not?"

Taylor hadn't heard anyone at the CIA utter those words since his training at Camp Peary. But this was not the moment to argue. "Yes, Madam Chairwoman."

"Can you define those words for me?"

"Source capture occurs when a CIA officer becomes so overly protective of an agent that he can no longer determine the agent's value or reliability. It isn't the same as being doubled, where the officer winds up becoming an active spy for the other side. It's more subtle and insidious. It happens for any number of reasons. Sexual attraction, or even friendship over a long period. Usually, the officer doesn't even recognize what's happening. Ultimately, instead of running the source, he winds up quote-unquote captured by him."

"Did Reza capture you, Mr. Taylor?"

Not even Carcetti had asked the question so bluntly. "I assure you, Senator, that Reza and I were in no way friends. I always felt uncomfortable at our meetings, to be honest."

"But there's an even simpler form of source capture, yes?"

Stretch the at bat . . . "I'm not trying to be difficult, Senator, but I don't understand the question."

"Then I'll explain." Frommer didn't smile. "If an asset is providing uniquely valuable information, he will have a uniquely valuable effect on the career of the officer who's handling him, yes?"

"Possibly."

"You, for example. I'm sure you recognized Reza's importance to your career."

Taylor's cheeks reddened like Frommer had slapped him. *She's the boss,* Carcetti had said. *Don't fight her.* But Taylor couldn't help himself. He had joined the agency after 9-11, for the right reasons, to defend his country —

"Question my judgment, Senator, I can

live with that. But don't question my integrity. Don't call me a careerist. Believe it or not, I know my place. I'm a small cog in a very big machine. I don't have any plans to be DCI. Or even a station chief. I've never told anyone this before, but I figured on retiring after this posting. If I've been fooled, if I'm wrong, I expect to be disciplined. Or terminated. This isn't about me —"

"Mr. Taylor —"

Never cut her off. Taylor raised a hand. "With respect, you brought this up. I'd like the opportunity to finish —"

"Mr. Taylor —"

"This isn't about me. It's about what's best for the country. Making sure that a nuclear weapon never explodes on American soil. I can only tell you what I saw. And I saw a man who repeatedly gave us accurate and actionable intelligence. A man who led us to 1.3 kilograms of weapons-grade uranium. As I'm sure you know, that ingot is by far the biggest piece of nuclear material that anyone has ever found. If we prove it didn't come from Iran, so be it. If the Iranians let us talk to their scientists, inspect their plants so we can be sure they aren't enriching in secret, great. But until then, my money's on Reza."

Taylor folded his hands on the table, waited for Frommer to rip him a new one. Instead, a smile creased her filler-plumped lips. He'd turned her around. Not just her. Senators from both parties were nodding and smiling. Each of the fifteen faces above him looked down with new respect.

He'd *won.*

"Mr. Taylor. I am surprised. It's rare to have a CIA officer speak so bluntly to us. I appreciate your candor."

"Thank you, Senator."

"I know my fellow senators have questions. As is customary, members will speak in order of seniority. I remind you, you have six minutes each. Not that any of you would ever go over." Faint laughter. "The floor is yours, Mr. Vice Chairman."

A cakewalk followed. Three senators urged Taylor to reconsider his plans to retire. He was done and dismissed within an hour. Hebley and Carcetti, who had watched from the row behind him, met him and Hunt in an empty conference room down the hall.

"Had me worried," Hebley said. "But that was a complete one-eighty."

"Thank you, sir."

They shook his hand and then they were gone.

But the real verdict came from Hunt, as they settled into the black car that would take them to Langley for a full debrief. For the second time that day, she brought her lips to his right ear. "Well done, Brian. Play your cards right, you might get laid tonight."

His response was immediate. And would have been embarrassing if anyone besides Hunt had been there to see it.

"Hey ho," she said, looking at his crotch.

"Ho hey." Taylor had never felt better, not even on the day he'd found the uranium itself. He had not just survived the Lion's Den. He had made the lions eat out of his hand. Now he was due for his reward.

If only he hadn't been so very, very wrong.

5

TEL AVIV

No one had ever accused Vinny Duto of being a patient man.

Today he had no choice. For his flight to Israel, he had borrowed a jet from his friends at Boeing, who were still good for a favor or two. Nonetheless, he brought along a pair of bug zappers to make sure that the conversation he was going to have couldn't be recorded. He trusted the guys who'd lent him the plane. But not that much.

The jet itself was nothing fancy, just an old 757 that would need to refuel in Rome on its way to Tel Aviv. Duto didn't plan to touch Israeli soil, though. He would have a drink with Rudi in the cabin while his pilots stretched their legs, or whatever it was pilots did after a five-thousand-mile flight, and then go home. He wanted no Israeli immigration records of this trip.

But when they landed at Fiumicino, a

message from Rudi waited on his Samsung. *Not tonight. Chemo wiped me out.* Duto cursed to himself. He was not a sentimental man, and he didn't fear death. It came for everyone, and it would come for him, too. Meantime, he had choices to make, chits to cash, problems to solve. A preoccupation with mortality was an indulgence, a weakness.

Still. Lung cancer. He called Jerusalem.

"Vinny." A whisper.

"I hoped I'd get to see you tonight."

"My doctors have other ideas."

"I have a present for you." Duto nudged the box with his toe. A radio-controlled Hummer, almost two feet long, one-twelfth scale. RC cars were Rudi's only known indulgence.

"Unless it's a new lung, you can keep it."

"Better than a new lung."

A faint sound that Duto recognized as a laugh.

"What if I come to you tonight? In Jerusalem?" Though he hated to leave a trail.

"Vinny."

"Tomorrow?"

Another laugh. "I hope I live long enough to watch it happen to you, Vinny."

"Rudi."

"It's good. Everybody else treats me like

137

I'm dying. You're the same prick as ever. You landed already at Ben Gurion?"

"Rome."

"All right, stay there tonight. I feel better in the morning, I'll call you."

"Thank you —"

Rudi hung up.

Duto splurged, booked himself a room at the Artemide. He hadn't been to Rome in thirty years. By the time he checked in, the sun had set, but he had time at least to take a cab to St. Peter's, see the great dome, cross his chest and pretend to pray. Instead, he made the mistake of logging in to his email.

He spent the next six hours taking advantage of the time difference to keep his D.C. staffers busy. So be it. The Vatican wasn't going anywhere. And when he woke in the morning, he found a text from Rudi. *BG 4 p.m.* So he'd lose two full days to this chase. He hoped the conversation would go well, though he had reason to believe it wouldn't.

The man at the base of the 757's stairway looked only vaguely like the Mossad chief whom Duto remembered. He was a crumpled copy fished out of the trash. The old Rudi was lean and strong, with the ropy muscles of middle age and a shock of dark curly hair. The new Rudi was bald, even his eyebrows gone. His neck and shoulders had sunk into themselves, like a careless surgeon had taken them out and lost a bone or two before putting them back.

Duto started down the stairs. Rudi shook his head and dragged himself up, step by step. He reached the top step breathless, as if he'd just crested Everest. Duto wrapped him up, dragged him inside, where he flopped into a cracked leather recliner that had probably seemed luxurious in 1987.

"Don't die, Rudi. Trouble if you die." Duto poured him a glass of water and tried not to stare as five long minutes passed. Finally, Rudi sighed and put down the glass. He looked around the cabin, his eyes settling on the jammers, each the size of a deck of cards, with a single green light blinking steadily on top.

"I'm not sure I'm comforted by the fact you think we need those."

"With your accent, nobody could understand you anyway," Duto said.

"You don't like my English, learn Hebrew." Rudi coughed lightly into his hand. "This an agency ride?"

"Boeing. Tell me I'm seeing the chemo and not the cancer, Rudi."

"It's good I look like this. Means they're still trying to beat the thing. That's what I tell Esther." His wife. "I'm not sure she believes it."

"Do you?"

Rudi tapped his chest, like he was carrying a baby inside and not a tumor. "You want to hear all about it? My sad story?"

Duto found himself shaking his head.

"I didn't think so. So your turn to talk. And it better be worth my time, Vinny. My very limited time."

Duto explained the last month, how he'd gotten a tip that led Wells to Glenn Mason, how Wells tracked Mason to Turkey and killed him. How Duto and Shafer and Wells were convinced that the uranium in Istanbul hadn't come from Iran.

"You think some other service is setting Iran up?" Rudi said. His brow lifted as he tried to raise his nonexistent eyebrows. "Us? You think *we* did this?"

"I wanted to ask." *Even though I already know you didn't. Unless Aaron Duberman works for the Mossad, and that's a conspiracy too far.*

"No."

"You've been out of the loop —"

"Even if I were dead, I'd hear. And we'd never do it, if you caught the Mossad tricking you this way it would destroy the U.S.–Israel relationship forever. Come on, Vinny. You didn't fly all this way for that."

"I didn't."

"What, then? You think the FSB, Putin making a mess? Too risky."

"Agree."

"Then *what*?"

"What if it's not another country? What if it's a private group?"

"I'm supposed to be the one who's sick. Maybe you have a brain tumor, Vinny. It's impossible."

"How well do you know Aaron Duberman?"

Rudi leaned back in his seat. "Christ," he muttered.

Duto explained that Mason had lost millions of dollars at Duberman's 88 Gamma casino in Macao before quitting the CIA and disappearing. That a Pakistani ship captain connected to the smuggling had also lost tens of thousands of dollars at Duberman's casinos. That Duberman had never explained the rationale for his massive donations to the President.

Rudi stared him down. Duto knew the look well: *You expect me to believe this nonsense?* "It's thin, I know. But it fits."

"You haven't gone to anyone with this."

"Not yet."

"Because you know how crazy it sounds."

"It's the only explanation for Mason. Remember a few weeks ago, I asked you about those assassinations in Europe, the bankers and the others helping Iran?"

"You think it was the same group."

"Duberman's first try at stopping the program. When he saw it wasn't working, he decided on something more radical."

"All right. Say it's true." Though Rudi didn't sound convinced. "You don't think *we* asked Duberman for this?"

Duto lifted his hands. "Of course not. But he's important over here, newspapers, political donations, you must have a file on him."

"We started paying attention to him about ten years ago, he spent $135 million on Radio Zeta, that's a national channel here, lot of influence. We're going to look at someone like that. Then he donated $180 million to the Holocaust Museum for what they're calling the Memory Project, you know about that?"

Duto shook his head.

"They're keeping it quiet. A lot of people have tried to lock down the survivors, get them on video before they die, and they've been successful. This is coming at it from the other end —"

"The *Nazis?* Why would they —"

"It's not about putting anyone in jail. They're old, too. Find the ones who want to relieve their consciences. See if they have any physical evidence they want to share. It's controversial, because some people think it equates us and them, why should we need them to prove what we already know? And because we're paying them —"

"Paying?"

"Not interviews. Papers and pictures. Anyway, Duberman is funding it. Seven, eight years ago, he made the donation. Not a pledge, either. He promised on a Sunday, the money came by Wednesday. So the Prime Minister started to see him. Maybe twice a year. Two or three times, I sat in also. And I can tell you, yes, back then he was very worried about Iran. We told him the truth, we're doing what we can, but war is unrealistic, they have fifteen times as many people as we do, all we can do is push the levers we have."

"He ever hint he might do anything himself?"

Rudi considered. "No. Though in the last meeting, he said something I thought was strange, he asked me directly if I had the resources I needed. The PM didn't like that. He said, Aaron, we're a grown-up country, we have our own military, we set our own budgets for our foreign policy. Duberman knew he'd gone too far. He apologized."

"That was the last time you saw him?"

"Maybe we shook hands at a cocktail party. But the last time we ever talked seriously, yes. After that, I asked our analysts for a full report on him. They ultimately concluded he was honest in his support. He has homes here, and he dated Israelis even before he married Orli. Not one of these American Jews who constantly meddles but has never been here."

"Which gives him even more incentive."

"It's an interesting theory. But you know what happens if you go to the President or your new DCI with this. And no evidence." Rudi shook his head. "If we had strong leads that the uranium wasn't from Iran, I would know."

"I'd settle for a weak lead."

"I'll ask. But everyone knows I'm sick. They'll wonder why."

"Whatever you get, I'll be grateful." Now they had come to the question Duto didn't want to ask. "We have one more lead. Mason's boss was a woman."

"That leaves half the planet."

"This operation was put together right and tight. Somebody found Mason. Not

Duberman. He wouldn't have known where to look or how to make the approach. He had to have a cutout. This woman. She would be a professional, or at least a semi-pro."

"Just say it. You think she's Mossad. An Israeli. A *Jew.*"

"Do you think Aaron Duberman would have used someone who wasn't Jewish as a cutout?"

"A billionaire Jew pushing the United States into war. With the help of a mysterious Jewess." Rudi chomped down hard on the last word. "This is Protocols of the Elders of Zion stuff, Vinny. Tell me again how Israel benefits if it goes public."

What Duto had feared he'd say. "You want us to invade Iran, Rudi?"

"If that's the alternative to this, maybe."

"You have to get in front of it. It's gonna come out, Rudi. You help, I'll make sure you get credit."

"Here I thought you came all this way to ask me for a favor. Turns out you were looking out for me. Vinny Duto, King of the Jews."

Before Duto could answer, Rudi's eyes opened wide. He raised a hand to his mouth and began to cough, racking heaves that shook his body. Like if he coughed hard enough he would spit out the tumor. Duto rose from his chair, but Rudi shook his head, *no no no.* Duto ran into the bathroom for paper towels. By the time he came back, a film of bright red blood covered Rudi's palm. He lifted it to Duto almost triumphantly.

"In case you were wondering whether I was faking." Rudi mopped his hand. He sat back in his chair and closed his eyes. "I have to think about this, my friend." Weariness had replaced the anger in his voice. "I'm not sure I'll have anything even if I do decide to help." He pushed himself up, his arms shaking. Duto rose, too, but Rudi flapped a hand at him. "No."

"Let me, please —" Duto reached for him. Rudi grabbed his right index finger and twisted it back, the last trick of the weak against the strong.

"I'm serious. I'll show myself out."

6
NINE DAYS . . .

RIYADH, SAUDI ARABIA

The first king of Saudi Arabia, Abdul-Aziz, had procreated with a stallion's vigor. His progeny continued the tradition. Sixty years after Abdul-Aziz's death, more than a thousand men and women could claim him as a grandfather.

But General Nawwaf bin Salman was more important than most. The eldest son of the Defense Minister, he commanded the Saudi missile arsenal, more than a thousand Chinese-made Dongfengs that could reach any target in Iran or Israel. And as part of his job, Nawwaf ran the Saudi nuclear program.

Though *program* was not quite the right word. The Saudis had given billions of dollars to Pakistan to help that country build a nuclear arsenal. In return, Pakistan's generals had promised that if Iran built a nuke, they would hand over a half-dozen bombs.

147

The result would be the Persian Gulf version of mutually assured destruction, two sworn enemies with the power to obliterate each other's capital. Both Pakistan and the Kingdom denied the deal. *We have enough trouble with the North-West Frontier,* Pakistan's Defense Minister told the Secretary of State. *You think we want to take a chance on the Arabs, too? We give the Saudis a bomb and it winds up in Washington, we know you blame us.*

Maybe. In June 2008, American satellites had spotted a massive construction project at a military base near the village of al-Watah, one hundred seventy miles west of Riyadh, the center of the Arabian desert. In summer, the area was one of the most unpleasant places on earth. Temperatures topped one hundred thirty degrees. Even Bedouins stayed away. Yet the Saudis had evidently decided the project couldn't wait. Construction moved fast. After a few weeks, the satellites picked up the outlines of missile launchpads and fortified bunkers.

The Saudis already operated two other missile bases, but al-Watah attracted the attention of the CIA's Near East analysts. Its bunkers were set fifteen meters deep into the desert's stony soil. Their concrete walls were six meters thick. Putting so much effort into a storage site for conventional warheads made no sense, especially given the base's inhospitable location.

The agency and the White House watched the site with alarm, waiting for the armored convoys and helicopter flights that would signal that Pakistan had made good on its promise. But they never came. In fact, after rushing to build al-Watah, the Saudis never used the base. Only seventy men lived in its garrison, guarding the perimeter and opening and closing the empty bunkers twice a day. The CIA and the Defense Intelligence Agency had concluded that the base was a bluff of sorts. The Kingdom wanted to show the world that its military could handle nuclear weapons without actually committing to them.

Wells understood the reluctance. Nukes would be the ripest of targets for al-Qaeda's jihadis. Plus the Saudis preferred to outsource their national defense to the United States. For seventy years, the Kingdom had depended on the American military to protect it, most notably when Saddam Hussein invaded Kuwait in 1990. The biggest Saudi oil fields were a short tank ride from the Kuwaiti border. Even so, the Kingdom's primary contribution to the conflict had been teaming up with Kuwait to cut a $36 billion check to cover the majority of the cost of the war. Like the United States Army was nothing more than a for-hire force.

But Wells planned to let that bit of history be. He hadn't come to the Kingdom to discuss Saudi-American codependency or ask for a guided tour of al-Watah. Instead, he hoped that General Nawwaf might lead him to the source of the highly enriched uranium. Given the Saudi interest in nuclear weapons, someone sitting on a private stockpile of HEU might have approached the Kingdom as a potential buyer before turning to Duberman.

The trip was a long shot. But Wells's only alternative was to sit in Zurich while he waited for Kowalski to set up a meeting with Mikhail Buvchenko. Instead, as soon as Kowalski's driver dropped him at the Zurich airport, Wells called a Riyadh number whose true owner was known to only eight people. It rang the personal mobile phone of His Majesty Abdullah bin Abdul-Aziz, Custodian of the Two Holy Mosques, Prime Minister and King of Saudi Arabia.

Years before, Abdullah had asked Wells to find a Saudi terrorist cell. The King feared he could not trust his own security forces because other members of the royal family supported the jihadis. After the mission, Abdullah promised Wells the Kingdom's lifelong support. Wells had already called in the chit twice. He didn't like asking again, but under the circumstances the chance seemed worth taking.

"As-salaam aleikum." Abdullah answered this phone himself. As far as Wells could tell, he enjoyed having the chance to be a normal human being in this tiny way. He had a throaty smoker's baritone, a Saudi Jack Nicholson. The vigor in his voice hid the fact that the King, born in 1924, had entered his tenth decade.

"Aleikum salaam, Your Majesty."

A pause. Despite his age, Abdullah's mind and memory were intact. Wells imagined him looking at the phone, sorting through possibilities.

"John Wells?"

"Yes, sir. Sorry to bother you —"

"No matter."

Not quite the same as *no bother.* "With your permission, I wish to come to Riyadh. To put a question to one of your nephews. A general." Wells spoke formally now, conscious of just how rough his Arabic sounded.

"I have more than one nephew who's a

general."

"Nawwaf bin Salman, sir."

Abdullah didn't speak. Wells wondered if he'd overreached somehow.

"Where are you now?" the King finally said.

From Zurich, Wells flew to Rome, where he caught an overnight Saudi Arabian Airlines flight to Riyadh. Saudia — as the airline was known — had the quirks of the country it served. It was at once deeply religious and highly status-conscious. The 777 jet included two prayer rooms, one at the front of the plane for first-class passengers, one at the rear for everyone else.

The pilots were Saudi, but the flight attendants were Filipino women. Male Saudis considered working as cabin crew beneath their dignity, and no Saudi woman would ever be allowed a job where she could mix so closely with men. No alcohol was available, and every flight began with a prayer in Arabic: *Bismi-Allah wa al-Hamduli-Allah . . . In the name of Allah, Praise be to Allah, Glory to Him who made this transport for us, as we could never have created it.*

The words both comforted and disconcerted Wells. Arabic was the language of his time undercover in Afghanistan and Pakistan. For better or worse, those years had hardened him into the man he was now. He had fought alongside jihadis who hated the United States. Though he never accepted their beliefs, he admired their endurance and fearlessness. They weren't fools, most of them. They fought knowing that they could never overcome the United States. They would have been wiser to focus their energy on the corrupt regimes closer to home. Yet their choice had a certain peculiar logic: America was the devil, and fighting the devil was the highest calling, even if only Allah could overcome him.

So the jihadis were brave and tough. Callous and cruel, too. They cared little for the lives of the civilians around them, less for any enemy unlucky enough to fall into their hands. Facing a foe with overwhelming advantages, they used deceit as a tactic. They fought without uniforms or front lines, picking off one or two soldiers at a time, then disappearing. But was Wells any different? He had lived with these men for years, pretended to be one of them. All along he'd hoped to destroy them, and he'd killed more than one in cold blood. He had come back from those mountains almost a decade before. Yet he still couldn't talk about what had happened there. Not with

Shafer, not with Anne, not even with Exley. He couldn't find the words, in any language. He circled that time in his mind like a plane trying to land in heavy fog. A psychiatrist would probably say he had post-traumatic stress disorder, but Wells didn't plan to ask.

In the cabin around him, heavy-legged men in white robes and leather sandals settled back in their seats. Wells wondered what these Saudis would make of him, an American who had taken their religion as his own. In theory, Islam was the most equal of faiths. Becoming Muslim didn't require approval from a priest or rabbi. Anyone who read the Quran with honest effort could join the *umma,* the worldwide community of believers.

Yet the Saudis had a way of making other Muslims feel like outsiders. Blood, language, and land joined the Gulf Arabs to Islam. They could trace their lineage to the original tribesmen who had supported Muhammad. The Quran was written in their native tongue. Their country included Islam's holiest sites. Their very flag included the *Shahada,* the Islamic creed: *There is no God but Allah, and Muhammad is the messenger of Allah.*

No, Wells knew how they'd see him: misguided at best, a faker at worst.

He closed his eyes as the jet leveled off and found himself dreaming of the Kaaba, the forty-three-foot-high cube at the heart of the Grand Mosque in Mecca, tall black granite walls set on a marble base. The Kaaba protected *al-Hajar al-Aswad,* the Black Stone, a smooth piece of obsidian that was sometimes thought to have come from a meteorite. The people of Mecca had believed in the stone's mystical powers even before Muhammad brought Islam to them. Now it marked the spiritual center of the religion. Muslims faced the Kaaba when they knelt to pray.

Wells had been to Mecca, yet he hadn't seen the Grand Mosque. The failure seemed to summarize the contradictions of his life.

In his dream, he finally arrived at the Kaaba. But he'd made a mistake. Pilgrims were supposed to circle the cube counterclockwise. He was walking the wrong way, squeezing through the crowd. He tried to turn but found he could only march forward. Bodies pinballed off his, bouncing him side to side. At first the other pilgrims didn't notice. Then one yelled: *Imposter!* The cries spread: *American! Apostate!* Men linked their arms to form an unbreakable wedge. They jammed Wells backward. He knew that if he stumbled the crowd would swallow him whole. Then a final jolt threw him on his back and the men around him roared —

"Sir? Sir?" The words in English, not Arabic.

Wells opened his eyes. A flight attendant leaned over him, her hand poised above his shoulder, close enough for Wells to pick up the scent of her too-sweet perfume.

"I'm sorry to disturb you, but we've run into turbulence." Indeed, the cabin rattled as the plane passed through dirty air. "You'll need to buckle your belt."

Wells latched his belt and closed his eyes. He hoped the Kaaba would return, that he could win some spiritual succor in his dreams at least. But it was gone. He spent the rest of the flight listening to the snores of the men around him.

His only consolation came from the back of the cabin, where two women whispered intimately in Arabic. Wells couldn't hear their words, only the low lovely trill of their voices through the stale pressurized air. He wondered if they were sisters, wives to the same man, or both. He wished he could ask, but the question would have been beyond impolite.

Two men in the black uniforms worn by

Abdullah's elite guardsmen waited as Wells stepped off the Jetway at King Khalid Airport in Riyadh. Wordlessly, they led him to the front of a long immigration control line. A nervous customs officer hardly looked up before stamping his passport.

Outside the terminal, a cool, blustery wind rustled the date palms. Even Riyadh had winter. The men led Wells to a sleek black Mercedes limousine, where another uniformed officer waited. He ushered Wells into the limo as the two escorts stepped into a chase car, a black BMW sedan parked nose-to-tail with the Merc.

"As-salaam aleikum."

"Aleikum salaam."

"I'm Colonel Fahd Ghaith. Deputy Commander, First Special Division of the National Guard." The Mercedes rolled off. Its windows were thick and bullet-resistant, and Wells guessed it had an inch or so of steel armor in its doors, too.

"None of this was necessary."

"The King has asked me to ensure your trip is pleasant."

"I appreciate that." Though Wells feared the star treatment would only bring unwanted attention to his arrival. He watched through the back window as a third car pulled away from the terminal, a four-door white Nissan with a tinted windshield and a nick on the driver's door. The windshield and the distance hid the faces of the driver and passenger.

"That one yours, too?"

Ghaith followed Wells's gaze. "No. Are you concerned about it?"

"Should I be?"

"You're His Majesty's guest, Mr. Wells."

Not exactly an answer, as they both knew. Terrorists had attacked the royal family before. They would be glad for a chance at Wells. The Mercedes and BMW followed the signs for the airport exit, the Nissan a few cars back. Lack of sleep and that dream about the Grand Mosque were probably making Wells twitchy.

Probably.

"General Nawwaf will see you this evening. Eight-thirty. His office is in the Ministry of Defense at the Riyadh Air Base. In the meantime —"

The Mercedes sped through a police checkpoint and accelerated onto Route 535, a crowded highway that ran southwest from the airport to the center of Riyadh. The chase car remained a few lengths behind, the Nissan still coming.

"A hotel?"

"His Majesty's guests don't stay in hotels.

A small residence south of downtown."

"Small residence?"

"Very modest. You're still looking at that car?"

"He's still there."

"This is the main road from the airport. As you can see from the traffic. Nonetheless. I'd rather not have you worrying." Ghaith turned to the front seat. "At the house in twenty minutes, Khalid. Let's have your siren."

A moment later, the limousine's siren sang its high *Oo-oo, Oo-oo*. The traffic ahead cleared, and the Mercedes surged to fill the empty pavement.

Two minutes later, the limousine turned from 535 to Route 65, the main highway through central Riyadh. The Nissan had vanished. Wells relaxed as best he could, took in the city around him. Riyadh was flat, unapologetically ugly, and in the middle of a Shanghai-size construction boom. With oil at one hundred dollars a barrel, Abdullah was expanding universities and hospitals and building a skyscraper complex for banks and a stock exchange. Inevitably, the new development was called the King Abdullah Financial District. Abdullah was a more democratic monarch than his predecessors, but his modesty had limits. He shared the

159

Saud family fetish for spreading his name far and wide.

After carving through the downtown traffic, the Mercedes turned west onto an eight-lane highway that Saudis called the Mecca Road. The city's sprawl seemed endless, an infinite loop of concrete towers, asphalt roads, and dirt lots. Beige and black and brown blurred together, as if Riyadh's builders wanted the city to reflect the monochrome desert that surrounded it.

The limousine left the highway and turned south down Prince Turki Road, a six-lane boulevard. An oversize complex of buildings loomed to the left, with signs announcing "King Faisal Specialist Hospital and Research Centre" in English and Arabic.

"Best hospital in Saudi Arabia. World-class." Ghaith spoke the last two words in English, with relish. "We're almost there."

The Mercedes turned right, into a crowded residential neighborhood, a mix of blocky apartment buildings and new houses. Then left, right, and left again, before squealing through an open gate watched by two guards. It stopped outside a three-story mansion.

"Twenty minutes exactly. Well done, Khalid."

"Thank you, sir."

"This is the small residence?" Wells said.

"Only one thousand square meters." Ten thousand square feet. Ghaith stepped out, and Wells followed him into a foyer that had more marble than most churches. A gold-leaf chandelier hung overhead. The Saudis didn't consider subtlety a virtue.

Ghaith pointed down a corridor. "Kitchen's that way. There's a chef if you're hungry. *Halal* only, I'm afraid. Though I do believe there's a liquor cabinet in the closet of the master bathroom."

"I won't ask how you know."

"Also an indoor pool at the back of the house, an exercise room."

"Who stays here, Colonel?"

"Mostly Western doctors working at the hospital."

"Of course." Abdullah would hardly mind spending a few million dollars on mansions to entice the best specialists to come to Riyadh to treat him and his family.

"I'll be back at eight to pick you up, but my men will wait in front. If I can be of service, please call. Is there anything else you need, Mr. Wells?"

Wells thought of the mysterious Nissan. "Wouldn't mind a pistol. If you have one to spare."

"I assure you you're safe here. These are some of the King's best men."

"No doubt. But I prefer to look after myself."

"*Al-Hamdu lillah.*" Praise be to God. "I'll see you this evening, Mr. Wells."

Wells forced himself onto a treadmill for an hour, flipping on CNN International to see what he'd missed on the flight from Rome. Laura Frommer, the chairwoman of the Senate Intelligence Committee, had announced her support for the President. *The CIA offered a convincing case at our hearings,* Frommer said at a press conference. *And the Iranians can defuse this crisis very simply. Open your nuclear facilities, let us speak to your scientists. You say you aren't trying to build a bomb, but this uranium ingot tells a different story.*

The American government had found its line: *If war comes, it's Iran's fault, for refusing to open up.* The argument had traction. Polls showed that sixty-three percent of Americans favored military action, up eleven percent since the missile attack that downed United 49. If Duberman was behind the missile, it had worked even better than he expected. Wells briefly wondered if he should have gone to Mumbai instead of

162

coming here. But he had no leads in India. And he and Shafer and Duto were far better off staying off the agency's radar. That would be impossible in Mumbai.

Exhaustion overcame Wells as he stepped off the treadmill. He found his way to the master bedroom, set his phone for 7 p.m., pulled the shades. And slept.

He woke not to the beeping of his alarm but amplified Arabic voices in the distance. He didn't have the usual traveler's dislocation when his eyes snapped open. He knew exactly what he was hearing. The *Maghrib,* the sunset call to prayer, the fourth of the day. Wells felt an oddly urgent need to pray outside, launch his devotions into the setting sun, nothing but desert between him and Mecca.

He found a prayer rug in the bedroom's cavernous closet, made his way to the mansion's flat roof. The wind yanked the sleep from him and he prayed vigorously, purposefully. By the time he finished, the sun had nearly disappeared. He felt calmer and stronger than he had in weeks.

He stood, turned to go inside —

And saw the white Nissan from the airport rolling past the mansion's back gate. The scratch in the driver's door left no doubt.

Wells didn't panic. Whoever was inside

wouldn't try to storm the mansion. Far easier to attack as the Mercedes left the grounds, a natural choke point, or on the road to the Ministry of Defense.

He would shower, get ready for his meeting. When Ghaith returned, they'd talk.

As he was showering, his phone buzzed. He stepped out unwillingly, grabbed for it. Kowalski. "I don't know if this qualifies as good news or bad, but the Russian says he'll meet you. No surprise, you come to him. Fly into Volgograd."

"It's not back to Stalingrad?"

"Nor Putingrad. Yet."

"When?"

"He can do it as soon as tomorrow. If I were you, I'd get there before he changes his mind."

"What about the visa?"

"Get to any Russian embassy or consulate, he'll arrange it."

Buvchenko proving the power of his connections. Wells wondered if he could leave Riyadh tonight after his meeting with Nawwaf. A direct flight to Russia would be impossible, but Saudia or Turkish Airlines surely had overnight service to Istanbul. From there he could get the visa, be in Volgograd by the next night. He wished he could ask the Saudis for a private jet, but

164

had pushed Abdullah's generosity too far already.

"What did you tell him?"

"That you had a question for him, one you had to ask in person."

"That's all?"

"And that you would pay a lot of money for the right answer. He likes money. As do we all."

"Thank you, Pierre."

"Don't thank me until you get out."

Ghaith arrived as Wells was raiding the refrigerator, which was disappointingly empty.

"No chef?"

"Didn't want to bother him. I saw the Nissan again, Colonel. From the airport."

"You're sure?" His tone surprised Wells. More annoyed than nervous.

"I was on the roof. For the *Maghrib*."

"It's ours."

Wells's turn to be surprised. "You said —"

"I lied. I didn't want to worry you. I didn't think you'd make it. There's one other undercover car, too."

Wells crossed the kitchen in two big strides, put himself face-to-face with Ghaith, close enough to smell the sugary coffee on the colonel's breath. He had six

165

inches and fifty pounds on the Saudi.

"You didn't want to worry *me?"*

"An error. I apologize." Ghaith pulled his phone from his pocket. "I'm married to one of His Majesty's grandnieces. Check for yourself. If you're concerned whether you can trust me."

"If Abdullah sent you for me, then I trust you. I don't doubt your loyalty, Colonel —"

"Thank you."

"It's your judgment I'm not sure about. You have anything else to tell me, now's the time. A specific threat, whatever."

Ghaith shook his head. "Nothing like that."

"Then why all this? Four cars. How many men?"

"Eight. Plus the guards at the house."

"Eight agents. For what?"

"Word about your arrival has spread."

"In one day? Did someone email the whole country? John Wells is in town. Huntin' season."

"I told no one. Several of His Majesty's secretaries know. His brother. General Nawwaf, too."

"Nawwaf must be reliable or he wouldn't be running your missiles."

"He's reliable. But I don't know everyone on his staff. The wrong person hears. A ten-second call to AQAP." Al-Qaeda in the Arabian Peninsula.

"And you were planning to tell me when? When you dropped me back at the airport?"

"I am sorry." Ghaith's embarrassment seemed genuine.

"I'd like that pistol now. Don't tell me you don't have a spare somewhere in that Mercedes."

Ghaith pushed past Wells, out of the kitchen.

He came back a minute later with a big black pistol. A Glock 22. Forty-caliber.

"You didn't have anything bigger? Like a cannon?"

"It's too big for you?"

Point, Saudi Arabia.

"As long as it's loaded." Wells popped out the magazine, found it full. Fifteen fat copper-jacketed rounds.

"You understand you can't bring it inside the ministry offices."

"If I need it in the Ministry of Defense, we're really in trouble." Wells snapped the magazine back into the pistol. It would kick harder than the 9-millimeters he preferred. Still, he was glad to have it.

He stuffed it into his jacket pocket, the butt poking out. Not ideal, but better than shoving it into the back of his jeans like a

167

wannabe gangster. "Can we go now?"

At first glance, the security around Riyadh Air Base seemed more appropriate for an installation like Kandahar or Bagram, an American airfield in hostile territory. A high concrete wall stretched around the perimeter. Cameras were everywhere. Signs warned in Arabic and English: "Danger: Armed Guards — Do Not Approach Without Authorization!"

At first Wells didn't understand why the Saudi military had chosen to present such a hostile face to its capital city. Then he saw that hostility was precisely the point. The Sauds wanted their people to remember that they were *ruled,* that the concept of *consent of the governed* went only so far in Riyadh.

The base's walls extended for what seemed like miles. Finally, the Mercedes reached its main entrance, marked by a tall and strangely elegant arch of tan-colored concrete. Four soldiers in a fortified machine-gun nest targeted them with a spotlight as the limousine stopped at the outer gate guardhouse. Khalid lowered his window to hand over his identity card. After a brief conversation, he looked over his shoulder at Ghaith.

"Colonel. They say we aren't authorized."

Wells liked this day less and less. He rested his fingers on the butt of the Glock. But pulling it would only make the guards more nervous. Through the glare of the spotlight, he saw their chase car five meters behind. Both too close and too far to do any good. They would make a fat target for a suicide bomber.

Two guards stepped out of the gatehouse and motioned for the Mercedes to turn around. Ghaith pushed open his door. The guards lowered their rifles, but the weapons seemed only to make him angrier. "We'll sort this out in one minute, no more. Or by next week you simpletons will be in the Empty Quarter chasing scorpions." Ghaith meant it, Wells saw. Nobody pulled rank quite like the Saudis.

The guards looked at each other, then waved him into the guardhouse.

Three minutes passed before Ghaith stepped out of the guardhouse, back into the Mercedes. He slammed the door. Whatever he'd said seemed to have carried the day. The gate slid open. "Go, Khalid." The Mercedes eased inside.

"They still had us coming this morning. Oafs."

Another easy explanation. Or maybe

someone wanted to be sure that their arrival would attract notice instead of being quiet.

Finally, Wells walked into Nawwaf's office, a square room that overlooked the airfield's main north–south runway. Models of American, Russian, and Chinese missiles filled a glass cabinet by the door.

As was customary in Saudi offices, photos of Abdullah and Salman hung prominently. Wells expected to see personal photos of Nawwaf with Salman, a way for the general to remind visitors of his place in the hierarchy. There were none. The omission mildly impressed Wells. Nawwaf was confident enough in his own authority not to rely on his father.

Nawwaf was tall and thin, with a crisp uniform and a neatly trimmed beard that framed his narrow lips. He stood from behind his mahogany desk and saluted Wells, more than a hint of irony in the gesture. "Mr. Wells. Hello."

"*Salaam aleikum,* General."

"I'd prefer we stick to English, Mr. Wells. I studied physics at Oxford. I expect my English is adequate for your needs."

"*Nam.*" Yes.

Nawwaf didn't smile. Wells decided to

take a friendlier tack, get the general talking generally about the Iranian program before moving on to the questions he'd come to ask.

"I appreciate your taking the time to see me. Do you know why I'm here?"

"I was told only that it was not related to our base at Watah." Making sure Wells knew that the topic was off-limits.

"I have questions about the enrichment process. I've heard you're an expert."

"I doubt I can tell you anything your own scientists haven't."

"Humor me."

"As you wish."

"I'll start with the obvious. Could Iran have enriched uranium to weapons-grade? Even though we and the IAEA watch their stockpiles." The International Atomic Energy Agency.

"The Iranians acknowledge they've enriched several thousand kilos to twenty percent enrichment. If they hid a fraction of that, they could easily take the final step, from twenty percent to weapons-grade."

"But could they have hidden it?"

"Certainly. They had years when no one was watching on-site. The inspectors checked afterwards, but it's a matter of altering output tables, hiding the efficiency of the process."

"That simple."

"Did you know, Mr. Wells, that the United States has lost hundreds of kilograms of weapons-grade uranium over the last fifty years?"

Wells shook his head in genuine surprise.

"No one really thinks it's missing. Otherwise, Washington and London would be ghost towns. Probably it never existed at all. Uranium enrichment is an industrial process, and like all industrial processes it has a margin for error. Especially if you want it to."

"So they hide this uranium. Then? They build another plant without anyone noticing?"

"Possibly."

"Wouldn't it be huge?"

Nawwaf shook his head. "Once you reach twenty percent, you need only a hundred or so centrifuges running for a few weeks to reach the weapons-grade level. A small factory or warehouse could hide those."

"If they used an aboveground site, wouldn't there be emissions?"

"Only for a couple of hundred meters. You couldn't find it with a brute search. You'd need to narrow the target area first."

"So you think the Istanbul uranium came

from Iran?"

"I didn't say that, Mr. Wells. You asked me if the Iranians *could* have enriched uranium to weapons-grade. The answer is yes. Whether they have *actually* done so is another matter. That comes down to what you Americans found in Istanbul. What you claim to have found, I should say."

"You think we planted it?"

"Maybe you wanted an excuse to attack Tehran. On the other hand, if the Iranians did produce it, we have a problem. I'm not sure which is worse."

Wells saw his opening.

"What if I told you I agreed with you?"

"That the United States has planted the uranium?"

"Not the United States. Someone trying to get America to attack Iran."

Wells watched as Nawwaf reacted to the theory the same way everyone did: *Impossible.*

But what if it's not?

"Who? The Israelis would be the obvious choice."

"Suppose it's a private group?"

Nawwaf shook his head. "No private group could manage it."

"Unless they didn't enrich it themselves."

"I don't see what you mean."

"Has anyone ever tried to sell the Kingdom highly enriched uranium?"

Nawwaf laughed, an unexpected sound.

"At least now I understand why you're
here."

The general busied himself in his desk,
came up with a gold cigarette case and
lighter. "Do you smoke?"

Wells shook his head.

"You Americans all expect to live forever."

"At this point, I'd settle for next week."

Nawwaf lit up with a practiced hand,
dragged deep. "I smoke less than I used to,
and I enjoy it more. Now. You were asking if
I might know the real source of that ingot?"

For a moment, Wells let himself believe
the general might have the answer. "That's
right."

"I confess I find your theory interesting.
But I can't help. I was approached once the
way you suggest. Before you grow too
excited, it was by a North Korean. This was
a conference five or six years ago. He
claimed he had a working bomb. I went as
far as asking the price. Five billion dollars.
Two up front, three when they delivered."

North Korea again. Wells wondered
whether Duberman could possibly have
been desperate enough to deal with the
psychopaths in Pyongyang.

"Cheaper than the Pakistanis."

"Funnily enough, he said the same, too. But I couldn't take him seriously. I had no way of knowing if they could even build a competent bomb. Their tests were just past fizzle, the low single-kiloton range. No, we would have to buy at least two to have one to test, and if it failed we would hardly be in position to demand a refund."

"You think he was serious?"

"I think *he* thought he was. I didn't bother to tell anyone here. I would have been a laughingstock. And he wasn't offering raw HEU, you should understand. Not what your people found in Istanbul. Only a finished bomb. I don't think he's the one you want."

"And that was the only time?"

Nawwaf took another drag on the cigarette. If he wasn't actually searching his memory, he was a fine actor. "Yes, truly. I don't love your country, Mr. Wells. But my father and the King have told me to speak honestly, and I wouldn't dishonor them by lying to you."

"Then I thank you for your time."

"Good luck with your search."

"By the way, General, do you have any idea why we were stopped at the gate? We were told that the time for this meeting hadn't been updated."

"My assistants handle that. I hope it wasn't too much trouble."

"Not at all." Wells extended his hand and they shook over the general's giant desk.

"I'll try to find the Korean's name, for what it's worth. And if I think of anything else, I'll call you."

Wells saluted. *"Ma'a as-salaama."* Goodbye.

"Ma'a as-salaama."

"He was helpful?" Ghaith asked, as they walked side by side through the ministry's empty corridors.

"Maybe." Wells would talk to Duto and Shafer about North Korea, though the possibility was far-fetched at best. "So we can be at the airport?" He'd booked himself on a Turkish Airlines flight to Istanbul that left just before midnight.

"I should tell you. While you were speaking to Nawwaf, the King's office sent word. His Majesty wishes to see you tomorrow."

Wells wondered why. Maybe Abdullah wanted him to relay a message to the White House, though Wells wasn't sure why the King would bother with an intermediary. He could call the President directly.

Whatever the King's reasons, staying overnight in Riyadh meant Wells would have to postpone his trip to Russia for at least another day. Buvchenko might call off their meeting. But Wells could hardly say no. He didn't need to be an expert on royal etiquette to know that Abdullah had given him an order dressed as an invitation.

"Of course."

The Mercedes waited outside the ministry's front doors, its engine running. The wind was up, the night almost cold. Wells looked up, expecting a galaxy of stars. But light pollution from the base and the city blocked all but the brightest.

Riyadh was far from a late-night town. Most Saudi families ate dinner inside their high-walled compounds. The city had no bars or clubs, not even any movie theaters.

So aside from the trucks cutting through Riyadh on their late-night runs across the desert, the Makkah Road was nearly empty as the Mercedes sped home. The BMW followed fifty meters behind. The Nissan was ahead, with the final escort, a Toyota Land Cruiser, farther back. A stretched-out convoy, blazing down the left lane, passing the eighteen-wheelers in the right two lanes like they weren't moving at all.

From somewhere behind them came the whine of a motorcycle engine cranking at high revs, closing fast. Through the back window, Wells saw the bike accelerating past the Land Cruiser, closing on the BMW. It was a big black sportbike, 1,100 ccs or more. It had to be doing at least one hundred thirty miles an hour. The driver wore a black helmet with a striking gold face shield.

As it closed, Wells pulled his pistol. Not that the weapon would do him much good. The Mercedes didn't have firing ports, and the bullet-resistant windows worked both ways. Trying to fire through them from inside would send bullet fragments ricocheting around the passenger compartment.

The motorcycle pulled up beside them. It slowed beside the right rear door, next to Wells. Barely three feet of pavement separated them. The rider turned toward Wells, the body of the limousine reflected and distorted in his face shield. Wells lifted his pistol. The rider would have to respect the threat unless he knew about the bullet-resistant windows.

Maybe he did. He pulled his gloved hand from the left handlebar, cocked his thumb to make a finger pistol. He extended his arm close to the glass and pretended to shoot, raising and lowering his index finger, *pow pow pow.* Wells imagined the rider, eighteen, nineteen, twenty at most, the years when death wasn't even a whisper. No doubt he was grinning like a fool under his face shield. He returned his hand to the bars and raised himself off the seat and pulled backward, lifting the nose of the bike. Back and back until the motorcycle rose at forty-five degrees from the pavement, a highway wheelie —

After a few seconds he lowered the nose, settled himself behind the fairing, took off down the empty highway. The bike pulled away like Secretariat in the Belmont home-stretch. No license plate, at least not one that Wells could read. In fifteen seconds, it disappeared into the dark, its red taillight dimming, engine fading. Wells had spent plenty of time on motorcycles. He was comfortable with three-digit speeds. But he couldn't remember ever pushing that hard.

Ghaith leaned forward to Khalid. "How fast?"

"Two-fifty, two-sixty kph." One hundred and sixty miles an hour, give or take. Suicide speed.

Wells checked the back window but saw only their chase cars. He tucked the pistol away.

Ghaith's phone buzzed. He reached for it, listened briefly. "No. A ghost. Keep on exactly as you are. Text when you reach

Turki Road."

He hung up, turned to Wells. "I didn't think you were the nervous type."

"You're telling me that was a coincidence."

"We call them ghosts. You know how many times every year the ambulances clean up the accidents? Our sons, they have too much hormones, no women, nothing to do. They want to find out how fast they can go on these big empty highways. Know the police can't catch them. He's on his way into the desert. He sees the limousine, he stops. Sees who's inside. You think a jihadi acts like that?" Ghaith mimicked the rider's finger pistol.

"Or else he's tracking us, checking out the setup, the chase cars."

"Even if he is what you fear, he can't touch us in here. These windows stop an AK."

"VBIED." The letters, all too familiar to American soldiers, stood for vehicle-borne improvised explosive device.

"At one hundred fifty kilometers an hour?" Ghaith yawned.

"What time did you get up this morning, Colonel?"

"Five a.m."

"I'll bet you get up at five every morning."

"Yes. Why?"

Ghaith understood the danger, or he wouldn't be running an eight-man protective team. But fatigue was giving him tunnel vision. He wanted to explain away these obvious danger signs, because responding to them required energy he didn't have. He wanted to stick to his original plan — *get Wells home as quickly as possible, the most direct route* — instead of recalibrating.

Natural mistakes. Wells had made them himself. Which didn't make them any less dangerous.

"We should tighten up. Pointless to have four vehicles that can't cover each other."

"You want us to slow down?"

"I want time to react."

"You'll be at the house in three, four minutes. Tomorrow morning I promise you a ten-car police escort. A tank if you like. A helicopter."

Wells ignored the sarcasm, checked the door next to him. Its knob was low, locked. Wells tugged on it, couldn't raise it.

"Unlock the doors, Khalid."

Khalid stole a glance at Ghaith.

"What is this?" the colonel said.

"Just tell him."

"As long as you don't jump out at one hundred fifty kph. His Majesty will be very

181

angry if anything happens to you."

"I won't."

Ghaith muttered the order. Khalid popped the back locks.

They passed the King Faisal Hospital apartment buildings. Khalid pulled off the highway as he had that morning. Wells had a sense of déjà vu that could have come straight from *The Matrix*. He'd been in Afghanistan when the movie came out, but he caught up years later. He didn't watch many movies, but he had to admit he'd enjoyed that one. The super-slo-mo bullets. Keanu Reeves with his sleepy surfer's twang. All the techno mumbo jumbo. *Déjà vu is a glitch in the Matrix . . . It happens when they change something.*

Then the whole world exploding.

Ahead, the white Nissan ran a blinking yellow traffic signal, turned left onto Prince Turki Road. Hardly a second passed before Ghaith's phone buzzed with a text. He read it, leaned toward Khalid. "Go."

Khalid turned south on Turki Road, passing over the highway. Ahead, the big apartment buildings of the medical center were mostly dark. The chase cars followed. South of the overpass the boulevard turned oddly claustrophobic. The perimeter wall of the hospital complex hemmed the road to the east. To the right, apartment buildings and a block-long mosque loomed several stories high and extended nearly to the edge of the road, blocking any view of the intersecting streets. An attack could come from almost any direction, including overhead. Yet Ghaith seemed unconcerned. "Two more minutes," he said. And then Wells heard a pair of motorcycle engines screaming. To the north, behind them. Through the back window, he saw the headlights closing. The Toyota tried to block them, but it had no chance. They swerved around it as easily as a running back cutting past a fat defensive lineman.

The lead bike tucked itself off the back bumper of the BMW, which was about sixty meters behind the limousine. The rider extended his arm. This time the pistol in his hand was real. Three quick pops echoed through the night. The BMW slowed, swerved right, trying to force the rider off the road —

As the trailing bike cut left, closing on the limo —

The Mercedes roared ahead and swerved right, toward the curb. Khalid was trying to keep the motorcycle where he could see it, stop it from sneaking up on the passenger side.

And Wells saw the trap. The assassins knew the limo was armored. They couldn't hope to shoot out its windows. But they could flush it into a suicide attack, into a car pulling out from one of the side streets. By cutting to the curb, Khalid had given himself even less time to react —

"No —" But even as he spoke, Wells realized he couldn't possibly explain in time. He had only one move. He grabbed the door handle, swung open the door —

He braced himself, threw his body out of the car, angling backward onto the pavement, throwing his hands over his head so that his shoulders and back and arms would take the worst of the contact. He rolled left over right, bounced over the curb, scraped along the narrow strip of concrete and rocks that separated the roadbed from the four-story apartment building that fronted it. His left hand caught on the edge of a concrete slab. He heard a bone snap and his left pinky caught fire, the pain radiating up his arm. *Hold tight, hold tight . . .*

A moment later, he thumped against the side of the building. He blinked, but regained his bearings quickly enough to see a white minivan pull out from a cross street barely twenty feet in front of the Mercedes.

The motorcycle that had been tailing the limo suddenly cut hard left —

Much too late, the limo's brakes screeched —

Wells squeezed his eyes tight, but even from half a football field away the heat of the explosion singed him and its blast wave pummeled his face with gravel and dust, a devil's wind. He wiped his face clean as best he could and opened his eyes. An orange-yellow fireball rose as high as the tops of the apartment buildings. The minivan was obliterated, its frame twisted and shattered. The motorcycle was gone, too. Wells guessed that it had outrun the explosion and survived. The Mercedes was nothing more than a burning box. Its armored frame had hung together, but Ghaith and Khalid couldn't have survived. The buildings nearest the explosion had partially collapsed.

The BMW chase car was now past Wells. It had stopped short of the explosion. It was basically intact, but its windshield had been blown out. The motorcycle that had tailed it —

Sat stopped about fifty feet past Wells. The rider figured out what had happened at the same time as Wells did. He turned and looked at Wells with his gold faceplate. Wells reached for his pistol. It was gone. It had fallen from his pocket when he'd jumped from the limo. It was lying to his left. He dove for it as the rider reached across his body and fired three times, the first round close enough for Wells to hear it ding off the concrete.

Wells swept the Glock up with his busted left hand. He ignored the pain in his pinky and squeezed the trigger. He didn't have much chance at shooting the guy under these circumstances, but he didn't much care. As long as he could get the guy back on his bike and away. The rider fired twice more —

And then headlights lit up the bike and Wells heard a car roaring toward them. The rider dropped the pistol in frustration and turned back to his bike as the Toyota, the final car in the convoy, gave chase.

Close.

Wells breathed in deep, filled his lungs with foul gasoline-soaked air, pushed himself to his feet. Already the fireball had faded, and the motorcycle engine, too. Instead, screaming filled the night. *Help,* a woman sobbed from the corner, her voice somehow clear through the crackling of the fire. *Allah, please help!* All this carnage and chaos and suffering *for* him, because of him.

But he was still here.

Skill, and luck, too, though Wells wasn't feeling very lucky at the moment, feeling instead like a kind of perverse Pan, a small-*g* god who was a bringer of chaos instead of pleasure wherever he went. He longed to curse but instead he tucked the Glock into his jacket pocket and ran for the woman yelling under the rubble, her voice already losing strength, dulling and fading like a bad phone call. He doglegged around the wreckage of the Mercedes, the steel beams of its frame warped from the inferno, until he reached the wrecked concrete.

At his feet he found a strip of plain white plastic in the road, a piece of a shopping bag. Perfect. He bound his left pinky tight to his ring finger, pulling until the pain dried his mouth. The break was bad, just short of a compound fracture, but Wells didn't care. Even if the agony in his hand magnified until he screamed with each piece of concrete he pulled, he needed to make himself useful as best he could. He needed to *dig.*

7

WASHINGTON

When the President ordered that first drone strike on Iran, he'd felt a certain grim excitement.

But since the attack on United 49, the excitement had worn off, leaving only the grimness. This morning he'd woken at 3 a.m. with a sour stomach. He'd fought the urge to call the Secret Service and demand a low-profile ride through D.C. Not to go anywhere in particular, just to remind himself that the world outside his bulletproof windows existed. That drunks still stumbled home after the bars closed.

He hadn't understood the price he would pay for choosing this path. Nothing in the world — not the exhaustion of the primaries, not the tension of Election Day, not the elation of the Inaugural — compared to these last days for pure suffocating power. Only his predecessors in this office could truly understand. He wanted to call them, ask them how they'd borne it. But he felt somehow he'd be cheating, burdening them with a weight that wasn't theirs. This confrontation belonged to him, no one else.

The paradox was that the pressure made him more certain of the decisions he'd made. He knew how carefully he'd considered every alternative. He'd hoped that his surprise first strike would wake the Iranian government to the risks of its overreach. In daylight, American drones and stealth fighters had smashed Iran's air-defense system and flown straight through Tehran to target the military airport at its heart. He couldn't have sent a clearer message. *We don't want to attack you, but if we do, you can't possibly defend yourselves.*

He had three aircraft carriers in the Persian Gulf and the Indian Ocean. He had Marine regiments on the way to western Afghanistan and the 82nd Airborne headed for southeastern Turkey. He had said explicitly that he had no interest in regime change, that he merely wanted the Iranians to drop their nuclear program.

He hadn't expected that Iran would give way immediately. But he had figured it would try to deter an invasion by promising to negotiate over opening its weapons plants. That move would have made sense as a way to buy time. Instead, Iran's leaders had taken the opposite course. They'd accused him of lying and making up evidence. They had promised they would die before agreeing to a deal.

Then they had shot down a civilian jet.

Who were these people? How could he make them see?

At least he had Donna. Donna Green, his National Security Advisor, a skinny angular woman smarter than everyone else in the White House. Including him. They didn't always agree, but he trusted her completely. They were set to meet at 4 p.m., less than two hours from now. He'd insisted on forty-five minutes alone with her before the Secretary of Defense and the general who ran Central Command updated him on war plans.

In theory, Green was coming early to brief him on the investigation into United 49. In reality, he wanted the conversation with her that he couldn't have with anyone else outside his family, the one where he dropped the *I-am-President* mask enough to vent some of the pressure he felt.

First he had to endure the majority and minority leaders of the House and Senate.

He had tried to escape, telling his chief of staff, an old-school Boston Brahman who bore the unfortunate name of Harrison Hamilton, to reschedule. *They make me feel like an old lady with too many cats. Every time I focus on one, the other three start pissing on the floor. And I see in their beady little eyes that they're hoping I'll die so they can gnaw on my fingertips. Besides, I met them last week.*

But Hamilton had flat-out said no. *Sorry, Chief. Can't help you with this one. Half an hour will buy you goodwill you might need. If it makes you feel any better, they won't argue. They read the polls like everyone else. Closer, in fact. They just want to be able to tell the world they heard you make the case first-hand. In the Oval Office. Pretend they're potential donors, okay? Very attractive, very rich donors.*

So he spent precisely thirty-seven minutes with his four congressional house cats, and then at 2:45 p.m. went upstairs to his bedroom to read. He'd asked his staff for the best histories of the Cuban Missile Crisis, hoping for clues. But the only conclusion he reached was that Jack Kennedy had been crazy enough to walk to the edge of nuclear war and lucky enough that the Soviets backed down. If Kennedy's experi-

191

ence was any guide, the President would have to push hard before the Iranians folded.

More sleepless nights.

After an hour, he set aside the book and snuck a cigarette. Normally, his wife gave him grief for smoking in their private quarters instead of the specially ventilated corridor where he usually indulged. But she wasn't arguing this week.

He swigged a mouthful of Scope to clear the ashy taste from his mouth, fixed his tie, walked downstairs, settled himself behind his desk. At exactly 4 p.m., a steward opened the door to the Oval Office and Green walked in. She held a red-bordered file, rarely a good sign.

"Mr. President."

She settled herself in the simple wooden chair to the right of his desk. "Before I bring you up to speed on Mumbai, you should know that CIA is reporting a terrorist attack in Riyadh. A car bomb. The attack occurred two and a half hours ago, roughly 2230 local."

"Related to Iran?"

"Unclear. As you know, AQ has a robust presence in the Kingdom. The attack was on the southwest edge of the city. Several dead and injured, but no one in the royal family. We should know more after the sun comes up over there."

"Unless it's related to Iran or otherwise significant, I don't care. I don't need to hear about random terrorist attacks right now."

"Yes, sir." The rebuke didn't seem to ruffle Green. "Now. As to Mumbai. I have potentially good news. India's Minister of the Interior has told the FBI that his investigators have an informant who reports the men who fired the missiles are in hiding in a slum there. The police don't have the location locked down yet, but they believe they will within the next twenty-four hours."

"Any nationality on the perps?"

"The report is Middle Eastern."

"And they haven't gone home? Why?"

"Speculation is that the ship that was supposed to pick them up didn't show. Maybe because half the Indian navy was in the bay searching for pieces of the plane. But that's a guess. The Indians are keeping this guy to themselves. The minister has refused our requests to talk to him."

The President's left ear suddenly itched terribly. The ear *canal.* He had a powerful urge to dig a pinky inside. A Q-Tip. He wasn't prone to tics or itching, and he didn't need a psychiatrist to tell him why he had suddenly developed one. Back in the day,

Jack Kennedy had gotten by with muscle relaxants.

"Is this the usual sovereignty nonsense? *We are a great nation, not just cricket and lamb vindaloo.*" The last sentence in a mock Indian accent that wouldn't have won him any friends on the subcontinent.

"Yes, the usual sovereignty nonsense. We will push. I think they'll drop the pose soon enough."

"It's morning there, yes?"

"A little before three a.m. in Mumbai."

"I want us in there before noon their time. If I have to call Gupta directly to tell him, let me know." Anil Gupta, the Indian Prime Minister. "And I want Rooney in here to tell me exactly what they have and how we're going to make sure the Indians don't blow it." Tim Rooney, the FBI director. "I want these men taken alive."

"Yes, sir."

The itch migrated from the President's ear to his throat. At least that problem was fixable. He tapped a button discreetly attached to the underside of his desk. Almost before he lifted his finger, a steward opened the door to the hallway that connected the Oval Office with his private kitchen.

"Mr. President?"

"Club soda with lemon, please. Donna?"

"Sounds good," Green said.

"Yes, ma'am. Yes, Mr. President."

Sixty-four seconds later, the sodas arrived on a sterling silver tray.

The President raised his glass. "Salud."

"Salud."

"Let's assume the Indians are right. We get these guys, they turn out to be Iranian. Like I told you earlier. I want your best guess, why provoke us this way? Attack a civilian jet when we were so careful to stick to legitimate military targets?"

"I think it's dangerous to guess at motivation, sir. Especially when we have such poor intel into the Iranian government."

"Your objection is noted. For the record. Now, guess."

"A couple possibilities come to mind. Here's one you won't like. We're wrong. The Iranians aren't responsible for the HEU. They've decided that since we're attacking them on false pretenses, they might as well hurt us."

"Before I ordered the drones in, everyone agreed the evidence pointed to Iran. Everyone. DCI, DNI, our nuke experts. You, too."

"It did. It does. But it's still circumstantial. Even now, we don't have confirmation from communications intercepts or human sources."

"Then why don't they just let us in?"

"Would we let *them* in if the situation were reversed?"

The President suddenly found himself very tired.

"What about aliens?"

"Sir?"

"Maybe it's not Iran. Maybe a UFO dropped that uranium in Istanbul."

"You asked me to speculate, sir."

"I asked you to speculate. Not give me a stroke. I went on television and told the world that Iran was responsible. Are you seriously telling me that's open to question?"

Before the President took office, he'd vowed not to make the mistake of putting himself in a bubble, surrounded by staff too frightened to challenge him. But this situation was exceptional. The die was cast. He had made his choice. He could tolerate a lot of uncertainty. But not the possibility that he had just attacked another nation under false pretenses.

She cocked her head, looked at him, seemed to recognize how he felt. "No, sir. It's very unlikely."

"Then let's move on."

"Yes, sir. If the Iranians are committed to protecting their program at all costs, the jet could be a warning shot. Their way of telling us that if we invade them, we can expect terrorist attacks all over the world."

"That'll backfire in the worst way. People will want me to bomb Tehran into ash."

"In the short run. Imagine if it stretches for months. Not just planes. Attacks on military bases, police stations. Shootings in malls. Movie theaters. Almost a low-grade military campaign. The Iranians make sure we know that the attacks will continue as long as we have soldiers on their soil."

"They couldn't possibly pull that off."

"But if they could. We're not used to. being attacked. September 11 aside, we haven't had major civilian casualties since the Civil War. Maybe a pacifist groundswell starts? Why are we bothering about this bomb? Why are we interfering anyway?"

The President shook his head. "I can't believe they'd have the guts to try that."

"If more planes go down —"

"I'll reconsider. Next guess."

"This is the simplest. They're convinced we're going to attack and they can't do anything about it, so they're taking their pound of flesh in advance. It's not a strategy as much as a lashing-out."

"Don't you always say, never assume the enemy is irrational?"

"People get locked in and panic."

The President wondered whether that sentence held a second message for him.

"Anything else?"

Green nodded.

"One more, the most likely. Plenty of different factions inside Tehran. Plenty of folks over there were never on board with the program. They may not even have known about it. Now that we've busted it open, they feel like fools."

"They want to close it down."

"Plus they see a chance to break the conservatives for good. But the mullahs and generals who approved it know that if they walk away, they'll lose the government. Wind up dangling by their necks from cranes." The preferred form of execution in Iran.

"So they're doubling down."

"Correct. They don't care if we find out they shot down the plane. In fact, they'd rather we did. The worse it gets, the more control they have."

"Until the Airborne and the Marines level them."

"They may figure they can survive a limited invasion. Or that once they beat the liberals, they can walk back from the brink, open up the program at the eleventh hour long enough to stop us from coming over the border. They're dealing with the immediate problem and hoping the future will take care of itself."

"So do you have anything that's not speculation?"

"With any luck, the guys who shot the missiles can give us some answers. Especially if they're Hezbollah." The Lebanese Shiite militia group that Iran funded. "The hardliners are the ones with the lines into Lebanon. They'd rather use Hezbollah than their own security services and risk having the liberals find out."

"Okay. Say that last theory is right. The jet got taken down because of an internal Iranian power struggle. How do we hit back without helping the hardliners? Assuming a public attack would play into their hands."

"Agree. Better to come back with something quiet and with teeth."

"I'm sure SOCOM has options," the President said. Special Operations Command.

"No doubt. Meantime, this is more out there — but you might think about dangling a carrot as well, sir. Give Rouhani and the good guys something. So that the Iranians can't just say you want to give our program up and get nothing back."

"Hit 'em in secret, offer a way out in public."

Green nodded. The President's phone buzzed.

"Secretary Belk and General Warner have arrived, sir." Roger Belk, the Secretary of Defense, and Tom Warner, the four-star who ran Central Command.

"Thank you." He hung up. "I overreacted before, Donna. I know the sacrifices you make for this place. The hours you work."

Green clasped her hands. She seemed to be deciding if he was offering her another chance to talk over the first possibility she'd raised, that Iran wasn't involved with the uranium. He hoped she realized he wasn't.

"Sir. I can't even imagine the pressure you're under."

"I'm so glad to have you on my team."

"Yes, sir."

The President reached for his phone. "Send them in."

For twenty minutes, Belk and Warner walked the President through what both men insisted on calling the "positioning of assets." Pentagon-speak for moving the soldiers and Marines who might be fighting and dying at his command.

Within a week, all three of the 82nd

Airborne's brigade combat teams, with about six thousand soldiers each, would be encamped in Turkey. At the same time, four Marine regiments, totaling more than ten thousand Marines, would reach their forward operating bases in southwestern Afghanistan. Meanwhile, the 75th Ranger Regiment was en route to Kurdish-controlled territory in northeastern Iraq. Finally, the Saudis were allowing Delta, SEAL, and Marine Special Operations units to operate out of their giant air base in Khobar, on the condition that the United States never admit their presence.

"Basically, sir, the positioning is on schedule," Belk said. "Not entirely surprising, considering these are mostly elite units and don't have a huge amount of armor, which is what really screws up the logistics."

"So we'll have forces to the east, north, and south by the time my deadline hits?" the President said.

"Correct, sir," Warner said. Four-star generals fell into two categories, the President had discovered. The bantamweights compensated for their lack of size with doctorates in operations research and an incredible devotion to fitness. The heavyweights were solid and strong, with chests full of medals and decorations. At six feet and two hundred pounds, Warner belonged in the second camp. He had gray Prussian eyes and a private's quarter-inch haircut. "The three carriers will also be in place, so we'll have the ability to fly hundreds of sorties a day. And six guided-missile destroyers. That's the good news."

"And what's the bad news?"

"The bad news, sir, is that our options will still be somewhat limited. We'll have roughly thirty thousand soldiers and Marines around Iran at your deadline. Now, those are elite units with a high tip-to-tail ratio. But you may recall that we invaded Iraq with a force closer to one hundred fifty thousand. And we judge Iran's forces to be more capable than Saddam Hussein's and more likely to fight for the regime."

"So a sustained ground invasion is unrealistic. Much less an occupation."

"Correct, Mr. President. For that, we'd need heavy armor. Three divisions at least. 1st Cav, 1st Armored, 1st Infantry. Even then we'd be stretched. Our planners would be more comfortable with four or even five."

"And the Iranians are aware of this?"

"They can do the math as well as we can. The only possible way we could win a ground war with a force this size would be if the Iranians were foolish enough to mass their units near the border. Then we could decimate them with airpower. But none of our planners think they would make that mistake."

"So their strategy would be to let us advance?"

"Most likely. Fall back, engage us with irregular forces, attack our supply lines as they get stretched. Force us to thin our air cover over larger and larger territory. Hit back hard as we approach Tehran, and the heavy civilian presence limits the advantages of our airpower. That's what I'd do, sir."

"So what options do I have on deadline day?"

"That depends how much risk you'd like to take," Belk said. "The most realistic options are limited strikes, discreet locations."

"You know what I want. The nuclear sites."

Warner lifted his meaty right hand. "If I may, sir."

"Please."

"We won't have the advantage of surprise, and Natanz and Fordow are large and well-defended installations. We would start with missile and bomb strikes to soften the targets, degrade defenses. I believe the 82nd and the Marines are capable of taking those two sites even in the face of sustained

Iranian opposition, especially if they have help from the Special Forces.

"But understand, the longer they stay, the greater the risk. We estimate the Iranian army and Revolutionary Guard have sixty thousand men within one hundred kilometers of both those installations. That is a serious edge in manpower, and they have substantial air-defense capabilities, too, that will blunt our edge there. We'll be facing an army, not an insurgency, with artillery and tanks and helicopters."

The President stared into his glass of club soda as if it held the answer.

"You're starting to make me nervous, General."

"I don't mean to say we'll be overrun. The casualties will be significant. And once we're done, we have to get them out."

"I can see where this is going. It's always the same. You always want more. You never want to go in without the entire army."

"I'm sorry if that's how this is coming across, sir."

"Right now I am not even going to consider a full-scale invasion. But if I did, how long would it take to deploy the divisions you say we need?"

"Ten to twelve weeks, depending on how much the host countries will help. That's the absolute best case without any language or scenario training."

The President turned away from the men on the couch, looked out through his bulletproof, bombproof windows. He wanted to feel both angrier and calmer. He was the most powerful man in the world and yet now he feared he couldn't control the avalanche he'd started. *The only way out is through.* He couldn't back down. Not now.

"That's unfortunate. Since the deadline I set is not even nine days away. I want to see both of you back in this office exactly twenty-four hours from now. I want you to look like you haven't slept. I want a viable plan to hit those nuclear facilities. Do you understand me?"

"Yes, sir," Belk and Warner said simultaneously. The men stood to leave.

Green cleared her throat. "Sir. Shall I stay?"

He shook his head. She followed them out. And then he was alone in the Oval Office.

8
EIGHT DAYS . . .

RIYADH

Two platoons of National Guardsmen watched Wells overnight. In the morning, a dozen armored Humvees convoyed him to Abdullah's palace on highways that police had closed to all other traffic. Barn door closed with the horse long gone.

The King's palace was in northern Riyadh, close to the airport, convenient for meetings with visiting dignitaries. Wells couldn't begin to guess at its size. He'd seen smaller malls. Two attendants led Wells through the formal stateroom where the King usually met Western visitors, into a private sitting room decorated in a tropical theme. Brightly colored couches overlooked a glassed-in interior courtyard where parrots and macaws flitted among hanging vines that seemed to have been imported straight from the Amazon.

"Coffee? Tea?"

Wells shook his head.

"His Majesty will be along shortly. Please make yourself comfortable." The door locked with a faintly audible click as they left.

So Wells watched the parrots twitter. At this moment, hundreds of workers were cleaning up the carnage from last night, filling the eight-foot-deep crater in Prince Turki Road, shoring the damaged buildings. In a few hours they would hang heavy plastic drapes to hide the broken apartment façades. The intersection would look like just another construction site in a city full of them, a view as false as this tropical tableau. The Saud family preferred to pretend that terrorism didn't exist inside the Kingdom's borders.

A half hour passed before Abdullah entered, helped by a fifty-something man who could have been a younger clone. The King's hair was as black as ever. His eyes were still clear under his glasses. But three years had passed since Wells had first met him. And three years meant a lot to a man born in 1924. Abdullah's hands shook, and the folds of his robe couldn't hide the weight he'd lost. He wheezed gently as he walked. The King had genetics and the best doctors money could buy, but time always won.

"Your Majesty. *As-salaam aleikum.*"

"*Aleikum salaam.* Come, please, Mr. Wells."

Wells did. To his surprise, the King reached out, hugged him.

"You were injured."

The night before, a National Guard medic had strapped bandages on his cheeks and chin to cover the cuts from the blast wave and put a proper splint on his broken pinky. Wells had turned down the medic's offers of painkillers. The decision seemed like the right way to honor Ghaith. But as a result, Wells hardly slept. "It was nothing."

"My men failed you."

"No one could have stopped what happened." A lie, as Abdullah probably knew. "Your men gave everything. I'm the one who's alive."

"*Inshallah.*"

"*Inshallah.*"

The King lumbered to an armchair and sat.

"Sit, please." The King indicated the couch nearest his chair. "These men, they call themselves believers, soldiers, an army of Islam. *Soldiers?* They kill innocent Muslims —" Abdullah stopped himself, shook his head. "You know all this."

Wells nodded.

"Allah sends them all to hell, this I'm sure."

"Nam." The men who'd blown that bomb had their own theological explanations for what they'd done, but Abdullah was in no mood for debate. Besides, he was right. The killers belonged in hell.

Abdullah nodded at the fiftyish man who'd come in with him. "This is my nephew, Fahd bin Salman, commander of the National Guard. He has a few questions for you and then he'll tell you what his men have found so far. After that, you and I will talk."

Fahd extended a hand. "I'm sorry to meet you under such unpleasant circumstances, Mr. Wells." His resemblance to Abdullah ended when he opened his mouth. His voice was soft, vaguely fussy. Even at ninety, the King was more powerful.

"As am I." Wells felt the need for a certain formality around these men.

"May I ask what you saw last night?"

Wells explained everything, including the delay at the air base gate, the motorcycle on the Mecca Road, and the attack.

"Do you have any idea why Ghaith didn't respond more forcefully?" Fahd said when he finished.

"I think he felt we were adequately defended. With the armored limousine and the convoy." *Too many 5 a.m. wake-up calls left him punchy* didn't strike Wells as the right answer, even if it was true.

"But you disagreed."

"I guessed."

"You were right. Did you see the license numbers of the motorcycles? Or their makes?"

"I'm almost sure they didn't have plates. They were big, a thousand ccs or more. Black. Sportbike fairings. I think they were identical, both the same model. Beyond that, I can't say. I'm sorry."

"What about the bomb vehicle?"

"White, a minivan."

"And you didn't see the driver."

"No. I can't identify the men on the bikes either. They wore helmets with mirrored face shields. One dropped a pistol at the scene. I'm sure you've recovered that."

"A Makarov, yes. We're trying to trace it, but as you know they're very common. I wish I could tell you we had good leads, but we don't. We recovered the vehicle number of the van earlier today from a piece of the frame that survived. It was reported stolen about two months ago from a parking lot in

Jeddah. There were no cameras in the lot there and the police have no leads. Most likely, whoever stole it just drove it to Riyadh and parked it in a garage somewhere, waiting for this sort of chance. The driver, we haven't even found fragments. I think we'll be lucky even to recover enough for a DNA sample."

"How big was the bomb?"

"Based on the size of the crater and the damage to the buildings, we're estimating five hundred kilos of high explosive."

More than a thousand pounds. A huge bomb. They were lucky it hadn't done even more damage. "You have a list of guys who can put together a bomb that size?"

"We try to track them. But every month, more come home from Iraq and Syria."

Depressing. And true. "What about the bikes?"

"They reached the southern ring road, turned west. After that, we believe they went into the desert. We're looking, but I fear they were garaged before sunrise. Before the attack, they passed several intersections where we have cameras, so we're analyzing those. But we don't have plates, and as you said, the riders hid their faces."

"Professional job."

"Very much. Mr. Wells, do you think this

attack could in any way be related to the mission that brought you to the Kingdom?"

Wells had given that question plenty of thought during his sleepless night. "I doubt it. I'd be shocked if the people I'm going after have resources like that in Riyadh. I think someone heard I was here and decided to take a shot at me."

"I agree."

"So have you asked the FBI for forensic help?" Over the years, the Bureau had quietly worked with the Saudis to investigate terror attacks.

Fahd looked at Abdullah. "For now, no. We believe we have the situation in hand."

So the King didn't want the United States looking over his shoulder on this investigation. Wells knew why. "How about investigating from the other end?"

"The other end?"

"Who told the jihadis that I was in Riyadh?"

Fahd hesitated.

"I think before we can answer that question we'll need to find out who carried out the attack."

"Of course. I understand."

Wells did, too. The King was angry about the attack. But he knew that the tipster was probably inside his family. One of his nephews. He might even have a good idea which one. He didn't intend to disturb the fragile peace within the House of Saud by finding out if his hunch was right. He certainly didn't want the FBI poking around. Wells was his friend, and Ghaith his grandnephew by marriage, sure. But neither man was blood.

"You can only do so much. I appreciate the briefing."

"Go," Abdullah said.

Fahd hurried off.

Then Wells and the King were alone.

"I'm glad you see our position." Abdullah spoke without irony or apology. A statement of fact, honest and cold as a North Atlantic wave. *We're both grown-ups, and you know the reality I face.* The reason he was King.

"As long as you don't mind leaving me unfinished business." *They may be your family, but if they're foolish enough to leave these borders, if they give me the chance, in Europe, Dubai, wherever, I'll kill them.* The reason Wells was Wells.

Abdullah merely nodded. Wells was reminded of a phrase attributed to Earl Long, the three-time governor of Louisiana, Huey's less famous, more corrupt younger brother:

Don't write anything you can phone. Don't phone anything you can talk. Don't talk anything you can whisper. Don't whisper anything you can smile. Don't smile anything you can nod. Don't nod anything you can wink.

Long hadn't been around for the Internet, but Wells could guess what he would have made of email.

"So. Nawwaf briefed me this morning on your theory. I must tell you I don't think it's correct."

"You think that the uranium is Iran's?" Wells found himself genuinely surprised.

"Persians are Persians."

"I don't understand."

"Do you know what the Shah had in common with the religious ones who took over in 1979? They all see everything within two thousand kilometers as theirs. West to Mecca, east to Baluchistan, north over the Caucasus."

"They must know the Muslim world would never accept Shia control of the Kaaba."

"They know nothing of the sort. In fact, the opposite. They see it as their divine right. And the ones who aren't religious, for them we're just a bunch of uncultured Bedouin riding camels through the desert. As far as they're concerned, Iran is the only real nation in the region, the only one with any history. To them the bomb is a triumph. Not just military, but technical, scientific. It makes them a modern nation."

"Modern as North Korea."

Abdullah ignored the objection. "Also, the bomb makes us squirm and protects them from you. And the Jews, too."

"Until Pakistan gives you a bomb of your own."

"Maybe they're not so sure the Pakistanis will give us a bomb," Abdullah said.

"What about you, Your Majesty? Are you sure?"

"It doesn't matter, because we haven't made the request."

"I see all the reasons they might want a bomb. It doesn't mean they've achieved one."

"If they have, they need to be stopped. And if they haven't, maybe they need to be stopped from trying."

"You want the United States to invade Iran on rigged evidence, Your Majesty."

"What is rigged? What does it mean?"

"People on the left and the right in America, they already don't believe what the government says. After what happened

215

in Iraq, this would be a catastrophe. Maybe even cause a constitutional crisis."

"I don't believe it. *Because you're an absolute monarch. You buy off anyone who criticizes you, and destroy the ones who won't stay bought. Your biggest threats come from your nephews, not your citizens. You can't imagine millions of people filling the streets to challenge you.*

But Wells said only, "Believe me, Your Majesty. It's possible."

"There are still eight days left. Maybe Iran will see the light and you won't have to invade."

"So you won't help?"

Abdullah leaned forward, staring at Wells like a pitcher who needed just one more batter for his no-hitter. He might not have too many fastballs left, but Wells was about to see one.

"I *won't* help? Have I not helped already? I let you come here, speak to Nawwaf as you wished. Last month in Bangkok you asked for aid and we granted it immediately. And I promise that no one will tell the FBI and CIA that you were the actual target of this bombing. Unless you would rather that your name be part of our reports."

"No." Wells didn't know what the agency would do if it heard about his freelancing,

216

but the response certainly wouldn't be *you go girl!*

"Those courtesies will continue. I gave you my word and it holds. Even though I fear what you find may not help my country. Do you understand me, Mr. Wells?"

"Thank you."

"Then what more would you like?"

"That you might speak to the President."

"What shall I say?" Abdullah smiled gently, as much as telling Wells that he was making a fool of himself.

"That he should wait. That there's too much we don't know."

"So you want me to pass along a theory I don't believe, act against my country's interests."

"A war on false pretenses."

"Allahu akbar! Allahu akbar!" The shriek came from behind the glass, astonishingly loud. Wells spun in surprise — and found himself staring at a huge blue parrot. *"Allahu akbar! Allahu akbar!"* God is great.

"Glad you think so," Wells said.

"Allahu akbar?" A questioning tone this time, and then the parrot flew off.

"You know, this is my favorite room in the whole palace. These birds."

"I thought you were more of a falconer,

217

Your Majesty."

"In my old age, these amuse me. They remind me of my aides, the foolish ones who repeat whatever I say. I bring them here sometimes, but they never see the joke."

"That why I'm here?"

"You and I, we can speak honestly. So I tell you now. Even if I spoke to the President as you asked, it would make no difference. Do you know why?"

Wells shook his head.

"Because he listens to three or four people about this now. His NSA, maybe the Secretary of Defense, maybe the Vice President and chief of staff, if he trusts them. And even them, he hardly hears. In his mind, he's reached the point where it's his decision and his alone. This is what it means to command an army."

"And you think he's made his decision?"

"You'll need strong evidence to change his mind. Very strong."

Abdullah pushed himself up. "Will you stay for lunch with me?"

Wells looked at his watch. Almost noon. "I can't." He decided against asking Abdullah for a private jet to Russia. The King would have agreed, but Wells didn't know what Buvchenko would make of his arriving that way.

"All right, then." Abdullah took Wells's hands in his own. The king's hands were worn with age, dry and creased. *"Barak'allah fik."* May God bless you.

His tone was final, the meaning clear enough. Good-bye, not just now but forever.

9
SEVEN DAYS . . .

BETHESDA, MARYLAND

"Gentlemen?" the waiter at the Hyatt Regency said.

"Coffee, scrambled eggs, rye toast, hash browns. And a side of bacon." Shafer felt like a bad Jew when he ordered bacon. A bad Jew who was going to die of a heart attack. But the guy at the next table had a plateful, and it smelled delicious.

"Egg-white omelet with asparagus, and please ask the kitchen to cook it dry," Ian Duffy said.

"Yes, sir."

Bad enough that Duffy's gray suit had a rubbed metallic sheen that screamed Armani. *Real men don't eat egg whites.* Shafer wanted to despise the guy. But he couldn't.

Duffy had been chief of station in Hong Kong during Glenn Mason's tour there. Duffy had quit the agency two years before and come back to the United States. Now he consulted for multinational companies with investments in China. His company was called Global Asian Partners, or Asian Global Partners, or I Partner Asia Globally, or some such. Shafer had done his best to forget.

The clandestine side wasn't that big. Shafer must have met Duffy at least a couple times over the years. But when he looked Duffy up on LinkedIn, he had no recollection of the man. On-screen, Duffy wore a getting-it-done smile. His profile openly mentioned the CIA. He didn't specifically say he'd been Hong Kong station chief, but he came close: *200X–201X: Senior Management, Overseas Post, East Asia.* Shafer was astonished at first, then less so. Of course Duffy's prospective clients would want to know what he'd been doing all those years after the University of Michigan. The CIA was a lot more impressive than the State Department.

For a couple of days after Wells flew to Switzerland and Duto to Tel Aviv, Shafer didn't try to contact Duffy. Shafer justified his hesitation by telling himself that the CIA was waiting for him to make a mistake. Like the White House, the agency had gone all in on the theory that Iran was the source of the Istanbul uranium. The DCI's chief of staff and axman, Max Carcetti, had warned Shafer against trying to prove otherwise. Shafer would embarrass himself and the agency at a crucial moment, Carcetti said. And Carcetti had leverage, in the form of tapes of Shafer passing classified information to Wells and Duto — who no longer had CIA clearances.

The tapes gave Carcetti and Scott Hebley, the DCI, all the evidence they needed to fire Shafer. If they wanted to play hardball, they could even ask the Department of Justice to prosecute Shafer as a leaker. Shafer probably wouldn't go to prison. Duto was a senator and the former DCI, and Wells had worked for the agency for more than a decade. Even so, fighting a federal indictment would take years and cost Shafer his life savings. Shafer figured the only reason Hebley and Carcetti hadn't gotten rid of him already was that they wanted him in the office, where they could watch him easily. Best to tread lightly, especially since Duffy probably didn't have anything useful anyway.

But the morning before, not long after the agency received reports of a terrorist attack in Riyadh, Shafer saw a message in his inbox from 2belizeprincess45@gmail.com. The body text was a cut-and-paste for counterfeit Viagra. The point of the message was contained in the sender's address: Wells wanted Shafer to call him on his second burner phone in forty-five minutes.

For a moment, Shafer found himself oddly sympathetic to the jihadis he'd spent fifteen years chasing. Did he and Wells think they would beat the all-seeing NSA with these simple tricks? *Inshallah,* my man. Forty-three minutes later, he stood outside his car in the parking lot of the Tysons Corner Galleria as Wells recounted his conversation with General Nawwaf.

North Korea?

I don't believe it either, Wells said. *But since it's all I got, I figured I'd mention it. Anyone you can ask?*

I'll think about it.

What about this bombing? We just got the reports. Were you —

I don't want to talk about it. If I thought it was relevant, I would have mentioned it.

I'm sorry, John.

The show never ends. And I'm starting to think I know all the lyrics by heart.

Get some sleep. If you can.

Keep an eye on Evan and Heather, okay?

Of course. You'll feel better in the morning.

223

Shafer wasn't sure if he was trying to convince Wells, or himself. Either way, he was talking to dead air. Wells was gone. And Shafer was furious with himself for his cowardice. Wells risked his life in the field every day, and Shafer was sitting on his hands because he was afraid to irritate the seventh floor? He left the burner in his glove compartment, found a cab to take him to the Clarendon Metro, the orange line. He didn't think Carcetti and Hebley would bother with a live tail. But they might have stuck a GPS tracker on his car.

From Clarendon he headed east to Rosslyn. South to Crystal City on the blue line. Northeast to L'Enfant Plaza on the yellow. To the street, a brisk walk from the entrance at 9th and D to the one at 7th and Maryland, then back underground. Again the blue line. The run took nearly an hour and was probably unnecessary, a blur of silver trains puffing in and out under waffle-shaped concrete ceilings. But Shafer wanted to work his countersurveillance muscles. Feel like a real case officer again. He got off at Benning Road. The massive growth in the government and the lobbyists who sucked its teats had made Washington wealthier than it had ever been. Neighborhoods around Capitol Hill and all over

Northwest had been prettied past recognition. But the gentrification boom hadn't touched the low-slung housing projects that speckled the hills east of the Anacostia River. Here, crack vials still littered the sidewalks, and convenience-store clerks cowered behind bulletproof glass.

Shafer trudged along East Capitol until he saw the neon lights of a check-cashing outlet glowing in the dusk. In a world of cheap prepaid mobile handsets, check cashers were among the last places that could be counted on for old-fashioned pay phones. Of the four phones outside Ready-Chek!-Go, one had no handset. Another had inexplicably been mummified with electrical tape. Burns and scratches that couldn't even be called graffiti covered the last two. As Shafer tried to pick the one less likely to give him hepatitis, two women in miniskirts sidled toward him. They were either prostitutes or doing their best to freeze to death. He expected an approach, but apparently he was too old for them to bother. The one on the left said something under her breath to the other, and they both giggled and kept walking. An entirely inappropriate flush of self-pity seized him. *When even the whores ignore you, you might as well be dead.*

He shoved quarters into the phone and

225

dialed. "Global Pan-Asia Partners," a woman said, her voice crackling through the broken plastic.

"Ian Duffy, please." Shafer was shouting, trying to keep the mouthpiece away from his lips.

"Who may I say is calling?"

"Ellis Shafer."

"And will he know what this is in reference to, Mr. Shafer?"

"Tell him it's Farm business."

Three full minutes passed. Shafer started to lose feeling in his fingers. He was nearly ready to hang up.

"This is an unexpected pleasure. The famous Ellis Shafer. How may I help you?"

Shafer didn't know why Duffy was so chummy. Maybe they had met after all. "I'd love to tell you over a drink tonight," he said with as much conviction as he could muster.

"Tonight's no good. Breakfast? Tomorrow?" Duffy's voice combined his Michigan childhood and the decades he'd spent in former British colonies. The flat nasal tones of the Midwest and the elongated consonants of Hyde Park. He sounded like an aristocrat with a cold.

"Tomorrow would be great."

"Eight a.m.? The Hyatt in Bethesda?"

"Looking forward to it." Though Shafer wasn't. He'd have to set his alarm at 5:30 for another Metro run.

"See you then."

The sky was dark when he left his house the next morning. But not so dark that he didn't notice the unmarked white van that picked him up when he turned onto Washington Boulevard. Then again, he would have had to be blind to miss it. It was a dented Ford Econoline with tinted windows and no commercial insignia, which only heightened its obviousness. Shafer looked for a front license plate to memorize, but the van didn't have one. The omission wasn't necessarily illegal. Several nearby states, including North Carolina and West Virginia, didn't require front plates.

The van seemed to Shafer less a tail than a signal. *We're watching. We know where you live.* The agency had already sent that message loud and clear. Which left Duberman.

He called home. "Sweetie. Can you do me a favor and look outside?"

She walked to the window. They'd been together forty years. Shafer believed he'd know his wife by her footsteps alone.

"I'm looking."

"See anything out of place? Unmarked

227

vans, anything like that?"

"Everything looks okay. What's going on, Ellis?" He'd learned in Africa a generation ago that she didn't scare easy. She didn't sound scared now. Not for herself, anyway.

"I'll tell you when I get home. As much as I can."

As a rule, she didn't ask him about work, but in this case she deserved to know.

"If I see anything, I'll call you."

"And the police. And the neighbors." Shafer thought of the pistol he kept in the basement, but the suggestion would only make her laugh.

"That bad?"

"Better safe than sorry. Love you."

"Likely story."

He drove on, eyeing the van in his mirror, trying to push down his fury, keep his mind clear. They wanted to come at him, fine. But not his wife. Real spy agencies didn't play these games. They were too easy, and too easy to escalate. Shafer decided to let them tail him for now. He'd find out at the Metro station if they were serious about following him.

The East Falls Church lot was already almost half full when he arrived. D.C.'s rush hour started early. Shafer drove slowly through the lot, waiting for the van to follow. But it stopped outside the entrance, as if the men inside weren't sure what to do. After a few seconds, it rumbled off. Shafer suspected its disappearance meant that the driver didn't want him to see its rear license plate and run a trace. More proof they were private investigators. FBI or CIA operatives wouldn't have cared. Shafer wondered if he ought to follow them, but they had a decent lead and he wasn't in the mood for a high-speed chase through suburban Virginia. Anyway, they'd be back.

The morning's countersurveillance run on the Metro gave Shafer plenty of time to consider why Duberman and the woman who worked for him had sent the van. The move seemed unnecessarily provocative. They knew the agency and White House had bought their scheme. But for whatever reason, they still felt the need to pressure Shafer. Maybe he and Wells were closer than they imagined.

Shafer walked out of the red line Bethesda Metro stop at 7:45. As far as he could tell, he hadn't been followed. It was always possible that the agency or the FBI was running a twenty-agent team on him, but those were basically impossible to spot, and Shafer didn't know why they would bother.

Duffy arrived at eight, exactly on time. Shafer didn't recognize him, didn't think they had ever spoken, but Duffy was as cordial as he'd been the day before. Duffy was a common agency type, tall and lanky, with blue eyes that seemed friendly at first and then less so. The CIA contained a surprising number of Midwesterners and Mormons. Shafer didn't know why. Maybe they saw espionage as a way to channel their murderous ids into the noble task of protecting the homeland. They unsettled Shafer. He knew he was being unfair, but he had no trouble imagining them setting railroad schedules for trains to Auschwitz in 1944.

"You live close by?" Shafer said, as the waiter walked away.

"Chevy Chase. We were lucky enough to buy a house twenty years ago and sublet it all these years I was in Asia."

"And business is good?"

"Fantastic."

Shafer was sure Duffy would have given that answer even if he was on the verge of bankruptcy. "You don't mind my asking, who do you work for?"

"Everyone from pharmaceutical companies trying to keep counterfeit Chinese drugs out of the supply chain to movie studios dealing with DVD knockoffs. Software, auto parts, it doesn't matter, if the Chinese can copy it, they will. Hedge funds hire us to help with investments gone wrong. Ask us to figure out if hiring some minister's son will cause more problems than it's worth. Western companies are only just realizing now how complex doing business in China is. Only problem is that I wind up spending half my time on planes to Hong Kong."

"And I guess they're willing to pay."

"I'm not afraid to tell you, Ellis. I charge a thousand-fifty an hour. And flying counts, too. Just to put me on a plane to HK costs twenty grand. But then, if you have seven hundred million dollars sunk into some truck plant there, twenty grand doesn't sound so bad."

Duffy didn't bother to hide his pleasure. His cynicism was so deep that it had molted into something like optimism. *Why shouldn't I get rich? Everyone else is.*

And he was right, more or less. Duffy had put in twenty-four years at the agency, retired at fifty-one. If he wanted to make a few bucks now, have all the egg-white omelets he can eat, Shafer understood.

Sometimes he wondered if he should have taken that path himself. Though it had never really been open to him. Years before, Duto had told Shafer that he was the ultimate agency loyalist, that as much as he claimed to stand apart, he couldn't exist without the CIA. Shafer had wanted to disagree, but in his heart he knew that Duto spoke true. In his twisted way, Duto was a keen judge of character.

"How about you, Ellis? How are you?"

"Getting by. Day at a time." Waiting for the blade to drop. "I have to ask, Ian. We ever work together?"

Duffy shook his head.

"Then why did you agree to meet me on such short notice?"

Duffy grinned. "I figured it'd be interesting, that's all. And I thought maybe you wanted to come work for me. It's not too late."

"I don't know anything about China."

"You wouldn't have to. The companies I work for do business all over."

"Not why I called. Though I appreciate the thought."

The waiter returned, bearing their breakfast, and they sat in silence until he left.

"You remember Glenn Mason?"

"Sure. Weirdest episode I had in all my years."

"You know what happened to him?"

"After we got rid of him, you mean? He

flaked. Disappeared."

"You never heard that he drowned in Thailand?"

"When?" Duffy sounded genuinely surprised.

"A few months after you fired him. Rented a boat near Phuket and fell overboard."

Duffy busied himself cutting a piece of omelet. "And it was never reported to us?"

"So it seems. Best I can tell, no one cared enough to bother. His parents were dead, he never married, no kids. And I'm guessing he didn't have anyone in Hong Kong."

"Not at the station, anyway. I'd like to tell you I've spent a lot of time thinking about him, but I haven't. Maybe once a year."

"You don't sound too cut-up."

"I hardly knew him. He had a breakdown in Baghdad, and for some reason he decided he wanted Hong Kong, and personnel figured they owed him one. Which they did. But he was burned out even before he started. Didn't come in half the time and was drunk when he did. He didn't recruit a single agent."

"You knew he lost all that money gambling."

"Of course. He didn't try to hide it. Part of me thought he was proud of it."

"At that casino called 88 Gamma? Aaron

Duberman's place?"

"Yeah. Which, coincidentally enough, I started working for a couple months ago."

Bile filled Shafer's throat. *Think.* Was this Duffy's wink-and-a-nod way of telling Shafer that he knew what Duberman had done? Doubtful. Shafer couldn't imagine that Duffy would risk being charged with treason.

Much more likely that the woman running the plot for Duberman had hired Duffy and other ex–CIA officers as an early warning system. This way she would hear if Shafer or anyone else went fishing for information about 88 Gamma. And no one would wonder why a casino company was hiring guys like Duffy. Casinos were a rough business, lots of political interference and cash sloshing around.

"What do you do for them, if you don't mind my asking?" Shafer had to tread lightly here. If he pushed too hard, Duffy would surely report this conversation back to 88 Gamma. *This guy Ellis Shafer was asking about Aaron.*

"They want to be sure they can collect on the credit they extend. Which, if someone is too connected in Beijing, gets tricky."

"Makes sense."

"So that's it? You came here to tell me that

Glenn Mason was dead?"

"Not really." Shafer wondered if he could pull this pivot. Distract Duffy from his interest in Duberman, and at the same time find out if North Korea could possibly have supplied the Istanbul uranium. The odds were hugely against Pyongyang being involved, but the question was still worth asking.

Shafer slathered butter over his toast, took a bite, buying a few seconds, thinking through the story he was about to tell. "The reason I got onto Mason at all, I've been looking into the North Korean nuclear program. We got this weird report that an FBI agent who'd been stationed in Hong Kong defected to North Korea and he lives in Pyongyang now."

"I don't get it."

"Neither did I. The report came from a North Korean defector talking to the South Koreans. They sent it to the Bureau and they said it was ridiculous. Got filed under *C* for crazy. But like I said, I was looking at defectors' reports about North Korea, and I realized that the guy might have said FBI when he meant CIA. So I looked for case officers from Hong Kong station who left in the last few years. That's how I found Mason. Now I'm wondering if there's any chance he might have faked his death and defected to North Korea."

Shafer worried now that the story sounded a little *too* real, that Duffy might get interested enough to ask questions of his old friends back at Langley.

"So he fakes his death in Thailand and then goes to Pyongyang?" Duffy said.

"I know it seems like a long shot. The defector said this American was working with the North Koreans to look for buyers for nukes and raw uranium. That they'd tried to approach Saudi Arabia and gotten laughed off."

Duffy shook his head emphatically. "Makes no sense. On either side. North Korea doesn't have any nuclear weapons to spare, and if they were trying to sell them, why would they need some burned-out CIA op to help? And Mason, he struck me as desperate, not stupid. He would know that North Korea's pure roach motel. He would last in Pyongyang until somebody high up got nervous. Then they'd shoot him. If he was lucky. More likely they'd find some even more unpleasant way to get rid of him. You heard about the air force general they fed to a bear?"

"Nice. So the North Koreans aren't trying to sell their nukes?"

"That was really Seoul's AOR." Area of

responsibility. "But I never heard anything serious."

"Fair enough."

"So. What are people saying inside? Are we really going to war with Iran over this?"

Shafer thought of the way Duberman had blocked them at every turn, even as the President's deadline crept ever closer.

"It's not looking good."

10

VOLGOGRAD, RUSSIA

The Yuzhniy Hotel was the best in Volgograd. The faintest praise imaginable. The restaurant beside its bland lobby doubled as a cabaret, complete with techno music, pulsing blue lights, and a smoke machine. Near the front, a single flabby stripper twisted halfheartedly around a pole. A late-afternoon special for bored businessmen.

At the counter, the receptionist made a copy of Wells's passport, handed it back with a key.

"You are in room three-zero-six. We have free breakfast from six a.m. to nine."

"In there?" Wells nodded at the restaurant, where the stripper was now jiggling on a low platform. "Sounds delicious."

"Yes. If I can help you with anything, please tell me." Her voice bordered on robotic. Wells sensed that if he presented himself at the desk again in five minutes, she would repeat herself word for word as if they'd never met. He was sorry for mocking her about the restaurant. Russian provinces weren't the poorest places on earth, but they might have been the saddest.

He bypassed the hotel's elevator to walk up the concrete staircase. Halfway between the first and second floors, he smelled cigarette smoke and stopped. Two male voices overhead, quiet, Russian. Wells was sure the men were here for him. He trudged up. He hoped they wouldn't feel the need to work him over before taking him to see their boss. But then Russians liked a bit of drama, even when it didn't serve their interests.

As their Ukrainian adventure proved. The protesters who'd started the trouble by begging Russia for help had obviously been agents provocateurs paid by the FSB. The entire episode was as badly acted as an elementary school play. Yet Vladimir Putin hadn't let the West's disdain stop them. And by the time he finished, he owned much of eastern Ukraine.

At the third-floor landing, Wells found two twenty-something men dressed in the mandatory uniform of Russian gangsters, black leather jackets and dark blue jeans. Though, weirdly, under their coats they wore thick white wool sweaters that could have come from L.L. Bean. Where the sweaters ended, ornate blue tattoos flared up their necks. Their faces were pouty, their fists meaty. The taller of the two wore an expensive version of brass knuckles, thick gold rings on nine fingers. Wells presumed he would have preferred ten, but he didn't have the option. His left pinky was missing. Wells's sudden appearance puzzled him for a moment. Then he dropped his cigarette and pulled his pistol, a snubnose, tiny in his hand. He didn't look puzzled anymore. "You are Wells."

"If you say so. You?"

"Why you take stairs?"

"Why not?"

Apparently, the right answer. The guy tucked away his pistol. "Hands —" He nodded toward the ceiling.

He stood back while his partner gave Wells an efficient frisk.

"You come with us."

"Mind if I take a shower first?"

"You come with us."

Volgograd was best known for being the place where Russia turned the tide of World War II. A five-month battle in late 1942 and early 1943 reduced the city, then known as

Stalingrad, to rubble. In November, with the German Sixth Army near victory, more than a million Soviet soldiers counterattacked. Two months later, as the Soviets encircled the Germans, Hitler ordered his generals not to surrender or retreat. The Sixth Army would fight to the last man, he said. It very nearly did. By some estimates, the Battle of Stalingrad was the deadliest single engagement in the history of war. Nearly a million German soldiers died, along with hundreds of thousands of Russians. Germany alone lost nearly as many soldiers that winter as the United States had in all the wars it had ever fought — combined.

Stalin wasted no time rebuilding the city that bore his name. But after he died, Khrushchev renamed it Volgograd, part of the effort to end the cult of personality around Uncle Joe. By any name, the city remained a backwater. It subsisted on agriculture and heavy industry, with none of the glamour of St. Petersburg or the wealth of Moscow. The arms dealer Wells was about to meet might be the richest man in the entire province.

Outside the hotel, a BMW 7 Series waited. Wells's escorts pushed him into the front passenger seat. They didn't even bother to take his phone, more proof they didn't think he represented much of a threat. Dusk was fading into night, and the Yuzhniy's red neon sign glowed against the blue-black sky.

Volgograd's streets were wide and quiet. The BMW quickly left the city behind and sped northwest along a provincial highway. Low apartment buildings and chunky concrete houses gave way to empty fields. Wells's escorts seemed content to ride in silence, and he didn't argue.

Then his burner buzzed. Shafer. They hadn't talked in more than a day.

"Ellis."

"Evan's threatening to walk."

Wells wasn't entirely surprised. His son was headstrong and surely hated having FBI agents watching him. Especially since Wells hadn't told him much about the threat.

"You told him to sit tight?"

"He said he has to hear it from you."

"I'll call him."

"In person."

"You told him that's not possible?"

"Of course."

"Make him stay, Ellis."

"I can't *make* him do anything. He's a grown-up. It gets worse. Our friends are watching me. Our private friends, not the public ones, *capisce*?"

242

Meaning Duberman's operatives, not the CIA.

"They come at you?"

"Not exactly. More like that they wanted me to know that they could find me. I don't know if it means they think we're close."

"I'm on the way to see the Russian." Wells kept his voice steady. "So you need to take care of this."

"I'll tell Evan you'll call him as soon as you can."

"And I will. But if there's heavy hand-holding required, you need to make yourself useful. That means getting on a plane to see him, talk him down, you do it."

"All right."

"But make sure nobody's watching. Let's not give anyone a road map to that safe house by accident."

"Save the tradecraft lessons, John."

"I'll let you know if my new friend tells me anything."

"Don't piss him off too much, okay? Files say he has a temper."

"Got my knee pads right here, Ellis." He hung up before Shafer could answer.

"Everything okay?" the driver said.

"Perfect." Wells stared out as dusk fled and the road sank into black.

■ ■ ■ ■

The BMW drove an hour before turning onto a dirt track. Stands of fir and pine dotted the hills around them. Wells sensed that when the sun rose the land would be pretty. After a few minutes, the sedan turned onto a paved driveway that ran between twin lanes of spruce trees. What looked like a model of the Arc de Triomphe straddled the road ahead.

The BMW passed beneath the arch, crested a low rise. Buvchenko's mansion lay in the dale below, tall and wide. Imposing. A Russian armored personnel carrier sat out front, its 100-millimeter main gun pointed at the road. The BMW drove past the mansion and finally parked beside a windowless concrete building. It was either a badly designed garage or a firing range. Wells figured on the latter.

Mikhail Buvchenko waited outside, a pistol strapped to each hip. He was a giant, well over six feet tall. He had hugely defined muscles that came from hours lifting weights every day, augmented with pharmaceutical help. He reminded Wells of a Slavic version of the movie star The Rock.

Despite the midwinter chill, Buvchenko

wore only sweatpants and a black T-shirt that stretched tightly over his deltoids and biceps. His head was shaved and the skin of his face unnaturally smooth. His eyes flickered like he was watching a movie no one else could see. Wells detected a slight theatricality in the pose. Kowalski sold his clients Swiss urbanity to go with their AKs and rocket-propelled grenades. Buvchenko offered the opposite. *I strong like bull. Buy my guns, you will be, too.* Good for business, as long as he remembered he was only posing.

Buvchenko reached out, squeezed Wells's hand, the grip just short of bone-crushing. "John Wells."

"Mr. Buvchenko. Pleasure to meet you."

Buvchenko smirked. *We'll see about that.*

"You have your own range."

"Ranges. Indoor and outdoor. Please, come with me." He led Wells around the side of the building. "So Pierre Kowalski sent you to me. Very nice of him." Buvchenko's accent was almost absurdly thick. *Verrri nus ahv heeem.* Again, Wells sensed that the Russian was exaggerating for his own amusement.

"He's a good guy, Pierre."

"You weren't always so friendly." Telling Wells he knew their history.

"I'm more of a people person now."

Behind the building's back wall was the outdoor firing area, a concrete patio lined with sandbags and fronting an open field. An earthen berm a couple of hundred meters away marked the end of the range, which was lit by a bank of halogens.

Along the left and right edges of the field, signs marked the distance every ten meters. Wells didn't get them. Then he saw the buckets of golf balls. Buvchenko had built himself a combined firing and golf range. Cute. A dozen men stood around, smirking and smoking.

The range had several firing positions, all empty besides one in the center, where a Russian 12.7-millimeter Kord heavy machine gun had been set up. The Kord was comparable to an American .50-caliber, a mean, lethal-looking weapon, belt-fed, with a long black barrel. Wells didn't know why Buvchenko had brought him here. But the presence of the Kord and the audience suggested he wouldn't like the answer.

"Ever fired a Kord, John?"

"Only an NSV." An older version.

"The Kord is far superior. You're about to have a treat." Buvchenko whistled. A few seconds later, a horse trotted around the corner. The rider slowed him, walked him over to Buvchenko and Wells. A gelding, its eyes rheumy and its roan coat flecked with gray.

"As it happens, both the horse and the rider are named Peter." Buvchenko tapped the horse on its flank. It took a half step back, tilted its head, regarded him warily. Buvchenko grunted a command in Russian, and Peter the rider led Peter the gelding over the sandbags. Wells saw now that a stake with a metal ring attached had been planted a hundred meters away, in line with the Kord's firing position.

He and Buvchenko watched in silence as the two Peters reached the stake. The rider hopped off, loosely tied the horse to the ring. He scattered a half-dozen carrots on the ground, gave Buvchenko a lazy salute. Buvckheno yelled, "Go," in English, and the rider walked off range. Wells expected the horse to be nervous, but the carrots had distracted it. It nosed at them, then picked one up and crunched away.

"There are two ways to do this," Buvchenko said. "If you're more interested in the Kord's performance, you just open up on old Peter. On the other hand, if you feel like a challenge you can fire a couple in the air. I promise you he'll take off. And that knot won't hold him."

"No."

"Da."

Wells shook his head.

"Mr. Wells, am I to understand that you're too good to shoot a horse?" Buvchenko drew the pistol on his right hip, held it loose at his side. "He's eighteen, you know, he's had a long life. Now he's just taking up space. A gelding. Can't even breed."

He stared at Wells like his eyes could bore through his skull. Wells stared right back.

"Put a bullet in his brain, it's more humane than a slaughterhouse. Look at him, eating carrots. He won't even know."

"Those steroids, they turn your balls into jelly beans, don't they, Mikhail? All the Viagra in the world and you can't get it up."

Buvchenko raised his pistol. "I count to ten. Then either the horse dies, or you do. One. Two —"

"Let me help. Ten."

Buvchenko looked genuinely surprised.

"Wahid, ithnan, thalaatha, arba'a, hamsa, sitta, sab'a, thamania, tiss'a, 'ashra." One to ten in Arabic. Wells raised his fingers as he counted, pronouncing as carefully as a kindergarten teacher.

Buvchenko stepped toward Wells, barked something in Russian. Then spat a gob at Wells's feet. "I tell you, *Idi na khuy.* Means, go to the dick. Eff yourself."

"See, we both learned something new to-day."

"You aren't going to shoot that horse."

"You had any brains, you wouldn't let me near that Kord."

Buvchenko smirked. "It's locked down."

He turned toward the horse, raised the pistol over his head, fired twice. The horse whinnied wildly and reared in panic. It dragged the stake out of the ground and turned and galloped back toward them. Buvchenko raised both pistols and fired a half-dozen times, pumping his arms forward and back, a parody of an old-school gun-slinger, used rounds littering the ground around him.

Flesh and bone exploded off the horse's chest. It *screamed,* the only word for the sound, not a whinny but an oddly human cry of pain, and turned and galloped paral-lel to the firing line. Buvchenko kept shoot-ing, and three geysers of blood erupted from the horse's flank. It reared up. Then its back legs sagged and it fell forward, not all at once but slowly as its strength ebbed. Its scream became a low moan as it looked at the men on the firing line. Its tongue flopped out, and it slumped over, blood coursing over its belly and pooling on the frozen ground, wisps of steam rising from the black puddles.

"You showed him," Wells said.

"To the dick with him. Like all of us," Buvchenko said. He shouted in Russian, and one of his men walked onto the range and shot the horse in the head.

Buvchenko tucked away his pistols and clapped a massive hand on Wells's shoulder. "He would have had a much easier time if you'd taken care of it." And without waiting for an answer, "Come. Let's have dinner."

Dinner was traditional Russian, plates of blinis with sides of caviar and sour cream and smoked sturgeon. The boiled meat dumplings called *pelmeni* followed, with butter, horseradish, and vinegar. Then grilled salmon and *shashlik,* marinated lamb skewers. Buvchenko ate with relish and without irony and hardly spoke as the courses came and went. Wells pushed the horse out of his mind and forced himself to eat. The food was delicious and beautifully presented, served on robin's-egg-blue china, with crystal glasses, sterling silver knives and forks, and a lace tablecloth. Buvchenko might be a gangster in every other way, but he ate like a nineteenth-century Russian noble.

A bottle of Stolichnaya vodka sat on ice in a silver champagne bowl at Buvchenko's elbow. As the meal started, Buvchenko poured shots for them both, but he didn't push when Wells declined. "More for me," he said. Maybe he figured he had made his point on the firing range. *My horse, my men, my mansion, my city, my country. Be glad I let you live.*

After ninety high-calorie minutes, the waiters swept away the last of the dishes. Buvchenko burped mightily. "What do you think?"

Wells wasn't surprised that the vodka had lessened rather than thickened his host's accent. "Excellent."

"My chef comes from the Four Seasons in St. Petersburg. Down here there isn't much. Even the best whores wind up in Moscow. I wanted decent food, anyway." Buvchenko poured two fresh shots, offered one to Wells. Wells shook his head.

"Pierre says you're Muslim."

"Yes."

"I don't understand this, but also I don't care." Buvchenko downed both glasses. A faint flush rose in his cheeks. Spit moistened his lips. He'd had at least a dozen shots over dinner. "So you came all this way to see me, you showed stupidity and courage both with the horse, we've eaten, you are a guest under my roof, you know who I am."

"Yes."

"You know my business. So I speak frankly to you. I supply weapons and soldiers. I don't care who you are, what you want them for, that's your business. If you can pay, I give them over. I have helicopters, BMPs, up to two thousand infantry, the planes to take them anywhere in Africa or Asia. Trained men who obey commands, don't make a mess with civilians. Unless that's what you want. Mines, SAMs, antitank. Jets and tanks are harder. I may be able to arrange those, but I can't guarantee. My prices are high, but they're fair. When Putin decided to go into Ukraine, I don't mind telling you I supplied that first wave of men."

"You're good with Moscow."

"If not, I would be in exile in London or in jail in Siberia. One doesn't anger the tsar. And you? Who pays you?"

"Once, I worked for the agency. Now I freelance." The answer was true as far as it went.

Buvchenko poured himself another shot. "Pierre didn't tell me what you wanted. So, please, ask whatever questions you like. Be direct, I tell you, before I'm too drunk to answer."

The offer seemed too good to be true, but Wells didn't plan to argue.

"Suppose I wanted to buy plutonium or HEU."

"A nuclear bomb."

"Not a bomb's worth. Just a kilogram or two."

"And who do you represent? Who wants this?"

"Let's say it doesn't matter. But I have the money."

"How much?"

"As much as I need."

"I don't understand. This is a real offer, or a test?"

"Real."

"And you have the money, you say?"

"I can get it."

Buvchenko shook his head. "Still, I don't think it's possible."

"What about the depots in Chelyabinsk?" Where the Russians stored their nuclear weapons. A few years ago, a terrorist had stolen two weapons out of Chelyabinsk and barely missed blowing up Washington. The story remained a highly classified secret in both the United States and Russia; Wells knew only because he'd helped find the nukes.

"No. Security there is tight now. Even I don't have those connections, and if anyone did, it would be me."

"There's nothing loose floating around? Someone must know. In Moscow, wherever. Even for a clue, I can pay."

"I would gladly take your money if I had something to tell you. But why do you ask?"

Wells decided to give Buvchenko a two-sentence version of the story. "Someone's trying to trick the United States into invading Iran. The HEU in Istanbul isn't Iranian."

"You mean the American president is lying?" Buvchenko wagged his finger. "Mr. Wells, I am ashamed you say such a thing as this." His accent thickened. *Meester Wheelles.* A natural ham. He should have played dinner theater.

"Not lying. Fooled."

"And now set this deadline for war. A red line like Syria, but this time I think he has no choice but to go forward."

"Yes."

"And who do you think has done this? Not the FSB."

Wells hesitated. But maybe Duberman's name would shake loose a connection in his host's vodka-soaked mind. "An American billionaire named Aaron Duberman. He owns casinos."

"Duberman?" Buvchenko rolled the name out: *Dooobermannn.* "A Jew, yes? And you say we Russians are anti-Semites."

"I don't care if he's the Dalai Lama."

"Yet you are Muslim. And here claiming this Jew tries to make the United States go to war."

Wells shook his head. He was guilty of a thousand sins, but prejudice wasn't one.

"All right, that is between you and your Allah. So what is your evidence for this?"

"Doesn't matter."

Buvchenko leaned across the table to Wells. "Meaning you don't have any?"

"Some."

"But not enough."

"Not yet." Somehow the Russian, despite all the vodka, had turned the questions back on Wells. "What about North Korea?"

"I don't think so. I won't do business with them. They can't be trusted."

Quite a statement coming from a man who'd shot a horse for predinner entertainment. Once again Wells had traveled to another country, another continent, and found nothing but a brick wall. Worst of all, he was hardly even surprised. He was now expecting to fail. A terrible attitude in the middle of a mission.

At least tonight nobody had died in a car bomb.

"Excuse me a minute, Mr. Wells." Buvchenko pushed himself up from the table, moving with the exaggerated care of a man who wanted to seem more sober than he was. "I must —" He was gone, leaving Wells to guess at what he had to do.

He returned a few minutes later, holding a bottle of Baltika, Russian beer. "Mr. Wells. I'm sorry to disappoint you after your long drive. I hope you'll stay over tonight, catch up on your sleep. I'd be offended if you didn't allow me to show you hospitality."

"I appreciate the offer, but —"

"In fact, I insist." Buvchenko's smile left no doubt what he meant. Wells had no idea why the Russian wanted to keep him overnight. Buvchenko's moods were impossible to read. But arguing would be pointless. Even if he could convince Buvchenko to let him out tonight, the Volgograd airport would be closed for the night by the time he got back to the city. Plus Wells wasn't even sure where to go next. Buvchenko was his last real lead. All he'd miss was the free breakfast at the hotel, and he'd count himself lucky.

"I have your word I'll leave in the morning?"

"Of course."

"All right. As long as I don't have to sleep with you."

As an answer Buvchenko poured himself another shot.

Wells's bedroom was vaguely anachronistic in the style of a Russian country manor, with oversize oak dressers and a heavy down comforter splayed across a narrow twin bed. Wells didn't try to pray in this place, but instead kicked off his shoes and lay down. The windows had been left narrowly open, allowing the winter chill to sneak in, but the comforter warmed Wells instantly. He was asleep almost as soon as he closed his eyes.

A light knock on the door woke him.

"Mr. Wells. I am to take you back to Volgograd." Eight a.m., according to the old-fashioned winding clock beside the bed. Wells couldn't remember the last time he'd slept through the night. Cold air and a warm blanket. Maybe the Russians had a few customs worth importing. Wells pushed himself up.

Buvchenko seemed gone, and Wells didn't look too hard for him. Ninety minutes later, the BMW dropped him at the hotel. He nodded at the receptionist, walked up the empty stairs, along the third-floor corridor. 306.

He reached for his keycard. But the door was already open, propped with a pen.

He reached for the pistol he wasn't carrying, cursed silently, pushed the door open.

"Come in." A woman. He knew her voice but couldn't place it.

Wells stepped inside, his shoulder against the door. 306 followed a setup familiar to anyone who'd ever stayed in a hotel. The front door opened into a short corridor that ran past the bathroom and into the main living space, which had a bed against one wall, a dresser and television on the other. Wells couldn't pass the bathroom without exposing himself to anyone inside. On the other hand, if they'd wanted to shoot him, they wouldn't have left the front door open.

"Don't worry. I won't hurt you." A faintly mocking tone, and then he knew. A dark street in a run-down slum in Istanbul. Headlights blinding him. *This will sting.*

She sat casually on the bed, legs crossed. Medium brown hair, brown eyes. A runner's body, tight and athletic, underneath a dark blue suit-and-pants set and sneakers. No weapon that he could see. She could have passed for a lawyer on the way to work. Pretty enough.

"John." She waved casually. "I'm Salome. We've met before, though you may not recognize me. I'm sorry to say you were in some distress at the time." Her words ironic in their formality.

"No worries," Wells said. "I remember."

PART TWO

11
SIX DAYS . . .

Nine a.m. in Volgograd meant 1 a.m. on the
East Coast. Just as Wells greeted Salome,
Vinny Duto arrived to meet his own *femme
fatale.* Donna Green. Duto would have
preferred POTUS, but the big man wasn't
interested. Duto couldn't even blame his
staff for the failure to set the meeting. He
had tried to arrange it himself the morning
after he returned from Tel Aviv, calling Len
Gilman, the President's scheduler. Duto
knew he was risking embarrassment. In
Washington, as Hollywood, making your
own calls screamed of desperation.

Gilman wasted no time shooting him
down.

"The President doesn't see senators one-
on-one," he said. "Simple fairness. He takes
a meeting with you, the other ninety-nine
will demand the same treatment. He just
doesn't have time for that."

"I'm sure the President can handle the slings and arrows of my fellow senators."

"Of course he *can,* Vinny. My job is making sure he doesn't have to. Can't you give me any idea what this is about?"

"I already told you. Iran."

"But *beyond* that. Whatever you tell me will remain in the strictest confidence."

"If I wanted you to know, I would have told you already."

"Then we seem to have reached an impasse. If something changes, I'll call you. This is your personal line, yes?"

Twisting the knife. Duto knew the President didn't like him. He had only run for Senate when he'd realized the White House was preparing to force him out as DCI. Still, he wasn't sure what he'd done to deserve this meat-locker treatment. He'd never feuded openly with the President, never embarrassed the White House.

For the first time in his life, he understood the impulse to leak. He'd always hated leakers. *Don't like it? Then quit. But you signed an oath of secrecy and you'd best keep it.* Now he saw the other side of the equation. *You won't listen, boss? Maybe the world will.*

The next night, his phone lit up. A blocked number.

"Vinny?"

Duto knew that flat female voice. "Donna."

He didn't like Green any better than Gilman. She had spent her whole life inside the Beltway, second-guessing the guys in the field. Duto knew that guys like Wells leveled the same charge against him. They forgot he had been one of them back in the day. He'd given blood for the job, and not metaphorically.

"Len says you have something to tell us. I'm listening."

Either Green or the President himself had decided Duto was too important to be ignored entirely.

"No phones for this."

Green sighed, an *I'm-too-busy-for-this-nonsense* sound. Duto was glad they weren't face-to-face. Whatever his sins, he'd never hit a woman. He wanted to go to the grave that way. "Next you're going to tell me this has to be today?"

"If possible."

"Can you come over?"

"It's in your interest not to have it logged." The Secret Service recorded all visitors to the White House for both security and historical purposes. The logs were sacrosanct. Any effort to remove an entry would only call attention to it.

"I'll call you later, location, time."

"Great." Duto tried to hang up, but Green beat him to it.

Now his two-car detail turned into a Home Depot parking lot just off the Little River Turnpike. Acres of empty blacktop at this hour. Convenient for a meet, if not exactly sexy.

"She's not here," his chief bodyguard said.

"Any other blinding glimpses of the obvious?" Duto knew his reputation. Short-tempered, verging on nasty. He didn't mind. Better feared than loved. He rode in an armored Tahoe, with two guards up front. Two others in the chase car, a Crown Vic. Most senators didn't rate that much protection, but Duto's years as DCI had put him high on al-Qaeda's wish list.

They parked in the center of the lot, which was surprisingly clean. No stray carts or trash. The beige husk of the store filled the west end of the lot. Duto reached for his phone, a reflex. Waiting meant downtime. He hated downtime. Much as he had disliked running for senator, putting his fate in the hands of millions of people who had no idea how Washington actually worked, he enjoyed the fact that the campaign never ended. His staff could always schedule another rally, radio interview, debate prep session, briefing book. By the end he had memorized the minutiae of the federal budget, the projects it funded in Pennsylvania, the most important issues in every town with more than five thousand people. He'd turned his opponent into a likable simpleton.

But at this hour Duto had no one to call. Wells was in Volgograd, no doubt arm-wrestling a bear for his life. Shafer was asleep. In the morning, Shafer would fly to Utah to convince Wells's son Evan not to ditch his FBI minders. The kid was an ungrateful brat. Duto had pulled big favors to get him in that safe house. If Evan was too dumb to realize he needed the protection, so be it. Like his father, he was too bullheaded to take good advice.

The difference was that Wells knew how to survive.

It was morning in Jerusalem. Duto was tempted to call Rudi. Four days since their meeting, and the Israeli hadn't called. Maybe he had decided that he could serve his country best by keeping his mouth shut. Maybe he was too sick to help. Maybe he had asked and found nothing. Whatever the answer, Duto had made his best case back at Ben Gurion Airport. Pushing would be counterproductive. Duto shoved his phone away and waited.

Downtime.

Green's motorcade showed up fifteen minutes later. Duto was surprised to see it was only three SUVs — two black Suburbans, one blue Jeep Grand Cherokee with the distinctive long antenna of a coms vehicle. The detail parked nose-to-tail about twenty feet from his Tahoe. Two men stepped out of each Suburban, surveyed the empty asphalt, fanned out toward the corners of the lot, muttering to each other on their shoulder-mounted TAC radios.

Only then did the real convoy arrive. Two more Suburbans, two Explorers, and another Cherokee for coms. Eight trucks in all, at least twenty guards. Like Green was going to Baghdad, not suburban Virginia. Though Duto could hardly complain. He had traveled in similar style as DCI.

The wind came straight from the Appalachians, chilling Duto through his overcoat. Green was dressed for the weather, in wool-lined boots and a green down jacket that plumped around her like she'd shoplifted it from a Salvation Army. Whatever the President saw in her, it wasn't her fashion sense.

Duto extended a hand. "Donna."

"Vinny. I'd say it's good to see you, but that would be a lie. And I'm planning to keep the lies to a minimum tonight."

"The pleasure's mine, then. Mind if we walk?"

"I'd prefer if you stayed close," the guard nearest Green said.

"I think we'll be okay," Duto said.

"I'd prefer if you stayed close." Like Duto hadn't spoken at all.

"I trust you to protect us from fifty feet, Kyle," Green said.

The guard nodded. His master's voice. They strolled side by side toward the Home Depot.

"I'm here, Senator. So talk." She spoke straight ahead, not looking at him.

"Whatever you have planned for Iran, it needs to wait."

"Because?"

"The HEU wasn't Iranian. Someone's setting you up."

"That possibility has been considered and rejected."

"You saw what you wanted to see."

She stopped. Looked at him. "Okay, Vinny. Say it's not Iranian. Whose, then?"

"I don't know who enriched it. But I can

tell you a private team working for Aaron Duberman put it there."

Every time Duto made the accusation, it sounded crazier. He knew he was right, yet he felt like a nutty conspiracy theorist. Green seemed to sense his embarrassment. She looked at him, let him see her smirking.

"So I'm clear. We're talking about the guy who spent two hundred million dollars to elect my boss."

Duto nodded.

"Are you saying that we're conspiring with him to produce false evidence to invade Iran? Because that sounds like treason. And I'll need to double-check the Constitution I keep in my office, but I do believe treason is punishable by death."

"I'm not saying you knew."

"What exactly are you saying, then?"

"This is the best false-flag op I've ever seen."

"Oh, false flag. So we *didn't* know. I'm so relieved." Every word more sarcastic than the last. "Is this where you hand me a thumb drive that proves we have aliens at Roswell?"

Her disregard finally got to him. He grabbed her arm. Unfortunately, or maybe not, the down kept him from getting a grip. Kyle ran at them, his feet pounding the asphalt. He hadn't drawn his pistol, but his hand was inside his jacket.

"Everything okay?"

"Fine." Duto dropped her arm.

Green let the question hang for a couple long seconds before she finally nodded.

"You sure, Ms. Green?"

"Your boss and I are having a full and frank exchange of views. Run along, now."

"I wasn't asking you, Senator."

Green nodded again, and they watched Kyle retreat.

"It'll take more than that. I hope you're properly humiliated," Green said under her breath.

"I'll tell you a secret, Vinny. You probably wonder why POTUS wanted you gone so bad. It was me. I remember Fred Whitby."

The chill in Duto's bones didn't come from the wind. Whitby had been Director of National Intelligence when Duto was DCI. They'd fought to control the agency and the entire intel community. Duto won. Through Wells and Shafer, he used Whitby's involvement in the death of a detainee at a secret prison to force Whitby to resign. Wells quit the agency in protest when he realized what Duto had done. At the time, Duto hardly cared. Losing Wells was a small price to pay to control all of American intelligence.

"They called it 'The Midnight House,' right? Neatest knifing I ever saw. Your boys got rid of him, it didn't even touch you."

Duto didn't bother to ask how she knew the details. She knew because knowing was her job. At least now he saw why everyone called her the smartest person in the White House.

"You're missing the point of that story."

"Enlighten me."

"I was *right*. He was dirty."

"You were, too. Up to your neck in rendition. But *he* went down."

"And Duberman's dirty, too. If you could stop trying to destroy me for a minute, you'd see I'm helping you."

"The President's biggest donor is behind all this?"

"Yes."

"And I'm guessing it's because he hates Iran, thinks it's a threat to Israel, doesn't trust the deal we made."

"I haven't asked him, Donna, but yes. I'm sure he's said as much to you."

"Not since this started, though. Man hasn't called me once."

"Because you're doing exactly what he wants."

"So it doesn't matter what Duberman does or doesn't do at this point. He calls, he doesn't call, it's all evidence."

"Ask yourself why I would tell you this if it isn't true. Or at least if I didn't believe it."

"Because you hate the Senate already. Think you're too good for it. But you know there's no way you're ever going to be more than the junior senator from Pennsylvania unless lightning strikes. And this feels like lightning. Your friends inside Langley, and you still have a few, have told you the evidence isn't as airtight as we'd like. You know we still can't find the colonel who tipped us."

News to Duto, valuable news, not that he was about to tell Green the mistake she'd made in revealing it. "All true."

"Now you're making the same mistake as Tehran. Underestimating POTUS, thinking that he doesn't have the stones to attack. You know if I listen to you and we back down, we'll owe you the kind of favor that will give you a whole new career. State. Defense. Whatever."

"And *John Wells* is helping me with this?"

"Probably he doesn't have the full picture. Just like you did with Whitby."

"It's a good theory, Donna." Duto raised

his right hand. "Only problem is it's wrong. I'll swear on whatever you like. I'll swear on Home Depot."

She shook her head. "I want evidence. Any at all."

Duto realized he'd misplayed his hand terribly. He'd figured his time as DCI would count for something. And it had. The opposite of the way he'd hoped. He should have held off on calling the White House until he had something tangible.

Donna Green was even more cynical than he was. An impossible feat.

"I don't have anything concrete to show you."

"That's no, then."

Duto hadn't planned to go into details, but he felt the need to explain. "A former case officer named Mason was running the op, but if you ask Hebley about him, he'll say the guy died four years ago in Thailand."

"But this Mason is actually alive."

"No. He's dead." Duto remembered now why he hadn't planned to go into details. "Last week. Wells killed him."

"Where's the body?"

Duto opened his mouth, but no words came out. Alarm flashed in Green's eyes. Like she couldn't decide if he was playing her or simply losing his mind.

"Gone. I know it sounds far-fetched. But it's not like you have a ton of evidence tying the uranium to Iran either."

"If it's not Iranian, where'd Duberman get it?"

"We're looking."

"You must at least have a working theory."

"We have several."

Duto realized that as DCI, he would have fired any deputy who made a presentation this bad.

Green turned back to the convoy, giving him no choice but to follow. A signal that the conversation was over. "Vinny. Let me tell you something you won't want to hear. If you don't mind." Her tone had a new breeziness that didn't comfort Duto. She sounded like a cop trying to talk down a jumper. "The Indians found the guys who shot down United 49. We took 'em six hours ago. Predawn in Mumbai. A Delta team."

"Delhi signed off on the Deltas?"

"We didn't give them a choice. POTUS wanted to be sure we brought them in alive. And the Indians are embarrassed. We warned them about Chhatrapati. Years ago."

"I know." Duto had been DCI at the time. The Federal Aviation Administration had even considered banning American carriers from flying to Mumbai. But the Indian government protested and promised to improve security, and the FAA backed down. "So who has the shooters now?"

"They're in the bath." Meaning the Navy was holding them offshore. "They're Lebanese. And we're a hundred percent sure they're Hezbollah."

"They're talking?"

"They're *bragging.*"

For the first time, Duto wondered if he and Wells and Shafer had made a mistake. Maybe they couldn't connect Mason to Duberman because the connection didn't exist. But no. The thread they'd followed was real.

"If Tehran thinks we're going to invade on false evidence, they'd have every reason to shoot down our planes. Doesn't it strike you as odd that they haven't even hinted at making a deal since we hit them? That they went straight to the wall?"

"Interesting theory, Senator." The chill was back in her voice. As much as saying: *I tried to make you see reason. And I failed. We're done.* "Two choices here. I go back to POTUS, tell him you've accused his largest campaign donor of treason without evidence. Get it in the record. When we hit Iran, find all that HEU you say doesn't exist, that file magically finds air."

"WikiLeaks?"

"Call me old-fashioned, but I just love the idea of it on the front page of the *Times*. Terrible way for a distinguished public servant like you to end his career. Second choice, we pretend this was a bad orange-flavored dream."

The threat snapped Duto's shoulders back, puffed his chest. Fight or flight. The amazing part was that for once his conscience was clear. He'd told the truth. He'd tried to warn her.

Last time he made that mistake.

"Do what you like, Donna. But I promise I'm gonna figure out where Duberman scored that uranium." Duto raised his voice. "Then I'm going to call you and tell you. Just you and me, face-to-face. Then I'm gonna turn you around and bend you over so hard you won't sit for a month. Like I did to Whitby."

All the guards, hers and his, were listening openly, not even pretending they hadn't heard. Kyle trotted toward them.

"Get that, buddy? Do I need to repeat it?"

"*Enough,* Senator." Kyle inserted himself between Duto and Green, close enough for Duto to see what was left of the spinach Kyle had eaten for dinner. Duto hoped beyond hope that the guard would put a hand on him. He still worked the heavy bag four days a week.

Green guided Kyle aside. "No worries. We're done here."

Duto stepped back as Kyle hurried Green to her Tahoe. The rest of her guards followed. Doors slammed. Forty-five seconds later, the last of the SUVs crunched out of the parking lot and turned onto the turnpike, running lights flashing, no sirens.

Duto watched in silence, replaying snatches of the conversation, his adrenaline fading. Had he really threatened to quote-unquote *bend over* the National Security Advisor? In front of two dozen witnesses?

They better find that uranium.

12

The woman who called herself Salome wasn't alone. A man stood beside the bed. His face was faintly asymmetrical, the left side wider than the right, like he'd had an accident that surgery hadn't fully fixed. His right hand hovered over his hip. His eyes stuck to Wells's hands.

A pro.

Wells stepped toward the bed.

"Close enough," Salome said.

"All friends here."

A smile spread from Salome's lips up her cheeks to her eyes. North like a warm front. While it lasted, she was pretty. Alive. Then it was gone. She looked at him as coolly as a research scientist checking out a chimp. *Don't mind this old needle, Mr. Chips. Won't hurt a bit . . .*

In happier news, they'd left the window curtains open. So they didn't plan to kill him. Not here, anyway. A tour bus idled in the parking lot below. As Wells watched, an old couple tottered toward it, hand in hand. He thought of Anne and all the lives he'd left behind.

"Mason told me you were trouble," Salome said. Her English was measured, almost too perfect, a hint of eastern Mediterranean. She could have passed for first-generation American, the accent left over from her native-speaking parents. She wore only a wedding ring, no nail polish or makeup. All business.

Except the smile.

"You come see me in person, I guess I'm moving up the ladder." Wells figured he'd take his best shot first. "You work for Aaron Duberman."

She shook her head, not so much denying what he'd said as declaring it irrelevant.

"For money, or because you're crazy?"

She muttered in Hebrew and a pistol appeared in the guard's right hand. That fast. Too bad. At least now Wells knew what he was up against.

"Be more polite," Salome said. "Who looks out for you? A broken-down CIA man and a senator no one trusts."

"I'll worry when I see you throw carrots on the carpet to distract me."

Wells saw she didn't get the reference. So she hadn't been at Buvchenko's.

"I didn't think I'd have the pleasure of seeing you again," Wells said. "Salome? That's your name?" A biblical reference, but Wells couldn't remember the details. "Your real name?"

"As real as any."

Ask a stupid question . . . Still, Wells was content to joust for the moment.

"And you're Israeli?"

"Why do you keep bothering me about this?"

"You're asking why I'm trying to stop a war?"

"I don't want war." She winked.

Wells couldn't read her at all. She was playing with him like a cat batting a mouse. "If you're worried about bugs, I never got here last night."

"I'm not worried. You know, my friend here thinks I shouldn't talk to you at all. He wants to shoot you in the face and be done with it."

"Lucky for me you're in charge."

"It seems so."

They looked steadily at each other, the only sound the rumbling of the bus outside. Wells couldn't deny the truth: He felt *connected* to this woman. They were both endless travelers, perpetual outsiders who had spent their lives in crummy hotel rooms, giving fake names to anyone who asked. They both knew how easy lying became after you'd done it too much, how boring the simplicity of truth became.

"You came all the way to Volgograd to tell me you weren't going to shoot me in the face?"

"And see you for myself, the man who killed five of mine. But mainly I came to tell you it's over."

The fact that she felt the need to say so suggested otherwise. "Buvchenko told you I was here."

"Of course."

Had the Russian supplied the uranium, then? Wells thought not. Then he would be a prisoner at the mansion, or more likely another target on the firing range. No, Salome had asked Buvchenko to watch out for Wells, and if he appeared to find out what he knew. No matter which direction he went, she was a step ahead.

"Last night, after dinner, he called you, told you I was asking about you. You said, hold me overnight, you'd come to Russia."

"I appreciate your" — she hesitated, trying to remember the word — "perseverance, yes? But understand, you only make trouble for yourself and your family."

Family. The magic word. What she had come to say. Wells stepped toward her. The guard lifted his pistol.

"Listen," she said. "You promise Buvchenko a million dollars? I pay ten. You don't know anything. Not even my name. You think these men in Washington look after you, but if Mason hadn't been a fool, you would be dead already."

"Concrete shoes."

"A joke to prove your bravery. What I tell you, bravery doesn't matter."

"Maybe I came here knowing you'd come for me. Maybe there's a Delta squad one room over."

She smiled, but this time her eyes stayed cold. "You're not that clever. You run here and there, hoping for a clue. How does the song go? Know when to hold 'em, know when to fold 'em —"

"If you're so confident, why threaten my family?"

"Don't you see they mean nothing to me?" Her voice was level, a teacher trying to stay patient with a not-very-bright student. "A whole country is in danger if Iran gets the bomb. I mention Evan and Heather only to remind you that you have something to risk, too. Because I know your life doesn't matter to you. Only the mission."

What she was really saying was that she felt the same. That they *were* the same. But they weren't. She was a fanatic. She saw the world in abstraction. *Us. Them. White. Black.* Who would close her eyes to reality if it didn't agree with her mind's vision. Wells was the opposite. He lied to the world, yes, but alone he drank truth until it filled his belly and choked his throat.

"Everything I read says Iran doesn't even *want* the bomb anymore," Wells said. "They're giving it up. All this for nothing."

"If you believe that, I don't know how you've survived so long."

"If I could get to my gun, I'd show you." She laughed.

In the distance a siren whistled, *ooh-ooh, ooh-OOH.* Then another. Wells wanted to believe the sirens were a coincidence. He knew better.

No wonder she wasn't in a hurry.

Salome murmured something to the bodyguard. He didn't answer. She spoke again, a tone that brooked no argument, and this time he tucked his pistol away.

"You think the Iranians are nice people? You know they shot down that plane."

"If you say so."

"It's true. You should *help* us, John. These men, they're your enemy, too. Look how they made the United States bleed in Iraq. How they treat their own people."

The sirens rang louder. Wells saw two police cars swinging into the parking lot. A black SUV followed. Now more sirens in the distance, a beat that needed remixing.

Salome pushed herself off the bed. Two quick steps to the window. She tipped her nose to the glass like a cat that had spotted a particularly tasty bird.

"Your welcoming party. A Muslim convert comes to Russia to meet an arms dealer? FSB will love that. So fortunate for the motherland that Buvchenko did his duty, told them you were here. Or maybe you tell them you're American, ex-CIA? Even better. They'll hold you a month, more, before all this gets sorted. So, good. You stay here, your son is safe."

She had him. Running was impossible. He had nowhere to go. He would have to give himself up, talk the FSB into letting him call home. Duto still had Kremlin contacts. Once the Russians knew who he was, maybe they'd figure a one-way ticket to the border was the easiest way to deal with him.

Maybe.

The guard muttered.

285

"My friend asks you to step into the bathtub while we take our leave."

Wells shook his head. The guard pointed the pistol at Wells's feet.

"A Russian jail with a hole in your foot. No fun."

Wells knew she was serious. He went to the tub, his muddy shoes staining the white plastic. At least she hadn't made him turn on the water. This woman had outplayed him twice now.

"Good luck." She smiled, the real smile, the one that warmed her face. She stepped into the bathroom, raised her right hand to his face, ran her fingers along his chin. Then touched her flat palm to his chest. The warmth of her skin stunned him. "Allah will protect you, I'm sure."

The words lifted the spell. Wells didn't like the glancing reference to his religion. Or the intimacy she'd presumed. He pulled her hand from his chest. "Touch my son, I'll kill you."

"Of course you will."

Then she was gone.

The room door closed. Wells waited a few seconds before going to the window. The police didn't seem to be in any rush. They stood in the parking lot, rubbing their hands against the cold. Wells counted nine in all, plus a German shepherd, sniffing the air as one of the uniformed officers stroked its head.

The shepherd bugged Wells. He wasn't sure why, and then he was. The dog answered a question he hadn't thought to ask. Salome knew how dangerous he was. She didn't have to risk seeing him in this little room. She could have met him at Buvchenko's mansion, where he could be controlled more easily. Why here?

Cops brought dogs to find explosives.

Or drugs.

Wells pulled open the drawers of the cheap wooden dresser. Empty, empty, empty. The nightstand, too. He flattened his cheek to the carpet, peered beneath the bed. There. A bundle the size of a brick, wedged against the bed's center support. He snaked his arm under, tugged it out. It was brown, plastic-wrapped. Heroin. A kilo or more.

No wonder Salome hadn't bothered to shoot him. Wells didn't work for the agency. He couldn't claim diplomatic immunity. He'd spend the rest of his life in a Russian prison. Another name for hell on earth.

Wells wished they'd left him something less dangerous. Like a grenade.

Outside, another SUV rolled up. Two

plainclothes officers drifted toward the front entrance. Wells grabbed his backpack, checked the peephole to be sure that Salome wasn't still in the hall, stepped out. The hotel was a simple rectangle with a single internal north–south hallway. The guest elevators occupied the north end, three doors from Wells's room. Wells ran the other way, south.

The hallway ended at a gray-painted door with a push bar. A red sign warned "Emergency Exit! ALARM!" in Russian and English. Wells didn't think so. The hotel wouldn't want sirens screeching every time a guest took the fire stairs. Anyway, he had no choice. Just ditching the brick down a trash chute wouldn't be good enough. The cops would scrub the hotel when they didn't find the heroin in his room. He had to make it disappear permanently.

Wells pushed the bar. No alarm. He scrambled up the stairs two at a time, quads burning, heart pounding. Past the fifth floor, the sixth. To the fire door to the roof. Atop the stairs, he found a fire door wedged open with a VCR tape. Old-school.

Outside, a mess of crumpled cigarette butts and empty vodka bottles. Wells ran for the rusty metal flues that rose side by side from the center of the roof, pumping inky black smoke into the gray sky. The smoke-stacks extended about six feet off the roof and had old-style mushroom caps mounted loosely atop the flues to keep rain and snow from pouring inside.

Wells carried a butterfly knife in his backpack. As he reached the flues he pulled it out, flipped it open. He had never been quite so conscious of time passing, of the seconds escaping with every motion. How long before the cops downstairs moved? Two minutes? Three? How much time had he used already?

The smoke was greasy and lukewarm after its trip up the flue. Wells reached under the cap, sliced at the bag. A river of brown poison poured down the steel pipe into the furnace below. Where it belonged. When the bag was empty, Wells tossed it down the chute, dropped in the knife, too. He ran for the door, leapt down the stairs. His hands were black now, slick with oil sludge. He didn't want to leave a trail. He balled them up, didn't touch the railing. He took the stairs in twos and threes, half running, half falling.

At the third floor, he stopped. If the cops had already reached the hallway, he would have no choice but to go downstairs and surrender in the parking lot. But the corridor was quiet. He ran for his room. The electronic lock on its door beeped green. No doubt the cops had made the clerk downstairs disable it. They were on their way up. He'd beaten them by seconds.

In his bathroom, Wells washed his hands to clean off the grease and whatever heroin residue might be stuck on them. As he finished, he heard footsteps, Russian voices mumbling. The door creaked open. Something skittered across the carpet. Wells saw it in the bathroom doorway. A green sphere. A grenade, and then another.

Wells almost laughed. He'd asked for a grenade. The Russians had seen fit to give him two. He spun, went to his knees, clapped his hands over his ears, and squeezed his eyes closed. If the grenade was a standard frag, he was dead, but if it was a flash-bang, a concussion —

The explosion seemed to come from *inside* his head. He was nowhere, and then in the hills north of Missoula, caught in a massive thunderstorm. He ran for cover as the skies exploded again —

No. Not Montana. Russia. Wells opened his eyes, found himself back in a shadowy version of the bathroom. Spiderwebs shrouded his eyes. A whistling scream filled his ears. He reached for the toilet and hung his mouth open, trying to vomit, failing. Only a thin trickle of spittle hung from his mouth. He knew the police had to have followed the grenades into the room, but the idea of turning his head to see them was impossible. He stared at the stained white bowl until men pulled him up, jerked his arms behind his back, cuffed them tight.

They shoved him in the chair in the corner. With his hearing gone, he watched the search play out like a silent movie, a comedy starring one smart dog and a bunch of dumb cops. The shepherd walked through the room, didn't alert. His handler took him out, brought him back in, tried again. When he still didn't alert, the handler got into a heated argument with the guy who seemed to be in charge, a tall thin man who wore a suit and thick black plastic glasses that would have passed for hip in Brooklyn. Wells didn't need to hear them to know what they were saying:

It's here. Why can't your idiot dog find it?

Because it's not here!

It's here.

They tried to talk to Wells, but he pointed at his ears and they seemed to believe him. They patted him down, like the dog wouldn't have sniffed the stuff on him. Then they tore up the room. Pulled open the drawers, flipped over the bed, cut his bag open, and found his second passport. The discovery made them happy, but not for long.

After a half hour, two cops pulled Wells up, hustled him into the empty room across the hall, threw him on the bed. They were big men, with pale skin and dull blue eyes. They looked at him like they were waiting for an order to work him over. Wells took limited comfort in the fact that it hadn't come. The police weren't one hundred percent sure about him.

The man with the glasses walked in. Up close his suit was cheap and his shoes scuffed. He looked like a Depression-era traveling salesman. No way was he FSB. Wells's fears had been right. Salome and Buvchenko must have used a local trafficker to tip the police — *American drug trafficker in 306, bring a dog, all the proof you need is in his room.* They found the perfect way to put Wells in a hole without having to call in chits in Moscow.

He tapped his ear. "You can hear now."

"Yes." Barely. Static still filled Wells's ears. The cop sounded like an FM station disappearing behind a hill.

"Which one?" The Russian held up his passports.

Wells pointed at the one with his real name.

"John Wells. You smuggle drugs?"

"I don't know who told you that, but he's wrong."

"You smuggle drugs." Not a question this time. "Heroin."

"No."

"You know the penalty we have in Russia for drug smuggling?"

"I came here to meet Mikhail Buvchenko. You know who I mean?"

"Of course I know him. He lives in the country. Nothing to do with this."

"I went to his mansion last night to talk to him. Not about drugs. I said something he didn't like. I guess today he got mad, called you."

"He didn't call me." The guy flipped through Wells's second passport, the one in the name of Roger Bishop. "This is yours also."

"Yes."

Wells wondered if the cop would ask why he had two passports, but he was stuck on the drug angle. "Last month you go to Guatemala. Panama. Thailand. Turkey."

"Looking for someone."

"For cocaine. Heroin. Now you come here, spread your poison."

"Sir. May I ask you your name?"

The man pulled his wallet, flipped it open to show his police identification. "Boris Nemkov."

Despite the hole he was in, Wells couldn't help but remember a line from the second season of *The Wire: Why always Boris?*

"You're a detective."

"I am head of narcotics police for Volgograd oblast."

A drug cop. An honest one, too, if Wells could trust the cheap suit.

"Don't you think it's odd I have two working U.S. passports?"

"Plenty of smugglers have extra passports."

"The dog in my room, it found nothing."

"So far."

"There's nothing to find."

"Maybe you see us coming, you hide it. In the cart of the maids. The trash. I promise, we find it. Then —" Nemkov sliced his hand across his neck and walked out of the room.

Five minutes later, he was back. Scowling. "The longer it takes, the madder I become."

"I swear on my son's life. No drugs."

"All this tells me is that your son means nothing to you."

Wells felt his temper rise. "I landed in Volgograd yesterday, I came to this hotel, Buvchenko's men picked me up. I stayed overnight, they dropped me back here. Then you came. Where would I have found these drugs?"

"Don't talk to me about Buvchenko." Boris went to the door. He pulled it open, stopped, looked at Wells. "The next time I come back, I have it. Then we take you in. But first I give my men ten minutes alone with you, punishment for wasting my time." Boris murmured in Russian. The cops laughed. "Tell me now."

"Nothing to tell."

Boris shook his head with what seemed to be genuine disappointment and walked out.

Wells thought of Salome, how very wrong he had been about her. Had he tried to convince himself she saw him as anything but an obstacle to her plans? Was he so lonely? So desperate for connection? Maybe she respected him vaguely for his courage, the way the Germans and Russians who had once fought here had respected each other. But even so, they had killed each other without pity or remorse.

An hour passed. Another lost hour, another hour closer to war.

Finally, the door swung open. Nemkov stalked in, tugged a cheap wheeled suitcase, hard-sided gray plastic. Wells stared at it, wondering if it was filled with heroin. He didn't know if Nemkov was crazy enough to plant evidence on an American he'd never met. Maybe. Any Russian policeman who didn't take bribes had to be crazy.

"That's not mine."

"It is."

Wells shook his head. Nemkov dropped the suitcase at Wells's feet. He stood over Wells, tugged at Wells's left ear like an angry nineteenth-century schoolmaster.

"We found it."

Wells tried to shake his head, but Nemkov held him fast. Wells couldn't help feeling the ear-tugging was childish for both sides. Like the detective had decided he was unworthy of a proper beating.

Nemkov said something in Russian. One of the cops went to his knees. Snapped open the clasps and opened the suitcase.

Revealing an empty compartment. Wells looked down at the molded plastic, wondering what he could be missing.

"Where is it?"

It's nowhere and everywhere. It went to the dick. H. E. Roin, born Helmand Province, Afghanistan, died Volgograd, Russia. Poppies to ashes and dust to dust. Wells's concussion talking. "Where is what?"

Nemkov pulled harder, twisting Wells sideways. Wells feared the detective might take his ear off. "This whole hotel. My men, they want me to make the evidence. You understand what I mean?"

"Plant it."

"Prison for you forever. But I don't do that."

Nemkov stepped away from Wells, reached behind his back, for a 9-millimeter. First Buvchenko, then Salome's guard, now this cop. For the third time in eighteen hours, Wells stared at a pistol's unblinking eye. *Maybe it's time to think about your life choices, son.* But Nemkov had to be bluffing. A man who wouldn't plant evidence wouldn't shoot a handcuffed prisoner.

Unless his fury ran away with him.

Nemkov stepped around the bed, knelt behind Wells. Wells felt the pistol kiss his neck, the tip of the barrel oddly warm.

"Last time. Where is it?"

This interrogation had gone as far it could. Nemkov would pull the trigger. Or he wouldn't. For the first time in all his years, Wells understood the words *death wish.* He was well and truly tired of being so close, of feeling the Reaper creep past, smirking and winking at him. Tired, too, of all the killing he'd done over the years to survive. *Do it, then. Let me rest.*

But as quickly as the words came to him, he pushed them away, forced the shameful weakness from his mind. And of course Nemkov didn't kill him. He grabbed Wells's cuffed arms and pulled him off the bed.

"This suitcase, it's yours. I give it to you to replace the bag they cut. You see it's empty, no trick. I give you back your money." Nemkov held up the passports. "Even these."

"Thank you."

"Now it's time for you to go. In one hour, there's a plane to Domodedovo." The largest of the three airports that served Moscow. "What you do after that is up to you, but I advise you, leave Russia as soon as possible."

An excellent idea.

Nemkov drove Wells to the airport himself, in silence. As they stopped at the terminal, Wells tried to open his door, found it locked. Nemkov reached over, squeezed his wrist.

"Tell me the truth, why you were here?"

"I swear it wasn't drugs."

"But the *truth.*" Nemkov shook his head.

Somewhere in his concussion-scrambled mind, Wells wondered if Nemkov wanted to help. And why not ask? "Detective —"

"Colonel."

"Colonel. I'm sorry. The hotel has surveillance cameras, yes?"

"Of course."

"If your men can find a shot of a man and a woman leaving together a few minutes before you arrived —"

"A few?"

"Five or less. Send me that picture, I promise I'll tell you the whole story when it's over. Whatever happens."

"You *promise*?"

"And what I did with the drugs they tried to plant on me. You know, the ones you and your dog and the whole 23rd Precinct couldn't find." The concussion talking for sure. For a moment, Wells feared he had said too much, that Nemkov would drive him back to the hotel and start the beating anew. Nemkov seemed to be trying to decide, too. But finally he nodded.

"And if I find them, what? You want me to arrest them? Use the police for your work?"

"They're probably already gone from Russia. I just want you to email me the picture." Wells gave one of his new email addresses. Having an image of her to show other people might make the trip worthwhile.

"If I decide to help you, it's not for pay, you understand. It's for —" Nemkov opened his door and spat onto the pavement.

As soon as the cop had pulled away, Wells emptied his new suitcase and ran his hands over the plastic, feeling for compartments where Nemkov might have hidden drugs or weapons. But he didn't expect to find anything, and he didn't. The suitcase was what it seemed, a cheap Samsonite knock-off, its walls too thin for any secret panels.

After security, he found an Internet kiosk, booked himself a business-class seat on a 5:40 p.m. Lufthansa flight, Domodedovo to Frankfurt. Then he emailed Shafer and Duto: *B no help. LH 1447. Talk from Germany.* He needed Shafer to know where to look for him in case he vanished again. Salome would hear soon enough that Wells had beaten her trap. When she did, she would have Buvchenko call his friends at the FSB. How fast the FSB sounded an alarm for Wells would depend on the story Buvchenko told. But Wells would be at risk until the moment that Lufthansa plane left Russian airspace.

The Transaero flight to Moscow was mostly empty. He settled back in his seat, closed his eyes, imagined how he would relax when this mission was done. Hiking the Grand Canyon. Buying a big new motorcycle and ramrodding it across the Montana plains at a buck-ten. Seeing Evan suit up for the Aztecs, a pleasure he'd never had.

Daydreaming had its dangers. In Afghanistan, Wells had seen that men who relied too much on fantasy for comfort rarely lasted long. But after the madness of the last day, he needed a few minutes of relief. Better yet, a good night's sleep. When he landed in Frankfurt, he would take a cab to the most efficient, boring hotel in the city. He would pull the shades and close his eyes. And he would wake ready for war.

As the Transaero 737 touched down on the Domodedovo tarmac, a concussive fog crept back into his brain. Wells blamed the change in air pressure. Black spots flitted across his eyes as he trudged through the massive steel-and-glass terminal that connected Domodedovo's domestic and international wings. A suicide bomber in the international arrivals hall had killed thirty-four people here in 2011. Now explosives-sniffing dogs and teams of commandos in spiffy blue-and-black camouflage paced the check-in counters.

301

At this hour, the airport was heavy on business travelers, well-dressed Europeans who looked relieved to be leaving. A high school ski team waited to check in for an Alitalia flight to Milan, the children of Moscow's elite, girls wearing diamond bracelets flirting with boys in Prada jackets. Wells watched the world through Saran wrap. His muzzy head accounted for only part of the disconnect. He couldn't help remembering the way Salome had touched him. Then walked away to leave him to his fate. He didn't know what she'd been trying to tell him, or why that moment seemed so much more real than this one.

He forced himself to move, find the Lufthansa counters. No surprise, they were quieter and more organized than the rest of the terminal. He printed out his boarding pass and joined the line for border control. Fifteen minutes later, an unsmiling woman waved him forward to her kiosk, where she took his passport with the practiced boredom displayed by immigration agents everywhere.

She flipped through it. "Mr. Wells."

"That's me." He'd had to use his real passport for this trip, since Buvchenko arranged the visa.

"This is not a conversation, yes? If I have

302

a question, I ask." *Stupid Americans always think they need to talk.*

"Right. I mean, was that a question? Did I need to answer?" Wells laying it on too thick now. She put a finger to her lips, ran the passport through her scanner.

The moment of truth. If Buvchenko had reached the FSB, she'd ask him to wait a moment, then pull him out of line. *A few questions in our office, nothing to worry about —*

"You've traveled a lot lately, yes?"

"Yes, ma'am. Work."

"And for this trip you stayed in Russia only two days. Why?"

"I met a business associate in Volgograd. The meeting's done —"

"Fine. I see." She typed away on her keyboard. "There's a problem."

Here it comes.

"A business associate, you said?"

"Yes."

"But you came on a tourist visa."

Wells didn't know whether to laugh or cry. He'd liked *business associate,* thought it sounded slick. Professional. "I'm sorry about that. My associate arranged the visa. Short notice."

She pecked away on her computer. "I'm noting this in our files. Do you plan to come back to Russia?"

"Of course, yes —"

"Then make sure you have the proper visa. Next time the penalty is serious." She shoved his passport back to him.

"I'm so sorry —"

She waved him on. "Next."

He had half an hour before the flight boarded. He sucked down four Tylenols, a Coke, a liter of water, trying to ratchet his brain back into gear. As the minutes ticked down, he sat two gates from his own and watched for any sign that the FSB was looking for him, uniformed or plainclothes police, hushed conversations between the Lufthansa agents.

Part of him wished he'd made a trickier move, checked in and then left the airport. He could have caught a cab to downtown Moscow, found a train or a bus heading west to Poland. But that would have taken yet another day, time he didn't have. Unless he found a smuggler to lead him over the border, he would still have to clear an immigration post that would be on the same computer network as the one he'd just passed. By tomorrow the FSB would surely have sounded the alarm.

When the flight opened, he was the first

to board. He settled himself in seat 2C, watched placidly as the plane filled around him. A pretty thirtyish woman with bobbed blond hair took the seat beside him, looked him over, buried her face in a German gossip magazine. Fine by Wells. With any luck, he'd be asleep by the time this plane left the runway.

The last passenger boarded. The purser made the usual preflight announcements in German, Russian, and English. And then finally closed the cabin door. Wells had never been so happy to hear the solid *thunk* of metal fitting metal, the low hum of air seeping from the vents over his seat. The flight attendants took their seats and the Airbus 319 rolled back from the Jetway. Diana Ross sang to Wells: *Set me free, why don't you, baby,/Get out my life, why don't you —*

The plane slowed.

Stopped.

The intercom alert chimed. The purser grabbed a headset. Listened. Made a short announcement in German that sent a brief hum through the passengers around him.

"What's he saying?" Wells said to his seatmate. Though he already knew. The knot in his stomach was all the translation he needed.

"He says we need to return to the gate for a moment. A sick passenger."

I'd much rather be treated in Frankfurt, thank you very much.

She gave Wells the thinnest of smiles, and he knew she knew. He wondered if he should ask her to call Shafer when they landed. But the story was too tricky to explain in the few seconds he had, and she didn't seem the type to do favors for strangers.

The plane inched forward. Stopped. 2C was near enough to the cabin door for Wells to hear the electric motors inching the Jetway forward. The death rattle of his bid for freedom.

The Jetway skimmed into place.

The purser stood, kept his eyes on Wells as he raised the big handle and pushed open the door. Wells found himself unbuckling his belt. No need to be difficult. And where could he go, anyway?

"Viel glück," the woman murmured. Maybe Wells had misjudged her. Too late now.

A man in a suit stepped inside, two cops in tow.

These are not the droids you're looking for.

"You are Mr. Wells?"

Wells nodded. The man flicked two fingers. *Up. Up.* The simple perfect command

306

of a police officer in a police state, a man who knew his orders would be followed without question, much less argument.

"Come with me. Please."

13

PROVO, UTAH

Mormons creeped Shafer out.

A ridiculous prejudice. Yet he couldn't shake it. The long underwear. The polygamy. The promise that believers might receive their own planets after death. Most of all, the unfailing perky friendliness. He didn't trust anyone who smiled so easily.

But here he was in Provo, the spiritual heart of Mormonism. He'd flown to Denver on United in the morning, supposedly heading for San Diego. At Denver International, he'd shucked his connecting flight, bought a fresh ticket on Southwest to Oakland via Salt Lake. Simple countersurveillance. He'd walked the United flight three times, scanning faces. He didn't see any of them on the Southwest flight.

In Salt Lake, he rented a car, drove to the wide boulevards south of downtown, found a long-term lot. He locked his phones in the glove compartment, taking only a burner he'd never used. He walked east and south until he found Great Deals Used Cars on State. He carried eight thousand dollars in cash, crisp hundred-dollar bills he'd pulled from his basement safe the night before.

The showroom was nicer than he'd hoped. A salesman in jeans and cowboy boots bee-lined for him. "Afternoon. I'm Rick. What can I do you for today?"

"Put the preposition in the right place."

Rick's smile faded, then came back stronger. "Sir?"

"Your cheapest car."

"We can do that. Naturally." Rick laid a friendly hand on Shafer's shoulder. "But maybe I can show you something nicer first, credit problems are no problem at Great Deals —"

Shafer was in no mood for cute. He twitched his shoulder like he was having a seizure until Rick pulled his hand away. "Cash. You want the quickest sale of your life, or not?"

Rick cleared his throat. "In that case. I think you're looking at a 2000 Regal. A Buick." Rick nodded over his shoulder at a fenced-in corner filled with junkers. "Hundred sixty thousand miles. Sticker's nineteen hundred, totally fair, but maybe I can knock fifty bucks off for a cash sale —"

"It'll get me to Provo?"

"Heck, it'll get you all the way to New York City" — those last three words spoken as if New York were Mars — "if that's where you want to go. All our cars go through a ninety-point checklist, we call 'em Great Deals certified —"

"Done." Shafer pulled out his wallet. "If you can get me out the door in ten minutes."

"No problem, sir, no problem at all —"

"And *shut up* while you're doing it."

Nine minutes later, Shafer had himself a new used car, legally registered and insured. The Regal was the saddest vehicle he'd ever driven. Someone had sprayed its pleather seats with mint air freshener in a futile effort to hide the smell of ten thousand cigarettes. Its steering wheel clicked ominously when Shafer switched lanes. Its brakes worked like a radio call-in show, with a seven-second delay.

No matter. Shafer had made himself as untraceable as any American could. Even if Salome's crew tracked the credit card he'd used for the rental, the trail would dead-end in Salt Lake. The Regal was too old and cheap to have a GPS. He'd ditched his phones. He could head to the safe house, where Evan and Heather were hiding, with a clear conscience.

This visit counted as a rear-guard action at best. Not that Wells and Duto were making much progress. Shafer had stopped at Duto's house predawn, on his way to Dulles. Duto stood in the doorway in black silk pajamas, reading glasses dangling from a lanyard. He didn't invite Shafer in.

"Told her I was gonna rape her," he said before Shafer could ask about Donna Green.

Shafer thought he'd misheard. "You threatened to tape her?"

"Rape. R-A-P-E. Rape." Emphatically. Like he was trying to win a prison spelling bee.

"The National Security Advisor? Of the United States? Of America? All these years learning to hide what a psychopath you are, you choose this moment to blow it?"

"She said I was making a play. I told her I'd be back with the truth, and when I was done with her she wouldn't sit down for a month."

"More like buggery, then."

Duto folded his arms over his chest and smirked. He reminded Shafer of an old-school Hollywood mogul, the kind who made every starlet spend time on his couch.

311

"That better or worse? I'm telling you, there was no convincing her. She knows about the Midnight House, how I got to Whitby."

Now Shafer understood. Green had waved the red flag, told Duto that she'd taken the agency from him. And Duto had charged, just as she'd expected.

"Nothing's changed," Duto said.

"Sounds like a productive meeting."

"More than you think. Donna told me we got the guys who took out the jet. Delta grabbed 'em in Mumbai last night. They're Hezbollah."

"So we're going to come back at them?"

"Yes. She wouldn't say how."

Another step toward war.

"And Wells busted out, too." The text had come in a few minutes before, Wells reporting that Volgograd was headed for Moscow and then Frankfurt. "I think he's in rough shape."

"He's a big boy." Duto's standard answer when Shafer worried about Wells. Like Wells was a horse who could be worked forever without consequence. "Call him when you work it out with Evan. That'll cheer him up." Duto edged the front door toward Shafer's foot. "Anything else? I gotta take a piss."

"Me, John, you against the world, you still

need me to know you're in charge."

As an answer, Duto shut the door.

Now Shafer parked the Regal outside a gray two-story house in the snow-dusted foothills on Provo's east side. A wooden stockade fence hid the building's first floor. The blinds were pulled tight on the second. A bubble camera watched the locked front gate. Shafer buzzed.

"Hello?" A woman's voice.

"Heather? It's Ellis."

"I need to see your identification, sir."

Not Heather. An FBI agent. Shafer held his license to the camera. A fresh westerly wind blew from the desert, dragging lacy clouds across the blue Utah sky. Shafer listened to the weekday sounds floating up from the streets below, school buses idling, kids yelling. Footsteps crossed the yard, and the gate opened to reveal an olive-skinned woman, late twenties.

"I'm Special Agent Rosatto. Hands against the fence." She frisked him thoroughly. "Come with me."

In the living room, Evan and Heather, Wells's ex-wife, played Scrabble on a beige couch. They grunted insincere greetings. They'd wanted Wells.

Heather was in her early forties now, still

pretty, but with the hollowed-out face of a compulsive exerciser. Shafer had met her long before, when Evan was a toddler and Wells was on his way to Afghanistan to infiltrate al-Qaeda. She and Wells had fallen in love in high school, married young, had a baby. Then she'd left. Like Exley. And now Anne. They'd all seen that the field was Wells's true mistress.

As for Evan, Shafer didn't need a DNA test to know that he was John's son. He was tall and rangy like his father, the same strong nose and thick brown hair. But his cheeks were unlined, his eyes soft. *I used to care . . . but I take a pill for that now,* his T-shirt explained. Shafer didn't know if Evan was weaker than John or just younger. Not even nineteen. Not one but two generations behind Shafer. Shafer knew he'd been that young once. He had pictures to prove it. But his memories of those years were lighter than dreams.

"We need a few minutes outside," he said to Rosatto.

"If she's okay with it."

Heather nodded.

"Just please stay in the yard."

So they stood around an empty sandbox, Heather and Evan on one side, Shafer on the other. Heather took a half step back,

314

letting her son do the speaking.

"I saw you on TV a couple weeks ago, Evan," Shafer said. "At Fresno State. That one-three must have been thirty feet out." He'd checked YouTube highlights the night before.

Evan looked at Shafer the same way Shafer had looked at Rick the used-car salesman. "Where is he?"

"Flying from Russia to Germany, or he may already have landed."

"What's he doing?"

"It's complicated."

"Then he should tell us himself."

Evan's voice was cool. Composed. Maybe he was more like John than he seemed, snarky T-shirt and all.

"He can't call. He'd have to come here, and he can't spare the time."

"Because of the NSA?"

"Among other things."

"That woman in there, she's FBI, yes? And you're CIA."

"Yes."

"So why are we worrying about the NSA?"

"It's complicated."

"Enough of that."

"I wish it weren't."

"Ellis. I haven't forgotten what John did in Kenya. But this, we've been here a week.

315

You know she won't let us leave the house? Haven't even been outside until now."

"A few more days."

"Give us *something,* Ellis."

Shafer had known they would reach this point sooner or later. Now he realized he wanted to tell them. Everything. He shouldn't, but he did. If only to unburden himself.

"You want to know?"

"Yes," Evan said.

"No," Heather said.

"Go inside, Mom."

"Don't do this. It's not *fair.*" She looked at Shafer with wide pleading eyes. He understood. She had lost Wells to this shadow war. She feared Evan would be next.

"Fair's got nothing to do with it," Evan said.

The kid was eighteen. Old enough to enlist, if he wanted. He had the right to know.

Heather turned away, walked into the house. So Shafer told Evan the story. It took an hour. He didn't mention Duberman by name, but he gave up everything else. Evan looked at him in disbelief when he finished.

"This mysterious billionaire might kill us to get at John?"

"Your father's lots of things. Not crazy.

316

Neither am I. It's all true. And we would both feel better if you stayed here until we figure out where the uranium came from."

"Or we, the country, I mean, invade Iran," Evan said. "This guy won't care after that, right?"

"Probably not."

"So John's running to every country that ever had this stuff, and they're all blowing him off. And in another week, we'll attack and it'll be moot."

Something about what Evan had said bugged Shafer. And it wasn't the dig, either.

"Say that again."

"I said, John'll be in Libya, chasing some guy who worked at some reactor in 1983" — as if the year was the dawn of recorded history — "and meanwhile the President will come on television to tell us all about Operation Irani Freedom or whatever. And Richie Rich will buy himself a new spaceship because he's so excited his plot worked."

Some reactor in 1983. That fast, Shafer saw what he'd missed. He was a fool. It had taken an eighteen-year-old kid to spot the hole.

A country running an active nuclear weapons project would track its HEU to

317

the milligram. It wouldn't sell the stuff at any price. But what about a country that had stockpiled a chunk of weapons-grade uranium and then ended its program? The material instantly would be a liability. It would be locked in a vault and after a few years forgotten. Waiting for someone — for Salome — to find it and pry it out for the right price.

A long shot, sure. But no longer than the possibilities that had taken Wells to Russia and Duto to Israel. Plus Shafer had an edge. Of all the countries that had walked away from enrichment programs over the years, South Africa had gotten the furthest. It was the natural place to start. Shafer's first agency posting had been in Kinshasa, the capital of Zaire — the country now known as Congo. This was the late seventies. Kinshasa was rife with officers for the South African Bureau of State Security — infamously known as B.O.S.S. All over Africa, the CIA worked hand-in-glove, white-hand-in-white-glove, with South Africa. It saw the white-run government in Pretoria as a buffer against the Communist-supported African National Congress.

In Kinshasa, Shafer had worked with a dozen South African intelligence officers. They were for the most part unapologetically racist, especially after a few drinks. *The blacks can't be trusted to manage their own affairs,* one told Shafer. *You don't let the animals run the zoo.* Yet when they weren't talking politics, they were pleasant enough. And Shafer, cynical to his core, nonetheless believed that some forms of government were worse than others. Communism would make Africa even poorer and more miserable. Eventually, sooner than they expected, white South Africans would have no choice but to give the vote to the black majority. Meantime, he would work with them when the need arose.

So Shafer told himself. Though he wondered if he was just making excuses.

The white regime took longer to fall than he expected. But it did. And in the mid-nineties a couple of the guys he'd known in Congo emigrated to the United States. Shafer couldn't remember where they'd wound up, but he could find out easily enough. Lucky for him, they all had these weird Afrikaner names. He wouldn't need fancy databases to track them. He was guessing the United States had only one Joost Claassen.

A poke in the ribs from Evan brought him back to Provo.

319

"I gotta go. Promise you'll stay." If Evan sat tight, so would Heather. "Even if you think it's BS."

"For that story, I'll give you a week. On two conditions. One for you, one for my dad. First. Whatever happens, promise when it's over you'll give me the after-action report." The kid raised his eyebrows, at once acknowledging and mocking the lingo.

"Done. What's the other?"

"You tell John, I want him to come out here, come skiing with me. If I'm stuck in Utah, I might as well get to Alta. Pow-pow."

"What about basketball?"

"I'm already out of the rotation."

"All right, I'll tell him. Though I bet he hasn't skied in at least twenty years."

Evan grinned, and Shafer saw he'd chosen the sport for exactly that reason. An easy way to show his superiority over the old man. Shafer turned for the gate. "Tell your mother I had to run."

"I'd like to see that," Evan said.

Shafer found a copy shop that had workstations with Internet access. In forty-six seconds, he found Joost and Linda Claassen, in Henderson, Nevada. He bought himself a phone card, hoping Joost hadn't moved. Or gone unlisted. Or died.

"Hallo?" The voice was thirty-five years

rougher than Shafer remembered, but the accent was unmistakable.

"Joost."

"Who's calling, please?"

"Ellis Shafer. We knew each other back in Kinshasa."

"I never lived in Kinshasa."

Shafer wondered if he had the wrong man. But no. Old spy habits died hard. "Come on, Joost. Remember that party you threw, Christmas, you brought in the witch to cast spells on us? Betty Nye, she hid in the closet. Orson had to drag her out." Orson Nye had been Shafer's first chief of station.

Joost laughed. "Okay, then. I remember. Where is Orson these days?"

"Nursing home in Virginia. Alzheimer's."

"That is unfortunate."

Shafer had forgotten how Afrikaners talked, these oddly flat statements. "Sure is. I need to see you, Joost."

"Where are you?"

"I can be in Henderson tonight."

"Ellis —"

"It's not about back then, Joost. I'm hoping you can help me find something."

Joost went silent. Shafer had only payphone static for company. He wondered if he'd pushed too hard, lost the old man.

"I've left all that behind."

"I swear. Nothing to be worried about."

"Then I look forward to seeing you tonight."

Henderson was on the outskirts of Vegas, four hundred miles down I-15 from Provo. Shafer decided to stick to the Regal instead of flying out of Salt Lake, a way to avoid using credit cards and the TSA.

Still, as the mile markers rolled by and the Buick's gauges rose toward red, Shafer wished he'd splurged for the *second*-cheapest car on the lot. The ninety-point checklist at Great Deals Used Cars didn't seem to include the engine. Shafer turned the Regal's heat to high to relieve the radiator and kept the speedometer steady at fifty-three. Anything beat blowing the engine in the Utah desert.

The six-hour trip took eight hours. But finally Shafer knocked on the door of Joost's house in Henderson. A tidy ranch in a tidy subdivision, as far from the chaos of Kinshasa as Shafer could imagine. The Regal had cooled after sunset. Shafer believed it might even survive the return trip north.

The door swung wide open. Joost looked surprisingly like the man Shafer had known a generation before. Gray hair and age spots notwithstanding, he held himself ramrod-straight, ready to head upriver into the heart of darkness.

"Joost. You look good."

"So do you." To Shafer's surprise, Joost opened his arms and wrapped him up. "Come, come."

Joost's living room was covered with pictures of Joost and a stout Hispanic woman maybe twenty years younger. She definitely hadn't been his wife in Kinshasa. Shafer vaguely remembered that woman as tall and blond. "Is that —"

"Janneke died in 2005. Cancer."

"I'm sorry."

"Linda was her nurse. She thinks I was a mining engineer over there."

Now Shafer understood why Joost had been wary of his call. "She's out tonight?"

"She plays poker with the tourists once a week. You'd be surprised how much she wins. Sit, please. If you'd like a drink —" On the coffee table Joost had set out a bottle of Johnnie Walker Black and a bowl of ice. "I don't drink much these days, but I thought tonight. Just a taste."

"Please."

Joost poured them two shallow drinks. "Cheers."

"It's good to see you, Joost."

And it was. Not because Joost had been a

good intelligence officer, or even a good man. He'd had a long-running affair with a secretary at the Dutch embassy, if Shafer remembered right. But Joost had kept his promises, a rare trait in their business. In any case, seeing him offered a more intimate version of a college reunion, a reminder that everyone was headed the same way.

"You're still working, Ellis?"

"For now."

"Can you believe Zaire is even worse now than it was back then?"

"We didn't exactly leave them a winning hand."

"Always this excuse. They've been independent fifty years now. Time to take responsibility for themselves. I remember you saying something like that to one of the big men. You were never afraid to say what you thought. Though you must have known after a few months that you were wasting your breath."

Story of my life.

"Worst that could happen, they send me back to Langley, I stop getting malaria."

"You remember the time when Mobutu's secretary called you in, that crazy one who drove the pink Rolls-Royce —"

For an hour, they talked about nothing but the past.

"So," Shafer said finally. "There was something I wanted to ask you about."

Joost tapped his wrist. "Now we come to the point."

"We can talk all night."

"Please, Ellis. You didn't come all this way to reminisce about Mobutu."

Shafer poured them both fresh splashes of whiskey.

"Were you ever involved with the nuclear stuff?"

"Our program? So, so, so." All one word: *sososo*. "No."

"Joost, I promise, I'm not here officially. I'm not fishing to get you in trouble."

"You see the life I live, Ellis. I don't want reporters at the door."

Shafer waited.

Joost sipped his drink and seemed to decide he had to give Shafer something. "Look, South Africa isn't like the States. Inside the apparatus, we all knew each other."

"After '77, it wasn't any great secret," Shafer said, hoping to encourage him.

In 1977, South Africa had been close to conducting an underground nuclear test when the United States discovered its preparations.

"One of the scientists, a little man named

Alfred, he's dead now, we grew up together in the Transvaal. When I came back from Zaire, he told me bits and pieces."

"You were working with Israel."

"Yes. The Jews didn't care about the sanctions. People hated them even more than us. We had money and uranium ore. They had the scientists. We traded."

"And the enrichment project succeeded."

"These stories you see now that we had six nuclear weapons, that's an exaggeration. Cubs trying to be lions, we say. But we did make enough for one."

"This was in the eighties."

"Yes. I can't remember exactly which year."

"And what happened to it? That highly enriched uranium."

Joost poured himself another whiskey, a big one this time, and offered the bottle to Shafer, who covered his glass.

"I don't suppose all these questions have anything to do with what you found in Istanbul."

"You know I can't answer that." Shafer already regretted telling the story to Evan.

"For what it's worth, the stuff we produced was very pure. Just like the uranium you found over there."

"You're sure."

"It was a point of pride."

"So the stuff is still in a vault in Pretoria?" Shafer couldn't believe finding it would be this easy. Wells and Duto had gone all over the world, and Shafer was about to get the answer.

"Of course not. We wouldn't have left it for the ANC. It's not even in Africa anymore."

Shafer's elation vanished. "So where?"

"Where do you think? We sent it to the Jews as a present. Why not? At least they'd helped us."

"All of it?"

"Yes."

Another brick wall. If the South Africans had given up the uranium twenty years before, the Israelis had no doubt long since blended it into a nuclear warhead now pointing at Iran.

Still, he'd come too far not to finish his questions.

"How much HEU was it, anyway?"

"A bit more than fifteen kilos."

Shafer hadn't expected such a precise answer. "That's oddly specific."

"Because fifteen was always the amount we needed to reach for a bomb. The scientists celebrated for a week when they reached it, my friend told me. But then the

Defense Ministry and the Foreign Ministry had a big fight and de Klerk halted the program."

"Because you knew what was coming."

"What could we do with it? Blow up Soweto?" The giant slum southwest of Johannesburg. "The joke was that it would look better after."

"So the program stopped at fifteen kilos. One bomb."

"Fifteen-point-three sticks with me, for some reason. But it's all gone now. Ask your friends in Tel Aviv."

"Did Israel pay for it? How did you arrange the transfer?"

Joost splashed more Johnnie Walker into his glass. He seemed to have forgotten his promise of "just a taste." "Now you've dug too deep for me. You need someone closer to the program. But none of them came to the States."

"The planes go both ways. If I wanted to chase this, who would I ask?"

"A lot of the scientists, they're gone now. But the bugger who ran the program at the end is still around. Real jackal, that one."

Joost drained the last of his whiskey. It seemed to hit him all at once. He closed his eyes, flicked his tongue across his lips. "Were we ever friends, Ellis?"

Shafer flashed back to a long night at the British embassy, Joost drunkenly wrapping an arm around the ambassador's wife, whispering in her ear until Janneke peeled him away.

All these years later, he was still a sloppy drunk.

"Sure we were." The truth could wait. Forever.

"How come you never looked me up until now?"

"I wanted to leave you in peace. But this is too important. So? This jackal who ran the program?"

"What about him?"

"His name, Joost. What's his name?"

14
FIVE DAYS . . .

MOSCOW

All anyone needed to know about the new Russia was that Lubyanka was still open.

Sure, the Soviet Union had crumbled a generation before, and Russia was now theoretically a democracy. Sure, the very name Lubyanka sent a shiver through Russians of a certain age. The building was synonymous with the bad old days, secret trials and one-way trips to Siberia. No one knew how many prisoners had been tortured to death in its basement cells. For generations, it had served as the headquarters of the Committee on State Security, the *Komitet gosudarstvennoy bezopasnosti.*

The KGB.

The KGB had vanished with the USSR, replaced by the more polite-sounding Federal Security Service, known in English as the FSB. Yet the FSB was in no hurry to leave Lubyanka. Moving was such a headache. Lubyanka was a beautiful building, conveniently located just a few blocks from the Kremlin.

Besides, many senior FSB officers had a more positive perspective on the KGB than the average Russian. After all, they were KGB veterans themselves. As was Vladimir Putin. He wasn't about to punish his old buddies. Putin and his oligarchs had more to lose from a revolution than Mikhail Gorbachev and the Soviet *apparatchiks* ever had.

So, by any name, the secret police stayed in business. And inside Lubyanka's walls, the cruelties continued.

The FSB held Wells at Domodedovo through the evening. The airport cell was big enough for a dozen men, but besides Wells, its only occupant was a baby-faced Southeast Asian. Wells tried English and Arabic on the guy, but he only shook his head and pointed to his belly. Wells guessed he was a drug mule. His skin was waxy and soft, like he was melting from the inside out.

Wells had endured more unpleasant cells. This one was warm, quiet, and windowless, a tonic for his concussion. The fog in his mind lifted and the black spots in his vision disappeared. He was left to consider the wreckage of this mission. Had Custer felt this way when he rode over the hill at Little Bighorn? Wells had traveled all over the world and earned only a broken finger and a shaken brain for his troubles.

He hadn't always won before, but he had never felt so outclassed.

He tried to tilt his anger to Salome and Duberman. But after a few minutes, the revenge fantasy lost its appeal. He changed his tack, closed his eyes, found his favorite Quranic verses. He didn't believe for a minute that Muhammad had received messages straight from Allah. Yet he sometimes sensed divine inspiration in the text. Not just in the obvious places, the rhythms and melodies of famous Surahs like *The Overturning,* with its bizarrely poetic promise of the apocalypse:

When the sun is overturned
When the stars fall away
When the mountains are moved
When the ten-month pregnant camels are
    abandoned
When the beasts of the wild are herded
    together
When the seas are boiled over
When the souls are coupled . . .

But contradictions and digressions filled the Quran's lesser chapters, verses that sounded sweet in Arabic but could barely be translated into any other language. Only a truly confident God would allow such malarkey in His revealed word. *I command you to believe no matter what I say . . .*

Wells slept. He must have, for the jangle of metal against metal stirred him. He opened his eyes to see a man in a windbreaker at the bars. Behind him, a digital clock read *00:23.* He waved Wells over, cuffed his hands behind his back through the bars, slid the cell door open.

"Bye," the Asian kid said.

"Good luck." Though Wells wasn't even sure what *luck* would mean for the guy. He might be better off having the package break inside him, a brief euphoria before he tumbled into the void.

"Bye-bye-bye." Like a toddler who knew only one word.

Wells's captor tugged his shoulder. Wells looked at him. "You're FSB, yes?"

"Da."

"How 'bout you tell me what's going on?"

"Lubyanka."

The word even *sounded* cold. For a moment, Wells considered trying to make a break. But the idea was beyond foolish. He

333

didn't speak Russian, didn't have money or a car waiting. He wouldn't clear the airport before they shot him down. He would get out of this mess with his wits, or not at all. *And Duto and Shafer think I'm just the muscle.*

They brought him to the center of the city in style, a big Mercedes. The ride took twenty minutes, the Merc's blue light clearing a path better than any siren. Even as Wells was still getting his bearings, they reached a plaza dominated by a single massive building on its northeastern side.

"Lubyanka," the FSB agent said again.

"I get the tour? Excellent. Didn't think that was part of the package."

The guy patted Wells's cheek, the touch more menacing than any punch.

The Mercedes stopped at a manned gate on the building's north side, away from the square. As they waited for the guard to examine the driver's identification, Wells found himself *wanting* to be inside. He was tired of the uncertainty of this twilight struggle. If they planned to torture him because they believed he was a spy, or a troublemaker, or just because they could, so be it. Give him a battle to fight.

His wish came true. The gate came up. The Merc rolled down a long curved ramp and stopped before a steel door where two men waited, pale guys with meaty hands and crumpled noses. A heavyweight welcoming committee. They yanked Wells out, shoved him inside, down a long staircase that ended in a narrow corridor lit with dim red bulbs, like a predigital photo lab. Wells figured he had to be fifty feet below street level. With no natural light or sound to anchor him, he would quickly lose any sense of time. They could destroy his sleep cycle in a day or two just by playing with the lights.

A woman stood at the end of the corridor. For a moment, Wells thought he was looking at Salome. But when the guards brought him closer, he realized his mistake. This woman had the same narrow hips, the same confident stance. But she was older, with a pinched nose, a wattled neck. She pulled open the door behind her.

"Ready for a shower?" she said in English.

The guards dragged him through the doorway into a white-tiled room about fifteen feet square, lit with standard white bulbs. A dozen showerheads were mounted from the ceiling. A camera and speaker hung in each corner.

The lead guard turned, gave him a right-left-right combination to the stomach. Wells doubled over, stared at the narrow tiles at his feet. He caught his breath, tried to straighten. But the second guard grabbed his cuffed hands, pulled them up and back, driving Wells's head down toward the floor. Over the years, his shoulders had been dislocated more times than he could remember. They loosened in their sockets. The pain arced like a firework about to burst. But just before they popped out, the cuffs came off. His hands were free. Wells needed a moment to realize that the guard had unlocked him.

Wells didn't question why. Instinct took over. He straightened up, trying to spin around, get in a quick right hook. Before he even got his arm all the way up, the first guard kicked out his legs, sending him sprawling. The fall didn't hurt much, but it was humiliating. As he pushed himself up to go after them, they walked out of the room, locked the door. Perfect choreography. Wells wondered how many times they had pulled this routine.

"Remove your clothes," a man said, a voice so empty it might have been computer-generated.

"I don't even know why I'm here."

"Five seconds."

"Let me call my embassy. Please. *Spasibo*." The pose of confused tourist was a weak play, but he didn't see other options.

The room went dark. And then water drummed his head, soaked his clothes. It was frigid at first. Wells moved to a corner, but the room had been designed so that the showerheads covered it. The water warmed to lukewarm. Then comfortable. Wells didn't need an engineering degree to figure that in a couple of minutes it would be scalding.

He pulled off his shirt, stepped out of his jeans. A psychological ploy to make him follow their orders without violence, show him that they were in complete control. And a good one. He doubted they would boil him to death in here if he refused to comply. But he couldn't take the chance.

As he finished undressing, the water again went frigid. He closed his eyes, saw Afghanistan. For months on end he had bathed only in the bone-chilling streams that flowed down the sides of the Kush. The memory relaxed him, and maybe his captors saw that the cold wasn't bothering him, because the water stopped quickly and the lights came up.

Wells forced himself to remember that the FSB had no reason to keep him for long. Moscow was two hours ahead of Frankfurt, eight ahead of the East Coast. At this moment, Duto and Shafer thought they were doing Wells a favor by letting him get a good night's sleep in Germany. But when they realized he hadn't reached Frankfurt, they would call Moscow. Duto still had FSB connections. Wells would spend no more than a day here. Two at most.

He hoped.

The two big guys stepped into the shower. With his hands free, Wells considered taking a pop. But clothes — and shoes — offered a huge advantage in close quarters combat. A boot strike would break his unprotected feet. Other body parts were even more vulnerable.

He let them cuff him.

They led him to an unmarked room at the other end of the hall. The woman waited inside, sitting behind a big and heavily scarred oak desk that looked strangely out of place in here. A relic dating back to the KGB, maybe even the Cheka. There were no other chairs. Wells had no choice but to stand naked in front of her. Water puddled at his feet. Goose pimples covered his arms and legs. He forced himself to stand straight, make no effort to hide himself. Let her look. Her smirk widened. She barked a command and the guards turned him around as slowly as a pig on a spit.

"Let me go," Wells said.

"Shut up." Her English was perfect, her tone as dismissive as a Valley Girl's. He wondered if she'd spent time in California. "You must know we have a hundred ways to hurt you in this place, no marks. You leave, complain, no one cares. A crazy American telling lies about Russia. What do you think we were doing when we had you at the airport? We checked with Moscow station, they say you're not one of them. Not listed. Not NOC."

The letters stood for non-official cover. Most CIA case officers operated under diplomatic cover. They worked out of embassies and had immunity from arrest and prosecution. Only a few worked without that protection. Even they usually could count on their stations for help when they got in serious trouble. The FSB had its own operatives under non-official cover in the United States, so both sides tried to keep from playing too rough.

"NOC?" Wells said. "What's that?"

She barked in Russian, and the guard to Wells's right rabbit-punched him in the kidney. The pain spread up, slow-cooking his viscera and ribs. Wells forced himself to stay steady.

"Next time, I tell him to kick you in those big balls of yours."

Wells nodded. He wasn't sure he could speak. These guys did maximum damage with minimum effort.

"You play games with me, this takes until morning. I don't want that. I want to get home, turn on the television, go to sleep. And you, I see even from the way you took that last punch, you're a professional. Please, treat me with respect."

She stared at him with her lumpy black eyes, almost daring him to argue. But she'd made her point. His best bet was to answer her questions as honestly as possible.

"Da."

"Good." She fetched the suitcase that Boris had given him from under her desk, pulled his passports. "Which is real?"

"Both real, both USG issued."

"Is either your real name?"

"Wells."

She flipped through it. "John Wells. Where were you born?"

"What it says. Hamilton, Montana."

"But you use the other also. In the name Roger Bishop."

"Yes."

"Are these your only passports?"

"The only ones I've used recently."

"Good."

Wells didn't know if she was complimenting him for his honesty or herself for having found such a valuable prisoner. She reached into the desk for a pen and a tiny notebook, scratched out a note. "You come to Russia when?"

"Two days ago."

"Where did you arrive?"

"Here. On my way to Volgograd."

"Why?"

"To meet Mikhail Buvchenko."

Another quick note.

"From where?"

"Saudi Arabia via Istanbul." No reason to lie. She wouldn't even need to check flight manifests. The passport stamps told the tale.

"Saudi Arabia. You are Muslim?"

"I am."

"This is very unusual. A white American becomes Muslim."

He didn't answer. She made another note. Wells wondered if she'd press him, but instead she said only, "Fine. Volgograd. You met Buvchenko?"

"Yes."

"For how long?"

"Overnight. His men brought me directly from my hotel. We had dinner, and then he asked me to stay at his house." Wells left out the tale of Peter the horse. "He didn't give me much choice, so I stayed. Then, yesterday morning, he brought me back to Volgograd."

"Where the police come to your room." Showing him she knew everything that had happened, he shouldn't bother to lie.

"They said I was carrying drugs."

"Were you?"

"No. I don't know why they had that idea. They searched the hotel and didn't find any."

He wondered if she'd ask about Salome, but she didn't.

"Then they put you on a plane to Moscow."

"The lead detective, Boris, he told me I needed to leave Russia. I didn't argue."

"You have much misfortune on this trip. People accusing you of drugs for no reason. The FSB comes for you."

"I've had better weeks."

She stood up, leaned across the desk, eyed him tip to toe. Wells couldn't help thinking of the witch in the gingerbread house. *Good enough to eat, my dearies.* "So why all this travel? You are businessman? You do oil?"

"We both know I don't do oil." Wells shivered. His adrenaline was wearing off. His feet felt numb, like he was turning to a statue from the ground up. He couldn't remember where he'd read that legend. Another fairy tale? A Greek myth? Tolkien?

A snap of her fingers brought him back to the room.

"You are tired? You need my men to wake you?"

"No, ma'am."

"Then answer my question. So much travel? Such nasty places. CIA says you don't work for them? Maybe you are bounty hunter? Like the American one? Dog the Bounty Hunter?" She said something to the guards, and they laughed.

She wasn't a great interrogator, Wells decided. Too eager to impress with her knowledge of American culture. The realization strengthened him. He could beat her. He twitched his legs, jogged his feet against the floor. Probably he looked like he was having a seizure, but he needed to keep active, not give in to this slow hypothermia clouding his mind. Get out of here without mentioning Duberman's name. He couldn't risk that. He couldn't be sure how it would play.

"Not a bounty hunter. I was CIA, yes. I quit."

"You admit this?"

"It's not illegal."

"Did you ever travel to Russia before?"

"No." A lie, a dangerous one. Wells had no choice. Years before, he'd come to Moscow chasing a Russian hit squad. He'd killed a carful of men, while the one he wanted escaped. But he didn't think the FSB could connect him to the case. He'd used a different fake passport, and back then the Russians hadn't gone for retinal scans or fingerprints.

"Never?"

"Never. I don't speak Russian."

"Where were you posted?"

"Mostly Afghanistan and Pakistan. But I tell you, I quit years ago."

"Yet here you are."

"Sometimes people ask me to do things."

She waited.

"In this case, Senator Duto. From Pennsylvania. The former DCI, as I'm sure you know."

"He sent you to Buvchenko."

"Yes."

"Why?"

The question. The FSB obviously wasn't sure who he was, or what to do with him. They didn't have any reason to provoke another diplomatic incident over a guy who had agency connections and might have a legitimate reason to be here. At the same time, Buvchenko had told them enough to get Wells brought to Lubyanka. This interview was a test. They hadn't drugged him, or beaten him badly enough to do permanent damage. They didn't have a team interrogating him. They were giving themselves the option to let him walk. If Wells could give this woman the right answer, the words she wanted to hear, she might. And as he tried to figure out what those words might be, he had one edge.

Salome had played their meeting in Volgograd brilliantly. But she'd made one mistake, telling Wells the story she and Buvchenko planned to peddle to the FSB. Of course, she'd done so to distract him from the fact that she didn't expect to involve the secret police at all. She'd planned to seal his fate with a block of heroin. But Wells had beaten that trap. And thanks to Salome, he knew exactly why the FSB had brought him here. Buvchenko had told them he had come to Russia to buy weapons for the Syrian jihadis. This interrogator had signaled as much by making Wells admit he was Muslim.

All at once Wells saw the play. *Lean in.*

"I told Buvchenko I was looking for guns. For Syria."

"You confess this?"

"I'm telling you that's what I told him. But really it was a sting. Someone in Washington, I don't know who, tipped Duto about rumors that Buvchenko was shipping weapons to the jihadis. So Duto asked me to get involved. I'm a Muslim, I have credibility, I could go to Saudi Arabia first and tell Buvchenko I raised money from the sheiks there."

"I don't believe you. Duto would just have told the CIA."

"No, he's angry because they dumped him. Wants to embarrass them. He thought if he could get the truth about Buvchenko, he could use it against them."

She nodded, and Wells knew the story rang true to her. Why not? The Russians specialized in this kind of palace intrigue.

"Use it how?"

"I don't know. He doesn't tell me that."

"He sends you to Russia to stand in a cell with your *khuy* shriveled up and doesn't even tell you his plans, and you say yes."

"When I get home, I'll ask for a raise."

"This was a stupid game. Very stupid."

"I had an arms dealer who knows Buvchenko set up the meeting. I thought I was safe. I didn't know Buvchenko would go running to the FSB. Bad for business."

"He's loyal to his country. Russia doesn't

help these terrorists."

No, Russia helped Bashar al-Assad, who killed kids with nerve gas. But they could have that talk another time.

"It was a mistake. I'm sorry."

"Duto should have asked us himself."

"I guess so."

She made more notes. "If this story is a lie —"

"Call Duto. Tell him you have me. He'll confirm it."

Assuming he figures out what I said while he's talking to you. If not, Wells and his shriveled *khuy* would be staying in these cells. He wondered if Buvchenko could play back. But the man couldn't change his accusation at this point, and he might not want to press his FSB masters any harder. Salome was just one client, and no matter how much money she could offer Buvchenko, he'd lose it all and more if he angered Moscow.

As for Salome, she'd no doubt already left Russia. Whatever other contacts she and Duberman had here, she couldn't risk involving them. Like Wells, she couldn't be sure how the Kremlin would react if it discovered what Duberman had done. It might see the chance to tell the White House, put the President hugely in its debt.

Plus she had no need to take risks. She won by running out the clock.

And the clock was still running.

"Don't look so sad, Mr. Wells," the woman said. "I think I believe you."

"Glad to hear it."

"Poor baby." She said something in Russian, and the guards laughed. Wells didn't mind. The less of a threat he presented, the more likely she would be to let him go. "If I unlock you, you'll be a good boy?"

"You unlock me, I'll do whatever you want."

Five minutes later, Wells found himself in a cell all his own. Aside from the fact that it was underground and thus windowless, it wouldn't have been out of place in a maximum-security American prison. It had a cot with an inch-thick mattress, a pillow that smelled like a locker room, and a plastic gallon jug half filled with water that Wells hoped wouldn't make him sick. His clothes were too wet to wear, but the guards had fetched him underwear, a T-shirt, and sweatpants, all in the same shade of gray.

The day had gone worse than a country song. Wells wouldn't know until the morning at least if the interrogator had bought his story. Still, he counted his blessings. If he hadn't found that brick of heroin in his hotel room, he'd still be in Volgograd, in a cell far less inviting than this one.

Sometimes the only sane move was to lie down and sleep.

So he did.

15

BEKAA VALLEY, LEBANON

Hussein Ayoub considered himself lucky.

More than lucky. Blessed.

Ayoub commanded the soldiers and militia who fought for Hezbollah, the Shia political party that dominated Lebanon. His army totaled more than ten thousand fighters, three thousand full-time and the rest irregulars. Despite its small size, it was highly capable. When Israel invaded Lebanon in 2006, his people fought the IDF nearly to a draw.

Ayoub was forty-one, and tall. He wore his thick black hair swept up and back, in what was almost a pompadour. A handsome man. He had made his reputation in the '06 invasion. Wearing a stolen Israeli uniform, he had walked up to four IDF soldiers at an outpost near the southern Lebanese city of Tyre and killed them at point-blank range.

Ayoub had commanded Hezbollah's army

for a year. Twice already he should have been killed. Once in Syria, fifteen kilometers south of Damascus. Rebels strafed his convoy with rockets, blowing up the cars behind and in front of his. Six of his guards died. The second time in Beirut, just a month before. A van loaded with artillery shells leveled an office building. Ayoub was supposed to be inside, but he was running late.

Inshallah. Truly. He had stopped fearing his own death after that morning outside Tyre. Dawn, the best hour for a surprise attack. The night watchers were worn out. Everyone else was still half asleep. He came in from the east, knowing the sun would be behind him, in their eyes. Still. They should have cut him down before he got close. His Hebrew was good, not great. The uniform was good, but his shoes were wrong. But back then the Jews were used to fighting kids in Gaza who threw rocks and Molotovs. They didn't know what real war looked like.

Worse, for them, they didn't know they didn't know. Ayoub would never forget the way they'd yelled in surprise when he raised his rifle.

So he lived. But his life belonged only to Allah, and one day Allah would call for him.

Until then he would fight for his people. At this moment, with the Israelis keeping to their side of the border, the fight was mainly in Syria. Years before, Hezbollah had joined the Syrian civil war, siding with Bashar al-Assad against the rebels who wanted to demolish his regime.

Ayoub disliked Assad. He and his friends drank, gambled, used drugs. Charity was one of the five pillars of Islam, but Assad lived in a palace while his countrymen starved. As the war ground on, Assad's crimes multiplied.

Yet Ayoub never questioned Hezbollah's choice. The rebels on the other side raged against Shia like Ayoub. No matter that Shia and Sunni were all Muslims, that they all believed that Allah was the only God, and Muhammad his messenger. The Sunnis ruled the Islamic world from Morocco to Indonesia. There were five Sunni for every Shia. But that dominance wasn't enough for them. They wanted to eliminate the Shia entirely.

Ayoub had seen the torture videos. Mostly they came from Iraq. Men begging for mercy as their eyes were gouged out, their faces sliced apart. Men led stumbling through the empty desert on the Iraq–Syria border. Held down. Chains strapped to their arms and legs. Each chain locked to a car. Each car driven a different way. He'd made himself stop watching them. He'd tried to forget.

But one he couldn't. It was the simplest of all. No sound, a fixed camera focused on a plain wooden table. On it, a ten-liter bucket of water beside a cardboard box filled with puppies. Ayoub didn't know the breed. In truth, he didn't like dogs. But these creatures were impossible to hate. They curled over one another, full of life. They couldn't have been more than a few days old. Eight in all.

A pair of gloved hands picked them up one by one, held them underwater as they squirmed and tried to breathe, their desperation obvious even without sound. Until their wriggling stopped. Then the hands threw the sodden corpses back in the box. They twisted over each other like broken vines. The hands pointed, proudly: *See what I've done?*

The screen went black. A single Arabic line splayed across it: *The Shia are worse than dogs.*

If the video had ended there, it would have been one more piece of Sunni propaganda. Not the stuff of nightmares. But it went on. The table reappeared. The bucket of water sat alone now. Until the gloved hands reached out, set a baby boy beside it. An infant, black-haired, black-eyed, naked, newly circumcised, his skin light Persian brown. He wriggled. He opened his mouth, screamed soundlessly at the camera. The gloved hands picked him up, carried him toward the bucket —

And the video ended.

What had happened to that boy? Ayoub wanted to believe that whoever had made the video had put him down after the camera was off. Maybe he was a prop, not Shia at all. But Ayoub knew these Sunnis. They had turned from Allah. Hezbollah could be cruel, but never without reason. Never with the joy the desert Arabs took in the suffering they inflicted.

They weren't beasts. They were something worse, men with the souls of beasts.

And one had held that boy under the water until he drowned. In a basement somewhere in Syria or Iraq, a laptop held the truth. On nights when the wind stirred the dust in the Bekaa and kept him from sleeping, Ayoub promised himself that one day he'd find that computer and the man who owned it.

So, yes, Hezbollah had sent men to fight with Assad. As had Iran. The Iranians were

354

Shia, too, the most powerful Shia nation by far. Naturally, Iran worked with Hezbollah. It gave the group seventy million dollars a year, trained Ayoub's soldiers at bases outside Tehran, snuck freighters loaded with weapons through the Suez Canal and past the Israeli coast to Beirut.

And eight days before, when an Iranian friend of Ayoub's sent a courier to tell him they needed to meet in Beirut, *now*, that very hour, Ayoub didn't hesitate. He canceled his meetings, locked his phones in his desk, grabbed an old Honda motorcycle for the ride over the Dahr al Baydar pass into Beirut. He would make this trip with no guards. He preferred two wheels when he traveled alone.

The Iranian was a senior officer in the Quds Force, the foreign intelligence arm of the Revolutionary Guard. A very senior officer. He reported directly to Qassem Suleimani, who ran Quds. He called himself Ali, though Ayoub couldn't be sure that was his name. They had met twice before. Both times Ali asked for help in Syria. Both times Ayoub agreed, sending more than a thousand paramilitaries. Ali didn't explicitly promise what Hezbollah would receive in return. But weeks later, Hezbollah's charities took in millions of dollars from Iranian expatriates in Europe.

On this third trip, Ayoub parked his motorcycle outside an apartment building in Haret Hreik, a crowded suburb south of downtown Beirut. Ayoub had never seen the building before. Each meeting with Ali happened at a different safe house. Not that Hezbollah would be foolish enough to try to monitor Ali's comings and goings. And not that any other faction in Lebanon had any idea who he was. Ayoub knew how dearly Ali prized his anonymity. The Jews or the Americans would pay dearly for him if they stumbled across him.

Ali was small, hollow-cheeked, in his fifties. He had close-cropped salt-and-pepper hair, a neat beard. He dressed modestly, Western-style, button-down shirts and sneakers. He hadn't wasted time with small talk in their earlier meetings, and he didn't today. No offers of tea or platters of hummus and big green olives.

"I need your help. Hezbollah's help."

"Of course."

"This is about the Americans. As you can imagine. You saw the President's speech?"

Twenty-four hours before, the United States had brazenly attacked the airport at the center of Tehran. Then the President gave Iran two weeks to open its borders or face invasion.

"Of course."

"What he says, it's a lie. He stares at the camera, lies to the whole world. I swear to you."

"They lie always."

In fact, Ayoub wasn't sure the President had lied. Iran kept its nuclear strategy secret even from Hezbollah. Only a few people in Tehran knew the truth. Maybe the Iranians were trying to smuggle a bomb into America. So be it. Some part of Ayoub *hoped* that the President was telling the truth. Let the people in Washington or New York fear an Iranian bomb. The Americans were no friends of Hezbollah. They called Ayoub and his men terrorists. Never mind that Hezbollah ran medical clinics and handed out food all over Lebanon.

Worse, the United States sent billions of dollars to Israel every year, money the Jews used to buy jets and tanks to invade Lebanon. Worst of all, the United States fed the carnage in Syria.

"Why do you think the Americans have done this?" Ayoub said.

"Isn't it obvious? They want an excuse to attack us. We have too much power for them. They're angry about Iraq, how we outsmarted them. They fight a war to over-throw Saddam Hussein, replace him with their friends. Instead, the Shia take over." Meaning one who did what Iran wanted. "They see now in Syria their choices are Assad or the Islamic State, and they hate that they must work with us to help Assad. So they make this up."

"To go to so much trouble —"

· "They know their people are tired of war. They need a reason to send their soldiers against us."

The explanation made sense to Ayoub. Which didn't mean it was true.

"And you can't open your doors, prove to the world it's a lie."

"Ayoub, if the Jews said that Hezbollah was making bombs to blow up the Qubbat al-Sakhrah" — the Dome of the Rock, the holy shrine that sat atop the Temple Mount in Jerusalem —

"I understand."

"That they would blow up your camps un-less you let them in —"

"We would never agree."

"Just so. We'll fill the streets with martyrs before we do what they ask." Ali leaned close enough for Ayoub to smell the mint tea on his breath.

"What, then?"

"They must know the price they'll pay if they keep on this path."

Now they reached the heart of the matter. Ali explained what he wanted, and where. He would provide the surface-to-air missiles in Mumbai, Ayoub the men. Hezbollah had no shortage of soldiers trained to use SAMs. Missiles were its best defense against the Israeli air force.

The mission disturbed Ayoub, though not for the obvious reason. He didn't question the morality of blowing up this plane. A couple hundred innocents would die. So be it. The Syrian war killed more civilians than that every week. No, Ayoub's concern was tactical. He didn't see why Ali didn't just use his own men. But he couldn't ask directly. Ali was polite enough to phrase his orders as requests, but he was the master in this room. Hezbollah depended on Iranian support to survive.

Instead of asking Ali directly, Ayoub tried a different tack. "You're sure my men can do this? Without advance training."

"Did you have training when you walked up to those Jews in Tyre?"

"I knew their post. I'd watched them all night. These men, they've never been to India, much less Mumbai. The airport must have security."

"The airport, yes. But the slums are around it, and police there, they're too lazy to go inside. Not even for bribes. Trust me. I've been there. Your men come tonight. My officer meets them. Walks them through the slum, shows them where to set up. No missiles. Tomorrow afternoon, they come back in daylight to see for themselves. Then, tomorrow night, they bring the missiles, they aim —" Ali raised his hands, hoisting an imaginary surface-to-air missile launcher. He cocked his head to look through the sight, squeezed the trigger. "Just like you and those Jews, Ayoub. Only a bigger explosion at the end."

Ali sounded almost wistful.

"And your man can't do it?"

"Better if he's not there."

So he wouldn't be caught when the Americans went crazy afterward. "And my men? Do you get them out after? Or is that up to me?"

"Neither."

Ayoub needed a few seconds to realize what Ali meant.

"You want them caught? But when the Americans see they're Lebanese —" Then Ayoub understood the game. Ali was playing both sides. He wanted the United States to know that Iran had ordered the shooting.

But he didn't want to give it proof. He, or his boss Suleimani, wanted the flexibility to deny Iran's involvement. The Iranians used proxies whenever they could. Though *puppets* might be a better word.

Ayoub remembered a saying of his father's: *When a mouse mocks a cat, you can be sure there's a hole nearby.* For this mission the Iranians had chosen Hezbollah as the hole. But Ayoub wouldn't waste his breath protesting. "My friend, if this is what you want, my men will be proud to help."

"You have someone in mind."

"Yes." Two cousins who ran a truck-repair shop in Baalbek. Jafar and Haider. Late twenties and fearless. Ayoub wondered what to tell them. Only bare outlines, and nothing about Ali, of course. They were smart enough to figure out for themselves that Iran was behind the mission.

But he would have to make sure they knew they wouldn't be coming home.

"I think through Dubai is the shortest route," Ali said. "MEA" — Middle East Airlines, the national Lebanese carrier — "has a flight at two p.m. Then Emirates to Mumbai."

Telling, not asking.

"Done. Once they land in Mumbai, they're yours."

"And clean phones, of course."

"I'll get your courier the numbers. Anything more, my brother?"

"Later this week. Five more teams."

Five more pairs of soldiers? Five more *planes*? Ayoub's mask of civility must have dropped for half a second. Ali grabbed Ayoub's wrist. "All right?"

"Of course. Will these be" — Ayoub hesitated — "active missions?"

"Not yet."

Ninety minutes later, at a supermarket two kilometers from Hariri International Airport, Ayoub met Jafar and Haider. As he'd expected, they came without question when he called. And they didn't flinch when he described the mission.

"An American jet," Jafar, the older cousin, said. His meaning was clear enough. *The Americans have this coming.*

Ayoub didn't expect the cousins to escape capture for long, but he gave them six thousand dollars and told them to hide, come back to the Bekaa Valley once the pressure lifted. They laughed.

"When they find us, do we tell them that this was a Hezbollah action?" Jafar asked.

"Yes." The Americans would know the truth anyway.

"Good."

The next night, the reports came in from India. They'd lit the sky with United 49.

Ayoub sent a third man to Mumbai, too, a truly clean operative who could travel on a Turkish passport. Not to help the other two, just to walk the streets and watch the local television channels so Ayoub might have a few minutes of advance word when they were caught. But the cousins managed better than he'd expected. A week passed with no word of their arrest. Ayoub wondered if the Americans had snatched them in secret.

He heard nothing from Ali, either. Probably the man wasn't even in Lebanon.

Meanwhile, he had other concerns. That morning, the Syrian Minister of Defense had called to tell him that the Sunnis were preparing a major offensive. No surprise, they figured a potential war with the United States might distract Iran from helping the Syrian government. The minister asked Ayoub to send another two thousand men. Ayoub put him off, spent the day debating with his deputies what course to recommend to Sayyed Nasrallah, Hezbollah's ultimate leader. If America invaded Iran, Hezbollah would be on its own. Maybe this wasn't the moment to risk fighters he might need to defend Hezbollah's own territory from the IDF.

The debate was exhausting. They all felt the pressure of war rising. Finally, after dinner, Ayoub sent his men home. The choice was ultimately Nasrallah's anyway.

Ayoub arrived at 10 p.m. to a dark house, his wife Rima and their five children asleep. Rather than wake her, he pulled out the cot in his office. He could have slept on a stone pillow this night. He closed his eyes —

Bees surrounded him, buzzing wildly. He pulled himself from the dream, reached for his phone. His fourth phone, the least used and most important. Even Rima didn't have the number. It was one of six that Hezbollah's most senior commanders used to send one another coded text messages, a way to set meetings when they didn't have time to rely on couriers.

Adhan Habibi, Nasrallah's second deputy and his top military advisor, had sent the message. It consisted of the first five words of the fifth verse of the Quran's first Surah: *You alone do we worship . . .* A few seconds later, another message popped up from the same phone: *10059.*

The system was simple. The first message set the meeting's location, in this case a disused warehouse fifteen kilometers west of Baalbek, near the town of Zahle. Habibi and Ayoub had met there once before. The commanders had five pre-agreed meeting sites, each signaled by a different Quranic verse. The second message set the time: one hour from now. *One hour . . . fifty-nine minutes . . .*

It was 1:45 a.m. Ayoub had no idea why Habibi would call a meeting so late, but when they created the system, they agreed never to question these summonses. They all knew that the more they used the phones, the more vulnerable they would be to American and Israeli spies. Ayoub would have to trust that Habibi had a good reason to ask for him.

Ayoub rubbed the sleep from his eyes, washed his hands and face. In his bedroom he pulled on a light jacket and the hundred-euro Adidas sneakers that were his only indulgence. He had fifty pairs, in every conceivable color.

His wife snored lightly, her arms cradled around their youngest daughter. He wished Rima wouldn't keep the girl in their bed, but his wife didn't care. *I need something warm to hold when you're not around.* He kissed her cheek. She mumbled his name but didn't wake.

He walked through the lemon grove that separated his house from the outbuildings where his driver and personal guards lived. A cool wind rustled the empty branches, and a low ceiling of gray clouds obscured the stars. This night's watchman was the weakest of Ayoub's men, a dullard named Hamid. He sat on a folding chair, his eyes focused on what seemed to be an Arabic translation of a vampire novel. Not exactly full combat readiness. Ayoub crept close, tossed a pebble, hitting Hamid in the arm. He grabbed his rifle and jumped, the book sliding off his lap. Ayoub had never seen him move so fast.

"Halt!" His eyes opened wide as he looked at his commander. "Sir?"

"Vampires, Hamid?"

Hamid bowed his head, as if the paperback would become a Quran if he stared at it long enough.

"We'll talk about that later. Wake the others. We have a meeting in Zahle."

Baalbek was dark, its streets empty, its eighty thousand inhabitants tucked away until dawn. At the Hezbollah guard post that watched the intersection of the Beirut and Tripoli roads, Ayoub's two-car convoy stopped only long enough to be waved through. Twenty minutes later, they reached the dirt lot behind the warehouse.

A lemon grove had once sat behind this building, but a mysterious blight had hit the trees years before. The farmer who owned the orchard had burned it to keep the sickness from spreading. Now charred stumps covered the fields, speckled with a few taller trunks that had survived the fire. Hamid wandered into the field, then pulled back, like a scared child.

"You want vampires, go that way." Ayoub pointed east. Toward the Anti-Lebanon range, the low mountains that split the Bekaa from Syria and the brutal fighters of the Islamic State.

"Sir?"

"If you weren't so useless, I'd send you there now."

The inside of the warehouse still smelled faintly of lemons. Ayoub's lantern revealed a space twenty meters by forty. Empty crates lined the walls, awaiting the day when the groves were replanted. Ayoub's guards waited by the door. He'd waved them off when they tried to follow him inside. He needed a few minutes to himself. He'd beaten Habibi here. No surprise. Habibi lived in West Beirut, an apartment overlooking the Mediterranean. After the 2006 invasion, Hezbollah had decided that not all of its leaders should live in the Bekaa Valley, its strongest territory but also the easiest to blockade.

Fifteen minutes passed before tires crunched on the gravel outside. At least four vehicles. Through the open warehouse door, Ayoub glimpsed their lights. Suddenly, he worried he'd made a mistake coming here. Maybe a Maronite hit squad had somehow cracked their code. Then he heard his men shouting greetings at Habibi's guards.

He walked outside as Habibi's men poured out. Habibi never traveled without at least a dozen guards. He was in the middle of the scrum, a heavy man with a beard too dark to be anything but dyed. He pushed his way through his guards, reached out for Ayoub.

"Hussein."

"Habibi. *Habibi!*"

"Habibi," Habibi said. A minor joke. *Habibi* translated into "friend." "You drag me out of bed, over the pass in the middle of the night. This better be important."

"I dragged *you* out? It's the opposite, my friend." He reached for his phone. "Look, look —"

But Habibi was already pulling out his own phone —

Both men realized at once.

"NSA."

"NSA."

Ayoub's stomach lurched. He had mis-judged his enemy, underestimated its cunning. He hadn't known what he didn't know. Just like those Israeli soldiers in Tyre. For a moment, he felt their anguish —

Habibi pushed him away, turned for his Toyota. "Go —"

Two miles overhead, two F-22A Raptor stealth fighters looped, hidden from the ground by the clouds and from Lebanon's air-defense systems by their radar-defeating composite skins.

The Air Force had initially envisioned the Raptor as a pure air-combat fighter. But aerial dogfights were in short supply these days. The Raptor had a three-hundred-sixty-million-dollar price tag and not enough to do. So the Air Force had modified the jet's missile bays to carry a pair of thousand-pound bombs. With stealth a priority for this operation, the Raptors were the natural choice.

The jets took off at 0130 from Incirlik, the giant NATO base in southeastern Turkey, on what was pegged as a routine night-training flight. They flew south over the

Mediterranean until they were fifty kilometers northwest of Beirut, then east over the Mount Lebanon range, the mountains that separated the coast from the Bekaa Valley. After crossing the mountains, they made a ninety-degree right turn, south again.

The Raptor could reach nearly Mach 2 with its afterburners at full power, but these jets flew at four hundred knots. No need to speed. They had time, and if radar did scrape them they'd get less attention flying slowly.

But neither plane picked up a hint that it had been painted. No surprise. The Raptor's twenty-year-old technology was no longer unbeatable. China and Russia had developed radar systems powerful enough to pick up its electronic traces. But the F-22A's magic still worked in Lebanon.

At 0210, the jets reached the target — named Tango United, an unsubtle reference to the reason for the mission. They would have to stay in Lebanese airspace at least thirty minutes. But since Israel had the only jets within two hundred miles remotely capable of engaging an F-22A, having to stay on station a few extra minutes shouldn't matter.

The Raptors weren't the only planes the Air Force had sent to Lebanon. As Ayoub left his compound and headed for the warehouse, an Avenger drone followed. The Avenger was the newest drone in the American fleet, a major advance over the Predator and Reaper. Unlike its predecessors, the Avenger was powered with a jet engine. It could fly eighteen hundred miles at twice the speed of the propeller drones, without producing the distinctive mosquito-like buzz that jihadis all over the world now recognized — and ran from.

The Avenger didn't carry bombs or missiles. But its payload was arguably even more lethal: the newest radar, cameras, and electronics intercept systems in the American arsenal. Now it was flying at four thousand feet, inside a thick cloud layer, so its optical cameras were no use. But it didn't need them. Nestled in its wings were two infrared cameras sensitive enough to track the heat signature of a groundhog in a burrow, much less a man in a basement. In its tail was a radar system whose software could monitor two hundred different targets simultaneously.

But the Avenger's most important tracking device was the three-foot dimpled sphere that hung below its composite belly. The ball was an electromagnetic sniffer as powerful as sixty-five cell phone towers. It could be used only when the Avenger was airborne. On the ground it emitted enough radiation to cause permanent damage. It was so precise that it could distinguish the signature of an iPhone from a Samsung Galaxy at a mile away. The Air Force techs who serviced the Avenger called it the Great Ball of Death.

Ayoub thought he'd taken adequate precautions. He thought he was safe.

He had all the protection of an ant under a magnifying glass.

The brave new world of drone warfare had pushed tricky technical issues on the Air Force. Foremost among them was the fact that drones were controlled through encrypted satellite links, while fighter pilots mostly radioed to local bases or E-3 Sentries that were effectively airborne command posts. Called AWACS — Airborne Warning and Control System — the E-3s were modified Boeing 707s instantly recognizable by the thirty-foot radar domes attached to their fuselages. The satellite and radio networks didn't overlap. As the Air Force integrated drones into its fleet, the need for real-time links between drone controllers and fighter jocks became more obvious by the day. The service was now installing drone workstations in the cabins of five E-3 Sentries, a tricky and expensive proposition. The first retrofit had been finished only a few weeks before to a Sentry that was flying a slow loop one hundred kilometers off the coast of Beirut.

For the first time ever, a drone pilot was actually airborne.

The Avenger had arrived at Ayoub's house a few minutes before the NSA spoofed the phones belonging to Ayoub and Habibi. The Hezbollah commanders had made one crucial mistake. They'd believed that they could risk leaving the phones on as long as they didn't use them. They were wrong. Twelve months before, an analyst at Fort Meade had noticed an odd coincidence, a series of phones with sequential numbers that were rarely used but popped up only in houses and offices belonging to Hezbollah's most senior leaders.

Ayoub and the other Hezbollah commanders used the phones to set up only a handful of meetings in the year that followed. But the connection was obvious once the NSA looked, the code even more so. The Quranic verses were not encrypted, merely correlated with meeting sites.

The broken coms system neatly solved the issue of how to kill Ayoub and Habibi without civilian casualties — a problem acute in the case of Habibi, who lived in a fifteen-story apartment building filled with families and who surrounded himself with women and children in his rare public appearances. As a bonus, the operation would grab the attention of Hezbollah and Quds Force in a way that a simpler bombing would not. At its best, the NSA's technical wizardry came off as nearly Godlike, and not every commander in Baalbek or Tehran contemplated his own mortality with as much detachment as Ayoub. This mission would send the message clearly: *Worry less about* Allah *and more about* America, *habibis.*

Meanwhile, if Ayoub and Habibi no longer used the phones or had switched to a more sophisticated code, they simply wouldn't leave their houses. No harm.

But the messages did the trick. Eight minutes after Ayoub received his, the Avenger's sensors spotted a man leaving his house. Seven minutes after that, it picked up two cars leaving the compound. The Avenger then took the only real chance of the operation, dropping below the cloud layer for eleven seconds, long enough to get its optics on the convoy. At Langley and the Pentagon, analysts agreed they were looking at Ayoub. A few seconds later, the Sentry's coms officer radioed the Raptors.

"Tiger 1, Tiger 2, this is Sorcerer. We have confirmation on Alpha." Ayoub. "Repeat, Alpha has left his nest."

"Copy. ETA to our station?"

"Fifteen to eighteen minutes. Two vehicles. Small arms only, no SAMs."

"Copy. Fifteen to eighteen. We are at eleven thousand, all quiet. Anything to the east?"

A few seconds of silence, then: "Nothing unusual." The radar dome atop the E-3 could see all the way across Syria. If it wasn't picking up Syrian jets, the Syrians didn't have any jets in the air to pick up.

"Good to hear. Any word on Beta?" Habibi.

"Tiger 1, you read my mind. We have just received visual confirm that Beta has left his nest. Four vehicles, approximately fifteen men. ETA thirty-five minutes. Small arms only." The report came not from the Avenger but from a CIA spotter in Beirut, the only American on the ground in the whole operation. Unlike Baalbek, Beirut was big and dense and easy for watchers.

"Copy. Beta arrival at zero-two-four-five local. Breaking off."

"Roger that, Tiger 1."

Then the pilots had nothing to do but wait. Tad Easterman, Tiger 1's pilot, had eight years' experience in the Raptor. As a technical challenge for him, this mission was right up there with a stadium overflight. In fact, stadium overflights were trickier. He was flying in circles waiting to drop satellite-guided bombs on a target that he would never see firsthand. Part of him wanted to break the cloud layer so that he'd at least have eyes on the men below. Instead, he focused on his displays and made himself stay as patient as a hunter in a blind.

Fifteen minutes later, right on schedule, Easterman picked up Ayoub's convoy on his air-to-ground radar and infrared sensors. The F-22A's downward-facing systems were less advanced than the Avenger's, but the road was empty. Easterman had no problem spotting the two cars speeding east on the road that led past the warehouse. He watched as the vehicles parked behind the building and men stepped out.

"Sorcerer, Tiger 1 here. I have Alpha at the target. That your read?"

"Roger that, Tiger 1. Avenger agrees Alpha has reached your location."

"Copy. We'll stand by for Beta and your green. Breaking off."

Nineteen minutes later, Easterman's radar picked up four blips speeding toward the warehouse, this time coming from Beirut.

"Sorcerer, this is Tiger 1. I have four more vehicles on Route Chicago —" The name the Air Force had assigned to the road that passed the warehouse.

"Roger that, Tiger 1. Avenger agrees. ETA is sixty seconds. Tiger 1 and Tiger 2, you are green as soon as Beta reaches Tango United."

Back at Incirlik, the briefers had explained that Ayoub and Habibi would recognize what had happened within a few seconds after they met. Thus the Raptors needed to be ready to drop their bombs as soon as the second convoy reached the lot behind the warehouse.

"Copy. Tiger 2?"

"Copy."

Easterman waited another fifteen seconds, then shoved the yoke forward, aiming to bring his Raptor down to five thousand feet in a decreasing-radius loop around the warehouse. The next few seconds were the only technically tricky part of the mission. He would be in a steep dive when he dropped the bombs in the Raptor's bays, to minimize their forward momentum relative to the stationary target below.

The bombs could and would guide themselves after release. But unlike missiles, they didn't have their own engines, so Easterman had a narrow window for the drop. For this mission, the bombs had been preprogrammed with the location of the warehouse. Unless he retargeted them, the software that controlled them wouldn't let him release them without what Air Force engineers called a "true path" to the target, a route that didn't violate the laws of physics. Easterman couldn't do that math, but his on-board computers could. At the same time, the Raptor couldn't be fully vertical at release, or else the bombs wouldn't clear their bays. Ideally, he would have the Raptor in a fifty- to fifty-five-degree dive as he dropped the bombs.

Fortunately for Easterman, air-to-air combat required exactly these sorts of maneuvers, and the F-22A handled them as well as any jet that had ever been built. For the next few seconds, Easterman and the Raptor were in perfect harmony. The plane weighed twenty tons and had a forty-four-foot wingspan, yet it anticipated his moves as nimbly as his four-hundred-pound sportbike. Meanwhile, his ground-facing radar showed the convoy slowing, turning left around the warehouse. Another left and they were in the lot behind the building. Men poured out, glowing on his infrared monitor.

"Sorcerer, we are green. Target acquired. Engaging."

The two Raptors carried four bombs, four thousand pounds of high explosive in all. The two convoys on the ground below totaled six vehicles, all standard civilian, no armor or blast-resistant windows. They were parked in a lot about one hundred twenty feet long and fifty wide. The laws of physics were brutal and simple. The Pentagon planners who simulated the attack reported odds of 99.2 percent that everyone in the target zone would die, whether they were on the ground or still inside a vehicle. *As for the 0.8 percent, you don't want to be that guy,* the lead planner said. *Unless you like skin grafts.*

Easterman reached for a two-inch-high joystick on the console above his right knee, pushed it up and right like he was switching gears on a manual transmission. The heads-up display inside his helmet flashed yellow. The bomb was armed. Then green. The software agreed that the bomb could hit its preprogrammed target. Easterman thumbed the red button on top of the joystick for two seconds. The Raptor tugged slightly as the right missile bay slid open and a thousand-pound bomb released. Easterman pulled the joystick down and left, pushed the button again. His left missile bay opened. The second bomb dropped out. The plane immediately felt lighter and more agile. He leveled out, swung the Raptor north. The hard part, such as it was, was over.

"Sorcerer, this is Tiger 1. GBUs out."

"Tiger 2 here," the second Raptor pilot chimed in. "GBUs out."

The letters stood for Guided Bomb Unit. Each bomb carried a Global Positioning System receiver and a package of software, gyroscopes, and motion sensors. The gyroscopes and sensors predicted the bomb's direction in real time. The software controlled motorized fins on the bomb's tail to guide the bomb to the coordinates preprogrammed into the GPS.

The bombs were shockingly accurate. Ninety-six percent of the time, they landed within ten feet of their target coordinates. Even in crowded cities, they had sharply reduced civilian casualties. Tonight civilians weren't an issue. No one lived within a quarter mile of the warehouse. A bomb dropped from an aircraft in level flight required eighteen seconds to fall five thousand feet. But these bombs had a head start, because the Raptor had released them in a dive. Easterman dropped them almost exactly as Ayoub and Habibi realized the trap. They had seven seconds of warning.

Theoretically, the men on the ground might have survived if they had reacted immediately. A fit man could sprint as far as fifty meters in seven seconds, enough under ideal circumstances to escape the worst of the blast wave. But in the real world almost no one had the situational awareness to take off at a full run with no warning. And the bigger the group, the more time required for the warning to spread and men to get out of each other's way.

Ayoub had time to hear a high whistle, and then another and another. The men around him looked at one another, processed the danger, scattered, running in every direction, a starburst pattern, an uncanny echo of the blast wave that was about to hit. Ayoub made for the lemon grove, hoping somehow that he'd find safety in the burned stumps —

■ ■ ■ ■

As they'd been programmed to do, the bombs landed in a one-hundred-twenty-degree arc centered on the back door of the warehouse. The Pentagon's simulators had predicted that configuration would produce maximum lethality. It did. Four superheated overpressure waves tore through the parking lot, each moving faster than the speed of sound, powerful enough to tear through metal and glass, hot enough to incinerate anything they touched. Seventeen of the eighteen men in the parking lot died instantly, twelve cut into pieces barely recognizable as human. Ayoub ran farther and faster than anyone else. The blast picked him up, tore the skin off his back, threw him twenty-five feet. For just a moment, he thought he'd survived. He might have, too, if not for a freakish bit of bad luck. He landed headfirst on a stump and cracked his neck. A million buzzing honeybees filled his brain and then, *Inshàllah* —

Easterman wished he could check the damage for himself. But the briefers at Incirlik had said in no uncertain terms they wanted the Raptors out of Lebanese airspace as soon as possible after the mission was done. So he and Tiger 2 set a course northwest at twenty-five thousand feet, Mach 0.98. No sonic booms tonight, please.

The after-action survey came from the Avenger. The drone descended to two thousand feet, below the cloud layer, for a brief live feed of the carnage below. Its cameras picked up only six bodies, but the fact that the others had vanished didn't surprise anyone. Five of the six vehicles in the convoy were pulverized past recognition, and the back half of the warehouse had collapsed. After two quick passes over the site, the drone pulled back to five thousand feet and made another loop, this one wider. Anyone who had escaped would have to be on foot or hiding inside the warehouse, leaving an obvious signature on radar or the infrared cameras. But the Avenger found nothing. The analysts and drone pilot agreed. Eighteen enemy killed in action, no wounded, no survivors, no friendly casualties. Success.

The President didn't watch the mission. He was eating dinner with his wife and kids. He wanted the illusion of normalcy for at least a few minutes. The White House chef seemed to have caught his mood. Tonight's meal was spaghetti and meatballs with a simple tossed salad.

The President was just tucking into his second meatball when his steward stepped into the dining room, phone in hand. "Sir. I have Ms. Green."

"Donna."

"I'm sorry to interrupt you, sir."

"I asked you to." He had told her to call as soon as the bombs hit.

"It's done. We count eighteen red KIA. Including Ayoub and Habibi. No survivors."

"Anything I need to worry about?"

"No, sir. The Raptors are en route to Incirlik."

"And you're sure we got them."

"Unless they had a teleporter."

In the past, these missions had knotted the President's stomach. He didn't love playing judge and jury. He wanted to believe the best about his enemies, that they might disagree with America's intentions but that they shared the same morals and values.

Not tonight. Green had briefed him on Ayoub's background, how he'd killed the IDF soldiers in 2006. No surprise the man was happy to do Tehran's foul bidding, destroy a jet filled with innocent people from a dozen different countries. The world was better off without him.

"Good. Please congratulate the team on my behalf. All the way down."

"Yes, sir."

"I'll see you tomorrow morning."

His steward took the phone and vanished.

"Everything okay?" his wife said. Dinner was supposed to be a bubble for her, too.

"Sorry about that."

"No calls at dinner, Daddy," his daughter said.

"You're right."

The President looked around the table at his family and, not for the first time, considered how lucky he was.

More than lucky. Blessed.

16
FOUR DAYS . . .

WADI ARABA CROSSING, ISRAEL–
JORDAN BORDER

Israel and Jordan had signed a peace treaty in 1994, making Jordan the second Arab state to recognize Israel's right to exist. But the end of war didn't make the countries the best of friends. Israel still closed its borders to millions of Palestinian refugees that Jordan desperately wanted to send back to Israel. And Israel knew that Jordan's rulers had agreed to peace for practical reasons rather than any love for the concept of a Jewish state.

The Wadi Araba border station between the Jordanian resort town of Aqaba and its Israeli counterpart Eilat reflected that wariness. Hundreds of tourists crossed each day, many on their way from Eilat to Petra, the ancient rock city in the Jordanian desert that had provided the spectacular backdrop for *Raiders of the Lost Ark.*

But neither side allowed vehicles registered in the opposite country on its roads. To cross, tourists had to trudge across hundreds of meters of empty blacktop hemmed in by high fences as bored soldiers watched. The scene was half Checkpoint Charlie, half baggage claim. The stations themselves were blocky concrete buildings, ugly and utilitarian, though the Jordanian side included a souvenir shop for any traveler who had somehow escaped Petra with a few dinars.

Now Wells walked past the hookahs inside the shop's dusty windows and handed his passport to the final border guard. After his troubles in Russia, part of him expected another hassle. But the guard merely nodded and handed back his passport. Wells stepped past a white-lettered blue sign that read "The Hashemite Kingdom of Jordan Good Bye," the broken English oddly pleasant, and entered the no-man's-land.

He had the walk west to himself. The checkpoint had just opened. Everyone else was heading the other direction, looking forward to a day among the ruins. Wells felt a little like Petra himself, battered and eroded but still standing.

The day before, in Lubyanka, a splash of

cold water had woken him. He opened his eyes to find his interrogator smirking, a bucket in her hand. "Wake up, pretty. It's nearly two."

So she'd let him sleep. A kindness Wells hadn't expected, and the reason he felt halfway human. Though he realized he was famished. He hadn't eaten properly since the dinner at Buvchenko's mansion the night before last. Too bad he wouldn't have a chance at those *pelmeni* again.

She threw him his jeans and shirt and boxers and stood in the doorway as he pulled on his clothes. Let her look. Let her do whatever she wanted, as long as she let him go.

"So many scars," she said.

Mostly on his back, where the surgeons had saved him after Omar Khadri shot him. He hadn't thought of Khadri in a long time. The living left the dead behind. For a while.

"Want to touch them?"

"Broken bones, too. I see where they've healed. Though they never fully heal, do they?"

Her fortune-cookie psychoanalysis irritated him. "I assume you're not getting me dressed to leave me in here."

"Domodedovo."

Again. "Didn't think that word could

388

sound so good."

On the ride to the airport she told him that Duto had backed his story, and the FSB had decided keeping him wouldn't be worth the trouble. "I told him you'd missed somehow your flight yesterday," she said, the misplaced word making her sound more Russian than she had the night before. "That you'd taken sick and we brought you to the hospital, but you felt much better now. He asked you to buy a ticket to Amman. There's a flight this afternoon, a nonstop."

Amman. Jordan. *Why?* But Wells didn't bother to ask. Duto would never have told this woman. Wells wondered if the United States and Iran had moved closer to war in the last day and a half, or if, perhaps, Duto or Shafer had made progress. By the time he reached Amman, the sun would be down. Another day wasted. Three lost in Russia. Before that, two in Saudi Arabia. By the morning, they would be less than one hundred hours from the President's deadline —

Wells stopped himself. Obsessing over the ticking clock wouldn't help. Besides, maybe Shafer had found the uranium already. Wells could imagine Shafer's glee. *Yeah, I just Googled "HEU where to buy" and there it was.*

389

Domodedovo was déjà vu all over again, the same business travelers and rich kids, the same blue-uniformed paramilitaries giving Wells the stink-eye. Wells bought a ticket on Royal Jordanian and his interrogator led him to a VIP line at the exit station. After a ten-second conversation and a flashed badge, the border guard nodded and stamped Wells's passport.

They sat in silence at the gate until boarding began.

"Before you go, want to tell me the truth? Why you were here?"

"Looking for a pony."

"Stand."

He did. She reached between his legs, wrapped her fingers around his crotch, squeezed. He wasn't sure if she was trying to hurt or arouse him. Maybe both. "You're still in my country. Be polite."

"Bad touching." Wells peeled off her hand.

"You know, some of us wanted to kill you. Dump you in the forest like those Poles." The Katyn Wood massacre. In 1940, on Stalin's orders, the NKVD, the predecessor to the KGB, had executed thousands of defenseless Polish prisoners of war.

"No man, no problem," Wells said. One of Stalin's most famous sayings: *Death solves all problems. No man, no problem.*

"I told them, no, a little girl like you, not even worth the bullet."

"Thanks for the vote of confidence." Wells turned away.

She reached for his shoulder, twisted him toward her, hissed in his ear.

"Don't come back to Russia, Mr. Wells."

In Amman, he called Duto from a fresh prepaid mobile.

"Fun trip?"

Wells didn't curse much, but he was sorely tempted. "The best."

"I don't suppose I get any thanks for bailing you out."

Now he did curse, potently and in Arabic.

"Don't know what that means, but I'm guessing *Miss you sweetheart.* Sounds like you didn't suffer any permanent damage."

Wells didn't see any reason to answer.

"Get anything?" Duto said after a few seconds.

"Bumped into my buddy from Istanbul. We had a nice chat. She's sweet as ever."

"How about a photo?"

"Maybe." Wells wondered if Nemkov, the narcotics colonel, had sent the surveillance shots of Salome from the hotel. He'd check as soon as he could find a semi-safe Internet connection. A photo would get them

Salome's real name and new paths to chase.

"What does *maybe* mean?"

"It means maybe."

"Your friend have anything to say?"

"Nothing we didn't know." Aside from the threat to his family. "Heather and Evan —"

"They're fine."

Wells felt a weight real as a barbell come off his shoulders. "Thank you."

"Thank Robin." Meaning Shafer.

"Tell me we're making progress, I'm in Jordan for a reason."

"Just getting to that. Someone wants to meet you at the Wadi Araba border crossing. That's down in Aqaba, by the Red Sea. The Israeli side. Eight a.m. tomorrow. He's not well, so don't make him wait."

Meaning Rudi, Duto's old friend, the former chief of the Mossad. It was now past 9 p.m. in Amman, and Aqaba was several hours south. Another long night.

"You know what he has?"

"No. But I know we have something to ask him, too. Call Robin. He'll explain."

"Anything else?"

"I think that's it."

Wells hung up without saying good-bye and called Shafer.

"Your Audi 5000?"

Shafer was showing his age. Audi hadn't

made that model in decades.

"They told me not to come back to Mother Russia, and I think that's advice I'm going to take."

"You'll always have your memories."

Wells could only laugh.

"I saw your favorite hoops player, by the way. And his mommy. They're fine. Staying put, and they seem safe."

"Vinny told me. He also told me you had something for me."

"You know who you're meeting tomorrow?"

"I think so."

"Ask him what he knows about a deal his people made a few years back to bring in stuff from South Africa."

"I assume we're talking about the stuff we've been looking for."

"No, we're talking about contraband Viagra," Shafer said.

"Point taken. Why South Africa?"

"I think closed programs may be our best bet, and they got the furthest."

Wells couldn't argue the logic. "You know how much?"

"I have on good authority it was just over fifteen kilos. Fifteen point three, to be exact. The guy on the RSA side was named Rand Witwans."

"I'll ask."

"Stay cool."

"As a cucumber."

The only cabbie in all of Amman willing to take Wells to Aqaba in the dark had a lazy eye and a habit of steering with his knees. The ride on the Desert Highway proved more frightening than the previous night in Lubyanka. Still, they arrived in Aqaba intact a little past midnight. Despite the lateness of the hour, the town bustled with European and Arab tourists. Wells found an Internet café, emailed Evan and Heather asking for patience. Then he logged on to the account he'd given Nemkov.

There it was.

A photo of Salome and her bodyguard, sent from a Yahoo account in the name of Roger Bishop, Wells's own pseudonym. The quality was better than Wells expected, Salome's face clear. Nemkov had cropped it so it couldn't be directly identified as having come from the hotel, but still he'd taken an enormous risk. *I am not sure why but I trust you,* the message said. Volgograd hadn't been a dead end after all. Wells would show the photo to Rudi in the morning. The Mossad and the other Israeli security services were tiny by American standards. If Salome had been part of them, Rudi would know her.

Now Wells walked through the empty space where Israel met Jordan, toward two men who stood at the gate at the edge of the Israeli border station. They could have been a diorama representing the stages of life, the first a soldier, young and strapping, the second withered, barely holding himself upright. As Wells walked close, the second man stepped into the neutral zone, extended a dry hand to Wells.

"Rudi. You're a legend." In truth, Wells knew very little about Ari Rudin or the Mossad. He'd never operated in Israel.

"Save it. I'm not dead." Rudi brought a hand to his mouth, began the impossible process of clearing his throat. "Yet. Since we're such friends, let me ask you a question. How would you spend your last few weeks? Family? Skydiving? Lying on the beach looking at the beautiful girls you'll never see in the afterlife? Apologizing for your sins?"

Wells had never heard the question posed quite so baldly. The right answer had to be *family,* he supposed, even if he was no longer sure who his family was. "Family, sure."

"Everyone says that. You know what you

wind up doing? Nothing. Watching TV. Grunting on the toilet like a monkey because the pills make it impossible to . . . Bitching at your wife about dinner, the lights she left on, the electric bill, everything, and really what it's about is you're dying. All of it. Every last sentence and thought and breath. *Family.*"

"Tell me how you really feel, Rudi. I'm tired of the sugarcoating."

Rudi patted his arm. "When your time comes, just hope it's a bullet in the back of the head. Nice and easy. Meanwhile, I'm wasting time, and we're both short on that. Tell me, where have you been?"

"Russia. And Saudi." Duto had arranged this meeting, so Wells saw no reason to lie.

"Find anything?"

"Only that a lot of people don't like me."

Rudi laughed. He sounded like he was chewing gravel. "An honorary Jew. You know, we think the Americans are going to invade. Especially after the Bekaa."

Wells had seen the reports at his hotel in Aqaba. A bomb had killed Hezbollah's top general. No survivors, no civilian casualties. Sayyed Nasrallah, Hezbollah's leader, had issued a statement promising revenge on the United States. *The Americans have again proven their devilry. Just as they attacked our*

Iranian cousins last week, so do they turn their weapons on us. We will not be intimidated. We remain the faithful servants of Allah, and we will respond at the time and place of His choosing.

"Hezbollah isn't even blaming us," Rudi said. "Unusual for them. If they have more of those SA-24s, I wouldn't want to be on an American plane anywhere within ten thousand kilometers of here." His smile revealed brown misshapen teeth. "Though I guess it doesn't matter so much for me."

Wells liked this tough dying Jew. "War. Off one kilo of HEU."

"You're the American, not me. But it feels like a lot of things coming together. So many reasons to be angry with Iran. Iraq, Afghanistan, Syria. You have considered that letting it happen would be best, maybe? A new regime."

"Not my choice."

"Of course. You can't be bothered with these big thoughts."

"Your people say they expect a war," Wells said. "Seen any casualty estimates?"

"A few thousand dead —"

But Rudi's voice faded, as if he found the argument too tiring to continue. The sun peeked out from behind the brown mountains east of the checkpoint. Rudi lifted his

397

head like a basilisk. "Sunshine on my face. That I'll miss."

"Vinny said —"

"I *tried* to answer his questions." Rudi went silent. Wells thought he might explain why he was helping, even at the risk of betraying Israel. But he said only, "I have a few names. I'm not sure any of them are right. Maybe I'm not good at this anymore."

Wells handed him the photo of Salome he'd printed. "Is she one of them?"

"You're sure this is her?"

Wells nodded.

Rudi's face tightened like the cancer had clenched him. He balled up the paper, threw it down on the blacktop. "If I'm this stupid, I might as well be dead already."

"You know her?" A break. At last. For the first time since he'd seen Glenn Mason in Istanbul, Wells was doing more than groping blindly in the dark.

"I didn't think of her, because she was never Mossad. Name is Adina Leffetz. Adina means 'gentle.' "

"She goes by Salome now."

"Never spoken to her, but she worked for a right-winger in the Knesset who takes money from your friend Duberman. Daniel Raban. Raban's on the Defense Committee, which means he gets regular briefings

398

from the Mossad."

"Worked? Or works?"

"I haven't heard her name come up for a few years, so I doubt she still works for him. But Raban's dumb enough to keep talking to her even if she isn't on his staff anymore."

Another mystery solved. Salome hadn't needed a source at Langley giving her information, as Wells and Shafer had always assumed. The CIA and Mossad worked closely on Iran, so she would have heard plenty through Raban. Of course, Wells still couldn't figure out how she'd found Mason, but that question was less important.

Rudi reached down, picked up the crumpled-up photo, unfolded it. "Lot of ifs. You're sure that's her."

"Yes. Can you get me her mobile number? An email?"

Rudi fell silent as an Israeli fighter jet passed northeast, tracing the line of the border.

"Number, yes. But I'm not going to find her for you. That you have to do yourself."

"Thank you." Wells paused. "I have one more question. Not about her."

"What, then?" Rudi looked exhausted, with Wells and himself. Wells reminded himself the man had spent his whole life stealing other people's secrets while keeping his own. Trading information was fine, but in this case Wells had nothing to give. Yet another reason Rudi must find this conversation painful.

"You remember, in the nineties, a deal where the South Africans transferred all their highly enriched uranium to you? Gave it or sold it, I'm not sure which."

Rudi nodded. "This was '90, maybe '91. The Afrikaners knew they couldn't hold on much longer. They just wanted to be rid of the stuff. The Defense Minister brought us in, asked us if we saw any reason not to take it. We said no."

"You know how much it was?"

Rudi shook his head. "Not much. Maybe enough for one bomb. It wasn't like we needed it. We didn't even pay for it."

The story matched what Shafer had said. Another dead end.

"But the deal did have one odd bit," Rudi said. "Probably why I remember it after all this time. The South Africans insisted on bringing us the stuff themselves. In fact, one of their guys literally flew the stuff up in a shielded trunk on a commercial jet. HEU, you know, it's not that dangerous."

"Why do it that way?"

"If they gave us a reason, I wasn't close enough to hear. My impression was that the

South Africans wanted the stuff to disappear quietly, and we were fine with that."

"Can you find out exactly who brought it, not who did the deal, but who actually brought it, and how much he brought? I know it's a long time ago —"

Rudi coughed, lightly, then harder. Harder. His eyes bulged and his veins strained at his throat. Finally, he opened his mouth and spat a peach pit of phlegm and blood, beige and brown and crimson, liquid and fibrous. As rich and repulsive as an alien life-form that demanded to be vaporized by a plasma rifle.

Rudi raised his hands like a magician: *See what I've given you?*

"The ladies must love that."

Rudi's eyes were wide with hate. Wells wasn't sure if it was meant for him, or the world. "I'll try to get you what you ask. It may take a day or two. But we all have so much time."

Rudi opened the gate, stepped in. Wells wasn't sure whether to follow.

"You plan to stay out there?" Rudi said.

"I didn't know if Israel would have me."

"I'll take you to Taba —" The station on Israel's border with Egypt, about ten kilometers south of this one. "Walk you through with no stamps on our side. What you do from there is up to you. I hear you get on fine in Arabic countries. But I want no record you were here. This dies with me."

"*Shokran,*" Wells murmured. The Arabic word for "thank you."

"*Shokran* yourself."

On the way to Taba, Rudi made three quick phone calls. When he was done, he scribbled an Israeli phone number and an email address on a notepad and pushed it at Wells without explanation.

"The email is strong, the phone not so much," Rudi said.

"Hers?"

"Smart boy."

"You ever meet Ellis Shafer, Rudi?"

Rudi shook his head.

"You two would get along."

Rudi marched him to the Taba exit gate. In place of good-bye, his last words were: *Please don't try to come back this way after I've left. It won't go well.*

Getting into Egypt wasn't a problem. The border guard was far more concerned with making sure that Wells had the proper entry fee than his lack of an Israeli exit stamp. Wells bought yet another fresh phone, called Shafer.

"I'll call you back."

Thirty seconds later, Wells's new phone buzzed, another number. Burner to burner. "Go," Shafer said.

"First, Vinny's friend confirms what you said about the stuff. Enough for one bomb. He says there was one odd part. Whoever delivered it insisted on bringing it in person. As in, flying up with it."

"Like in an icebox? A kidney to transplant."

"He didn't have details, but yes, more or less."

"He know who flew it up?"

"He didn't have a name. I asked."

"Even before he comes back with an answer, I think you should go down there, talk to Witwans."

"Every time we guess wrong, we lose another two days."

"You have a better idea?"

"I have the woman. Her real name." Wells hesitated, decided that if the NSA was already up and listening on these new phones they had less than no chance. "Adina Leffetz. A-D-I-N-A —"

"Nice Jewish girl."

"L-E-F-F-E-T-Z. She worked for an Israeli MP named Raban. Who was in the pocket of our friend in HK."

"You're sure?"

"I showed Vinny's friend her picture. He knew right away."

"You did good, John. I'll find her."

"I want to shake her. Make her play defense."

A pause.

"That business or pleasure?"

Sometimes Wells wondered if Shafer was psychic. Despite everything, Wells couldn't stop remembering Salome's hand on him in that hotel bathroom. He hated her, but even hate meant something. "You have anything better?"

"I made my suggestion. South for the winter."

"I'll consider it. Anything else I should know?"

"Just that our friend from Pennsylvania burned his last bridge with POTUS. More than burned. Nuked. We'll need something airtight to get another audience over there."

Wells wanted to ask Shafer what he meant, ask about the Bekaa, too. But even on a new burner three minutes was too long. And the men around him were giving him odd looks. With his perfect Arabic, Wells could pass for Jordanian or maybe even Egyptian under the right circumstances, but right now he was whispering in English. "I gotta go."

Wells hung up, considered his next move.

Cairo. A five-hour drive west from Taba. Cabbies were happy to make the trip. From Cairo International, he could be in Western Europe in four hours or South Africa in eight. He could hide in Cairo, too. He had before. The city had no shortage of hostels and one-star hotels that were happy to take cash and not picky about identification. Worst case, he could sleep on the street.

Meantime, Wells decided to press his luck. He found another Internet kiosk. Set up another dummy email account. She could probably trace it here, but by the time she did, Wells would be gone.

He typed: *Adina. John Wells here. You weren't nice to me in Volgograd but I'm the forgiving sort.* He reread the last sentence. No. Less whiny, more vaguely menacing. He deleted it, replaced it with —

Sorry you had to run in Volgograd, but now that I know how to find you I look forward to seeing you soon. Maybe I'll even drop by.

He looked it over. Just so. Send.

17

FREE STATE PROVINCE, SOUTH AFRICA
The job was babysitting, and Amos Frankel hated it.

Frankel was Salome's bodyguard, the man who'd drawn on Wells in Volgograd. He'd never been to South Africa before. If he wanted lions and elephants and giraffes, he would go to the zoo. Right now he belonged at Salome's side, not a twelve-hour plane ride away. He'd told her so. She disagreed.

For that matter, he wished she had let him shoot Wells in Volgograd. A simple trigger squeeze. A few kilograms of pressure with his index finger. Nothing Wells could have done. They could have left the body in the hotel, been gone from Russia in two hours. Buvchenko had a jet at the airport. But Salome wouldn't let him. Duberman didn't want them to kill Wells, and anyway the drugs they'd planted would destroy him, she said. *By the time the Russians are finished*

406

with him, he'll wish he was dead.

Frankel believed Salome had other reasons, ones she wouldn't admit. He'd seen how they looked at each other in Volgograd. Alpha males provoked her. Years before, Frankel had caught her staring at a photo of Duberman's supermodel wife Orli in a bikini. Frankel wondered sometimes if Salome had proposed this whole scheme to impress Duberman. *She may be the stuff of a million slack-jawed teenage fantasies, Aaron, but can she start a war for you?*

Lust and love and lust chasing each other in a circle without end, as Frankel watched the follies from afar. A decade before, he'd skidded his motorcycle onto gravel to avoid a stump-tailed dog, sliding off the blacktop at one hundred thirty kilometers an hour. He'd broken his jaw and his hip. Worse, the stones had scraped his legs and face past raw. The pain from the accident and the botched surgeries afterward unwound his interest in sex. He hadn't been with a woman since. He saw himself as almost a eunuch now, emotionally if not physically.

He loved Salome, but without heat. He felt at once close to her and a million kilometers away, like the childhood friend of a famous actor. He knew what drove her, or thought he did. Yet what she'd achieved

shocked him. Her intensity and focus un-
nerved him. They'd grown up together in
the Tel Aviv suburbs. After the accident and
the surgeries, she had come to his hospital
bed and sat with him in silence. By an
alchemy even Frankel did not fully understand, he belonged to her now.

Frankel didn't know if she understood his
feelings for her. He didn't plan to ask, not
ever. When she'd asked for his help with
this scheme, he'd figured that they wouldn't
last long. The CIA or Mossad would dis-
cover their plans. But somehow they'd
survived long enough for Frankel to imagine
that they might succeed. He tried not to
think what Salome might become then.

First they had to make sure that Wells didn't
blow up their plan at one minute to midnight. The man had escaped the trap Salome
had set in Volgograd. Talked his way out of
Lubyanka. He was harder to kill than a Ne-
gev spider. And Salome was worried that
he'd heard about Rand Witwans. *They might
have found him,* she said. She didn't explain
how she knew.

Can't we trust Witwans to be quiet? Frankel
said.

*He's a whipped old man. We can't trust him
with anything. He drinks.*

Why don't I just kill him, then?

If I let you, you'd kill everyone in sight, Amos.

Only the ones who deserve it.

Long as he's alive, no one cares about him. If he dies suddenly, the CIA and the Mossad will notice.

What about Wells? What if he comes for you?

I can handle Wells.

So Frankel took an overnight flight from Istanbul to Johannesburg and drove to the Free State province, the rural heart of South Africa, where Witwans had an estate.

Now Frankel arrived at the man's front gate, two meters of wrought iron set between two brick pillars. "Witwans Manor," a bronze plaque announced. Atop a hill behind the gate was a tall brick house that wouldn't have been out of place in the fanciest London suburbs, set on a manicured lawn where two beautiful brown horses munched grass. In truth, the Free State was too dry for such greenery. The estate radiated a dedication to appearance at any cost. Frankel hated it on sight. He pressed the gate buzzer, rang it long and hard. Nothing happened. He rang again, this time gluing his finger to the buzzer.

His patience was gone by the time Witwans walked down the driveway, a shotgun slung over his shoulder, a German shepherd trotting beside him. The gates swung about a half meter and Witwans stood between them. Up close Frankel could see that the dog and the weapon were both more annoyance than threat. Witwans was a gnarled old man, mid-seventies at least, with a drinker's red nose.

Frankel stepped out of his rented SUV, keeping both hands visible. "Rand."

"Who are you?"

"From Natalie." Natalie was the name Salome used with Witwans. "She told you I'd be coming." A moment later, the gates swung open. Had Witwans really been too frightened or stupid to remember? Frankel saw why Salome had sent him here.

They sat on Witwans's back porch, drinking coffee, eating fresh blueberries and clotted cream. *He's old-style Afrikaans,* Salome had told Frankel. *Thinks the natives exist to serve him. Even worse, thinks they* want *to. Don't talk politics with him or you'll throw up. Just ask him what I told you and put the taps on his phone and wait.*

Babysitting.

"So what's happened?"

Witwans raised the porcelain cup to his

lips with a shaking hand. "I've told Natalie all this. One call from my old friend Joost. Two days ago. Wish I'd never mentioned it. Natalie asked me to call if anything seems wrong, so I called. I didn't tell her to send *you*. I take care of myself."

As far as Frankel could see, all Witwans could take care of was a bottle of scotch. "Since Joost called, has anything out of the ordinary happened?"

"I don't know what you mean."

"No calls from the police."

"Of course not."

"Has anyone come around? The electrician. The plumber —"

"The plumbing's fine."

"You know what I mean. Has anyone shown up who shouldn't be here?"

"Only you."

Frankel reached out, squeezed Witwans's biceps. He forced himself to be gentle, though he wanted to tear the old man's arm clean off.

"You haven't told anyone about Natalie? Or what you sold her?"

"Never, never."

"Your children."

"You think I want them mixed up in this? You know, Natalie told me she'd burn all this down if I did. With me inside."

411

If the tremor in his voice was any indication, the threat had stuck.

"John Wells?"

"Who?" Witwans's face registered genuine surprise.

"And there's no way anyone could know what you'd done?"

"No. I told Natalie when she bought the stuff. We produced fifteen-point-three kilos, I brought the Israelis fourteen, stored the difference here. One HEU ingot, thirteen hundred grams in all. It was in a safe downstairs. I destroyed the records. Back then, everything was paper. No computers. There were three sets of files, two with us, one at the Defense Ministry. I took them all, burned them. No way for anyone on either side to know." Witwans rubbed his hands together, *gone like this.*

"No one asked questions about you destroying the files."

"Nobody wanted anything to do with them. They were afraid the blacks would take revenge on all of us in the secret services."

"You're sure there were only three copies."

"I suppose it's possible the Defense Ministry made another set, they're in an archive somewhere. But I don't think so. And all the years the blacks have been in power, no one's ever asked me about the program. Until Natalie. You see?"

"Sure."

Though Frankel saw only that Witwans was lucky. If Frankel had been in charge instead of Salome, he would have put a round in the man and sent him and his story to the grave.

"She seems to have put what I sold her to good use."

"If I were you, I wouldn't say another word about that. Not even dream about it."

"Of course. Now what? You go back to Natalie, tell her everything is fine."

"Oh no, Rand. I've come all this way. I'm staying."

"No need — I promise —"

Frankel shook his head and Witwans trailed off.

"That's fine, then." Trying to play the country squire. "I have plenty of room."

"What about weapons? Beyond your shotgun." Because he'd flown commercial, Frankel had needed to leave his pistol in Istanbul.

"Of course. A whole cabinet, pistols, rifles. Out here you can't be too careful."

For the first time since he'd arrived in South Africa, Frankel felt a smile crease his lips.

18

BUCHAREST, ROMANIA

Hey Adina!

The subject line was strangely cheery. But the sender's name was what froze her.

John Wells.

Some part of Salome had known this moment was coming. Even wanted it, maybe. She clicked the email open.

She had come to Bucharest the night before, from Istanbul, after Buvchenko told her that the FSB had let Wells go. The Romanian capital was unpleasant at the best of times. In winter, when the sidewalks and buildings and sky blended into the same pallid gray, the city induced despair and an overwhelming desire to flee to Brazil.

But Bucharest also had some of the best hackers around. So Salome had a safe house here, occupied by a young man named Igor. He wore cheap leather jackets and heavy cologne that didn't hide his disinterest in showering. Online, where he spent most of his life, he called himself *IbalL*.

"Didn't expect to see you again," he said over his shoulder as she walked in. She didn't need to wonder how he knew who she was. No one else came here. In her experience, hackers were either compulsively neat or crazily messy. Igor was the latter. Like he'd moved his consciousness onto the Internet already and no longer cared about the space his body occupied. Empty Red Bull cans and pizza boxes covered the scuffed wood floor. Dozens of partly disassembled laptops filled the couch and the coffee table. Generations of PlayStations, Xboxes, Nintendo Wiis occupied the kitchen. Amazingly enough, the place was bug-free. Igor had sprayed it a few months before with an insecticide banned everywhere in the world except Romania and Africa.

"I missed you," Salome said.

"I think one day you come to kill me."

"Never."

"No. You send your boyfriend." What Igor called Frankel.

Good call. She stood behind him, but he didn't look up. He was simultaneously playing online poker, Gchatting with four different people, and on the third and highest-resolution screen watching truly foul pornography.

"Is that a dog?"

"Be glad it's not a horse."

"Off, Igor." He hated when she used his real name. "And get out."

"I'm in a tournament —"

"A *tournament* —"

"Poker." He pointed at the first monitor. "See, a horse." Indeed, a stallion was now being led onto the third screen. "Always a horse sooner or later."

Salome kept a pistol and silencer in a safe in the apartment's bedroom. She was tempted to blow out the monitors and the boy-man sitting at them. Maybe the fanatics were right. Maybe the modern world was so mired in sin that God needed to wipe it away, start anew. "Igor —"

"Fine." He flicked off the screens. She knew he didn't want to make her too angry. He liked her, or at least liked the jobs she offered, more interesting than credit-card scams. He dragged himself up. He spent so much time on his rear and so little on his feet that he sometimes seemed unacquainted with gravity, his bones brittle as needles.

"Not far. I may need you."

He nodded.

"If I want to get online —"

"They're all clean. Safe to use, I mean. I wouldn't touch the one in the bathroom."

"Lovely. Phones?"

He walked into the kitchen, came back with three. "These."

She opened the windows as he left. The Bucharest air wasn't great, but at least it didn't coat her mouth like the inside of a paint can.

Thirty hours before, she had left Volgograd assuming she was done with Wells. But even before Buvchenko's private jet landed at Ataturk Airport in Istanbul, she'd learned she was wrong. She and Buvchenko went to their backup plan, convincing the FSB to pick Wells up. She'd much preferred the local police. Buvchenko had told her the plan couldn't fail. *When they find the heroin —* he drew a hand across his throat.

What about a bribe?

Buvchenko shook his head. *This colonel, he's the only clean police officer in all of Russia.*

But somehow Wells had gotten out, and they were stuck with the FSB, which acted solely in its own interest. She wasn't sure how the FSB would view Wells. But she imagined it would keep him at least a couple days while it sorted him out.

And from what she saw when she landed in Istanbul, Wells was very short on time. Though the city was fifteen hundred kilometers from the Iranian border, the Turkish police and army were gearing up for war. Soldiers stood at the terminal doors, their faces hard and ready. Five-ton army trucks were lined up along the runway fence and outside the airport's main gate. Plainclothes police officers looked over every vehicle coming in and out.

The security made sense. Turkey was run by conservative Sunni Muslims who supported the rebels in Syria and didn't want Iran to get a nuclear weapon. The Turkish government was letting the United States use its mountainous eastern border with Iran as a base for the invasion. It had every reason to fear that Tehran would respond with terrorist attacks.

Salome's safe house was in the city's wealthy Nisantasi District. By the time she and Frankel reached it, the winter sun had slid behind the luxury apartment buildings that dominated the area's narrow streets. At this hour, shoppers and commuters should have filled the sidewalks. Instead, they were nearly empty. A neighborhood full of Western luxury brands was a ripe target for a Hezbollah bomb.

"They think it's coming," Frankel said.

"Looks that way."

"Let's hope they're right."

Frankel had never before expressed an opinion about what they were doing. "Now you tell me," Salome said.

He smiled at her in the rearview mirror. "Everyone loves a good war."

The apartment was a big two-bedroom with a view that stretched over central Istanbul from the Bosphorus Bridge to Topkapi Palace. All the wealth of a country in these blocks. Frankel brought up her bags and was about to leave when her phone buzzed.

Rand Witwans.

"Natalie." His voice slurred, a day of drinks clogging his tongue.

Frankel opened the door to leave. She shook her head. She was sure Witwans would have unpleasant news. She was right. He didn't want to tell her, but ten minutes later she had teased the story out of him. Ellis Shafer had found his name from a man in Nevada, some other South African fossil named Joost. Then Joost called Witwans like the tattletale he was. Playing all sides. Why couldn't the old Afrikaners have the good sense to die?

"Don't worry about it," she said when he finished. Keeping him calm was her first priority. "What does he know about the program?"

"That I ran it. Nothing more."

"Then you'll be fine. And has anyone contacted you?"

"Besides Joost?"

"Yes. Called or come to the house."

"The manor?" Even now he insisted on playing a country gentleman. "No."

She had questions, but she wasn't asking them over the phone. "I'm going to send someone to you."

"There's no need, Natalie."

"Would you rather I come myself?" They both knew she terrified him. She clicked off, checked schedules. Turkish Airlines had an overnight flight to Johannesburg that left in a few hours. A lucky break. Frankel wanted to stay with her, as she knew he would, but she ignored his objection. She told him he was not to kill Witwans. He was there to watch the man, keep him from calling the police or doing anything dumb. If the police came, Frankel was to leave Witwans to them. Killing him would raise a red flag that even the CIA couldn't ignore.

If Wells showed up, on the other hand . . .

■ ■ ■ ■

Her mood darkened after Frankel left. She sat in bed, watching Italian game shows, big-breasted hostesses leering at the contestants. They didn't soothe her. She was conscious of a creeping feeling that she pretended she didn't recognize. *The hole.* Strange that her brain's sickness began with physical symptoms. Her peripheral vision furred, as if the world's edges were coming apart.

She shouldn't be depressed right now. Excited. Or fearful that the tide was turning. Not depressed. All the years of scheming and hiding and lying were almost over. But, of course, the end of the mission *was* the problem. If she lost, she knew what would happen. A bullet to the temple, a needle in her arm. The prospect scared her only theoretically. But what if she won? What would replace the mad beauty of this double-triple-quadruple life? Nothing. She should have asked Wells in Volgograd how he walked away when his missions were done.

Of course, Wells had his own problems. No doubt the FSB interrogators were working him over at this moment. She imagined him enduring his punishment, blaming her, knowing that she had put him there. Would he ask for mercy if she came to Lubyanka? She would bet everything she had that he wasn't the begging type.

Thinking of him chased the black from her mind. She settled back in her bed, turned off the television, closed her eyes, and slept.

The buzzing of her phone woke her. In her confusion, she imagined that Wells was calling. But the number was Israeli and included three eights, the code that meant it belonged to Duberman. She sat up, fully awake. 4:40 a.m. Outside, Istanbul was as dark as it would ever be.

"Shalom."

"Did you hear?" he said in Hebrew. As soon as he spoke, she knew the news was good. When Duberman was pleased, his voice turned soft and guttural, like a late-night radio host's. "They took the bait. The Americans. In Lebanon. You'll see." Then he was gone.

Duberman now had a half-dozen ex–Mossad agents on his staff, mainly to protect Orli. Salome assumed that one had passed along gossip about the United States attacking Lebanon. Meaning Hezbollah. The hit must have been big enough for

Israel to find out quickly.

She gave up on sleep and spent the pre-dawn hours flipping through news channels. By 6:30 a.m., the Lebanese Broadcasting Corporation had live footage of a building smoldering in the Bekaa. Soot-coated men tossed broken bricks into piles.

We are told that at least two senior Hezbol-lah officials were killed in an attack on this warehouse in Zahle early this morning. No word yet on who is behind this attack. Stay with LBC for more . . .

No wonder Duberman was excited. The FSB had Wells. Now the United States was bombing Hezbollah's leaders, a move just short of attacking Iran outright.

They were going to win.

A few hours later, Buvchenko ruined her mood. Wells had talked his way free of the FSB. "They just wanted to be rid of him," he said. "They didn't know what he wanted or why he'd come, and they decided he was more trouble than he was worth."

"I know the feeling."

"They sent him to Amman. Not sure why. But don't even try looking for him there. He speaks Arabic. Unless he wants you to find him, you won't. Not there."

She asked a few useless questions, hung

up. She assumed Wells would land in Amman and board the next plane to Istanbul, less than two hours by air. He could easily track Buvchenko's jet to Istanbul. He knew she had a safe house in Nisantasi.

She'd underestimated him too many times. She decided to hop to Bucharest, just a ninety-minute flight from Ataturk. Wells wouldn't look for her there, and she could play the card she'd been holding for just this moment.

Jess Bunshaft.

She had nurtured her relationship with Bunshaft for three years. He had no idea she was behind this plot. But he knew who she was and that she worked for Duberman. She had met him years before. At the time, he was a mid-level civilian aide to Hebley, who had just earned his fourth star. Salome saw he was sensitive about his role. The Marines treated him like they treated all their male civilian employees, as a eunuch who didn't have the guts to do what they did.

She took Bunshaft to lunch every few months, usually at the Capital Grille, which she couldn't stand but he seemed to like. She was careful never to ask him for war stories from Afghanistan. Instead, they traded Jerusalem and Washington gossip,

424

and she begged his opinions on geopolitics. *No, Jess, I want to hear what* you *think* . . . In all her years, Salome had never met a man immune to that flattery. She always kept her work for Duberman vague. *I'm a consultant. A problem solver.* Bunshaft never asked. He was more interested in talking about himself than hearing about her.

A year before, she pushed the conversation to Iran. At the time, nuclear disarmament talks were progressing in Vienna. "You know what my boss thinks about the ayatollahs," Salome said. "Trusts them about as much as the Hitler Youth."

"Scott feels the same." Bunshaft loved to call Hebley *Scott.*

"But your side must believe the Iranians want a deal or you wouldn't be going ahead with these talks. Your Guard sources —"

"Our Guard sources?" Bunshaft's tone was ironic. "All those Guard sources."

"That bad."

He nodded.

"You know I can't go into details —"

"Say no more, Jess."

He wasn't quite done. "Let's just say that there's some space between my boss and those midgets at the State Department. But the President, he wants this deal, you know. This would be a big hit for him. And he doesn't have a lot of those."

She came away from the lunch confident that if she could find enough highly enriched uranium and tell a plausible story, the CIA would run with it.

In the year since, she'd spoken with Bunshaft a half-dozen times. She left Iran alone and instead dangled a job with Duberman. At first he denied interest. Then she told him Duberman would sign a seven-figure contract for someone with his skill set.

"My connections, you mean," he said.

"Look, you ought to meet with him. I'll set a time. Doesn't have to be soon."

"All right."

So she sent him an email, vaguely worded, but not vaguely enough. Anyone who saw it would understand that Bunshaft was thinking about taking a payday from Duberman. Perfect.

Now Wells was on the loose. Again. Salome needed Bunshaft to see where he stood. From the rancid apartment in Bucharest, she picked the cleanest of the phones that Igor had left. It was early evening in Romania, about noon in Washington.

Bunshaft didn't answer. Probably he wasn't in the habit of picking up random calls. She called again, and a third time.

Finally, he picked up.

"Jess. It's Adina Leffetz."

"This is not a good time."

"I need your help. Please." He had a chivalrous streak, or pretended to.

"What's this about?"

"I think you know."

A faint grunt.

"Jess?"

"I'll get out of here, call you in ten."

Not ideal. He could easily get the NSA involved in ten minutes. But he probably didn't want anyone listening to this call either. A half hour later, her phone buzzed.

"Adina."

"My boss is furious, Jess."

"But we know there's no truth to it, he has nothing to worry about —"

"*He's* not the one who needs to worry."

"Excuse me?"

"You need to stop this man Shafer who's running around telling these lies. And everyone who's helping him. If this goes public, Aaron will lose his mind. He'll blame me and you."

"What?" Bunshaft's voice jumped an octave.

"He's afraid that Shafer will use the connection between us against him. All those meetings, and me offering you a job —"

"I didn't *take* it." Now he was practically a soprano. "Adina. None of this matters, because what Shafer is saying isn't true."

A question in the form of a statement.

"Of course not. But that doesn't make it any less toxic. People hate Aaron. A rich Jew with a beautiful wife. Any excuse to smear him."

"I'm telling you, we're watching Shafer. His email accounts, his phones."

Not closely enough, since Shafer had learned Rand Witwans's name without the CIA finding out. But that bit of information was one Salome didn't plan to share.

"Whatever you're doing hasn't stopped him spreading this story."

"Your name has never come up."

Wrong again. Wells knew her name, so Shafer surely did, too.

"You need to stop watching and *do* something. Not just Shafer. His friend, too. John Wells. He was in Russia, and the FSB picked him up and then let him go —"

"How do you know?"

She let the question hang. She had entered dangerous territory. She was playing both sides, insisting that Duberman had nothing to do with the plot and was only worried about his reputation, and at the same time disclosing information she probably

428

shouldn't have had in order to force Bun-shaft to act.

If Bunshaft were stronger, he might have confronted her over the contradiction. But he was afraid. He didn't want to know how she could be so connected. The reason she'd chosen him for this call.

"What you should be asking, Jess, is why these men are pursuing this crazy agenda. When the only ones who benefit are the Iranians."

"All right."

"You understand."

"Yes."

"And what it means if my name comes up. For *both* of us."

"I said all right." His voice was soft. Beaten. "I'll deal with it. I can't do anything before tomorrow, though."

"If I hear more, I'll let you know."

"I'd rather you didn't." But his tone suggested he didn't have much say in the matter.

"Good-bye, Jess." She hung up. She'd given him a way to handle Shafer: accuse him and Wells of working for Iran, wittingly or not. Now she just had to hope he, and more important his betters on Langley's seventh floor, would follow it.

■ ■ ■ ■

Bucharest sank into night. She lowered the bedroom's blackout shades and watched the news. CNN was calling its coverage "The March to War," and alternating between shots of American troop transports taking off from North Carolina and the aftermath of the attack in the Bekaa, now eighteen hours old. The United States still wouldn't confirm it had dropped the bombs. But at a White House press conference, the President's spokesman said that the United States and India had captured two Lebanese men who had confessed to shooting down United Airlines 49 for Hezbollah.

"Given the relationship between Hezbollah and the Iranian government, we must conclude that Hezbollah carried out this missile strike for its Iranian sponsors," the spokesman, Josh Galper, said. "Again we call on Iran to agree to the very reasonable terms the United States has set. We do not want war with Iran. But if the Iranians give us no choice, rest assured that we will fight."

Asked where the men were, Galper would say only that they were "en route" to the United States but might not arrive for some time. "We are trying to learn exactly what they know and whether other aircraft are at risk."

Salome fell asleep with the television on. She dreamed she was sitting in a plane with Wells and Duberman on either side of her. She knew she was dreaming because they were in economy class, not a private jet. Wells turned to her, opened his mouth. She thought he might kiss her. She raised a hand to block him, but his jaw opened wider, like he was a snake eating a rat, and he stuck his arm down his throat and pulled out a plastic-wrapped brick, the same brick she'd left under the bed in his room in Volgograd. *You shouldn't have done that.*

I thought you'd like it.

But her voice was squeaking like Bunshaft's. They both knew she was lying. The plane raced down the runway, and Salome knew suddenly that the brick was not heroin at all but a bomb. Wells shoved it at her, and she cradled it like a baby.

The plane leapt from the runway and the brick glowed red in her hands and —

She woke. She imagined when she pulled the shades she'd find dawn still hours off. But the sun glowed wanly through the city's haze. She couldn't imagine how but she'd slept through the night. She stretched, showered, dressed. And only then checked her email:

Adina. John Wells here. Sorry you had to run in Volgograd, but now that I know how to find you I look forward to seeing you soon. Maybe I'll even drop by.

He'd sent it about three hours before. Bad luck she'd slept so long.

She read it a dozen times. But the only word that mattered was the first. *Adina.* He had found her real name. Disaster. Now that Wells knew who she was, he could easily link her to Duberman. She hadn't advertised the connection, but she hadn't buried it either. And if Wells knew, Shafer did, too. She wasn't sure how quickly he could hook her to Bunshaft, but he surely could search the Langley visitor records and figure out how she'd found Glenn Mason.

Wells and Shafer still couldn't prove that she was behind what Mason had done. Mason was the only man who could connect her to it, and he was dead. But her protection was suddenly paper-thin. All along, she had known her plan would only succeed if the uranium fanned the latent distrust and anger between the United States and Iran. And it had. Both sides had reacted as if war wasn't just inevitable but overdue, the only way to settle their generation-long battle for influence in Iraq and all over the Middle East.

But if Wells and Shafer convinced the President that the uranium might not be from Iran, the momentum for war would fade. The appeasers would raise their voices and beg for time. And if the President used that time to order the NSA and CIA to look at Duberman, they would find him. All the shell companies and wire transfers and single-use phones in the world couldn't keep the American government at bay.

She should have listened to Frankel, disobeyed Duberman. She should have learned from the way Wells had broken out of his shackles in Istanbul two weeks before. She should have shot Wells in Volgograd.

But she hadn't. Now he was emailing her. Practically taunting her. *Look forward to seeing you soon.* She imagined him sitting at a station in an Internet café somewhere in Amman or Istanbul, his big hands poised over the keyboard, picking out one letter at a time. Those tired brown eyes of his would have some extra life, and when he was done he'd rub his thumb and forefinger over his square jaw, as she'd seen him do in Volgograd. He wanted to incite her.

So she had to stay cool.

First things first. She texted Bunshaft. *They have my name.* Nothing more. Even he was smart enough to know what she meant: *Move.*

Then she called Igor. "Are you close?"

"Maybe an hour."

"Come as soon as you can."

"I knew you wanted it."

"Idiot." She went out hunting for some drinkable coffee. Igor arrived seventy minutes later, freshly showered and shaved, wearing a shirt that passed for clean from him. He really was hoping to play horny hacker.

"Tell me where this was sent from." She had printed out the header, not the message.

"Can I see the email?"

"No." She wasn't letting him see her real name.

"It will help."

"No it won't." She knew that much.

He grabbed the page from her. Two minutes later: "Good news. Whoever sent it either didn't know how to route it through anonymizing servers or didn't care. I can narrow it down to Egypt. Eastern Egypt. The Sinai Peninsula."

"You're sure."

He didn't bother to answer.

"And there's nothing more you can tell me?"

"Past that you need government-grade technology. But if I had to guess, I would say somewhere on the Red Sea. Not so many Internet cafés in the desert."

Not what she had expected. Wells had gone south instead of north from Amman. And on the way, he picked up her name and her email address. He hadn't had them in Russia, she was sure.

Jordan. Egypt. Between them, Israel. Had someone there given her up? She couldn't believe another Jew would betray her, even if the chronology suggested otherwise.

"Do you want me to try to track him? I can send him an email with a virus, if he even clicks on it it'll infect whatever computer he's using. It's a long shot, because he'd have to use this account again, but there's no downside."

"Do it, then."

While Igor hunched over the laptop, Salome went into the bedroom. She dialed a number that wasn't written down anywhere. Hesitated. Hung up without hitting send.

But she had no choice. She redialed. Called.

Duberman picked up on the second ring. "Wait a moment."

In the background, she heard a toddler

435

yelling. "Not now, Rafael." Rafael was one of his twins. "Take him away." Then: "All right."

"They know my name."

"You said that was impossible."

"I thought it was. I don't know how. The one — the troublesome one who travels — he emailed me."

"So he has that, too. Anything else? What you ate for dinner?"

"I think he doesn't know as much as he's pretending."

"If there's other bad news, tell me now."

"They know about our friend in the southern hemisphere."

"If he talks." Duberman didn't need to finish the sentence.

"He won't. I have someone watching him. Believe me, he doesn't want trouble."

"I wish I shared your confidence. Tell me you're doing something more than watching the roof doesn't cave in."

"I'm dealing with the one who stays at home." She hoped.

"There are two of those."

"The Jew." Shafer. "The other" — Duto — "we can't touch. But he needs the others. He can't beat us himself."

"The one who travels. The one who emailed you. Any idea where he is?"

"He sent it from Egypt. The Sinai."

Duberman was silent. "That gives me an idea," he finally said. "How quickly can you get here? The beach?" Meaning Tel Aviv.

If she left for the Bucharest airport now, she could be in Istanbul by early afternoon, catch a quick flight to Tel Aviv. "Maybe six hours."

"Then come."

"You're not going to tell me why?"

He laughed. Nothing more. All these years, he was still a showman. "When we're face-to-face."

19

Shafer walked past the guard station to the glass-paned entry gates in the lobby of the New Headquarters Building, swiped his identification card —

And nodded with a confidence he did not feel as the glass parted. He had lived to spy another day. He had given up asking why Hebley and the seventh floor didn't put him on leave or flat-out fire him. Maybe he and Wells had stirred enough doubt that someone upstairs was letting them push as a just-in-case insurance policy. Over the years, Duto had used that strategy effectively. But Shafer figured another answer was more likely. Max Carcetti, Hebley's chief of staff and nut-cutter, wanted to keep him close. Better inside the tent pissing out, et cetera.

Outside, the sun hadn't yet risen. The Langley parking lots and garages were mostly empty. Wells had called around

438

1 a.m. Washington time with Adina Leffetz's name. Shafer had lain awake through the night debating whether to run it through the only classified database he could still use. Inevitably, someone on seven would see.

Just as inevitably, he decided to roll the dice.

He sat at his computer, plugged *Adina Leffetz* into the ACFND, the all-contacts foreign nationals database. The all-contacts log was not the master list of the CIA's foreign agents — the men and women who betrayed their countries to spy for the United States. The agency kept those names, and their associated cryptonyms, on coded disks that were not physically stored at Langley and were of course not connected to any network. Sometimes called the Kingdom List, the master database could be viewed only with the approval of the DCI, the deputy director for the clandestine service, or the President.

Of course, station chiefs and their bosses at Langley knew the real identities of the spies their case officers ran. But the agency strongly discouraged them from sharing those names with anyone who wasn't directly involved in handling them. Its caution was a legacy of the Aldrich Ames case. In the 1980s, Ames, a counterintelligence officer with a drinking problem and an expensive wife, sold the agency's Soviet networks to the KGB.

In turn, Ames was himself betrayed by a Russian defector in the early 1990s. He was now serving a life sentence at a maximum-security prison in Pennsylvania. But during its internal investigation of Ames's crimes, the CIA discovered that almost two hundred employees had access to the real names of its Russian spies. The agency had taken internal security more seriously ever since.

In the CIA's view, Edward Snowden's massive NSA leaks had vindicated that caution. Whether Snowden was a whistle-blower or a traitor — and arguments could be made on both sides — he had been a mid-level contractor at a minor NSA office in Hawaii at the time he stole the data. He should never have had access to so many crucial documents and programs.

Yet the agency could not ignore the fact that case officers and analysts needed to be able to trade data, rumors, and tips. The all-contacts log gave them that chance. The log was less sensitive than the Kingdom List, or even a third database where case officers reported serious relationships with foreign nationals. It wasn't tied to specific operations. Instead, it gave case officers a place to report contacts that had not offered actionable intelligence or clear recruiting opportunities. Officers had some discretion over reporting, but it wasn't unlimited. As instructors at the Farm told trainees, *Taking a cab in Paris is not a significant contact, no matter how chatty the driver. But if the same guy picks you up two days in a row, his name's probably worth logging.* The list was intentionally massive and unfiltered. The agency was trying to create a Top Secret Wikipedia of sorts, a way to draw on the day-to-day contacts of thousands of case officers.

Unlike the Kingdom List — or operational reports, of course — the database was broadly available. Anyone in the clandestine service could see or update it. After some initial resistance, case officers had bought in. The log now included tens of thousands of names. Some offered long, detailed biographies. Others were a single line. It was searchable by dozens of fields, including time of contact, station, reporting officer, and of course contact name.

Given the breadth of the list, Shafer figured he had a decent chance of finding Leffetz. Sure enough, he did. The surprise was not the entry but the photo, a head shot of an attractive if harsh-looking woman with deep brown eyes. The existence of the photo didn't result from any NSA wizardry. It had been taken at Langley about five years earlier. *She'd been here.* According to the log, Leffetz/Salome had come to discuss "Transnational Human Resources Strategies to Manage Troubled Case Officers, Based on the Israeli and American Experience." Like nearly all foreign nationals, she'd received a black-bordered badge, requiring her to have an escort anywhere on campus.

As he read the log, Shafer felt the cold thrill that only detectives and investigative reporters truly understood. The game was on now. She'd been so careful for so long, but the wind had turned, the fog lifted. He'd glimpsed her on a distant hillside. A speck, but clear enough. He didn't have to wonder anymore. She was out there, and he'd never let her go. *Across the river and through the trees, to Grandma's house or wherever you please . . .* Shafer wanted to howl at the moon, now setting over the parking lot.

Shafer had tried to explain this feeling to people outside the building a few times over the years. But knew he came off sounding creepy. Maybe he was. So be it. Wells played God in the most elemental way: *Who shall live and who shall die, who shall reach the end of his days and who shall not, who by water and who by fire, who by sword and who by beast . . .* But snatching the world's secrets from their graves gave Shafer his own taste of absolute power.

On a more practical level, the entry explained to Shafer how Leffetz had found Mason. *Hey, HR — I want to hear about your most screwed-up case officers. No worries, American friends. It's for a project. Trust me!* Shafer couldn't believe the human resources managers would have given her actual names, but with enough biographical details she could have backtraced Mason easily.

At the same time, the fact that Salome had told such an elaborate cover story suggested to Shafer that no one at the agency had known what she really wanted, at least back then. From the first day that he and Wells had stumbled onto Mason, Shafer had wondered. Politicians had used the CIA to pull the United States into war before. But this plot was so risky that Shafer couldn't imagine anyone would go near it.

Not before Scott Hebley became DCI, anyway.

■ ■ ■ ■

Leffetz's name popped up a few more times after that first entry, but not for anything interesting. She'd never come back to Langley. As far as Shafer could tell, she'd shown up occasionally on the lower rungs of D.C.'s lobbyist/embassy cocktail circuit, where wannabe arms dealers mingled with attachés looking for kickbacks. *Wondered if she was Mossad but I'm pretty sure she's not,* a Middle East desk officer wrote after a party at the Turkish embassy three years before. *Seems harmless/useless.* Another offered: *Casino consultant? Entry to Macao?*

Officers were not allowed to discuss recruiting potential agents on the all-contacts database because it was so widely read, but the entry hinted that someone had approached Leffetz. Shafer couldn't access those files, but he was sure that Leffetz would have brushed off the approach. She would have wanted to avoid the scrutiny that came with an official relationship.

Shafer left the log open as he considered his next move. The seventh floor had cut him off from other internal databases. But, probably because of simple bureaucratic oversight, he could still access some files outside Langley. He started with the National Crime Information Center, the FBI-managed database of property and court records that police officers used to investigate crimes and track fugitives. Adina Leffetz's name didn't return any hits. Other federal and state files also came back blank. Leffetz had never registered as a lobbyist for a foreign government, never filed an American tax return, never applied for citizenship or a driver's license. Local property and court records were incomplete, but her name didn't show up in those either. Immigration records would have told him when she'd entered the United States, but not what she'd done once she'd arrived, and they were off-limits to Shafer anyway.

The NSA might have credit-card or phone records for her. But if she'd been really careful, she could have used a card that belonged to a limited-liability shell company and carried a false name. For local travel, she could have hired a driver and paid cash. For hotel reservations, third-party services like Hotwire. For coms, all the usual tricks, single-use burners and email accounts. In any case, Shafer had no chance at the NSA, and he was less interested in finding Salome at this moment than dredging up her current link to the agency, if one existed.

He turned to open-source records, looking for Leffetz's name in newspaper archives, Internet gossip columns, photo databases, Facebook and Twitter. He found references to an Adina Leffetz, but not the one he wanted, not unless she moonlighted as a high school gymnast in Orlando. He tried translating her name into Hebrew and struck another blank on the Israeli newspapers.

Then he reverse-searched her badge photo. The NSA had sophisticated photo-recognition software, but Shafer didn't need it, thanks to the head-on shot. TinEye, a free site, did the trick. On DCsuperparty-.com, which advertised itself as "your source for Washington events," Shafer found a photo of Leffetz from a fund-raiser at the Brookings Institution almost three years before. She frowned at the camera, apparently not thrilled to have her photo taken. She stood next to a man Shafer knew well. The caption: *Jess Bunshaft and friend.*

Bunshaft might be a friend of Salome's, but he was no friend of Shafer's. A month before, when Shafer first tried to warn Hebley that he and Wells had stumbled onto a false-flag plot, Hebley sent Bunshaft to talk to Shafer. The conversation went badly. Shafer had found Glenn Mason, but at the time he didn't know that Mason was connected to Salome or Duberman. Bunshaft and his boss Max Carcetti later dismissed the theory on the apparently unimpeachable grounds that Glenn Mason was dead. Ever since, Shafer had been on the seventh floor's no-fly list.

Now — at last — Shafer could prove what he'd suspected all along. Salome was linked to the agency's new guard. Of course, the photo didn't prove that Bunshaft knew what Salome was doing. But, as Donna Green had told Duto at their midnight meeting, the White House had wanted for years to replace Duto with Hebley. Maybe Green or the President himself hinted at those plans to Duberman. A hundred ninety-six million bought a lot of access. Salome would have cultivated Bunshaft carefully. Maybe she'd told him she worked for Duberman. Maybe not. A case officer would have been innately suspicious of the approach, but Bunshaft wasn't a case officer.

Shafer knew he had entered the realm of guesswork, what his old friend and Wells's old love Jennifer Exley sometimes called his string theories. This lone photo just didn't prove anything. Maybe Salome had never seen Bunshaft again after that Brookings talk.

But Shafer could be sure of one thing: Salome hadn't wanted her photo taken with Bunshaft. She had refused to give her name, figuring that without it the Jpeg would be dumped into a forgotten file along with a million others. And it had, until now.

Shafer double-checked the dates in the all-contacts log. As he'd expected, the entries about Leffetz stopped after the photo. Probably she'd been more careful afterward, staying away from public events.

On one level, the depth of Salome's connection to the agency hardly mattered. At this point, everyone on seven would be destroyed if Shafer and Wells proved the plot was fake. Incompetence and naïveté would be treated nearly as harshly as outright treason. Shafer wondered if he ought to go straight at Bunshaft, figure he was a dupe rather than a traitor. Maybe he could convince Bunshaft that Iran and the United States could still avoid war. Whatever he did, he needed to let Duto know what he'd found. Better phone than email. Of course, the agency was monitoring both, but it could delete his outgoing emails before they left the Langley servers. Shafer reached for his handset —

And saw that his computer screens had gone blank. He jabbed at the keyboards on his desk. Nothing. His office phone was also dark. He grabbed his mobile, tried his wife. The screen showed five bars, but the call wouldn't go through. The voice of a *National Geographic* narrator played in his head: *Just that quickly, the hunter becomes the hunted . . .*

Had Adina Leffetz's name triggered an alarm? Or was Bunshaft watching Shafer's computers in real time?

Either way, Shafer needed to get off the campus. His office had been shoved to the fourth floor, a nowhere land of analysts and database managers. Fortunately, the New Headquarters Building had fire stairs at the corners as well as the core. Unfortunately, those corner stairs were alarmed at the ground and roof exits, and Langley's guard teams answered sirens in a hurry.

Shafer wondered if Hebley would risk a scene by grabbing him in the lobby. Probably not. In that case, the stairs by the elevators made sense. He ran for them, his feet flapping heavily. He was shocked how slowly he moved, like he was running through water. Luckily, it was still only 7:15 and the hallways were empty. No curious looks.

He reached the stairs, ducked inside. After barely a hundred feet, his lungs burned. He took three steps down the empty gray stairwell and wondered why he was bothering. Even without a fifteen-foot wire fence, Langley's perimeter was as well guarded as any supermax. Theoretically, the barriers were meant to keep intruders out, but they worked both ways. Even if he escaped the building, the guards could pick him up at an exit gate, a quick and almost surgical grab.

Of course they would. Like most traps, this one seemed head-slappingly obvious once Shafer saw it. They, whoever they were, wanted him to run. Why else turn off his computers instead of just grabbing him at his office? If he was a flight risk, the agency could justify holding him without charges. Eventually, of course, they'd have to present him to a judge, but when they did, they would lean heavily on the fact that he'd fled. *He ran, Judge. As soon as he realized we were looking for him. Under the circumstances, we had no choice but to search his office down to the studs, check phones, bank records, his house and car. We didn't realize we would need seventy-two hours, Judge, and we apologize. But here he is, safe and sound.*

Worst of all, even Shafer's wife wouldn't know exactly where he was. She would figure he'd gone to Langley this morning, but she couldn't be sure. He had left the house while she was still asleep.

No running, then. But Shafer needed someone he trusted to see him, to know what was happening. He didn't have much time. No doubt they had put sensors on his car and had the guards looking for him. They would be confident he couldn't escape the campus. Still, they wouldn't wait long. When they realized after a few minutes that he hadn't taken the bait, they'd come for him. At this hour, only one person he absolutely trusted was likely to be here. He hated to drag her into this mess, but he didn't see any choice.

The lights of her office suite were on. He knocked and without waiting for an answer stepped inside. "Lucy." Lucy Joyner, the CIA's human resources director, among Shafer's oldest friends at Langley. She was a brassy Texan who had handled the agency's most thankless jobs for thirty years. A month before, she'd helped him uncover Mason's role and start this roundelay. They both knew the seventh floor was looking hard at her.

"Ellis."

She sounded worse than wary.

"Why do I feel like I'm your crack addict kid and you're waiting for me to beg twenty bucks?" he said.

"Twenty doesn't buy much crack."

"Take my picture."

"Why would I do that?"

Shafer raised an imaginary iPhone to his eyes. "Snap snap. And sometime today tell my wife you saw me this morning."

"Why?"

"So she doesn't worry."

Joyner nodded, as if requests like this came her way all the time. "That all?"

"Yes. No. One more thing." Shafer tore a page from a sexual harassment reporting handbook on Joyner's desk, wrote *Salome-Jess Bunshaft-DCsuperparty.com* in the margin. "Give this to Vinny —"

"Duto —"

"Of course Duto. And do yourself a favor, don't look at it —"

"What's going on?"

"Long story."

"No one's going to disappear you, Ellis."

"They might misplace me for a few days."

"This ends badly for both of us."

"I don't know. Truly." Shafer tapped the nonexistent watch on his wrist. "Yes or no on the picture? Places to go, people to see."

She reached for her phone. "Smile."

He raised both middle fingers.

"Perfect. Everyone will know it's you."

The phone clicked.

"I think you left your lipstick at home, Lucy. Better get it." Meaning: leave Langley and store the photo somewhere safe.

"That bad?"

Shafer turned for the door, blew a kiss over his shoulder at Joyner. "Later, my love."

"I'm not even your like, Ellis —"

His mood swung between grim and weirdly jaunty as he made his way back to his office. Whatever Carcetti had planned would not be pleasant. On the other hand, now that Joyner had seen him they wouldn't be able to make him vanish.

He was not at all surprised to find Carcetti and Bunshaft waiting at his desk. As a lieutenant three decades earlier, Carcetti had been a heavyweight on the All-Marine boxing team. His gut had thickened notably since then, but his legs and shoulders were still solid. He looked like a bouncer at a biker bar.

"Mr. Shafer —" Bunshaft said.

"Jess. Max. Call me Ellis. As far as I'm concerned, it's first names for us."

"Where were you?" Carcetti said.

Shafer smirked.

"Believe it's known in the trade as dropping the kids off at the pool."

"We've been here fifteen minutes."

"I'm an old man." Shafer tapped his belly. "Things get stuck —" Shafer grinned, not even hiding what he was doing, riffing like a drunk comedian at the late show on Friday night. Carcetti had followed his boss Hebley up the Marine Corps ladder. He'd retired with three stars on his collar and the nickname Mad Max, a commander who shouted and intimidated subordinates into submission. Shafer had learned over the years that playing the fool worked surprisingly well against that personality type. He hoped to drive Carcetti into useless and counterproductive rage, as he had Duto a dozen times.

"Least you can't say I'm full of —"

"Enough." Carcetti's voice was level, but his eyes bulged like a blocked artery.

Now Shafer needed to shift gears, remind Carcetti that he wasn't a fool after all. "You think this is still the Corps, General? You have me confused with a terminal lance?" A Marine who ended his enlistment as a lance corporal, the lowest possible rank after four years. "You think you say jump and I say how high, sir?"

Carcetti grabbed Shafer's arm. "I think you're coming with us."

■ ■ ■ ■

Carcetti and Bunshaft had detained Shafer briefly a month before. Back then, they'd locked him in a cell disguised as an executive suite, a room meant to preserve the illusion of dignity. Not today. Today Carcetti led him through a tunnel that connected the New Headquarters Building with its older cousin, the Original Headquarters Building. Down a grimy fire staircase that dead-ended on a subbasement that Shafer had never seen before in all his years at Langley. Through a maze of corridors lined with aging air handlers. Carcetti seemed to know the layout by heart. Finally, they reached a room whose concrete floor and grease stains suggested that it had once housed a furnace. Now it was stagnant and empty but for a steel table and three chairs, two on one side, the third on the other.

Carcetti shoved Shafer into the third chair. "Where's John Wells?"

Good. He'd asked a question Shafer couldn't answer. "Dunno."

"We suspect him of aiding the Iranian government. And we suspect you of aiding him."

Shafer felt the ground shift. The accusation was desperate, proof of the pressure Carcetti and Hebley felt. But if they could convince the President to sign a finding that Wells was aiding a foreign government, the agency would be authorized to snatch Wells without warning. The finding wouldn't specifically call for Wells to be killed, but once black-ops teams were involved, anything could happen. If Wells pulled a gun, and he probably would, they'd shoot him in the street. A tragic accident.

And Shafer had no way to warn Wells.

"You can't seriously believe that."

"He's a Muslim convert."

"You know there's a difference between Sunni and Shia, right?"

"I know that about twenty-four hours ago the FSB released him from Lubyanka following a call from Iran's Foreign Minister to the Russian Interior Minister."

"Two things that have nothing to do with each other."

"I know he got on a plane from Moscow to Amman. And I know he hasn't been seen since. You tell us where he is, we can pick him up safely. Nobody wants him to get hurt."

"Why don't you check the files, find out what Wells has done for this agency, this *country,* before you accuse him of treason?"

"Like those Deltas he killed in Afghanistan, you mean? Or when he was five minutes late in Mecca?"

Shafer didn't think he was naïve. But he had never imagined anyone spinning Wells's record that way.

"Max —"

"Look, maybe he's got the best of intentions here, but he's acting as a foreign agent whether he means to or not." Carcetti nodded like a salesman trying to close a deal. "Do everyone a favor. You don't want to tell me where he is, I get it. Just tell him, go to an embassy. Somewhere safe for him and our guys, so nobody makes a mistake."

"Somewhere safe." The line a parody of good-cop reasonableness. In reality, the offer was poison. Wells would never agree to come in, and Shafer's phone call would give the agency and NSA a chance to pinpoint him.

Shafer closed his eyes, like the pressure was getting to him. Let Carcetti believe he'd won. He needed time to think through his next move, get Carcetti back inside the lines so that Wells wasn't at risk.

Carcetti's hand squeezed his wrist. "You know I'm right."

Shafer looked at Carcetti and Bunshaft. Their posture was telling. Carcetti sat forward, eager. Bunshaft was back, arms folded. Nervous. Shafer ticked his head at Bunshaft.

"Jess. You're sweating." The furnace room's harsh overheads highlighted the sheen of perspiration-occupying territory ceded by Bunshaft's receding hairline. "You on board with this? Bringing me someplace with no cameras. No warrant, nobody watching. Your boss doesn't like the law much."

"Exigent circumstances," Carcetti said. "National security exception."

"He's got to do it this way, because even Taylor wouldn't come near this." Cliff Taylor, the agency's new deputy legal counsel, handpicked by Hebley. Bunshaft glanced at Carcetti. Cleared his throat like he'd forgotten how to talk.

"Worry less about us, more about yourself," Carcetti said. "Maybe you've forgotten. Duto's a senator. He's protected. Not you. All those leaks to Wells and he doesn't have a security clearance —"

"We've gone from treason to leaking in two minutes. Next you'll accuse me of parking in a handicapped spot."

"This kind of leaking *is* treason. And, your age, twenty years in jail is a life sentence. Bright side, your wife's old, too. No worries about her leaving you."

Carcetti went silent and Shafer found that he, too, had nothing to say. They were both breathing hard. Like the bell had rung and they'd gone back to their corners to sit on their stools, get ready for the next round, the arena empty, only Bunshaft watching, a silent, unreliable referee.

Shafer realized he'd forgotten the most important question of all. He opened his palms and dropped his head like he was ready to surrender. Rope-a-dope.

"All right, General. I'd like to ask something. Tell me the truth, I'll call Wells."

"Why would I trust you?"

"Because I don't want him to get shot."

An answer Carcetti would believe. He nodded. *Now we're getting somewhere.*

"You really think Iran produced that HEU?"

Carcetti hesitated for half a second. "Yes. I mean, that's what our experts concluded —"

"Translation, you have no idea. And the worst part is *you don't care.* Like the Gulf of Tonkin or WMD." The excuses that Lyndon Johnson and George W. Bush, respectively, had offered for Vietnam and Iraq. "You've decided that invading Iran is the right war. Even if it's for the wrong reasons."

"You rather they get the bomb, Mr. Shafer? That what you're telling me?"

"Do the President and Donna Green agree?"

Carcetti's thick black eyebrows rose, the movement as surprising as an Easter Island statue coming to life. They came down fast, but Shafer saw that he'd scored. Carcetti didn't know what Hebley was telling the White House. Shafer suspected that Hebley was keeping his doubts, if he had any, to himself.

Shafer looked at Bunshaft. "Hebley's taking all of you over Niagara Falls. Except he's the only one with a barrel."

"If only you and Duto had actual evidence for this crazy theory you're peddling. Aaron Duberman, right? Who just happened to give two hundred million dollars to the same President who fired Duto."

"That's a feature, General. Not a bug."

"What?"

"Ask your friend here about Adina Leffetz."

Another score. Carcetti's big Marine head wobbled a fraction on his big Marine neck.

"You don't know her, but she ran the job for Duberman. Used to work for a Knesset member named Daniel Raban. Nice guy. One of those Jews who think Israel should treat the Palestinians like crap for the next two thousand years to make up for what happened in the last two thousand. I can say that because I'm Jewish. You can't." Shafer shifted his attention to Bunshaft. "Come on, tell the general about her."

Bunshaft shook his head.

"I still don't hear any evidence," Carcetti said.

Shafer wondered if he should mention Witwans and decided to hold off.

"You can do the right thing, General. You can walk this back."

"They blew up a plane." Carcetti tapped the table, clanking metal against metal.

For the first time, Shafer noticed that in addition to his heavy yellow gold wedding ring, Carcetti wore a thick platinum ring etched with the Marine Corps insignia. On his right hand was yet another ring, this one dull steel, almost black with wear. Intentionally or not, the rings looked like makeshift brass knuckles on Carcetti's meaty hands.

Carcetti caught Shafer's glance. He tapped the steel ring. "This was my granddad's. He died on Tarawa. November 22, 1943. My dad lost his right eye at Khe Sanh, March 7, '68."

461

"And now you get to start your own war, kill somebody else's father. Circle of death. Congratulations."

A crimson flush spread up Carcetti's neck. His big hands bent into fists. Shafer knew he'd gone too far.

"General," Bunshaft said.

Carcetti exhaled long and loud. "An angel on my shoulder. Lucky for you." He took a phone from his pocket. "I answered your question. Time for you to do your part."

"Call John, you mean? You get service down here?"

"We'll go outside."

If he hadn't just almost talked himself into a beating, Shafer would have laughed. "I don't know his number. He's on a different burner every time we call —"

"So email him, tell him you have to talk to him —"

"More important. Did you really think I'd call him for you?"

Bunshaft broke the silence that followed.

"But you *promised.*" The shock in his voice sounded genuine.

Carcetti looked from Shafer to Bunshaft like he was trying to figure out which one to shoot first. He grabbed Bunshaft's arm, tossed him off his chair. Bunshaft was hardly skinny, but he flew like a bag of sticks.

"Get out," Carcetti said. "Close the door. And walk. Until you can't hear anything."

Bunshaft opened his mouth and closed it again and did what Carcetti had told him. Shafer and Carcetti waited in silence as Bunshaft's footsteps receded down the hall.

When they were gone, Carcetti stood. "People fall down stairs." He swung his head side to side, rolled his shoulders like a boxer trying to get loose.

Shafer realized he needed to make sure Carcetti knew that Lucy Joyner knew what was happening. She had to have cleared the campus by now.

Carcetti stepped toward him —

Shafer bit back the words. Let Carcetti crack his ribs, blacken his eyes. He'd be digging an even deeper hole. And Shafer would prove, to himself, to Wells, or both, that he wasn't afraid.

Though he was.

Carcetti pushed over Shafer's chair, sent him sprawling, his knees clapping the concrete floor. Shafer lay on his back. That quick, his fear vanished. This was Langley, not North Korea. Carcetti hadn't earned three stars in the Marines by making dumb mistakes. He wasn't going to hurt Shafer, no matter how furious he was.

"Last chance." Carcetti squatted beside him. "I will break your neck." Carcetti put a hand on Shafer's throat, squeezed lightly.

Time to end this nonsense. "You will not. And fyi, Lucy Joyner saw me this morning. I was down at her office while you and Bunshaft were waiting for me. She's got a picture to prove it."

Carcetti cursed, stepped away from Shafer, kicked the table over. The metal clattered against the concrete, as loud and empty as Carcetti's threats.

"I'd say you have three options. Put us all under quarantine down here. Lucy and my wife and Vinny, too. It could get cramped. Though maybe if we have snacks. Everyone loves snacks." Shafer pulled himself to his feet, hoping Carcetti didn't notice the tremble in his legs. "Two, let me go. Though I have a feeling that isn't on the agenda. Three, go for a warrant, do this right."

"You want me to call that bluff? We have tapes of what you told Wells. We play them, you spend the rest of your life in prison."

Carcetti might be right. Federal judges didn't love CIA officers who disclosed classified information. Stopping a war would be a mitigating circumstance, but only if Shafer succeeded.

Yet at this point Shafer didn't care. To get a warrant, even in a case that supposedly presented an immediate national security threat, Carcetti and Hebley would have to talk to the CIA's lawyers, who would insist on calling the Justice Department. Justice would be predisposed to believe whatever version of the story Carcetti gave. But once they got involved, Hebley would have a much harder time ordering the CIA's black-ops teams after Wells — who, if nothing else, had constitutional protections as an American citizen.

Carcetti opened the door, stepped out. Then turned back, looked at Shafer from the doorway.

"Just one thing, Ellis. I know you and your buddy have looked all over the world for that HEU. So have we, believe it or not. We can't find it. Tell me, if it's not Iranian, whose is it?"

Shafer could only shake his head.

"Whose?" Carcetti shouted now. "Tell me. *Whose?*"

Shafer felt no choice but to answer "I don't know."

"And you know why? Because it's from *Iran.*" Carcetti slammed the door so hard as he left that the plaster wall beside it cracked from floor to ceiling.

Shafer sat alone, wondering how long Carcetti would leave him here, whether he'd have a warrant when he returned. Either way, Shafer believed he had done all he could to take the red dot off Wells's chest. He wasn't the praying type. Never had been. So he settled for crossing his fingers and hoping Wells would use that freedom.

20

Wells found a computer in the corner of a crowded café off Tahrir Square and logged into the account he'd created to email Adina Leffetz. He wasn't expecting a response. To his surprise, he found not one but two replies.

Both from her, though from two different accounts. The first was blank. Wells suspected it contained a tracking virus, because his computer briefly froze when he opened it. No matter. Let Salome try to find him in Cairo.

It was the second email, sent a few hours after the first, that stopped him. *John. So good to hear from you. And yes, I miss you, too. I'd love to see you. So would my boss. Let's meet in Tel Aviv tomorrow . . . Adina.*

She was offering the ultimate honeypot, a chance to talk to the man himself. Still, the meeting stank of a Hotel California trap.

Once she had him inside Duberman's mansion, why would she let him leave?

He ought to forget the offer, move on. He could book a flight to South Africa and Witwans. Or call Shafer again, see if he had anything new. Although Shafer had gone dark since the morning.

As for Witwans, Wells didn't want to go unless he knew the man had something. Without a private jet, he'd lose the next day getting to Johannesburg and then Witwans's home. If he was wrong, he'd lose yet another day getting back. He couldn't afford to waste that time. And he feared that the NSA was now up on the only passports he was carrying. As soon as he boarded an international flight, they and the CIA would know exactly where to find him. Until he knew if the agency wanted to bring him in, he couldn't take that chance.

Tel Aviv, for better or worse, was less than five hundred miles from Cairo, less than an hour by air if Wells could figure out how to fly there without being caught. Plus, truth be told, he wanted to see Duberman. He couldn't help himself. The offer tempted him. He was sniffing at it like a mouse at a hunk of cheese, trying to convince himself the net overhead wasn't a trap.

■ ■ ■ ■

No. He'd made this mistake in Istanbul. He needed someone with him to guarantee that Duberman wouldn't hold him indefinitely. Who? Shafer was out of pocket. Rudi was old and sick and had done all he could.

Which left Duto.

Wells bought yet another new phone, ducked into an alley off Talaat Harb, one of the avenues that spoked north off Tahrir. He pushed himself against a wall as men strolled by. Since the riots and the revolution and the counterrevolution and the gropes and rapes that had come with them, women were invisible around Tahrir after dark.

Duto answered after two rings.

"Get yourself arrested again?"

"Not yet."

"Too bad."

"I need a private plane. Now. With you on it."

"Where am I going?"

Wells debated being coy, but if anyone was tracing Duto's phone, they would see the Egyptian prefix anyway. "Cairo."

"Why?"

"Tell you when you get here."

Duto was silent.

"And don't forget the bag I left with Ellis." Before heading out from Washington the week before, Wells had left a knapsack stuffed with the kind of goodies that cause problems at border control. It would come in handy for the meeting with Duberman.

"Ellis." Duto stopped. Something he didn't want to tell Wells on an open line.

"It's at his house. Is that a problem?"

"No, but I need a few hours to put this together. Plus, what, eleven in the air?"

"As long as you can get here by noon tomorrow."

"If you aren't at the airport, I'll kill you."

Join the crowd. Wells hung up, found a two-window café and ordered an oversize pita stuffed with greasy chicken and falafel. Delicious. Before the 2011 revolution, some Cairo restaurants had served beer and wine. A handful had even served hard liquor. Although Islamic law banned alcohol, the sales were a concession to Western tourists, the millions of Coptic Christians who still lived in Egypt, and Cairo's own cosmopolitan past.

But after the revolution the Muslim Brotherhood had sharply raised taxes on alcohol. Some restaurants that served it had seen their windows smashed. Even though

470

the army had forced out the Brotherhood in 2013, the alcohol seemed to have disappeared, or at least been forced into the back rooms. Another way that Egypt had become more like Saudi Arabia, its neighbor across the Red Sea.

Wells washed down the last of his pita with a lukewarm Coke and set out on a countersurveillance run. He didn't think anyone was following him, but he wanted to be sure. Tahrir Square was an excellent place to find out. The passageways that ran underneath the plaza allowed for an almost infinite variety of moves. Wells spent twenty minutes wending his way through them and then doubled back and at a near run came back to the entrance on the square's northeast corner, where he'd entered. He stepped into one of the cabs that were ubiquitous in Tahrir.

"Salaam aleikum."

"Aleikum salaam. Where to, my friend?"

"Ramses Square." Another massive square to the northeast, this one home to the city's main railway station.

At a traffic light a block south of the square, Wells handed the cabbie his money.

"But we haven't arrived yet."

"I like to walk." Wells opened the door and stepped out, walking southeast, away from both Ramses and Tahrir. He was now sure no one was on him. He had run across the Egyptian security services before. They were decent trackers, but they weren't subtle. Americans would have stood out even more. He found a café with an Internet station and checked in. Shafer still hadn't replied, but Duto had, with a jet tail number and an arrival time. And something else, a phone number. *Col. Alim Bourak. Tell him I said hello.*

"Salaam aleikum."

Bourak's voice was wary.

"Colonel. A mutual friend suggested I call," Wells said, in English.

"Does he have a name?"

"Duto."

"Do you have a name?"

"No."

A long pause.

"All right. Where are you?"

Wells told him.

"Stay there."

Words that made Wells want to be anywhere else.

Bourak showed a half hour later. He was a tall man, mid-fifties, with a slight limp and the dull eyes of a *mukhabarat* officer who had seen more than he wished.

■ ■ ■

"Salaam aleikum."

"As-aleikum salaam."

"You speak Arabic."

"Nam."

"All right, come with me," Bourak said in Arabic. "But no talking."

Bourak turned out to live in a two-bedroom apartment in one of Cairo's better neighborhoods. Wells didn't know why the breadth of Duto's contacts still surprised him. The man had been DCI for almost a decade. "One night, yes?" Bourak said, as he closed the apartment door behind Wells. "Then you can tell your friend we're even."

"I can talk now?"

"As long as you don't tell me your name. Would you like something to drink? Unfortunately, I don't have alcohol."

Not a complete surprise. A five-foot-wide photo of the *hajj* pilgrimage to Mecca dominated the living room.

"I don't drink." Wells examined the photo.

"You know the *hajj*?"

"I'm Muslim."

Bourak squinted at Wells.

"Even without your name, I think I know you."

473

"Did you take the pilgrimage?"

"Yes."

"I've always wanted to go."

"What they say is true. It's difficult. So many people, not nearly enough space. The crush. The smells. No one has bathed properly in weeks. Yet sooner or later you stop fighting the pressure. Then something strange happens. I can't describe it exactly. Not so much that you're closer to Allah as that He's closer to you. If you die there, no matter. Maybe this is what heaven is, so many people and no space to think about anything. No thoughts of the heat and the dust and the thirst. No concerns about money or comfort. Just these people bending together under some will bigger than their own. I wish every Muslim could do it."

"Not exactly how the Quran describes paradise."

"Don't tell me you believe in seventy-two virgins."

"I'm not sure I believe in virgins, period."

Bourak laughed.

"How did a man with your convictions rise so far in the *muk*?" The secret police were not exactly fans of the Muslim Brotherhood.

"They need a few of us who know the

prayers. But colonel is as high as I'll ever get."

Wells put his hand over his heart. "Let's pray, then, Alim. For Egypt."

"And peace."

21
THREE DAYS . . .

CAIRO

Cairo International Airport was as ramshackle as everything else in Egypt, a maze of potholed access roads and unfinished construction. Hall 4, the airport's VIP wing, was the inevitable exception, modern and high-ceilinged. Nearly empty, too. Wealthy travelers weren't visiting Cairo much these days.

So Wells had a lounge to himself as he waited for Bourak. Duto's jet had landed, but Wells couldn't reach it without a new passport. Bourak didn't have the juice to walk Wells through border control without identification. And Wells didn't want to use either of his current passports. The NSA was surely watching for both John Wells and Roger Bishop.

Duto held the solution. The bag of toys he'd picked up at Shafer's house included a fresh passport. Wells had never used it before, and he was sure it wasn't on any watch lists. Even better, it was several years old, with a slightly blurred photo, so face-recognition software wouldn't jump it. Wells could again travel without fear of being picked up, at least for a few hours.

One day he'd run out of spares, and life would get even trickier. For now, he was still in the game. As soon as Bourak returned from the tarmac, Wells would be on his way to Duberman. He stuffed away his impatience and he watched the headlines scroll across CNN International:

AMERICAN DEADLINE LESS THAN 72 HOURS AWAY . . . NO TALKS SCHEDULED . . . PENTAGON: 82ND AIRBORNE FULLY DEPLOYED . . . IRANIAN PRESIDENT ROUHANI: NUCLEAR ENRICHMENT IS "RIGHT AND DUTY" . . . SUPREME LEADER KHAMENEI: "ALLAH WILL PROTECT US" . . .

Until the words BREAKING NEWS flashed in foot-high letters, and the scroll changed:

AMERICAN AIRLINES JET MISSING OFF SOUTH AMERICAN COAST . . . 767 LEFT RIO FOR JFK 7 HOURS AGO,

LOST FROM RADAR 2 HOURS AGO . . .
AA 964 CARRIED 229 PASSENGERS,
CREW . . . BRAZIL, US, VENEZUELA
SENDING SEARCH TEAMS . . . DEBRIS
FIELD REPORTED . . .

Then the real surprise:

SECOND PLANE FROM RIO ALSO MISS-
ING . . . DELTA FLIGHT LOST IN SOUTH-
ERN CARIBBEAN . . . DISAPPEARED
SAME TIME AS AA JET . . . DELTA: 257
PASSENGERS, 14 CREW ON BOARD . . .

Five hundred more people dead, and the
war hadn't even started. The odds that two
planes from the same airport had both
crashed accidentally at the same time were
infinitesimal. The Iranians were warning the
President that they would disrupt aviation
worldwide if the United States attacked.
This time, they had covered their tracks,
sending the evidence to the bottom of the
Atlantic. Washington would accuse, Tehran
would deny, and the deadline would tick
closer. Wells hated Duberman for causing
this chaos, and himself for not finding a way
to stop the man.

The lounge door swung open. Bourak
walked in, passport in hand. "Yours, I think,
Mr. Michael." The passport was in the name

of Michael Ishmael Jefferson. Wells made sure he had its biographical data memorized, then tucked it away and gave Bourak his other passports. They could only cause trouble.

"I should hold them?"

"Burn them." His lives, real and fake, turning to ash.

But nothing came easy this mission. The immigration agent took immediate exception to the new passport. "Bad photo."

"Sorry."

"No entry stamp. You came through Cairo?" The guard tapped at his keyboard. "I don't see it."

They'd run across the only government worker in Egypt who wanted to do his job. Bourak flipped out his *mukhabarat* identification. "This man has been a guest of mine."

"Then maybe you tell me why there's no record," the guard said in Arabic.

"Because your computers don't work," Bourak said. "I appreciate your boldness, taking this tone with a colonel in the GID." The General Intelligence Directorate, the *muk*'s official title. "Call your supervisor. I want to tell him you're such a good officer."

The guard muttered under his breath.

"What?"

"I said, I'll take his picture, and yours, too, and send him on."

A minute later, they were through. Wells followed Bourak downstairs to an unmarked door that led outside the terminal, onto the tarmac. Bourak embraced Wells, the emotion genuine. "Maybe one day we'll take the *hajj* together."

"I'd like that."

The jet was a Gulfstream G650, long, sleek, and white. No corporate insignia, nothing but the registration number tattooed on the engine. Duto didn't stand, instead offering Wells a cheap finger-to-temple sideways salute. "Cap'n."

"Crunch," Wells said. "Do I want to know whose ride this is?"

"For now, it's ours. I told the people who lent it to me you were good for it. More important, where are we going? Pilot says we have fifteen hundred miles of fuel left. We need to top up?"

"Not yet. Tel Aviv."

"You hear that?" Duto yelled through the open cockpit door to the pilots. "Ben Gurion. Refuel there. Make sure they know it's an American jet so they don't give us any trouble about landing rights."

480

"Yessir." The cockpit door swung shut.

"We meeting Rudi?"

"Duberman."

Duto grunted in surprise. "How'd you work that?"

"I didn't. He asked. Through Salome. Didn't say why, but I'm guessing it's not a confession."

"So he wants a meeting, and you come running to me to protect you." Duto gave Wells an *I'm-not-going-to-let-you-live-this-one-down* smirk.

"I don't know any other senators, and after what happened in Russia I needed someone who could guarantee safe passage." As soon as he explained, Wells wished he hadn't. Duto surely already understood. "Speaking of. Where's Ellis?"

Duto's momentary hesitation told Wells the news wasn't good.

"Lucy Joyner gets in early. Lucky for us. She came to me yesterday about an hour before you called. Shafer showed up at her office around seven a.m., made her take his picture. He thought the seventh floor was going to grab him, and he was right."

"He's under arrest?"

"Not yet. But Justice is involved. Best I can tell, they're holding him as a material witness right now, no charges."

"Any idea why now?"

"He passed Lucy the name of a website he found that connects Salome and Jess Bunshaft. I don't think you've met Bunshaft. He's a Hebley guy. Mid-level. It's nothing that proves anything, just a picture from a couple years ago. But maybe that freaked them out."

"But they can't hold him indefinitely —"

"Long enough. From their point of view the easiest move would be to toss him in a cell for a couple weeks. But maybe he told them that Lucy had his picture. So, for whatever reason, they decided to get Justice involved."

"Good, right?"

"Maybe. Means somebody's watching. But also a criminal process. Justice, they'll say he's a U.S. citizen, we can't hold him without charges. Fine. Hebley gives them enough for a one-count complaint for leaking classified material, a couple excerpts from the tapes."

The tapes of Shafer calling Wells. Wells had blocked them out.

"He was stupid, John. Should never have talked to you from his office. They don't mention your name in the complaint, just co-conspirator A. As long as you weren't cleared for the information, they don't even have to prove you misused it. The fact he passed it is enough."

"Then?"

"Then tonight they find some friendly federal judge who believes in hanging 'em high, and they ask for no bail. And they get it. Remember, Shafer doesn't even have a lawyer at this point, nobody's arguing the other side. Presto, they have an excuse to transfer him tomorrow to the detention center in Alexandria. And you know, short ride, but delays, he gets stuck in processing. All that time, he can't call anyone. That's tomorrow gone. Then, the next morning, his wife is screaming, finally somebody lets him make a phone call, he gets a lawyer. Even so, whoever he hires has to figure out what's going on and file for an emergency hearing. That's the day *after* tomorrow gone. Then, the hearing, Justice pushes back, says national security, they're still looking for safe-deposit boxes, secret bank accounts —"

"Anyway, we've attacked Iran by then." Wells hated the thought of Shafer in jail. He would backtalk a guard, get himself in trouble. "And you're so sure about this —"

"Because it's what I'd do."

The cockpit door swung open. "Plans filed," the pilot said. He was tall, with hair so blond it was almost white. "We'll push in a minute. I know you want privacy, so the flight attendant won't bother you, but please strap in. We should be in the air forty minutes, give or take." He disappeared again.

"All these years, everything you've seen," Duto said. "Still can't admit the game only has one rule."

"And what's that?" Though Wells knew what Duto would say.

"Just win, baby. I know you think Hebley should know better —"

The jet's engines spooled. Wells buckled up as the plane rolled back. He didn't want to hear this speech, yet he couldn't pretend he wasn't fascinated by Duto's cynicism.

"But he's neck-deep in this now, and the only way out is right through Tehran —"

"We can't go to war on a lie."

"We have the best army in the world, John. We can go to war because our beer was flat. And the guys in Tehran aren't our friends. Long as we win, this unpleasantness gets forgotten. One thing I've learned about the folks back home in my brief political career, they are results-oriented."

"And if we lose?"

"Nobody starts a war expecting to lose. I promise you what the Pentagon is telling the President right now is that we've learned from Iraq and Afghanistan, we'll roll right up to the nuclear factories, blast 'em open, see what's inside. Let the Rev Guard try to hit us from the flanks, the back, our airpower will destroy them as soon as they mass. That's one thing we know how to do. That this isn't about roadside bombs, that for a change we'll fight the war that we want and then get out. No occupation."

Duto made the case so enthusiastically that Wells wondered why he had come here at all. But of course he wanted the White House. Taking down this plot was his only chance. And with Shafer out of action, Wells had had no choice but to ask Duto for help.

Duto, who had betrayed him a half-dozen times.

Duto seemed to read Wells's mind. "Politics makes strange bedfellows."

"This isn't politics."

"Everything's politics."

The Gulfstream turned onto an access runway, bounced along the rough concrete.

"But Shafer will get out, right?"

"Make bail, sure."

"And after that?"

"You know the answer. Depends who wins."

■ ■ ■ ■

Wells feared yet more immigration head-
aches in Tel Aviv, but Duto's black VIP
passport smoothed the way.

"Before we tell Salome we're here, I want
to check in with the embassy," Duto said.
The American embassy to Israel was based
in Tel Aviv, not Jerusalem. The building was
the usual recessed-windows concrete fortress, though weirdly enough it sat only a
block from the beach. The juxtaposition
made for odd photos when protesters
showed.

So Duto wanted to be sure that the government knew he was in Israel. Duberman
probably wouldn't be crazy enough to
kidnap a senator, but the move was prudent
just in case.

Duto walked out of the embassy ninety
minutes later, joined Wells on the prom-
enade. The afternoon was unseasonably
warm, and the Israelis were taking advantage. Four bikinied women knocked a vol-
leyball.

"Nice scenery."

In fact, Wells was thinking mainly of the
three-inch blade he had taped to his left

thigh, just below the groin. It was ceramic, sharp enough to cut glass. On his right leg he'd taped the handle, two and a half inches of rigid plastic. A metal detector wouldn't pick either one up. A full-body airport-style scanner might, but even Duberman probably didn't have one of those at home. And no matter how well-trained they were, guards were reluctant to frisk too far up the thighs. Of course, the knife wasn't much use to Wells in its current spot either. He'd need an excuse to spend a couple of minutes in a bathroom once he got past the frisk.

"Embassy ask what you were doing?"

"I told them I was meeting Duberman. They were smart enough to leave it there. Equal branch of government and all that. Come on, let's go."

Wells had figured that Duto agreed to back him on this mission because he didn't see any choice, because he realized that after his fight with Donna Green he had gone too far to back out. But the enthusiasm in his voice suggested another possibility. The former DCI wanted to be here, back in the field. They found an Internet kiosk and Wells typed a six-word email: *In Tel Aviv. See you soon.* "Good?"

"Let's hope he's home."

"He's home." Wells hit send.

Duberman's mansion sat two blocks from the ocean, in Tel Aviv's fanciest neighborhood, north of downtown. A high concrete wall along the sidewalk blocked any view of the house. A Range Rover limousine was parked in front of the main gate. Two unsmiling men sat inside the Rover. Two more stood beside it.

Duto stepped onto the sidewalk as Wells pushed a hundred-dollar bill into the cabbie's palm. "Wait."

The driver nodded, but when Wells stepped out, he pulled away, tires screeching. The guards beside the Rover stepped forward. Thick, Slavic-looking men. Part of the Russian emigration to Israel, maybe.

"Your boss is waiting for us."

The lead guard murmured in Hebrew into a shoulder-mounted radio.

Five minutes passed before the door beside the main gate opened, and Salome stepped out. Despite himself, Wells couldn't help but notice that she wore a black T-shirt and calf-length gray pants that showed off her best feature, her smoothly muscled arms and legs.

"Senator. What a pleasant surprise. I'm Adina."

She smiled at Wells. He recognized the look from Volgograd. "John. Wonderful to see you again. Are you carrying a weapon?"

"To a fancy place like this? 'Course not."

"You don't mind if we check."

Wells stepped up, spread his hands against the wall. The bodyguard wanded him with a metal detector, then frisked him, a thorough, two-handed job, down one arm and the other from wrist to pits, around the torso. He squatted low and came up from the ankles. He reached mid-thigh and Wells had a moment of worry. But with a couple inches to spare, he pulled off.

"And you, Senator?" Salome said.

"You want to frisk me?"

"I want him to frisk you."

Duto stepped next to Wells.

Two more guards joined them as Salome led them into the mansion's fifty-foot-long front entrance gallery, filled with modern art that Wells didn't recognize, oversize balloon animals, and what looked like a massive pile of Play-Doh.

They walked up a staircase that tracked into a hallway with a half-dozen bubble surveillance cameras in the ceiling. The corridor ended at a windowless door. Its deadbolt snapped back even before they reached it. Salome pulled it open, waved in Wells and Duto. The guards stayed behind.

Inside, a square white room that Wells guessed was Duberman's outer office. Televisions displayed the casinos that formed the 88 Gamma empire, mostly night shots taken from helicopters. Their hotel towers were fifty stories or more of black glass and white neon, sleek futuristic cylinders that dominated the cities around them. Interspersed with the photos were corporate statistics: 88 Gamma had 49,000 employees in eighteen countries, yearly profits of $3.2 billion, a stock-market value of $60 billion. And Duberman owned almost half of it. No wonder he could afford to spend $200 million on a presidential campaign. He wasn't the richest man Wells had ever met. That honor, if honor was the right word, belonged to King Abdullah. But he was certainly the richest *self-made* man.

And the richest enemy.

Aside from the pictures, the outer office had two desks for assistants who were nowhere in sight, plus a white couch where anyone who got this far could wait to beg Duberman's favor. Based on its spotless leather, few people did. More than ever,

Wells wanted to meet Duberman, see for himself what drove the man. If he could.

Salome knocked on the inner door. It opened fractionally. She murmured in Hebrew. Waited. Turned to them. "Come."

22

ISTRES–LE TUBÉ AIR BASE, NEAR
  MARSEILLES, FRANCE

Since the first American drone strike, the
Iranian government had said it would never
meet the President's demands to open its
nuclear program. Both publicly and through
the French foreign ministry, which was
secretly passing messages between Tehran
and Washington, Iran insisted it would not
even consider negotiations until the United
States retracted its invasion threat.

But the previous afternoon, the Iranians
had seemed to blink. The French Foreign
Minister, Marie le Claire, called Green
herself. "Behzadi says he'll meet you tomorrow, if you wish."

Fardis Behzadi was an Iranian parliamen-
tary deputy, one of the few Iranian politicians trusted by both moderates and hardliners. As a teenager in Tehran in 1979, he
had helped lead the takeover of the Ameri-

can embassy. Four years later, as a junior officer in the Iran–Iraq war, he had lost both legs to a mine, forever ensuring his revolutionary bona fides. At the same time, he was known to believe that *Allah gives us life, but full bellies make full hearts.* Unpoetically translated, the slogan meant the Shia regime wouldn't survive unless it improved the Iranian economy and reduced unemployment.

Behzadi couldn't negotiate a deal himself, but Green could be certain that Hassan Rouhani, Iran's president, would hear whatever she told him. "Best news I've heard all week." She was tempted to agree on the spot, but her own president might not approve. "Give me five minutes."

She needed only two.

"This guy's the real deal?" POTUS said.

"The realest. Sir."

"Go, then."

They agreed to meet at 2 p.m. the next afternoon at Istres–Le Tubé, a big French air base near the Mediterranean coast. They would each bring one advisor/translator. No guards. The French would handle security.

Their only disagreement came over where exactly they should meet. Neither would board the other's plane. They were less worried about being kidnapped than taped. But neither wanted to give the French a chance to record them, either. Ultimately, they agreed to talk on the tarmac, a ridiculous but necessary solution.

Once she'd iced the details, Green spent a half hour going over talking points with the President and the SecDef. The only other officials who knew about the meeting were the DCI and the CIA's top Iran expert, a forty-something man named Ted Rodgers who would go with Green and serve as her translator and advisor.

Unfortunately, Rodgers couldn't give her much insight into what Behzadi might want. The CIA had no reliable sources inside the top ranks of the Iranian government, much less the Revolutionary Guard's Quds Force. And in recent years, the Iranians had grown expert at keeping the National Security Agency out of their computer and telecom systems. The NSA believed that military and Quds Force commanders used a network of motorcycle couriers to send written notes to one another. The couriers functioned almost as a mail service, running both point-to-point and through a central facility outside Tehran.

So Rodgers had no better idea than anyone else why Behzadi had asked for this meeting. Still, Green was glad to have him along. He spoke perfect Farsi and knew every detail of Behzadi's biography.

To preserve secrecy, Green insisted on flying on a NetJets charter rather than an Air Force jet. The Secret Service objected. *Only sat connection is in the cockpit,* her security chief told her. *You'll be unreachable.*

I'll manage, Green said. She didn't tell him she saw the lack of coms as a positive. For the first time in the years since she'd taken this job, she would have a few hours to herself.

She spent the hours before her flight reading the plans for the war that would come if her meeting failed. The attack would begin with two days of bombing raids and missile strikes to knock out Iran's fighters and air-defense systems. On the third day, with complete air superiority, the Air Force would level the Iranian nuclear reactor at Bushehr and attack border garrisons, setting the stage for a ground invasion at dawn on the fourth day. The 82nd Airborne Division would strike from Turkey while three Marine regiments would advance from Iraq, close to thirty thousand soldiers and Marines in all. They would aim for Natanz and Fordow, the two complexes where the

Iranians performed their most important nuclear work. Both were close to the holy city of Qom — and, not coincidentally, near the geographical center of Iran, hundreds of miles from any border.

Rather than trying to take both at once, the 82nd and the Marines would converge on Natanz, the most crucial site of all. Natanz was an underground factory housed inside a military base, protected by more than ten thousand soldiers and the best air-defense system anywhere in Iran. The United States would depend on speed and airpower to take Natanz within five days of crossing the border. Over the next forty-eight hours, the Marines and the 82nd would search and destroy the facility while using the base's airfield to resupply their troops and evacuate their wounded. They would then fight north to Fordow, the second crucial enrichment factory, where they would repeat the drill. They would then retreat almost five hundred miles south to the Persian Gulf for evacuation.

The 75th Ranger Regiment and a fourth Marine regiment would be held back in case the first invasion forces ran into trouble. If neither did, the twenty-two hundred Rangers and four thousand Marines in the reserve would be flown into Natanz to reinforce the initial units for the second half of the fight. Still, the total invasion force would be only about one-twentieth the size of the Iranian army, which included three hundred fifty thousand soldiers and an equal number of reservists. Of course, the United States had far superior weaponry, battlefield surveillance, and communications, but the sheer numerical imbalance was not comforting.

Even under the best case, the planners believed that several hundred American soldiers and Marines would die. The Iranians knew exactly the sites the United States was targeting. They could concentrate artillery and armor on the highways and bridges that led to Natanz and Fordow. American airpower would shred the Iranian positions, but not before they had inflicted plenty of casualties on the invading units. The Iranians would also try to lay the massive roadside bombs that guerrillas had used so lethally against Americans in Iraq, though the Pentagon had a countermeasure, round-the-clock drones overflying the roads the ground forces would use and destroying bomb-planting teams before they could even dig holes.

But the real concern was that Iran would block the advance of one or both invasion forces. Neither the 82nd nor the Marines had nearly enough men to protect long supply lines. Instead, they would advance in tight clusters, relying on the ammunition, fuel, and food that they brought with them until they reached Natanz and resupply. Along the way, they would have to depend on the Air Force to defend their flanks and rear. The attack would be almost a *blitzkrieg,* though aiming to take territory rather than encircle and destroy enemy armies. It ran counter to the doctrine the Pentagon had used to invade Iraq in 1991 and 2003. In both those cases, the United States had slowly assembled massive armies and then demolished the undermanned Iraqi forces that faced them.

The plan gave the United States the chance to destroy Iran's nuclear program quickly, and potentially with far fewer casualties than a multi-year occupation. But if it failed, the invading forces risked being surrounded and trapped in a way no American soldiers had been since the Battle of Chosin Reservoir in the Korean War. After three days of simulations, the Pentagon put the odds of rapid success at 75 percent, of a campaign that was longer and bloodier than expected but ended in American victory at 15 percent, and of failure at 10 percent.

Both the chairman of the Joint Chiefs and the Secretary of Defense told the President that 10 percent was too high a risk and that he should consider a bigger invasion force. "It will take longer, both to put together and to move once we cross the border, but it'll be safer."

"Maybe the first few days will be safer," the President said. "Then we're stuck. It's your job to make sure that ten percent doesn't happen."

As she reread the plan, Green understood the military's concerns. The United States had lost almost seven thousand soldiers in Iraq and Afghanistan, but those deaths had occurred during more than a decade of fighting. Here, the United States could see hundreds of soldiers killed in a day. And that wasn't even the worst case. The worst case was that the entire invasion collapsed and that the 82nd or the Marines were forced to retreat to their bases in Turkey or Afghanistan. Or to surrender. Americans couldn't even imagine that their soldiers would ever be forced to throw down their weapons and put up their hands. The psychic damage would be unthinkable. Green believed that a major defeat would cause America to retreat from the world, becoming isolationist in a way it had not been in

499

generations. And history suggested that whatever the problems with American leadership, the world was a more dangerous place without it.

But the President had made up his mind. Despite all the uncertainties, including the fact that the CIA still couldn't find the Revolutionary Guard colonel who had first told it about the highly enriched uranium in Istanbul, he would not back down from his ultimatum. At the same time, he did not want another long war in a Muslim country. He would live with a ninety percent chance of success. And the decision belonged to him, no one else.

Green had done her best to help him sort the pros and cons. But as she finished rereading the briefing book that night, Green was happy she hadn't had to decide.

She and Rodgers left Dulles just after midnight and ran into a winter storm over the western Atlantic. She was so tired that even the bumps couldn't keep her awake. She woke to bright blue skies, the sun already behind them. "Where are we?"

"Western France." Rodgers looked grim.

"What's wrong? Weather make us late?" She checked her watch: 7 a.m., so 1 p.m.

local. Right on time, a few minutes late at most.

He handed her his CIA BlackBerry. "Reception just kicked in."

The headline jumped out at her. *American Airlines Jet Lost Off South America . . .*

Iran's hardliners had just incinerated five hundred people to send her, and maybe their moderate counterparts in Tehran, a message: *You're wasting your time.* Point made. This meeting, their last best hope for peace, was over before it even began.

She wondered if she should order the pilots to land in Paris, refuel, turn around. But they were barely an hour from Marseilles. Might as well go ahead. At least she'd get to see Behzadi in person, judge for herself whether he'd had advance knowledge of the attack.

"I should call in," Rodgers said.

"No." Besides two hundred new emails, his BlackBerry had seventeen unheard voice mails. No doubt hers had dozens more. She didn't want advice or opinions. Not now. She handed it back to him. "Keep reading so we don't miss any updates, but don't send any emails, don't take any calls. I don't want to talk to *anyone* until I hear for myself what he has to say."

■ ■ ■ ■

The runway at Istres–Le Tubé stretched three-plus miles, the longest in Europe. NASA had considered using the base for emergency space shuttle landings. The Bombardier taxied for what seemed like an eternity. When they finally reached the apron at the end of the overrun, Behzadi's jet was nowhere in sight. Insult to injury. Instead, five armored SUVs waited, along with a dozen French paratroopers, red berets cocked jauntily, short sleeves cuffed smartly over their biceps. They rolled a Jetway to the cabin door. A French air force officer in a perfectly pressed uniform mounted the steps.

"Madame National Security Advisor" — only a Frenchman could make those four words sound like an invitation to dance — "I'm Colonel Muscoot. I regret to tell you your friend is not so punctual. We expect him within twenty minutes. Would you like something to eat while you wait? I have sandwiches."

Muscoot's manner suggested he hadn't heard yet about the downed jets, and Green couldn't bring herself to tell him. "No thanks."

"They're excellent, I assure you."

Why not? They would be back in the air soon enough. Might as well ride on a full stomach. "All right, then."

He whistled sharply and a paratrooper trotted up the stairs with a picnic basket, a ridiculous and perfect flourish. Under better circumstances, Green would have been thrilled. Muscoot took it and stepped past her into the cabin. She realized that the lunch had been an excuse for him to peek inside the Bombardier, make sure it didn't have a kidnap team stowed in back.

Still, she was glad she'd agreed. The basket held salads, tomato-and-mozzarella sandwiches on black bread, a thermos of steaming hot coffee. She had a feeling that if she'd asked for a bottle of wine, Muscoot would have snapped his fingers and produced it. While they ate, she asked about the SUVs on the tarmac, which seemed to have come straight from a *Mad Max* set.

"We call them VBLs. Not so armored as the Humvee, but quick. Also, it — how do you say this — it swims."

"Amphibious."

"*Oui,* amphibious." Muscoot gave her a thousand-watt smile. Before she could come up with a suitably witty answer, his radio buzzed. After a brief back-and-forth in

French: "Please excuse me. Monsieur Behzadi's plane is arriving." He trotted outside.

Green put down the sandwich. She had lost her appetite.

Ten minutes later, Behzadi's jet rolled close. Muscoot's men brought a wheelchair ramp to its front cabin door. A minute later, two men emerged, one pushing the other down the ramp. Green could wait no longer. She pushed open her own jet's cabin door, trotted down the staircase, across the tarmac. Rodgers followed.

She reached the base of the wheelchair ramp just as Behzadi rolled off it. He was in his fifties but looked older. His eyes were pouchy, his skin sallow. He wore a white short-sleeved shirt and an elaborately knitted shawl over the stumps of his legs.

He reached up with a fleshy hand. "Ms. Green," he said. "I'm Fardis."

Either he was the world's best liar, or he didn't know. Green didn't know which was worse. "Can we have a moment, Colonel?" she said to Muscoot. As the Frenchman retreated, Green pulled Rodgers close.

"No pleasantries. Ask him if he knows. If he doesn't, tell him. Make sure he understands that we're blaming his bosses for killing five hundred civilians." No matter how good Behzadi's English, she wanted this stretch of conversation in Farsi so she could be certain he understood.

Rodgers squatted beside the wheelchair, spoke for about thirty seconds. Behzadi shook his head, *no no no.* He interrupted, but Rodgers talked over him. After a few seconds more, Behzadi reached out and grabbed Green's wrist with his right hand. She pulled back, but hc held her tight, his grip strengthened by a lifetime working the wheelchair.

"I didn't know of this," he said in English.

She wrenched her arm away from Behzadi and squatted down beside Rodgers. International diplomacy at its finest. "You don't even deny your side did this?"

Behzadi spoke for a minute in Farsi. When he was done, Rodgers said, "He doesn't know who did it. He says he wishes that this hadn't happened, civilian deaths are always a tragedy, but it doesn't change the reality that an invasion would be a disaster for both our countries —"

The worst possible answer. Green felt a surge of pure fury. She wanted to tip the wheelchair over. "You were human for thirty seconds, now you're back to toeing the party line."

"Leave us," Behzadi said to Rodgers. "I speak English well enough for this."

"Donna?"

Green nodded. Rodgers stepped back.

"All right. Speak, then."

"Iran has no need to apologize. Your country provoked all this. Your President. On false evidence. As you must know."

"Prove it. Let us in."

"Never."

"When I left Dulles last night, I was in a good mood. Had my speech all planned out. I wanted to tell you, what the President's said publicly is true. That we have our differences with you, but we're not interested in regime change. Occupying Iran. We learned that lesson. We just want to be sure that your nuclear program isn't a threat. Give us a chance to see for ourselves and this ends." She shook her head. "Turns out you don't want it to end."

"I don't make these choices —"

"I know you don't. I don't know if you're a bad guy or not, Fardis. I don't even know what you came here to say. At this point, I don't care either. Here's what I know. You're just a guy with no legs who wastes my time while your bosses blow up planes full of Americans."

Green stood, walked around the wheel-chair, spun it to face the ramp. "Roll on home now, and tell Rouhani and everyone else they have two days to agree to what the President has asked. Otherwise, we're coming in. To Natanz, Fordow, every other factory you've ever built. We're going to figure out exactly what you've put there. How much uranium you've made. Then we're going to blow them up. Every last one of them. Then, if you're lucky, we'll leave."

Behzadi stared at her in silence.

"Your English good enough to pass that message on, Fardis? Or you need a translation?"

"You'll regret this. You think you frighten me? And eighty million of my people? You think we don't know what to do with Americans? I saw your guards at the embassy begging for their lives with my own eyes." Behzadi pointed at his eyes. "Those brave Marines. I watched them piss themselves."

Before she could do something truly foolish, like tip the wheelchair, Green walked away.

The last, best hope for peace.

23

Duberman's office had the windows the outer suite lacked, overlooking the city to the south and the flat sea to the west. The winter sun hung low over the water, reminding Wells that this day, too, was mostly done. So many lost hours in this chase, so few left.

Duberman leaned against his desk. He was bigger than Wells expected, handsome, with a wide, square face. His brown eyes were flecked with something lighter. Leonine. He wore linen pants and buttery brown shoes, a plain white shirt, a simple wedding ring.

The man next to him carried a stubby pistol on his hip, the only weapon openly displayed so far in this mansion. The bodyguard was in his early fifties, with a trim body, a hollow face, and eyes as mirrored as if he were wearing sunglasses. He would shoot them without question if Duberman gave the order, Wells knew.

Duberman grinned like they were gamblers who had shown up at his casino with a million dollars each and a reputation for bad luck. "Mr. Wells. Senator Duto. A pleasure. I'm Aaron. This is Gideon." The bodyguard shook his head. "Excuse him. He doesn't like strangers."

Duberman's voice carried a touch of Southern twang. He'd grown up in Atlanta, Wells remembered. Like the room and the clothes, his voice broadcast an easy, overwhelming confidence. Wells wondered whether the attitude had come with the money or vice versa. He wanted to hate the man, but he had nothing to grip yet. Duberman was a thousand-foot rock face with no visible holds.

Gideon mumbled in Hebrew. "He'd like to search you," Duberman said.

"Sure." Though Wells didn't want to be frisked again. He sensed Gideon would be unafraid to get up close and personal.

"No," Duto said. He knew about the knife. "He's got the gun. We were searched outside. Enough is enough."

Duberman said something in Hebrew to Salome and she answered, presumably explaining that they'd been thoroughly checked already. Wells realized that her personal bodyguard, the one with the scars, wasn't around. He ought to be. Wells couldn't imagine an errand more important than this meeting. But asking about him would only call attention to the fact that Wells had noticed his absence.

"All right. No frisk." Gideon muttered something else, and Duberman smiled. "But know he'll shoot you even faster then."

The office was thirty feet long, divided into three sections, with Duberman's desk in the center, a couch on one side, a square wooden table on the other. Duberman led them to the table and they sat, Wells facing Duto, and Duberman Salome. Like bridge teams.

"Mr. Wells. Senator. I'm sure you won't try to tape this meeting. If you do, know that this room has a jammer that disables microphones. Also, your mobile phones will not work here. Only the outer suite."

"Great," Duto said. "We can focus on work."

Duberman ignored him, leaned toward Wells. "Let me start by asking, do you think your religion is playing a role in your efforts here? Maybe subconsciously."

Wells knew Duberman wanted to provoke him, but he rose to the bait anyway. Duberman had insulted his faith, his honor, and his intelligence all at once. *Maybe subconsciously* suggested that Wells couldn't understand his own motives.

"You're Jewish, but your casinos stay open on Friday nights."

"That's business."

"So is this, for me. I don't want you to trick the United States into war."

"And that's all."

Wells decided to believe that Duberman's question was sincere. "I came to Islam to survive. In a place where I was the only American, surrounded by people who wanted to destroy my country. I needed something to hold on to and I had to choose, their religion or their hate. I chose their religion."

"All right. I respect that." Duberman spread his hands as if to push away the unpleasantness he'd created. He radiated charm like a banked furnace. "You strike me as a plainspoken man."

This close, Wells saw the unnatural tightening of the skin around Duberman's jaw, the fullness in his cheeks. "It's good."

"What's that?"

"Your face-lift."

"Thank you. For what I paid, it should be." *You'll need more than that to rattle me,*

511

his smile said. "You know our former operations officer is no longer with us. Early retirement." A sly joke. They all knew Wells had killed Mason. "We have a vacancy. I doubt the new DCI will invite you back to Langley. And you've seen my resources."

Could Duberman really be pitching? He was using a classic technique. Unbalance Wells by opening the conversation with an unpleasant question, then dismiss it and focus on what they had in common. *E and E,* Wells remembered an instructor at the Farm telling him. *Empathize and emphasize.*

"Even if we disagree about Iran, we have plenty in common. We both know the world would be safer without certain members of the Saudi royal family. Those Hamas cowards who live in Qatar and let their people serve as human shields. Salome tells me you have unique talents. The fact you've stayed alive for the last month suggests she's right." Duberman was laying on the flattery thick now.

"Mainly, I'm lucky."

"You would have complete operational freedom. We, the three of us, would choose projects together. But after that you'd make every decision. Hire one person, a hundred, none. I can give you whatever resources you need. Salome has spent years setting up safe houses and communications all over the world."

The offer tempted the way a syringe of heroin might. A bubble of sweet venom at the tip. *Try me. Once. Once can't hurt.* Wells wondered if Duberman had planned this offer all along or whether he'd invented it when Salome told him that Wells hadn't come alone.

"You're serious."

"Why not? I'd rather have you working for me than against."

"Killing people you don't like."

"We both know that's not what this is."

Wells looked at Salome. "You on board? We'd be working closely."

She gave him a real smile, the one that lit her face. "Oh, I think so. Look how much Mason pulled off. And that was Mason."

"What about Iran?"

"Forget Iran," Duberman said. "It's done."

"Maybe not." Wells nodded at Salome. "We have her CIA contact. Jess Bunshaft."

Duberman didn't blink. "So? My customers come from all over. China. Russia. I know who has money problems, who likes little boys, who's an addict. Of course she talks to the CIA sometimes. I admire you, Mr. Wells. Truly. But you have no chips left."

Duberman looked at Duto. "He's the only one who can protect you, and his enemies are even bigger than yours. You played as best you could, but the cards didn't come. Let's move forward. Please. For all of us and our families."

Families. The threat, again.

"My turn to ask a question."

"Anything."

"The Iranians say they don't even want the bomb. Why are you so sure you're doing the right thing? I'm sure you heard what happened today. Two more planes, five hundred more dead."

"Do you think that means we should trust Iran *more,* John?"

Wells didn't have an answer.

"What do you know about me? Besides that I'm rich."

"That you're *very* rich."

"I was lucky to be born. My parents were Austrian. Nathan and Gisa. They came to America from Shanghai. I know, I don't look Chinese." A wisp of a smile. A joke he'd made before. "They spent World War II in Shanghai. Before that, they lived in Vienna. They had a store on the north side of the city that specialized in trinkets and cameras. I never understood the connection, but that's what they sold. Silver candlesticks and Leicas. One day they saw the future goose-stepping in from Munich. They'd been successful. The kind of Jews the Nazis hated."

Salome said something in Hebrew. Duberman nodded.

"Right. How silly of me. The Nazis hated every Jew. The ones who prayed, and the ones who didn't. The ones in Berlin who spoke perfect German and the ones who never left their *shtetls*. The homosexuals and the ones with families of ten. The rich and the poor. They were all guilty of the same crime. They all received the same punishment. You see?"

Wells nodded.

"You think so, but you don't. Anyway. My parents had a piano, an apartment. They sold all of it in two weeks, took whatever they could get, so they could pay for visas and passage to China. Shanghai was practically the only place left still taking Jews by '38. The United States sent an ocean liner filled with them back to Europe. No more refugees, Roosevelt said. Except if they knew physics. Those Jews were fine."

"I didn't know that."

"Of course you didn't. Why would you? Your friends from Afghanistan, it's not on their curriculum. So. Shanghai was still open. Nathan's parents, Gisa's brother Josef, they said, *Don't go. The Germans want to scare us. Steal our money. They're jealous. Hitler doesn't mean those terrible things. He's playing to the crowds. We'll keep our heads down and this storm will pass. Like all the others.* You know what happened to those people, John?"

Wells didn't want to answer, but Duberman's stare insisted the question wasn't rhetorical. "They died."

"*Todt.* The Austrians were even more thorough than the Germans. Not one person my parents knew in Vienna survived. So excuse me when I tell you that when the Iranians publish maps that don't show Israel, that when Ahmadinejad" — Mahmoud Ahmadinejad, the former Iranian president — "says the Holocaust didn't happen, that the Jews must be eradicated, I listen. If I can manage it, those people will never have a nuclear weapon. Not now. Not ever." He leaned forward, squeezed Wells's biceps. "I want you on our side, John. The right side."

Duberman smiled like he believed Wells might agree. Maybe he did. All those billions would bolster anyone's confidence.

"Can I have a minute alone? To think."

"In here? You want us to leave —" Duberman shook his head in puzzlement.

"No, of course not. Bathroom's fine."

Duberman nodded at a door on the wall behind Duto. "Right there."

"You can't seriously be considering this," Duto said.

"Worried you'll need a new errand boy, Vinny?"

Wells closed the bathroom door, eyed the tired face in the mirror. Duberman had made a surprisingly persuasive pitch. Asking Wells about Islam had been a brilliant move. The question had planted a seed of doubt. Was it possible he was anti-Semitic? No. *No.* He knew himself that much, anyway.

What would Shafer say?

Don't let him play you, John. You can't let him start a war on faked evidence. End of story. Anyway, he isn't the only one who remembers the Holocaust. Israel doesn't depend on anyone else to defend itself. If it needs to attack Iran, it will.

Then, maybe, Shafer would smirk. And sing: *I'm starting with the man in the mirror / I'm asking him to grab his knife . . .*

"Shut up," Wells mumbled, unsure if he meant the words for Shafer, Michael Jackson, or himself. He turned on the tap, leaned over, and lapped from the sink like a dog, letting the water skid across his face, down his neck.

He left the taps on as he pushed his jeans down to expose the blade and handle attached to his legs. He pulled off the tape, snapped the pieces together. The assembled knife was five inches long, half blade, half handle. Any shorter and it wouldn't have been useful. But even at five inches, it was too big for Wells to hide in a pocket.

He had a nylon sheath tucked into his underwear. He pulled up the left leg of his jeans, strapped the sheath low on the inner calf, just above the nub of his ankle. An ankle sheath made a slow draw, but Wells feared Gideon would spot the knife anywhere else. He double-checked to be sure the jeans hid it. He flushed the toilet, washed and dried his face. Stepped out.

"You all right?" Duto said.

"Never better."

"And have you decided?" Duberman said.

"I'll do it."

"John —" Duto said.

Salome muttered in Hebrew.

"You're serious."

"That I am."

Duberman stood, extended his hand. "Welcome."

■ ■ ■

Wells left him hanging. "Just one condition. That you confess to the President."

"That's funny." But Duberman wasn't smiling.

"Or if that's too much, tell us where you got the HEU. We'll pass it on. Keep your name out."

Duberman's hand sank to his side with the slow finality of a castle gate dropping. He stared at Wells, an angry god who couldn't believe that a mortal had refused his wish. Behind him, Gideon the body-guard put a hand on his holstered pistol.

"I made a serious offer, John. I don't ap-preciate this."

Wells felt a familiar itch in his fingers. "Then we should go. We have a plane to catch."

"Mossad may feel differently." Duberman gave Wells a gargoyle's stone grin. "I prom-ised you safe passage. And you'll have it. Right to them."

"Come on, Aaron." The words were mean-ingless, a way to buy a few seconds as Wells figured out how to get to his knife and cor-ral Duberman before Gideon shot him. He could imagine his move, could *see* it —

He'd take a big step forward with his left leg, almost a squat, pulling up his jeans, exposing the knife. He'd reach down and across his body with his right hand as he grabbed Duberman with his left and reeled him in —

But Gideon was too close, and watching too closely. Wells couldn't make the combination work without an extra second or two. A diversion.

Duto stood. "I'm not leaving without him. And you can't keep me. Embassy knows where I am."

"You're right," Duberman said. "Israel can't keep you. But it can send you home. Alone."

Duto reached down, flipped the table over, sending it toward the bodyguard. The distraction Wells needed. As the heavy wood cracked against the floor Gideon turned to Duto and drew his pistol —

And Wells lunged forward, came up with his knife, squeezed his left hand around Duberman's arm, pulled him close. Duberman was strong enough for a man past sixty, but against Wells he had no chance. Wells twined his arm across Duberman's chest, twisted him so that Duberman's body hid his own. Gideon half turned toward Wells. But he didn't raise the pistol. He didn't have a clear shot.

Wells touched the knife to Duberman's neck, tugged Duberman backward, toward the bathroom. Duberman sagged against Wells, not struggling but not helping either. Subtly looking for a way to free himself.

Wells jabbed the blade into Duberman's neck, hard enough to break the skin. Duberman yelped as his blood bubbled out. "No games."

"All right," Duberman said.

Gideon brought the pistol up, stepped to the right, looking for an angle.

"Drop it," Wells said. *"Now."*

Gideon hesitated. Then shook his head, turned the pistol on Duto.

"Let him go or I shoot."

"Then shoot." Wells probed the knife deeper. Blood flowed from Duberman's neck. "Tell him, Aaron. He kills Vinny, you die."

Wells meant his words. He would slice Duberman's throat open if Gideon shot Duto. His own life would end seconds later, but he didn't care. No one could hide the simultaneous deaths of a senator and one of the world's richest men. The United States and Israel would have to investigate. Maybe they'd uncover the plot.

Anyway, he and Duto wouldn't go down alone.

"Three —"

Gideon shook his head —

"Two —"

Cursed in Hebrew.

"One —"

Squatted. Laid down the pistol. Muttered at Duberman.

"Yes," Duberman said in English. "This is why we should have let you frisk him." He tilted his head into Wells. "What now, John? You're the expert." His voice was level, impassive. Like he was still in charge despite the knife against his neck.

"Now he kicks the pistol. To Vinny."

Duberman explained. Gideon nudged it with his foot. Too late, Wells realized Salome had a chance at it. It skittered close and she looked at it —

But let it slide. Duto grabbed it.

"Now tell him to sit on the floor."

Duberman translated, and Gideon complied.

"I'm figuring you didn't call the Mossad before I got here, because why would you? You didn't know Vinny was coming, so you assumed you could hold me as long as you liked. Is that true?"

"Yes."

"Is it?"

"Yes."

"Good. Here's what we're gonna do. Tell Gideon to take off his shoes. When he's done, he lies down on his stomach with his hands laced behind his head. Then bends his knees and lifts his lower legs off the floor."

"What is this? Yoga?"

"I'm going to cut his Achilles tendons so he can't follow us when we leave."

"*Cut* him?"

"That or a bullet in his head." Wells shifted the knife under the artificially tightened flesh of Duberman's chin. "You think I won't, ask Salome what I did in Istanbul."

"Listen to him," Salome said in English.

Duberman spoke and Gideon did what Wells had demanded.

"Now you two stand by the bathroom, so I can do it without you in the way." Wells spun Duberman, shoved him away, sending him stumbling against the wall.

"You're an animal," Salome said.

Maybe she wasn't his soul mate after all.

When Wells knelt on Gideon's back, the guard looked over his shoulder at him.

"Just one, please."

"You're too dangerous for that." Wells

523

grabbed Gideon's left ankle and slashed into the tough tendon there. Even with the sharp ceramic blade, he had to hack like he was sawing a rope. Gideon screamed, but Wells cut until the tendon snapped in two, its halves retracting, hiding under the skin. Gideon's foot hung limp and useless. Blood spurted from the hole in his ankle. He made a single mewling moan, a cat in a coyote's jaws.

Wells looked over the damage. "All right. Just one."

He stood, looked at Duto. Who waved him over with two fingers.

"We can end this now," he murmured. He nodded at Duberman and Salome, who stood with their backs pressed against the wall like they hoped to melt into it. "They know. Where it came from."

Meaning that Duberman or Salome could tell them where they'd bought the HEU.

"I won't hurt them, Vinny."

"Not saying that. Nothing permanent."

"What, then?"

Duto explained. A cruel play, revolting and brilliant. Wells shook his head.

"I'll do it," Duto said. "If you can't."

As an answer, Wells reached for Gideon's stainless-steel pistol, a little Sig Sauer that felt oddly small in his palm.

"Cute, isn't it?" Duto said.

"As long as it shoots."

"By the way. Would you really have let him shoot me?"

"In a heartbeat." Wells covered Salome and Duberman with the pistol. "Salome. Go in the corner. Stand facing out, hands flat against the walls. Aaron. Lie facedown on the floor next to your desk."

"No."

"If you don't I'll shoot you."

"How do I know you won't do that anyway?"

Wells shook his head: *You don't.* Duberman took two steps. Went to his knees. Lay down. The rustling of his linen pants was the room's only sound. Wells came over, racked the slide to be sure he had a round chambered. Duberman flinched at the metal-on-metal click.

"Put your hands behind your head." Wells put a knee into Duberman's back.

"I can pay. Whatever you like."

"Shh." Wells shoved the pistol into Duberman's neck — and flashed back to the hotel in Volgograd where Boris Nemkov had done the same to him. An *ouroboros* came to him, the mythical snake that ate its own tail. He should have let Duto handle this. It was Duto's idea —

No. He would own what happened next. No one else. Most of all, not Duto.

"It's time for you to tell us where you got the uranium."

Duberman shook his head. Wells pressed the pistol down harder, wrinkled the tanned skin of Duberman's neck. "Tell me. You have my word, we'll keep your name out of it. Your life goes on. Your wife, your kids —"

No.

This wasn't who he was. He didn't threaten to execute defenseless prisoners. Then he made himself think of the Americans and Iranians who would die by the thousands for Duberman's lies if the United States invaded. He tightened his grip, shoved the pistol harder into Duberman's neck, where the spine bent into the skull.

"I count to three. Then I blow your brains out."

"No."

"One."

"I don't know."

"Two."

"I swear, I don't, *I don't* —"

"Lie." Wells shifted the pistol, pressed it against the thin bone of Duberman's temple. Duberman tried to raise his head, but with his left hand Wells forced him down, forced him to see the pistol. "I want you to live, but you have to tell me."

"Tell him," Salome said. "Please. Aaron. *Please.*"

"She loves you." As Wells spoke, he knew the words were true. "Listen to her."

Duberman tried to shake his head under Wells's hand. Blood from the cut on his neck dribbled to the floor. Wells looked at Salome. He'd threatened Duberman instead of her because he'd expected she'd be the stronger of the two, more willing to die. Maybe he'd guessed wrong. "You tell me, then. Tell me and he lives."

"Aaron," she said.

Duberman answered in Hebrew.

"He says he'd rather die."

"Yes," Duberman said.

"Then you will," Wells said.

"Do it, then."

"Three. Last chance. Now."

But of course Wells didn't pull the trigger.

Duberman's body shook under Wells's knee, ripples that ran the length of his back. Wells wondered if Duberman was crying. No. Laughing. Maybe he had never believed Wells would shoot him. Maybe he truly was willing to sacrifice himself for this war. Either way, he had called Wells's bluff.

During all his years in the field, Wells had

sworn he would never torture. Mock executions might not leave bruises or broken bones, but they were psychic torture nonetheless. He had tossed aside one of his most important principles. Humiliated himself.

For nothing.

What would Anne say? Or Exley?

"John." Duto's voice brought Wells back to the room. They still had to escape.

Wells stood, nudged Duberman's leg. "Get up."

Duberman rose. His hands trembled, but he raised his head and stared at Wells, his eyes shining. Triumphant. At this moment, Wells wanted more violence not at all, but he needed to reestablish his authority quickly. He shifted the pistol to his left hand. With his right, he jabbed Duberman beneath the ribs, a single vicious punch. Duberman doubled over, his breath shallow and fast. With his left hand, Wells brought the Sig down on Duberman's skull. He didn't put all his weight into the blow. He didn't want to knock Duberman out or break bone. Duberman groaned, went to his hands and knees, his head hanging low, drool threading from his mouth. "What are you?"

"This meeting is officially over." Wells forced himself to keep his voice calm.

Steady. "But we're not done with each other yet. You're going to lead us out of here, Aaron. I'll be a step behind you. Salome behind me. Vinny's going to be the caboose. A happy little train. Right, Vinny?"

"Absolutely."

Wells pulled Duberman up. "Your job is to make sure your guards don't do anything dumb so I don't have to gut you. Understand?"

Duberman wiped the spittle from his lips, nodded.

"Say it."

"I understand."

"You have your passport in this office?"

"Yes."

Wells looked at Salome. "And you have yours on you, I'll bet."

She nodded.

"Good. We're taking a ride in that Range Rover outside. The four of us only. Guards and phones stay here. Salome drives, Vinny sits up front with her, I sit in back with you. We're going to Ben Gurion. Anyone tries to stop us, we kill you. You ask anyone for help, we kill you. At the airport, we go through the general aviation side. Vinny has a jet there. You two are coming with us. We'll fly to Cyprus and drop you off there."

"No," Salome said.

"Why would we agree to this?" Duberman said.

"I'll kill you if you don't."

"Another bluff."

Wells shook his head. "You think I want this? It's our only play. We can't leave you here. Soon as we go, you make a call, we're done. We have to keep you close until we're off Israeli soil. I just proved I won't kill you if you're my prisoner. But if you won't come, we'll shoot you and take our chances, see how far we get."

"Not a hundred meters."

"Probably. But you'll be dead already. Your choice."

Duberman looked Wells over, seemed to see he wasn't bluffing. "Fine. Cyprus. And Gideon?"

"He stays. Make sure he understands what happens if he calls anyone."

Duberman and Gideon spoke in Hebrew, and Duberman laughed.

"He says after you land there, he hopes you have a rocket to the moon, because nowhere in the world will be safe."

Thirty-five minutes later, they reached the general aviation terminal at Ben Gurion Airport. At the security checkpoint, Duto flashed his diplomatic passport, walked around the metal detector. A guard reached for him, and Duto shrugged him off.

"I'm sorry, sir —"

"I'm a United States senator."

"Not for long," Duberman muttered.

"I flew twelve hours here for a meeting, now I have to turn around. My back is killing me. Don't touch me."

"Sir —"

"You can walk me straight to my plane if you like, but don't put a finger on me."

The guard reached for a phone at the X-ray station, but Duberman said something in Hebrew and he stopped.

Five minutes later, they stepped into the G650. The blond-haired pilot poked his head out of the cockpit. "Four passengers? For Cyprus?" Duto had called on the drive over.

"Correct."

"No weather, no line, we should be airborne in five minutes. On the ground in forty-five."

As he closed the cockpit door, Wells pulled two pairs of plastic flex-cuffs from the bag that Duto had brought him. "I need you both to put your wrists together in front of you."

"Are we such a threat to a trained killer?" Duberman said. He let Wells cuff him and settled into his seat, his smirk wider than ever. He'd shaken off the mock execution and pistol-whipping in record time. Wells knew what he was thinking. That he would call his guards when they landed and be back in Israel within hours. That he had this jet's tail number and could track it. That he would either have Wells arrested right away or, more likely, let him flail until the deadline passed and then put Gideon on him. Most important, that Wells and Duto didn't have any idea where Salome had gotten the HEU and didn't have the time to find out.

Duberman was thinking that he'd won.

Wells feared he was right.

Where could they go after Cyprus? Their best bet would probably be to fly to the United States, see if they could shake Shafer loose from CIA custody. Maybe he'd come up with something before the seventh floor grabbed him.

And if they lost? *When* they lost? Being a senator gave Duto protection, though it wasn't unlimited. Wells would have to decide whether to take his chances with the Justice Department or go off the grid. Maybe a year or two in the mountains would do him good. Catching steelheads and salmon for supper. Sleeping in a one-room cabin without electricity or a toilet.

Chopping wood or going to bed cold. Good old-fashioned basic survival. Maybe this life had made him too hard and too soft at the same time. Or maybe he was deluding himself, pretending life as a fugitive would be anything but exhausting and lonely. He'd fall asleep each night wondering whether the FBI or Duberman would find him first.

A song he'd first heard lying in bed with Anne came to him:

If you can't hold on
If you can't hold on
Hold on

The singer's voice breathy and quiet. The band was called The Killers, Wells remembered now, the song "All These Things That I've Done." Both about right.

He wasn't beaten. Not as long as he breathed. Let the world break him. He wouldn't surrender.

He settled into his seat and waited for Cyprus.

24

BEN GURION AIRPORT, NEAR TEL AVIV
The Gulfstream's engines spooled up.

And Wells felt his phone buzzing in his pocket. An Israeli number. Had the Mossad tracked them already? He sent the call to voice mail.

The phone buzzed again. Same number. Wells knocked on the cockpit door. "Hold tight a minute." He stepped to the back of the jet. "Yes?"

"The question you asked me." Rudi's rasping voice. "About the stuff. The man who brought it, his name was Witwans."

"Rand Witwans?"

"That's right. First name R-A-N-D. The amount was fourteen kilos."

"One-four?" Wells's heart drummed a mad song in his chest.

"Yes, dummy. Fourteen. Fourteen exactly. Does that help?"

"Maybe." *Yes, yes, yes.*

"No more questions. No more favors."

"Thank you, Rudi."

"I don't want to hear it. I'll see you at my funeral. Unless yours comes first." *Click.*

Joost Claassen had told Shafer that South Africa produced 15.3 kilograms of highly enriched uranium. Joost remembered the amount because the program had beaten its goal of 15 kilos. But Rand Witwans had brought only 14 kilograms to Israel. He'd held on to those missing 1.3 kilograms all those years. Until Salome found him.

Witwans held the answer, if they could track him down in time. Cyprus was the wrong move, the wrong way. Wells needed at least twelve hours. To fly to South Africa, find Witwans's house. He'd be alone there, only his servants for company —

No. Wells suddenly realized why Salome's personal bodyguard hadn't been at their meeting. She'd sent him to watch Witwans. He needed to put Salome and Duberman someplace they couldn't immediately call the guard. Wells could think of only one place in the world from which Duberman couldn't use his billions to free himself immediately. The last card in the deck. His last play.

He reached for his phone.

"Again?" Abdullah said. "And after our conversation last week. Truly?"

"I know I've stretched your generosity, King."

"What you did for my family, I didn't think I could repay it, not in the time I had left. But maybe I've lived longer than I expected. What is it now?"

Wells explained.

"This is one of the richest men in the world, not some maid from Pakistan," Abdullah said. "You think no one notices?"

"A day, two at the most —"

"An American. A diplomatic nightmare. And what's our excuse? No, it's not possible."

"How about this? Not even a day. Just until the afternoon tomorrow, and then put him on a plane back to Amman." Amman was less than a hundred kilometers from Jerusalem, close enough that Duberman and Salome could find their way back to Israel without trouble. At the same time, the jet would stay outside Israeli airspace, so Abdullah wouldn't have to worry that it or its pilots would be detained. "Say it's a terrible mistake. Blame me."

"Of course I'll blame you."

The King laughed, and Wells knew he would agree. "All right. In return, I want a promise."

Wells waited for the inevitable.

"This repays our debt. Now and forever."

"It's already repaid, King."

"I know."

Wells came forward, ignored the others, knocked on the cockpit door.

"Ready to push?" the pilot said.

"Can I come in?"

The cockpit was sleek and black and angular, with four big flat-screen panels side by side under the windshield. It looked like a cross between a BMW dashboard and a video game.

"What can I do for you?"

"Mind if I ask your name?"

"On these sorts of missions, I go by Captain Kirk," the pilot said.

Fair enough. "We have a new destination. And I'd rather you not call it in until we're in the air."

"Where's that, sir?"

"Riyadh."

"We can get cleared to land? From Tel Aviv?"

Wells scribbled down the number for Abdullah's private secretary. "He'll arrange it. All he needs is the tail number and an ETA." Wells hesitated. "I don't suppose you can turn off the transponder."

Civilian jets carried transponders so that air-traffic control systems could track them and distinguish them from military aircraft. In response to radio signals from ground stations, a transponder emitted a unique call sign that included the location and altitude of the plane carrying it. Public tracking services like flightaware.com now tracked the transponder signals of planes worldwide in real time, which meant that Duberman's guards could easily follow this flight and would know when it changed course and turned away from Cyprus.

But pilots could turn off transponders from the cockpit, as had famously happened in the case of Malaysia Airlines 370. They were supposed to do so only in extraordinary circumstances, such as a malfunctioning transponder that was sending the wrong altitude, or an electrical fire. Any plane that wasn't sending transponder signals was presumed to be a military aircraft and risked being shot down.

The pilot shook his head. "Not in this neighborhood. The Israelis get squirrelly. In fact, even with it on, they won't like the change of plans. We'll have to give them plenty of room, go over the western Sinai and the Red Sea before we make the turn into Saudi airspace."

"How about when we get over the Kingdom?"

"I trust you, sir, but not that much."

Not what Wells wanted to hear, but he could hardly argue.

"I gotta ask." The pilot nodded at the door. "Do they know about this little course correction?"

Wells hesitated, all the answer the pilot needed.

"I can lock this door, get you where you need to go, but if you can't control them —"

"We can control them."

"Sure about this? Because it's about five felonies."

Just put 'em on my tab. "Ask the senator if you like."

"I don't even know who you're talking about. What happens in Riyadh?"

"We'll leave the two we brought now and go straight to Johannesburg."

The pilot shook his head. "By the time we land, it'll be midnight local, we'll have been flying about twenty-four hours straight. I'll do my best for you, but Spock and I have to sleep a few hours before we go. Can't be flying over Africa on a route we've never seen in the middle of the night with no rest."

More bad news. Wells would have to check, but he imagined Riyadh was at least eight hours from Johannesburg. If they left the Kingdom tomorrow morning, they wouldn't reach South Africa until mid-afternoon at best. By the time they found Witwans's mansion, night would have fallen. Even if they could grab him quickly, they'd have barely one full day left before the President's deadline, and South Africa was a sixteen- or seventeen-hour flight from Washington. Wells was sure that they would have to bring Witwans to the President or Donna Green in person to have any chance.

"You can't sleep in Joburg?"

The pilot shook his head. "Everyone thinks these things fly themselves, but there's a reason for the rules. We're over the duty limits already. And I'm guessing that won't be our last stop, that you'll want us to come back here or the U.S. or somewhere else pretty soon, maybe even tomorrow night."

"Possibly."

"Even more reason, then. If you have a relief crew in Saudi —"

Wells shook his head. He was out of favors with Abdullah.

"Then we need seven hours minimum in Riyadh."

Wells couldn't argue. The pilot had already done as much as Wells could have hoped. By changing his destination after takeoff, he was essentially kidnapping Duberman and Salome. "Thanks."

Back in the cabin, Duto, Duberman, and Salome waited expectantly.

"You'll be happy to hear that was Shafer," Wells said to Salome. As he'd expected, she shook her head, *not possible.* "If I can talk my way out of Lubyanka, you don't think he can outsmart those mouth breathers on the seventh floor?

"And that's why you went to the cockpit?" Salome said.

"He told me we had to talk on a clean phone. I asked the pilot for his, but he told me I had to wait until Cyprus. Anyway, I'm sure whatever he has to tell me is bad news for you."

The explanation didn't even qualify as paper-thin, but the engines went to full power before anyone could argue. "Buckle up," the pilot said through the intercom. "We should be in Cyprus in about forty-five minutes."

Ten minutes later, the G650 was high

above Israel's coast. The plane turned slowly right, to the northwest, and soared uneventfully toward Cyprus for fifteen minutes. And then they settled into an easy left turn. They were more than one hundred kilometers offshore already, with a thin scrim of clouds before them, nothing to provide any perspective. Even so, Salome figured out what was happening.

"What is this?"

This G650 had been equipped with two seats per row, one on each side of the aisle. Salome and Duberman were in the third row from the cockpit door. Wells was one seat up. He unbuckled his belt, stepped into the aisle, put one big hand on each of their shoulders.

"Change of plans. We're going to Riyadh."

"You think that's going to save you?" Duberman said. "You think Gideon can't track this plane? He'll find you even before you land. You think they don't know who I am in the Kingdom? Half the royal family has spent time at my tables. Those Gulf Arabs, they like roulette and baccarat. The classy games. Never craps. They don't like to touch the dice that the infidels have touched. They have such funny rules."

Wells had seen enough of the royal family

to know Duberman was telling the truth. "Sure."

"They're not great gamblers, they get bored, don't size their bets, blow through their bankrolls. They want big comps, too, always the fanciest brands, the biggest suites. One of Abdullah's grandsons, he lost three million dollars in Macao in a week, we gave him a Ferrari convertible, a Spider 458, a three-hundred-thousand-dollar car. You know what he said? 'Not bad, but I like the Bugatti.' Which runs more like a million, a million-one."

"Sounds like we're doing you a favor," Wells said. "You can set up shop in Riyadh."

"Or are you hoping they won't care who I am, they'll lock us up because we're Jews?"

A cheap shot, though Wells supposed he had it coming. "You'll be safe enough. I want a decent head start" — let Duberman think he was running — "and they're going to keep you for a couple of days."

"All the head start in the world won't help you."

"Then maybe I should just kill you now."

Duberman waved his hand, dismissing Wells, a remarkable gesture under the circumstances. "Whether I'm alive or dead, Gideon will hunt you down. And after what you did he won't be satisfied with just putting a bullet in you."

Wells sat back next to Duto, whose unhappiness was plain. He grabbed a pad, scribbled, *That really Shafer on the phone?*

Wells shook his head. *But good news,* he wrote.

What happens in Riyadh?

Tell you when we get there. Wells wasn't asking permission. Whatever Duto had expected when he came to Cairo, he was committed now. Duto shook his head, but wrote only, *Hope you know what you're doing.* Wells did, too.

Outside, the sky turned orange-pink for a few glorious minutes before night came. They were all silent as the jet followed the course the pilot had outlined to Wells, over the Sinai and the Red Sea. After almost two hours, the G650 turned left, over the Arabian Peninsula, the desert's blackness broken only by a few small outposts. Mecca and Medina were down there somewhere. Wells wondered if he'd ever see them properly. He thought not.

He stood, faced Duberman.

"That offer you made me, Aaron —"

"Off the table."

Wells smiled. "But you were serious?"

"You would have had to stay with me until

after the war started. But yes."

Wells believed him.

"You should have taken it. You know I've seen you at my casinos a dozen times."

"I don't —"

"All the years I've been doing this. You come and you're lucky, and you're lucky, and you're lucky. And it starts to feel like something more. Even the dealers, the bosses, the shift managers, they start to believe. That's when they call me. Guy came in with ten thousand last night, he's been playing craps, now he has six hundred K and the whole casino wants to bet with him. He's hit six straight blackjacks and let it ride every time, he wants to do it again for a quarter million."

"That happens?" Duto said from the seat ahead.

"You run a casino long enough, everything happens. I tried to figure out once how many separate bets I've taken over the years, not even counting the slots. I couldn't. It had to be billions. Sooner or later, you get these streaks. You know what I always tell my managers? *Take the bet.* In fact, they know what I'm going to say, they're not even calling to ask as much as to let me know what's going on. I like to hear. So we take the bet. In all those years, you know how many times the guy, it's always a guy, has walked out ahead? Once. In 1999. The blackjack guy, I couldn't believe it, I'll never forget it, he won that seventh bet."

"Another blackjack?" Wells didn't much care about gambling, but Duberman could tell a story.

"No, a six-card twenty-one to beat two tens for the dealer."

"Bull," Duto said.

"Why would I lie? I'm guessing you don't play much blackjack, John, but trust me when I tell you that's incredibly rare. I wasn't there, but my manager told me that he said, *That was fun. I guess I'm done.* Picked up a half-million dollars in chips and walked out. We never saw him again, either. My security guys looked at the tapes to make sure he wasn't cheating, colluding with the dealer. I still think that's probably what happened, but we could never find it. But every other time, those guys, they crashed and burned. Because it's just luck, John, that's all it is. That's all *you* are. The luck eventually runs out. The house always wins."

Wells had to fight not to mention the call from Rudi. Instead, he said only, "We'll see," an answer that sounded lame even to him. Duberman didn't bother to answer.

Wells turned away, looked at Salome, but he found no succor in her face. Only hate. He had questions for her: *Did you feel it, too?* And *How did you end up here?* But he didn't feel like asking. And he supposed he already knew what she'd say: *Yes.* And *How does anyone end up anywhere?*

"I should have killed you in Volgograd."

"I'm glad you didn't. I wouldn't have gotten to hear your boss's stories."

A reluctant smile creased her lips, and Wells knew her thoughts, knew they mirrored his. Ninety minutes later, the jet began to descend. "We'll be at King Khalid International Airport in approximately thirty minutes," the pilot said over the intercom. "After landing, we've been told to remain on the auxiliary runway, so that's what we'll do. Rendition Airways looks forward to serving you again soon."

As the jet stopped, a dozen unmarked police SUVs surrounded it. The armada taxied slowly away from the lights of the main terminal, to an apron beside a blocky concrete building at the airport's northeastern edge, as far from the city of Riyadh as possible. "Quarantine Station," its sign read in Arabic and English.

"If they offer us a welcome shower, I'm

going to get nervous," Duberman said.

"Holocaust humor," Duto said. "Classy."

The police trained a half-dozen spotlights on the jet and rolled a staircase to the front cabin door. The flight attendant, who had spent the entire flight in the rear galley with wraparound Beats headphones over his ears, the literal definition of hearing no evil, stepped forward and popped it open. The desert wind kicked dust inside as a spotlight glared through the open door.

Wells stepped forward. A uniformed Saudi officer stood at the base of the stairs and waved him down. Three soldiers stood around him, their rifles trained on Wells. Wells wondered if he might finally have exhausted his credit with Abdullah, if the Saudis might arrest him and everyone on the plane. But when he reached the stairs, the officer extended a friendly hand. He was short, stocky, and handsome, with the close-cut beard that Saudi royals favored. Wells tried to ignore the fact that he looked about twenty.

"Salaam aleikum."

"As-aleikum salaam."

"Mr. Wells. I'm Colonel Faisal. A grandson of Miteb." Prior to his death a year before, Prince Miteb had been Abdullah's closest ally in the royal family. If his grandson was here, Wells was safe.

"Thank you for coming here."

Faisal smiled. "Rami" — Abdullah's most senior secretary, basically his chief of staff — "said it might be the most interesting mission of my career. He said when you were involved, his life was never boring."

Wells had sometimes wondered why Abdullah let him draw so many favors over the years. He suspected that Faisal had given him the answer. Genuine excitement was as hard to find for a king as anyone else. Maybe harder.

"Do you know why you're here, Colonel?"

Faisal shook his head.

"A man and a woman aboard that plane have requested asylum in the Kingdom." This explanation failed to answer any number of important questions, including *Who are they? Why are they claiming asylum? What's your relationship with them?* And, even more obviously, *Why did you land here in the first place?* Whether out of deference, or, more likely, because he'd been told to keep his mouth shut and do what Wells said, Faisal asked none of them.

"Yes. I see."

"I imagine you don't get many asylum seekers, but I think it would be best if you kept them out here in the quarantine station. Instead of taking them back to the terminal to start a more formal process."

"Are they dangerous, sir?"

"Not unless you like to gamble." The joke sailed past Faisal. "No. They aren't."

"And shall I question them, sir? To determine whether they have legitimate business here?"

Absolutely, positively not. "Just hold them, make sure they're comfortable. Food, a hot shower, whatever they like. Don't touch them under any circumstances."

"But then how will I know what to do with them?"

"Tomorrow afternoon, you'll release them," Wells said. *Of course. Makes perfect sense.* "Rami will tell you exactly when, but it won't be too late. Certainly before dark."

"Release them where, sir?"

"A flight to Amman. Rami will arrange the jet. But don't tell them that you're going to let them go until Rami tells you so. Most important, don't let them make any phone calls. Whatever they promise or threaten, no communication of any kind."

"I understand, sir. And will you be leaving now?"

"Not yet. We'll sleep on the plane until morning and then take off." Wells figured the Gulfstream would be at least as comfortable as the quarantine rooms.

Faisal nodded, though his expression remained puzzled. "This seems like a lot of trouble, sir. If they're going to leave tomorrow anyway."

Wells shook the young Saudi's hand. "If you don't mind my asking, how old are you, Colonel?"

"Twenty-five, sir."

Nice to be a prince.

Back in the cabin, Duberman and Salome hadn't moved.

"Go on," Wells said. "I give you my word you won't be hurt."

Duberman stood, turned to Duto. "Senator. Your friend is obviously mentally ill. Are you going along with this? It'll destroy you, too."

"Good-bye, Aaron," Duto said.

At the cabin door, Duberman turned to Wells. "You're going to wish you'd killed me."

"I already do."

As they watched Faisal and his men usher Duberman and Salome into the station, Wells told Duto what had happened, beginning with Rudi's call.

"So all of this was to buy an extra day. Not even."

"Yes."

"Ever think that maybe we should just have shot them?"

"Shot Aaron Duberman."

"He's the one who suggested it. They're going to come at us as soon as they get out of here. And if we win he's dead anyway. You think the President's going to give Duberman a get-out-of-jail-free card?"

"I don't shoot prisoners, Vinny."

"All right. Better hope Witwans is home when we get down there."

A possibility Wells had not even considered. "He'll be home, Vinny."

Finally, the jet reached an apron where dozens of other private jets were parked. The pilot opened the cockpit door. "We'll sleep here. Wake at 0800 and be in the air by 0815."

"Thank you, Captain."

"Good night to all, and to all a good night."

25
Two Days . . .

AMMAN, JORDAN

With no bags, Salome and Duberman walked untouched past the customs posts at Queen Alia International Airport. They stepped into the arrival hall, a wide, low room crowded with money-changing stations, coffee stands, and men hawking hotel leaflets. Duberman stopped so abruptly that Salome had to dodge his heels and looked around as wide-eyed as an aquarium-bound fish. Salome thought she understood his confusion. The superrich never spent time by themselves in uncontrolled public spaces. Duberman had no guards or minders or drivers to tell him where to go, clear his path. Being threatened with execution didn't faze him. Having to find his way through this terminal on his own, on the other hand . . .

"Over here." She led him to a mobile

553

phone kiosk.

The previous night in Riyadh, the young colonel had ushered them inside the quarantine station, where a pair of cots were waiting. "Sleep," he said. "We will discuss in the morning."

"Discuss what?" Salome said. She lay down and, to her surprise, fell asleep almost immediately.

She woke in confusion, certain she'd had the strangest of dreams. Wells had taken her and Duberman to Riyadh. Then she tasted the desert dust in her mouth.

She'd slept in her clothes, but the Saudis had shielded her cot with a sheet anyway. She pulled it open to reveal a concrete room covered with posters encouraging handwashing. The colonel sat in the middle, playing a video game on his phone. Duberman was still asleep, lying on his back, his arms folded prayerfully across his chest. The world's richest monk.

She still couldn't believe that he hadn't cracked in Tel Aviv. *She* almost had. After seeing how Wells had eviscerated his guards in Istanbul, she was certain he would follow through on his threat to kill Duberman. She'd been trying to play out what might happen after she gave up Witwans's name.

Maybe they could still stop Wells from getting to him. Maybe she could buy time by giving Wells a fake name. Anything to get him away from Duberman. But she saw that once she spoke, Wells would keep threatening her until he was sure that she was telling the truth and that he had a way to Witwans.

Still, she wanted to tell. *She loves you,* Wells had said to Duberman. More accurate to say that Salome couldn't imagine a world without Duberman. She understood her hypocrisy. For five years, she had insisted they had to stop Iran from building a bomb at any cost. Now, with victory days away, she was about to risk their success to save one man.

Luckily, Duberman had somehow known that Wells wouldn't pull the trigger. He had called Wells's bluff.

Yet Wells still wasn't finished. She supposed his ability to adapt to crisis, never give up, was the reason he'd survived so long. So they had wound up at this concrete quarantine station at an airport in Riyadh, watched over by this ridiculously young colonel.

He put away his phone as Salome rose from her cot and approached him.

"Salaam aleikum."

"Don't pretend to be polite. We're your prisoners."

"Not at all."

"Then let us go."

"Miss" — he pulled her passport from his pocket, made a show of looking at it — "Leffetz. I understand you're upset, but there's nowhere for you *to* go. You're in quarantine."

"Then let me call my office. Or email."

He tucked away the passport. "Once you're out of quarantine."

"And when will that be?"

"Soon."

"Days, weeks, months?"

"Soon." He wasn't smiling, but she couldn't help feeling he was mocking her.

"What kind of quarantine is this, anyway? We're not sick." As she spoke, she knew she'd lost. Even speaking the word meant accepting his ridiculous premise.

"We are processing your request for asylum."

"We haven't —" She broke off, forced herself to keep her voice level. "That man over there. You know who he is?"

This time, he pulled Duberman's blue American passport. "Aaron Duberman. Born Atlanta, Georgia."

556

"He's worth almost thirty billion dollars. Why would he want asylum in Saudi Arabia?"

"We have excellent free health care."

Now she knew he was mocking her.

"When the processing is complete, we'll inform you of the outcome."

"I hope you're enjoying this, because it's going to end badly for you."

"Would you like some coffee?"

When Duberman woke, she explained what had happened.

"How long do you think they can hold us like this?"

They were speaking Hebrew, ignoring the stares of the guards.

"Not long. No doubt they're already getting calls from Jerusalem. Washington soon enough."

Gideon would have realized quickly that Riyadh was their most likely destination, especially since Duberman had investigated Wells and knew of his relationship to the Kingdom.

The more important question was *why* Wells had dumped them here instead of Cyprus. Presumably, the phone call he'd taken in the minutes before takeoff held the answer. He would have needed a good reason for such a desperate play, and Salome could think of only one.

"Someone told him where we got the stuff." Though she couldn't understand who'd tipped him off. Maybe Shafer really had talked his way clear of the CIA. "If he gets to Witwans —"

"I understand, Adina." He used her real name only when he was annoyed. "If I thought shouting would do any good, I'd shout. But it'll just piss them off. And no matter what, I'm sure they'll put us on a plane soon enough."

Once again Duberman's instincts proved right. As the digital wall clock over the door turned to 3:00, the colonel handed back their passports.

"I regret to inform you that the Kingdom of Saudi Arabia cannot accept your asylum request. You're going to have to leave Saudi soil."

"Too bad," Salome said.

"We will provide a flight to Jordan, free of charge. Further transport will be your responsibility." The colonel walked into a back room, returned with a dusty black abaya and headscarf. "You don't have to cover your face, but please put these on until you are clear of our airspace."

"Come on."

"Your flight leaves in forty-five minutes."

She would argue over Saudi dress codes for women another time. She wiped off the shapeless gown as best she could, threw it over her clothes, stuck her hair under the scarf.

"Gorgeous," Duberman said.

The colonel drove them to the main terminal, where they boarded a Saudi Arabian Airlines 737. Salome had figured they'd be given a private charter, but this was a standard public flight to Amman. More evidence that the Saudis wanted to resolve their detention without fanfare.

The colonel and a nameless man in a suit whom they'd picked up in the boarding area walked them into coach. Despite herself, Salome had to smile. She wondered when Duberman had last sat in cattle class. Three empty seats awaited them near the back. Salome took the window and smirked as the man in the suit gently steered Duberman to the middle seat.

"I'm sorry we weren't able to grant your request," the colonel said. "Gabir will accompany you to Amman. After that, as we've discussed, you're on your own. Safe journeys. *Ma-a salaama.*"

■ ■ ■ ■

Gabir didn't speak during the two-hour flight. Salome and Duberman didn't, either. It seemed safe to assume he was a *mukhabarat* officer who spoke Hebrew and English. But when they landed, he disappeared and the Jordanians treated them like ordinary passengers.

Now they were back in the world. It was just past 6 p.m. A day had passed since Wells kidnapped them, eighteen hours since he dumped them in Riyadh. If he and Duto had flown to Johannesburg overnight, they could already have found Witwans. Worse: They might already have grabbed him. They might already have put him on a plane to the United States.

"You call South Africa," Duberman said. "I'll call home, get us a jet."

Salome punched in Frankel's mobile number, wondering what she would do if he didn't answer. After five rings, the phone went to voice mail. She reminded herself that he would be seeing a Jordanian number on his screen, called again. One, two, three —

"Shalom."

"Amos."

"Adina? Where have you been?"

"Don't worry about it. What's important, do you still have Witwans?"

"Of course." He sounded surprised at the question.

"Can you control him? He'll do what you say?"

"Without a doubt. He's been drunk since I got here, and he's scared out of his mind."

"Take him and go."

"Whcrc?"

"Cape Town, a safe house not far from the airport. I'll fly down, meet you there." Witwans's mansion was in the Free State province, the middle of South Africa. She guessed it had to be eight or ten hours by car to Cape Town. The city was on the Atlantic Ocean, in the country's southwest corner. She had a safe house in Johannesburg, too, but keeping Frankel and Witwans on the road as long as possible seemed smart. For her, the difference was immaterial. Depending on how quickly Duberman arranged the jet, she would arrive in Cape Town a couple hours after Frankel and Witwans.

"That must be a thousand kilometers from here. More. You want me to leave now, drive all night? Why not just let me shoot him?"

"Wells is on his way to you. Get out of there. No bodies. Nothing to find. Give Witwans a few more drinks, he'll sleep the whole way."

"He smells terrible, you know. Old *shicker*—" Yiddish and Hebrew slang for drunk. "Probably throw up in the seat."

"Amos. Go."

"The address."

"I'll text it." She hung up.

Beside her, Duberman cooed into his phone in Hebrew, "No, everything's fine . . . I'll explain as soon as I'm home . . . I love you, too, babe. Bye."

Babe. She supposed she was happy to hear that he was as banal in love as everyone else.

"They were waiting for us to call. There's a jet fueled up at Ben Gurion. Be here in half an hour, forty minutes."

Salome explained the call with Frankel.

"So you're going to Cape Town?"

"Yes." She wanted to ask him to come, though she knew he wouldn't possibly.

"We'll stop at Tel Aviv, drop me off. Gideon has four guys on the jet. You can have two, I'll take two, just in case you're wrong and Wells somehow got back to Israel."

Wells wasn't in Israel, and Duberman no

doubt had another squad of guards at his mansion anyway. But two reinforcements was better than none.

Ninety minutes later, they were back in Israel, their round-trip complete. Salome suddenly was certain that she wouldn't see Duberman again.

As the cabin door opened, she hugged him, too long and too close. She bent her head to his chest and smelled his musk, his scent true and ripe after almost two days without a shower. "Aaron."

"Adina." His voice was gentle and as distant as the break of the ocean. She would have told him she loved him, but why? He didn't love her. The words would have been just one more coin for his fortune. So she pulled away, unwound her arms.

"I'm going to find him," she said instead. "And I'm going to kill him."

26

The countdown clock was more than ticking now.

Flying Riyadh to Johannesburg took eight hours. Even after gaining a time-zone hour, Wells and Duto didn't clear South African immigration until 4 p.m. local. Worse, they didn't have the prearranged help that would have come if they'd been on agency business. No car waiting in the O. R. Tambo International parking garage. No dossier with Witwans's address. Most important, no pistols, silencers, or box of ammunition in the trunk.

They solved the first two problems easily enough, thanks to Avis and the Internet. Thirty-five minutes after immigration, they had an Audi A3 and turn-by-turn directions to Witwans's mansion. He lived in farm country a couple hundred kilometers southwest of Johannesburg. The location was a blessing and a curse. They would waste at least three hours getting there. But once they did, they wouldn't have to worry about neighbors or a quick police response.

Their lack of weapons was far more serious. The bag that Duto had brought to Wells had all manner of helpful paraphernalia, including several pieces he'd already used. What it didn't have was a pistol. Wells hadn't packed one because he feared losing the entire bag to an airport screen. He hadn't known in advance Duto would be bringing it to him, or flying private. As a result, they had only one pistol, the Sig P238 that Duberman's bodyguard had handed over in Tel Aviv. It was an undercover weapon, small, underpowered, and with just a six-shot magazine. Salome's bodyguard would be waiting on them, and they didn't know how many guys he had with him.

"You have anyone who can hook us up?" Wells said.

"Not on this continent."

"Then let's find a gun shop." Given South Africa's crime rate and hunting culture, Wells expected that they could legally pick up a rifle or shotgun. He scrolled through the phone he'd picked up at the airport.

"How about this one? Great Guns of Sandton?" Sandton was a wealthy white neighborhood north of downtown Johannesburg.

But Wells was wrong. The Great Guns manager explained that South Africa had strict firearms laws. Police performed background checks on all buyers. "Backlog is years now. Typical of this regime."

The man's contempt for the black-run government gave Wells a glimmer of hope that he might break its laws. "Any way around it?"

"I wish," the manager said. He had the friendly but wary expression that Wells had seen before on gun enthusiasts. *Sure, we're buddies. For now.* "Why the rush? Come to Joburg on business, now you want to hunt the mighty dik-dik? Your guide will gladly supply everything you need."

Wells looked at Duto. "Can I talk to you outside?"

In the lot, Wells handed over the Audi's keys.

"I'm going to have to do something I don't like. Get in and keep it running."

"You're not —"

"No." Gun store robbers were instant Darwin Award finalists. *Sir, I see that you believe deeply in your right to use firearms to protect yourself, but please stand aside while*

566

I take these. "I'm going to ask. Politely. Even so, he might make a citizen's arrest."

"Good luck with that," Duto said.

The manager conspicuously laid a pistol on the counter when Wells reappeared. "More questions, brother?"

Wells had two choices here, wink-and-a-nod — *We're hunting, but not dik-dik, see what I'm saying* — and straight-up desperate. This guy didn't strike him as the wink-and-a-nod type. "My friend and I, we're in a bind."

"I wish I could help." Though his tone implied the opposite.

"If you know anyone. A friend who needs cash."

"What's your name?"

"John."

"Looking for anything in particular, John?"

A pop quiz to see whether Wells knew what he was talking about. "I used to be partial to Makarovs. I know they're junk, but they were popular where I operated. Plenty of ammo and spare parts. Then, a couple years ago, my girlfriend made me switch to a Glock. Which I admit is more accurate, more stopping power."

"What about your friend?"

"Never asked him."

The man shook his head. Wells felt weirdly negligent. *You've known him all these years and you can't even name his favorite pistol? What do you two talk about, anyway?*

"What were you doing, in the places you needed the Mak?"

So he still had the guy's interest. "About what you'd expect."

"And this? Today?"

Wells shook his head. "Better if I don't say." *You'd never believe me anyway.*

"You look like the real deal, John. But you can't trust me, I can't trust you. You'd best go."

Never argue with a man standing in front of an arsenal. Wells turned away.

"Where will you try next?"

"Soweto, maybe." The district lay on the other side of the city. Decades after the end of apartheid, it remained ninety-eight percent black and desperately poor.

"Foolishness. By the time you get there, it'll be dark. They'll take your money and your car and leave you in a ditch. That's if you're lucky. Otherwise, they'll just —" The man raised his index finger, *pop-pop.*

"My friend has a Sig if it comes to that." Wells barely kept himself from adding *You racist prick* as he opened the front door.

568

"John —"

Wells stopped.

"I can't help you. My boss finds out, he'll sack me on the spot. But Soweto, no. I know a man who might have something."

Now the guy's racism was working *for* Wells.

"In Roodepoort. West of here. Your saloon has a navvy?"

Wells needed a second to understand — *Does your car have a GPS?* "Yes."

The man scribbled a phone number and address, handed it over. "Name's Pieter. Tell him Marion sent you. Make sure you have plenty of geld." He rubbed his fingers together.

"Thank you."

"You look like you need a break."

Outside, Wells plugged the address into the GPS. "Twenty minutes. Let's go."

"Great." But Duto didn't sound happy.

"What?"

"I just talked to Roy Baumann. My chief of staff. Had to be sure my events are canceled for the next couple of days."

Chief of what? Wells almost said. With everything that had happened in the last day, he had nearly forgotten that Duto was still a senator. "So?"

"FBI came to my office yesterday. This morning they showed up at Roy's house. Six a.m. Four guys, wanting to know if he had any idea where I am."

"Does he?"

"Dummy. It doesn't matter. I'm traveling under my own name. On a diplo passport. They don't even have to ask the NSA to look, those get tracked automatically. And as soon as they look at the Tambo landing logs, they'll find the plane."

"So they know where you are —"

"Know what else they asked? Whether Roy knew who I was traveling with or what I was doing. He said no, which is true, because he's been smart enough not to ask. Then they brought up Shafer, did Roy know when I'd last spoken to him, what we'd talked about. Of course he said no to that, too. They asked him if he'd be willing to tell them if he got a call from me. That's when he told them that they'd gotten their three free questions at the top of the mountain and if they wanted more they'd better come back with a subpoena."

"Sounds like he handled it."

"He's been around. But you get what's happening here, right? They're looking to put us on Shafer's indictment, an excuse to bring us in as material witnesses. Or just arrest us."

"We knew it could happen."

"Difference between knowing it could and seeing that it *has.*"

"So they track you to Tambo. You dead-end there. I rented the car, not you. If they're smart, maybe they figure I'm with you, look for the alias I used to clear immigration. But that means getting the NSA involved to see who else arrived when you did. And correct me if I'm wrong, Vinny, that's a big step. Way bigger than sending the FBI to talk to your chief of staff. If that blows up, they just say they were worried that Shafer and I duped you, they wanted to give you a friendly heads-up. But that excuse won't wash with the NSA. Before it starts chasing a U.S. senator, it'll want paperwork. An active criminal investigation."

"At this point the AG" — Attorney General — "or even the President will have no problem signing off on that."

"Fine. Let's say they make that move today *and* NSA figures out who I am right away. Even then, they won't get the car that fast."

"Credit cards," Duto said.

"You may not have noticed, but the credit

card I used didn't exactly match the passport."

"That's why the rental guy was giving you a hard time?"

"Yes. Used my middle name instead of my first and misspelled the last by one letter, *Ishmael Jeferson* instead of Michael Jefferson." Shafer had taught Wells the trick. Amazing how big a difference a one-letter change could make.

"Then how come he let you rent it?"

"Because Ishmael's my middle name on the passport, and I gave him an extra five hundred bucks as a cash deposit. But the NSA isn't looking for Ishmael."

"If he hadn't bit —"

"I had a card with the right spelling if I needed it. Point is, it won't come up right away. They'll have to start canvassing hotels and car companies in person, and you can't do that from Langley. In fact, they can't do it without local help, no matter what. And guess what, it's past five here already and this is a tricky story for the chief of station to be giving South African intel. Much less the local cops. Way I figure it, we have at least until tomorrow morning, probably the afternoon, before we have to worry about this car being hot. If we can't find Witwans by then, we're done anyway. And if we do, and he confirms he sold Salome the HEU, it won't matter how many Feds are waiting when we land at Dulles, the White House has to listen."

Wells watched in silence as Duto considered the case he'd made.

"Starting to understand how you've lasted so long," he finally said.

"Let's just hope that Pieter in Roodepoort doesn't prove me wrong by shooting us both."

Pieter arranged to meet them in the parking lot of a Steers, a popular South African burger chain. *Orange Honda,* his text explained. He was there when they arrived, eating a messy-looking burger and leaning against a beat-up Accord. The car was more red than orange, but Wells wasn't arguing.

"You're the ones from Marion?" Pieter crammed down the last of his burger and stepped toward them. He was a wiry man with tattoos that curled up his neck like his chest was on fire. He wore a baggy T-shirt emblazoned with the South African rugby logo. Wells would have been shocked if the shirt *didn't* hide a pistol.

"That's us."

"Wait in your car," Pieter said to Duto. He led Wells to the back of the Honda and popped the trunk. Inside, an unzipped blue canvas bag held two Glock 19 pistols and a pump-action Mossberg shotgun, along with a box of 9-millimeter ammunition and a dozen or so 12-gauge shells loose in a plastic bag.

"Fifty thousand rand." About five thousand dollars. Almost three times what these weapons would cost in a store. A black-market price for black-market guns.

"I take a look?"

Pieter nodded. Wells reached into the bag. The pistols were unloaded. Wells racked their slides, made sure their magazine releases were smooth, dry-fired them. He couldn't be sure without actually shooting them, but they felt right. He didn't care about the shotgun. The pistols were what mattered.

"Okay, then, chief?"

"Can we give it to you in dollars. Five thousand?"

"What bills?"

"Hundreds, mainly. New." Guys like Pieter didn't always like hundreds, the denomination most targeted by counterfeiters.

"Six, then. Your friend has it?" Pieter dumped out the fries from his Steers paper bag and handed it to Wells. "Put it in the sack. I'll put the duffel on the ground. You toss me the sack and I drive off."

Wells didn't like the sequence. There was a tarp in the trunk behind the bag that could be hiding a second bag that looked identical to the first but was filled with junk instead of guns. Pieter could grab the second bag and throw it down while Wells got the money from Duto. By the time Wells looked inside it and realized the con, Pieter would be on his way out of the lot, the money in his pocket and the weapons still in his trunk. He'd be making a stupid move, since Wells and Duto were paying far more than the firearms were worth. But guys with neck tattoos were rarely strategic thinkers.

"Vinny. Bring over six thousand."

"I told him to stay," Pieter said. He stepped back from Wells, lifted his rugby shirt to reveal a black pistol tucked into his waistband. He made the move in a half-assed wannabe gangster way that told Wells he had no intention of using it.

"Good for you." Wells nodded at Duto. "He has one, too. Take out the bag, put it on the ground."

From the way Pieter looked at the trunk, Wells knew he'd tried to scam them.

"Seriously? After your buddy brought a tear to my eye with the white-solidarity speech?"

Pieter ignored him, tossed down the bag.

"We're going to pay you anyway. Give him two thousand dollars, Vinny."

"I said six."

"Before you tried to rob us. Two thousand is what they're worth." Now Wells was the one acting stupid. Two thousand or six thousand made no difference. But Wells was all out of patience. He felt like a walking incarnation of that T-shirt favored by bratty five-year-olds: *I only have one nerve left and you're getting on it.* The last month had been exhausting, and the longest night was still to come.

"He'll put it under the wiper, I'll grab the bag, and we're done."

Duto reached into his pocket, counted out the money, fanning the bills so Pieter could see them. He stuffed them under the wiper blade. Wells picked up the bag, backed away carefully. Pieter grabbed the money and made a show of counting it. "Good."

"Everybody's happy, then."

Pieter offered Wells his twin middle fingers.

The Audi's GPS led them southwest, toward the N1, the sun low in their eyes. "You think putting one over on that kid makes up for the way Duberman beat you in Tel Aviv?"

"Just drive, Vinny."

"You want to talk about it?"

Wells didn't want to talk about it. Not with Duto. Not now, not ever. He had let Duto bait him over a moral line he had sworn not to cross. Now the man wanted to — what, exactly? Absolve him? Condemn him for failing? Wells wasn't sure which choice repulsed him more.

He closed his eyes and recited the Quran's first Surah, *Bis-millahi rahmani rahim / Al hamdu-lillah rabbi alamin . . . In the name of Allah, the merciful, the compassionate / All praise due to Allah, Lord of the Worlds . . .*

"I know you're just spouting that to piss me off, John —"

Wells filled himself with the prayer, and soon enough Duto had nothing to say.

When he opened his eyes, the sky outside was full dark. He must have slept. They were deep in the countryside, speeding down a two-lane road that curved through fields cut as tightly as a Marine's first haircut and speckled with barrels of hay.

"You have a nice nap?"

Wells tilted back his head, rubbed his eyes. "We close?"

"We're not far, Sleeping Beauty."

"You must want me to start praying again."

"Dear Jesus, no." Duto's idea of a joke. "Any ideas how we're going to play this? Since I left the satellite shots at home."

"Look for the weak spot, then come in hard. Guns drawn. Don't waste time. Shoot first. Try not to kill anyone we shouldn't. The usual." Wells supposed the last two words were *his* idea of a joke.

"Sounds good."

Ten minutes later, the GPS told them that they had arrived. A fence marked by lightning-bolt pictographs ran along the road, ending at the property's main gate, eight feet of wrought iron set between brick posts. *Witwans Manor,* a bronze plaque announced.

"Classy," Duto said. The house itself stood on a low hill a couple hundred feet from the gate. Wells expected it would be mostly dark. Instead, the entire first floor was lit like Witwans was having a cocktail party. Between the Audi's high beams and the light coming out of the house, they could see up the driveway and the lawn around it. Empty, no guards visible.

Salome's bodyguard could have set up in a sniper's nest on the second floor of the mansion to pick off Wells as soon as he jumped the gate. But Wells didn't see a way around the risk. Shorting out the fence so he could climb it would take longer and be even more conspicuous. Anyway, he had a sinking feeling that they had arrived too late, that Salome's bodyguard had already left with Witwans.

"I'll go over the gate, pop it for you from the inside," Wells said.

"You think he's gone, don't you?"

Wells reached into the back seat for a Glock, jammed it into his waistband. He stepped out of the car and scaled the gate, ignoring the iron tines prodding his hands and feet. The gate's motor was on the inside of the right brick post. Wells turned it on and the gate churned open. Easy enough.

A dog's howl erased his satisfaction. Not one dog. Two, three, a pack. They tore down the driveway at him, three German shepherds and two Great Danes, their jaws wide open, galloping like they were thoroughbreds and Wells the finish line. Wells reached for his pistol and then realized that shooting them wasn't an option. Even if he could take out two or three, the survivors would shred him.

He ran for the corner where the gate met the brick post and scrabbled up the iron, a clumsy game of parkour. The pack leader, a giant gray Great Dane, arrived just as Wells pulled himself onto the post. The dog's jowls snapped shut an inch beneath Wells's feet. Wells stood atop the post as the pack growled and howled and snapped and jumped for him, *lemme at ya, come on down and fight fair, you can't stay up there forever.* Now Wells could shoot them all. But he didn't like shooting dogs. Anyway, killing them wouldn't gain him any points with Witwans or whoever was inside the house.

Duto edged the Audi forward and cracked his window. "Now what?"

"I'm gonna jump on the roof and you drive to the house."

"John —"

Wells jumped. His bad ankle nearly gave and he had a moment imagining himself on the ground with the dogs at him, but he steadied. Beneath him, the Audi rolled through the gate and up the driveway. The dogs followed the car, howling all the way, outriders from hell.

The mansion's wide front door swung open. An African man stepped onto the porch, pointing a shotgun at the Audi. From a window on the floor above, a second black man covered them with a pistol. Salome's bodyguard and Witwans were nowhere in sight.

Wells raised his hands.

"You have a gun?" the man on the porch said. He looked at least seventy, his skin wrinkled and his hair short and gray, but he held the shotgun steady.

"Yes."

"Throw it down."

"We're looking for Rand."

"Throw it down."

Wells plucked out the Glock by its butt and spun it softly to the right, onto the grass at the edge of the driveway. The man whistled sharply and shouted in Afrikaans. The dogs snapped their jaws shut and looked up at him. One by one, they backed away from the car. The man whistled again and they trotted through the front door. The gray Great Dane went last, unwillingly, eyeing Wells as he disappeared into the house.

"Get down," the man said. "This side." He nodded the shotgun to his right, the direction opposite where Wells had thrown the pistol. Smart. Wells jumped down.

The man stepped off the porch, keeping about fifteen feet from Wells. The man on the second floor shouted down in an African language Wells had never heard. The first man didn't answer. He seemed to be enjoying his control of this situation. Wells tried to imagine how he must feel, a servant who suddenly had absolute power over these

581

white men who had bizarrely come to the house where he worked. Yet he seemed polite, almost friendly.

"Your name?"

"John."

"I'm Martin. What is it you want?"

"We're looking for Rand."

"He's not here."

"The man with the scars took him?"

Martin hesitated, obviously wondering how Wells knew, then nodded. "Amos, yes. Around six p.m."

"Don't suppose he told you where?"

"No."

Wells grunted, just once. Like he'd taken a shot to the stomach. He and Duto had come so close. They'd missed Witwans by three hours, no more. But three hours or three months made no difference. Witwans could be anywhere, and they had no way of finding him. *In the wind,* the cops said.

"This man comes, now you. What is it you want with him?" Martin appeared sincerely interested.

"To stop a war."

"Rand? He can't get out of bed without a drink." The man upstairs laughed.

"Did a woman come here a few months ago? In her thirties, brown hair, pretty. Big nose. Maybe take something from the house?"

Martin's eyes widened. "Natalie, yes."

Wells tented his hands together in supplication. "I promise you, if you have any idea where he went — *please.*"

"Tell me more about why you want him."

"He sold that woman uranium — stuff for a nuclear bomb. She's pretending it's from Iran. And that's why America wants to attack Iran tomorrow."

"This is true?"

"I swear on my family."

"You catch him, then what?"

"We take him back to the States, to the people who need to know the truth." A more than slightly oversimplified answer. Wells hoped it was right.

"They put him in jail?"

"I don't know."

"Drunk greedful fool. You know he thinks we like him."

"So help us find him."

"I tell you I don't know."

Wells bowed his head. Maybe Martin would let them look through the house for clues. Though Wells couldn't imagine that Frankel had left anything useful.

Then Martin grinned, nodded to the man on the second floor. "But Jacob, my nephew, he does."

Inside, Jacob explained. Every couple of weeks, Witwans drove his Mercedes to bars around Bloemfontein and drank himself to blackout. The bartenders took his keys and called him taxis home. Their motive was not so much altruism as the cut of the fare they received. The next day, Jacob had to find the Merc. To simplify the process, he installed a GPS tracker.

This evening, when Frankel told Witwans that they would have to leave, Witwans had set only one condition, that they take the Mercedes. After a minute of arguing, Frankel agreed.

"Does Rand know about the tracker?" Duto said.

"Not sure. He loves the car. So maybe it was a fortune —"

"Coincidence —" Martin said.

"Or maybe he wants us to find him. No matter." Jacob pulled out his phone, a big-screen Samsung. "Here he is." A white dot pinged on a bright orange highway.

"That's the N1?"

"Yes. He's in the Northern Cape now. Almost three hundred kilometers from here. Going good, maybe one hundred kilos."

"Can we have the phone?" Wells said.

"No no no." Jacob tucked it away.

"Name your price."

"No price."

Not now. They couldn't afford more delays. Wells couldn't imagine hurting these people, but he would for the phone. "Please."

"This is too good. I'm coming." Jacob grinned. "What are we waiting for? Let's go."

27
ONE DAY . . .

BELLVILLE, SOUTH AFRICA
Wells expected to stay at the wheel until they caught the Mercedes. But just after midnight, the Audi demanded gas. At the station, Wells went inside for a pit stop of his own. He came out with coffee and water and found Duto in the driver's seat.

"Move."

Duto grabbed the coffee instead. "You're not the only control freak in this car. Besides, big day tomorrow. You need your beauty sleep."

So Wells took his place in the passenger seat. Their new friend Jacob sprawled across the back, cradling the phone that was his ticket to the party. He was a big man, and spherical, round eyes in a round head atop a round body, fat, but strong, too. Wells wasn't sure how they would make him stay in the car when they caught Frankel and

Witwans. He looked to be having too good a time.

Wells dozed fitfully as Duto raced down the N1. He hoped they might reel the Mercedes in over the night, but the road didn't give them much chance. It was not a divided highway but a single strip of asphalt, often with only one lane in each direction. A county road, with an interstate's traffic, even in the small hours of the night. Twice oncoming trucks forced them onto the shoulder.

Every few minutes, Jacob let them know that the Mercedes was still moving, still ahead of them. But Wells couldn't shake a creeping fear that Frankel had shucked them somehow. Maybe he knew about the tracker. Maybe he'd passed the car to another driver and taken Witwans the opposite direction, toward Johannesburg. Paranoia, yes, but Salome and Duberman had more than matched him this last month. Why wouldn't they have one more trick?

Around 6 a.m., Wells jerked out of a haze of not-quite-sleep to see a three-foot chunk of steel pipe bouncing at them from the bed of an overloaded pickup. Duto pulled the wheel hard left, and the Audi, down on its shocks, missed the pipe by six inches.

"I'd hate to disappoint Duberman by dying in a car accident," Wells said.

"Didn't you learn at the Farm that they're among the top risks case officers face?"

Indeed. Wells had joined the service in the halcyon days before 9-11, when drunk driving, paper cuts, and herpes were the major health threats in the clandestine service. A few minutes later, as they came through a bump of a town called Matjiesfontein, the sky went from black to blue, wisps of dawn creeping from the east. The light revealed an arid, scrubby land, low hills flecked with scattered shrubs and bushes.

"I thought the Cape was supposed to be beautiful," Duto said.

"This the Karoo," Jacob said.

"Did you sneeze?"

"Something else. Witwans off the N1."

"When?"

"Just now."

Wells reached back for the phone. Sure enough, the Mercedes had turned south off the highway about twenty kilometers east of central Cape Town. The giant slum called Khayelitsha lay a few kilometers south, as did the Cape Town airport. Wells feared Frankel might be taking Witwans to the airport, but he had chosen a strange route in that case, along surface streets rather than the R300 ring road, which ran directly to the airport.

After their all-night chase, the Mercedes held a lead of about two hundred kilometers, two and a half hours, give or take. Seeing the airport on the map reminded Wells that their jet was still in Johannesburg. They needed it in Cape Town.

The pilot answered on the first ring. "This is Kirk."

"Hope you and your first mate got a decent night's sleep, because you have a long day ahead."

"Tell me we're going home."

"We're going home." *Inshallah.* "Can you meet us in Cape Town this morning?"

"Done. I'll check the charts, but I think we can be there in two and a half hours, three at most. Quick turn?"

"With any luck. Back to Dulles. You can file the flight plan now. Three passengers." Wells hoped he wasn't jinxing himself. But better to do this now, with time, than as they were racing to the airport.

"Who's the third?"

"Rand Witwans. South African national. Shouldn't raise any flags."

"As long as you have his passport number."

"I do." Not just the number. The passport

itself. Witwans had left it in the bedroom safe at his mansion. His not-so-faithful servant Martin knew the combination.

On the ground, the Audi raced southwest. On Jacob's phone, the Mercedes turned right, left, right again. It stopped, then doubled back a few seconds later. Wells guessed Frankel was trying to find a safe house he'd never seen before. The Merc made another right and moved slowly south, into an area the map marked as Bellville Lot 3. There it stopped.

The squarish road grid and setting near highways and airport suggested a middle-class suburb. Wells imagined houses set on narrow lots, plenty of residents around to hear a gunfight and call the police. Worse, he and Duto would reach the neighborhood around 9 a.m. Some straggling commuters would still be heading out, along with parents taking their toddlers to day care. All potential victims of stray bullets.

But the location came with positives, too. The executive terminal at Cape Town International was barely ten kilometers down the M10, which the map indicated was a big surface road. Even in traffic, they ought to be able to reach it in under fifteen minutes. Better still, the police had no obvious choke points for roadblocks. Wells and Duto were looking at the human equivalent of smash-and-grab. Go in fast, take Witwans, stuff him in the Audi, dump him on the plane while the police were still making sense of what had happened.

They had a second edge. Martin had told them the night before that Frankel was the only guard watching Witwans. Of course, he might have reinforcements at the safe house, but then why hadn't they come to Bloemfontein and helped at the mansion? Duberman didn't have casinos in South Africa, so Wells doubted he had a local guard force. More likely that Salome had sent Frankel down by himself. Then, after the Saudis released her, she must have called him and told him to move Witwans from his mansion to this safe house a thousand kilometers away. The likely reason was that she had figured out that Wells was on his way to South Africa and wanted to hide Witwans from him. Her plan would have worked if not for the GPS tracker on the car, something she couldn't possibly have expected.

But if Frankel was alone at the mansion, he would have had to make the entire thousand-kilometer drive himself. Witwans had been too drunk to walk, much less drive, the night before, according to Jacob.

Frankel would be exhausted. No matter how good they were, exhausted soldiers made mistakes.

With that thought, Wells leaned back in his seat and made himself rest.

Ten minutes after Wells closed his eyes, the G650 carrying Salome went wheels-down at Cape Town International, the first landing of the new day. She'd flown in the darkness over Egypt, Sudan, Congo, Zambia, Botswana, South Africa, seeing none of them. The flight was smooth, and she'd slept the whole way.

She couldn't remember her dreams. But she woke with a clear-eyed, cold anger at Wells. Duberman had thrown him a lifeline in Tel Aviv, and he had not just rejected it but sneered at it. She hadn't understood until then how small-minded Wells was. He couldn't grasp the strategic catastrophe that would come if Iran built a nuclear weapon. Worse, he lacked the imagination to realize the elegance of the story she and Duberman had told. He was stuck on the fact that they'd *lied* about the uranium. Of course they had. Human beings lied every day in every conceivable way. Iran had lied about its nuclear program for twenty years.

How had she ever considered Wells her

match? He was a more skilled version of the men around her on this plane. A bruiser with a great survival instinct. Nothing more. She would shed no tears when she killed him.

At last, as their jet rolled to a stop, she saw the full significance of the name she'd given herself. The Bible told the tale of Salome, who danced for Herod and demanded the head of John the Baptist as her reward. But two millennia had passed. The new Salome didn't need a man to do her dirty work. She would kill Wells — John the American, John the Troublemaker, John the *Muslim* — herself.

First, though, she needed to run out the clock. South Africa was seven hours ahead of Washington, where it was now 11:30 p.m. In a half hour, the final day of the President's deadline would officially begin at the White House. She turned on her phone, found CNN.com reporting that in a speech from the Oval Office three hours before, the President had repeated his deadline. "Iran's efforts to terrorize the United States by killing innocent civilians and disrupting travel and commerce around the world will fail," he said. "Our resolve is unshaken. Iran must agree to open its nuclear facilities by midnight tomorrow, or face the consequences."

The *New York Times* wrote that the United States planned its first air raids "minutes or hours" after the cutoff passed. A ground invasion would follow "within days," though of course no one would say exactly when. Military analysts were split over the wisdom of the President's willingness to invade with a small and lightly armored force, instead of the massive armies it had mustered in Iraq. *Whole new way of fighting. If it works, it'll give the United States options all over the world,* one retired three-star said. *But if it doesn't, we'll lose more thousands of men. In a week.*

If that prospect worried the President, he wasn't admitting it publicly. "We will fight, we will win, and we will destroy the factories that you use to build weapons of mass destruction," he'd said at the end of his speech. "Do not doubt our resolve. The United States can never allow Iran to threaten it with nuclear attack. My fellow Americans, of every faith and creed, may God bless us all."

Her phone buzzed with a message, a single word from Frankel: *Here.*

Me, too, she wrote.

An hour later, after an unexpected and frustrating wait for immigration to open, she and her men stepped out of a taxi outside the safe house. She had never seen the place before. She had set up safe houses all over the world, but in cities like Cape Town, where she had no operations and no plans for any, she sometimes let real-estate agents choose their locations. In this case, she'd made a mistake. The neighborhood was anonymous and close to highways and the airport, as she liked, but the house was small and run-down. Worse, it stretched almost to the edges of the lot.

She preferred bigger houses in gated communities. Still, the place should be fine for a night, and Wells couldn't possibly find it. Of course, she couldn't find him either, not yet. But tomorrow morning, she would make Witwans call Wells, tell him they needed to meet. Wells would be suspicious, but he would know that the FBI and CIA were closing in on him and that Witwans was his only hope. He would take the chance. This time Salome wouldn't leave Wells to Russian cops or Glenn Mason. She would pull the trigger herself. And after Wells was finally gone, Witwans would get what he deserved, a bullet in the back of the head.

Then she would rest.

Frankel barely looked up when she walked

into the house. He sat on the couch, a pistol on the coffee table in front of him, a bag at his feet stretched by the shotguns inside. The scars on his chin shone and he stank of cheap coffee and too many hours behind the wheel.

"Amos." She knelt on the couch, wrapped an arm around him. "Long drive?"

"Fine."

"Wells —"

"No way could he have followed me."

"Rand?"

"In the bedroom. He was all right. Spent most of the ride with his tongue hanging out."

"Once he gets us Wells, you can do whatever you like with him."

Frankel smiled. Put his head against Salome. Almost that quickly, he slept.

She gave him two minutes, then extricated herself and unzipped the bag. Inside, she found a pistol and two shotguns. She kept the pistol, gave the shotguns to Binyamin and Gil, the reinforcements Duberman had sent down with her.

"There shouldn't be any problem, but just in case."

Wells opened his eyes and found himself in a tunnel. Not a metaphorical tunnel, a real one, cut through rock, with headlights speeding uncomfortably close. He couldn't see entrance or exit, but the grumbling in his stomach assured him he was very much alive and not in purgatory.

"Where are we?"

"Huguenot Tunnel, it's called. We get out, we're fifty klicks from Bellville."

Seconds later, the exit came into view, a white speck that grew steadily. Wells felt his pulse kick up. Past 8 a.m. now, 1 a.m. in Washington. Twenty-three hours to go. Plenty of time.

Only it wasn't. South Africa was a long way from anywhere, and a very long way from North America. The eight-thousand-mile flight from Cape Town to Dulles would take at least sixteen hours, more if the Atlantic headwinds were strong, plus a refueling stop in Dakar that added another hour.

Seventeen hours minimum, less a seven-hour time difference. If everything went right and they captured Witwans with no hitches and took off from Cape Town by 11 a.m., they still wouldn't arrive at Dulles until at least 9 p.m. Washington time. And at some point during that flight, they would need to convince Donna Green to talk to them rather than send the FBI to arrest them on landing. The equation was simple but punishing. They had used every inch of their slack and could no longer afford a single misstep. Even an error as small as a botched refueling in Senegal might destroy their chances.

"What are you thinking?" Duto said.

"That I wish we had some silencers."

"And a teleporter." Duto could count, too.

They sped out of the tunnel, and Wells saw Table Mountain in the distance, the famous thirty-five-hundred-foot plateau that rose behind Cape Town and offered a perfect view of the city and ocean. A must-see destination, by all accounts, but Wells wouldn't. The world's worst tourist. He always missed the big sights.

"You have a plan?" Duto said. "Or pretty much the same as last time?"

"Pretty much. Loop around the block, once, see what we can see. If the houses are as close as they look on the map, maybe we try to come in from the side."

"What about me?" Jacob said.

"You're the wheelman. You know what that means?"

Jacob shook his head.

"Means we get Rand out, throw him in the back of the car, and you drive us to the airport."

"You want me to stay in the car?"

"That's what the wheelman does."

"You think I can't handle a gun? Covered you easy enough."

"Let's talk about it after we see the place."

After the tunnel, the N1 became a true divided highway, two lanes each side. Duto sluiced the Audi through the morning commuter traffic. Twenty-five minutes later, they reached Durban Road, which led into Bellville's commercial center, ten- and fifteen-story office towers.

South on Durban, east on another arterial, then south again on the M10, Robert Sobukwe Road, the big boulevard that connected Bellville to the airport. On the right, west, they passed a massive train yard. They were nearly on top of the Mercedes now, less than a kilometer away. It was parked in the residential neighborhood just east of Sobukwe.

"Left here."

Duto turned, and they were in Bellville Lot 3, not a slum but certainly scrappier than the city center to the north. The houses sprouted clotheslines, the cars rust. The neighborhood looked to be mainly *coloured*, the term South Africans used for people of mixed race. The Audi stuck out. The car's conspicuousness wouldn't matter before the attack, but it might afterward, when the neighbors made emergency calls. Wells wondered if they ought to park around the corner, but then they would have to drag Witwans from the house to the car. Street kidnappings were rarely a good idea.

"Right here," Wells said, as they reached Industry Road, which marked the district's eastern edge. The neighborhood had been laid out in an imperfect grid. Its east–west streets stacked neatly, but the north–south roads started and stopped. The GPS showed the Mercedes parked on one of the north–south stubs, Octovale Street between Kosmos and Lily Roads.

"You know where we're going?"

Even with time desperately short, Wells wanted to spin through the neighborhood's main streets once. They might see a parked police cruiser, or road construction that blocked an escape route. "Just drive. Right here —"

"On Mimosa? *Mimosa?*" Mimosa marked the south end of Octovale.

"Calm yourself, Vinny." Though Wells did like the jumble of names. He couldn't imagine a neighborhood back home having a similarly random set — American developers were too careful.

"Here. Right. Slow."

If the tracker was correct, then they would see the Mercedes almost two short blocks up, on the right side. "We're only going to take one pass, so go easy —"

"You think you're the only one who's ever been in the field?"

Wells focused on the street. He liked what he saw. American building codes wouldn't allow houses built as closely as these. In some cases, their eaves almost overlapped. If Witwans was inside one like that, Wells could jump roof to roof and break in from the back while Duto attacked from the front.

Duto touched his brakes as they rolled through the intersection of Octovale and Lily. The GPS showed the Mercedes just a few houses ahead. Duto eased the Audi up the street at twenty miles an hour. And —

"There," Jacob said. The car was parked nose-out for an easy getaway, in the gated driveway of a squat yellow house. Eighty-four Octovale. The house nearly touched its neighbor to the right, but it was a relative fortress, with gated front windows, high walls on both sides, and a five-foot-tall fence in front of a short front yard. Thick white curtains blocked Wells from seeing who might be inside, but he glimpsed lights.

Then the house was behind them. Duto

turned left on Kosmos, and Wells considered what he'd seen. Despite the possible roof access, the setup wasn't ideal. Duto would have no way to reach the front door easily. The back door was sure to be locked, the back windows gated. The pack that Duto had brought from Virginia included Wells's auto lock picker, a tool that had saved him before. Even so, Frankel would hear him enter.

"Fortress Octovale," Duto said.

"Maybe." Wells looked back at Jacob. "You said you wanted in. That still true?"

Jacob nodded.

"Sure about this," Duto muttered.

Wells ignored him. "You're going to distract them. You go next door, the house to the left, one up from Rand."

"Over the wall?" A four-foot-high concrete wall separated that house from the street.

"That Ford is parked right in front. You step over the wall, no problem."

"Then what?"

"Then you knock on the door, hammer it. You yell, *I know you're in there, come out.* Not in English. In Afrikaans. You speak Afrikaans?"

"No problem. But Rand *next* door —"

"We want to make them wonder what's going on. Get them looking the wrong way, toward you, while I'm coming from the other side. If we're lucky, Rand will recognize your voice and stick his head out the front door. He won't be able to see you because of the wall, but he'll wonder why you're there. He'll know what you're saying, but Amos won't. If we're *really* lucky, Amos'll come out himself and make himself a target."

"Don't know who's inside that house next door, what biscuit he got."

"You don't want to, you don't have to. In or out?"

Asked that bluntly, the question could only have one answer.

"In."

Duto made a right, north, driving slowly away from the house. "And while Jacob is yelling nonsense and hoping he doesn't get shot, what about you?"

"I'm going to the house on the other side, one down. With the carport on the right side. I'll pull myself up that, run across the roof —"

"They might have a biscuit, too," Duto said. "Even a gat."

"Thank you for that, Vinny. I didn't see any cars, so I'm guessing whoever lives there is at work. Even if they're home, by the time they figure out what's going on, I should be on top of Witwans's house."

"Where am I?"

"The way the timing works, Jacob and I will get out of the car at Mimosa and Octovale" — the intersection almost two blocks south of the house. "We'll walk up Octovale to Lily" — one block up — "while you circle around up to the top of the street, the Kosmos intersection. When we see you there, Jacob goes ahead of me, runs up, jumps the fence at the house on the left. Just about the time he starts yelling, I'll be scaling the carport. It shouldn't take me more than a few seconds to get across. By then, Vinny, you'll have swung the Audi onto Octovale to give yourself a view of the front door of Rand's house. If it opens and anyone comes out, you'll honk to let me know. If it's Amos, I'll pop him from the roof and jump down. It's only one story. Then I'll grab Witwans from the house and throw him in the Audi. If Witwans comes out instead, I'll have to decide whether to grab him right away or go in the back door. And if nobody comes out, I'm going in the back for sure."

"What do I do then?" Jacob said.

"No matter what, you go back to the car after two minutes."

"Let me make sure I have this right," Duto said. "This all hinges on whether Amos opens the front door when Jacob starts yelling? What if he doesn't? You think you're going to get across the roof of a one-story house and then in the back door without him hearing?"

"I think Amos, who hasn't slept all night, is all of a sudden going to have to figure out what's going on when the neighbors start yelling and the dogs start barking. His first thought is not going to be that someone's on the roof coming for him. If he goes outside, I can blow off his head, and if he doesn't, I'll just creep along the house while he's distracted and go through the back." Wells knew that he was trying to convince himself as much as Duto. *A plan so crazy it just might work.*

"Give me best case, John."

"Best case, Jacob shouts for a minute, Amos comes out, I pop him with one shot. It takes me thirty seconds to get in the house and grab Rand, another thirty to get him to the car. That's two minutes and one shot and we're gone. The cops won't even be close. By the time the first car responds, we're at the airport. Worst case, nobody opens the door after a couple minutes and I have to go in the back and it takes a little longer."

"Worst case, you and Rand both get killed."

"That would be worse. You have anything better? I'm open to suggestions."

Duto pulled over. They sat for two long minutes as cars rolled by. In the distance a train whistled, but inside the Audi no one spoke.

"SOG team would be nice," Duto said. "Real surveillance. A magical unicorn. How did I get myself into this?"

"You know exactly."

"True. And I still can't figure it. If you get caught in there, what then? I grab the Mossberg and come over the fence? Not entirely senatorial. But I guess I burned that bridge a while ago."

Duto folded his hands across his chest as the Audi's clock counted off another two minutes. Wells wished Shafer were here. He'd understand the absurdity of the situation better than anyone. *America's fate depends on three men in Bellville, South Africa. Two can't stand each other. The third is a civilian they met the night before. Will they kidnap the old racist drunk in time to fly him to D.C.? Or get killed trying?*

But long experience had taught Wells that

too much second-guessing at these moments was not just pointless but dangerous. Climbing a carport to jump a roof to kidnap Witwans might seem bizarre, but they had no better option, and no time to find one. The choices they had made over the last few weeks had led them here, and without a time machine those choices couldn't be undone.

Wells had rock climbed a few times in his teens and twenties. The best climbers weren't necessarily the strongest, the most agile, or even the bravest, though those qualities helped. They were the ones who resisted the temptation to look down, who spidered up the face, always recognizing where they were and looking for the best solution, and with luck, the best after that.

"Time's a-wasting," Wells said.

Duto put the car in gear. "What a cluster."

"So it's a go?"

"Like our friend in Tel Aviv would say, shuffle up and deal."

28

BELLVILLE

Salome was sitting in a wrinkled leather chair in the living room, watching the deadline clock tick away on CNN International: *21:35:42 . . . 21:35:41 . . .* when the party started. Fists banging metal, a man screaming in a language Salome guessed was Afrikaans. He seemed to be at the next house over, on the other side of the wall to the north. Seconds later, a woman began yelling back.

Maybe screaming fights were common in this neighborhood. And Frankel had been sure Wells couldn't have tracked him here. But in moments like these, she didn't believe in coincidence. She drew the curtain a few centimeters, peeked into the yard and the street beyond. Something was different, though she couldn't figure what.

"Go look," she said to Binyamin.

"Take the gun?"

"Yeah."

He grabbed the shotgun and stepped out as a dog on the other side of the house added its howl to the chorus. Salome looked at Frankel, still sleeping on the couch. "Amos!"

A car honked, once, long and loud. She realized what had bothered her outside. The car. She tugged aside the curtain to double-check. A white Audi was parked across the street, diagonally north, twenty or twenty-five meters away. She couldn't see if it was running or anyone was inside, but she was sure it hadn't been parked there when she came to the house.

"What's happening?" Frankel said behind her.

"I think Wells. Go check Rand for a phone."

"I already did —"

She flapped her hand, *Don't argue, just do it.*

Outside, Binyamin stepped toward the people yelling next door.

"This wall. I can't see anything —"

When Duto honked, Wells crept to the front of the roof. *Eureka.* The play had worked.

Only, it hadn't. The man in the yard wasn't Frankel. Even from the back, Wells

609

knew. He'd seen Frankel in that Volgograd hotel room. This guy was much taller and broader.

Maybe Frankel had found the tracker and shucked the Mercedes overnight. He and Rand were a thousand miles away, and Wells was about to cut down a sucker paid by Frankel to drive the Mercedes here.

Or else Frankel had brought in reinforcements somehow. In that case, Wells was about to start a gunfight without knowing how many guys he faced. Either choice was bad, but the first was worse. Wells couldn't shoot an innocent man. And just because the guy had a shotgun didn't prove he worked for Duberman. The man stepped close to the wall and the Mercedes, yelled back to the house —

In *Hebrew*.

Good. At least Wells didn't have to worry he was shooting a civilian. He pulled the Glock. The tile on the roof was cheap and cracked and didn't offer great footing. But the roof itself was only slightly sloped and Wells was not even twenty-five feet away from the guy. An easy shot. The man never looked back. Never even turned his head.

Wells sighted, wasted a second wondering if his target knew what was really happening here. Probably not. Probably he'd taken a bodyguard job for the pay, been told the night before to get on a plane. *Excellent benefits. Must be willing to travel on short notice.* An employee. Nothing more. Maybe he would have thrown down his shotgun and surrendered if Wells gave him the choice. Maybe not. The answer didn't matter. Wells had no choice himself.

Wells squeezed the trigger twice. He aimed center mass, missed a few inches high. The back of the guard's head exploded in a slaughterhouse spray of blood and bone and brain. He crumpled face-first onto the scrubby lawn next to the Mercedes, dead before he knew what death was. Rudi would have been jealous.

From the room below, a woman yelled, "Binyamin!" Wells knew that voice. Salome. She must have flown directly from Jordan. So she and Amos were inside. How many others? Only the Mercedes was in the driveway, and no other cars were parked in front. They had taken a cab here. Which meant two or three people. Unless they'd taken more than one cab.

Wells fired two shots into the air, hoping that Duto would understand his message: *That wasn't Frankel and this isn't over.* Now he had to move. Where?

■ ■ ■ ■

Two shots, then two more. From the roof. Of course Wells was on the roof. He was a vulture. A vampire. Salome looked out. Binyamin lay in the grass not ten meters away, his head a cracked egg. She lifted her pistol, hoping Wells would jump down.

"Wells!"

No answer. No noise at all.

"Wells! Don't be a woman! Quit hiding!"

Still nothing. Was he creeping around up there? Or keeping still, hoping she would come out? She wondered how far the nearest police station was, how many minutes they had. The cops would take everyone into custody. They would need to sort out this strange house where Americans and Israelis were slaughtering each other. When they realized Witwans was a South African citizen, they would separate him and question him alone. Salome couldn't imagine what he would say. She'd peeked in on him a few minutes before. He'd deteriorated badly since she'd last seen him. The broken blood vessels in his nose had advanced to his cheeks. Even in sleep he smelled sweet, sickly, his liver fighting a losing battle against the poison he poured down his throat.

And what if Duto was here? An American senator and the former CIA director. The police would listen to his story, no matter how bizarre it sounded. Salome's mere presence here would help to confirm his accusation. How could she explain her sudden trip to South Africa, or how she'd ended up in this house with the former director of the South African nuclear program?

No, she and Witwans had to disappear. As long as they could escape this neighborhood and reach the highway, they should be safe. South Africa was huge, and she had plenty of cash. They could take the N1 all the way to Johannesburg, or head along the coast to Port Elizabeth. The police would have no way to connect them to this house. They'd been here only a couple of hours. No one knew who they were.

But they couldn't go anywhere until they put a stake in the vampire on the roof.

Frankel ran back into the living room, his pistol drawn. "What happened?"

"Wells shot Binyamin. From the roof." Luckily, they could speak openly in Hebrew. "Stay with him in case Wells tries to break into his room. Now."

"What's happening?" Gil, the second

guard, yelled from the kitchen, at the back of the house.

"Guard the back door. Wells is on the roof."

"How's that?"

"Just watch it."

She imagined how Wells might attack. The house was only about fourteen meters wide, eight across. Forty-five feet by twenty-five. Its layout was simple. In front, the living room spanned the width of the building. In back, the kitchen did the same. A center hallway connected the two rooms. The main bedroom ran along the right side of the hallway. A smaller bedroom and a bathroom shared the left. Witwans had naturally grabbed the big bedroom. Even in a kidnapped alcoholic haze, he acted the king.

The shouting next door stopped. In the silence, Salome listened for Wells. Nothing. Yet she was sure he hadn't jumped down. The noise would have been obvious. She wondered why he hadn't already tried to come at them. He'd just blown a man's head off, so he couldn't be planning to stick around for the cops. But if he figured that they would run, he might wait on the roof for the chance to pick them off.

On the flatscreen, CNN's countdown clock ticked away. *21:34:51 . . . 21:34:50 . . .*

But she and Wells had their own countdown. She would give Wells exactly one minute to make his move. She hadn't heard any sirens, so they still had a little time before the police arrived. Ideally, Wells would blink first, come off the roof to attack the house. As long as he was up there, they couldn't touch him.

If Wells hadn't moved in sixty — now fifty-five — seconds, she would tell Frankel to grab Witwans and hustle him out the back door and along the north wall of the house to the Mercedes. Gil and his shotgun would lead the way. She would cover the front yard from the living room. They would dare Wells and his friends to stop them. The alleys along the north and south sides of the house were narrow, and the edge of the roof overhung them. Wells would have to perch over the eaves for a shot. He'd have to be accurate. Gil wouldn't.

Still, she'd rather have him on the ground.

She checked to be sure she had a round chambered and flattened herself beside the front door. As she waited, every cell in her body came to life. The opposite of the depression that had once swallowed her.

She knew she would kill Wells.

At that moment, Wells would have traded

what was left of his soul for a CS grenade, or even the homemade Molotov cocktail that had served him in Istanbul. Too bad the devil was serving other clients. Wells didn't even have the shotgun. He'd left it with Duto, knowing he would need both hands to shimmy up the carport.

After killing the bodyguard, Wells stepped off the roof onto the wall that divided Salome's house from its southern neighbor. The wall was no wider than a single concrete block, with glass bits embedded in its top, so Wells had to tread carefully. But the wall gave him the chance to move quietly, rather than pounding the roof and giving away his position.

As he tightroped along, he heard Salome yell twice to him. At him. Did she think he'd answer? That she could convince him to throw away his tactical edge by insulting his masculinity? He understood the trick. Still, the words goaded him.

A window was cut into the house's south wall about halfway down. Through its bare glass, Wells glimpsed an unmade bed. He saw a shadow in the room. He guessed Witwans was down there, but he couldn't be sure. He kept moving. Six inches past the back right corner of the house, he stopped. The wall on which he stood ran another six feet to the rear lot line, then swung left around the back of the house and left again around its north side. Cracked concrete covered most of the narrow backyard below, creating a patio with all the appeal of an exercise pen in a supermax prison.

Next door, Jacob stopped shouting. He'd done his job. In the silence, Wells listened for sirens, heard none. Yet. Nor any movement inside the house. Salome was playing defense. Probably she figured he was still up front staking out the Mercedes. She hoped he would come down, open himself to a counterattack. He understood. The house had only two obvious entry points, the doors in front and back, both easily covered. But Wells was left with no choice now but to do what Salome wanted. He had to move, and quickly.

The back of the house had two windows that looked out on the patio, one on each side of the back door. Wells inched to his right along the wall. Through the nearer window, he spotted a yellowish Formica countertop and a couple of glasses. Kitchen in back, living room in front.

He craned his head, but he couldn't see if anyone was inside. The kitchen lights were out, and the sun was hidden behind clouds. Keeping the room in shadow. Then, an answer to a prayer that Wells hadn't uttered, the sun broke through. Wells caught a glint of light off metal, a shotgun barrel. The man holding it was against the wall a few inches left of the back door.

Just that fast, the sun was gone. The break Wells needed. Now he knew where to aim.

His phone buzzed. He pulled it, found a text from Duto: *Where you?* Wells decided to take the seconds to respond. *Back of house. More men inside.*

He shoved away the phone and jumped into the backyard, as far from the wall as he could. He wanted to land close to the door. He could aim and fire the Glock faster than the guy could bring the shotgun around, a life-or-death advantage in a close quarters firefight.

He heard his left foot break almost before he felt the pain, a loud *pop* as he landed on the concrete and then an electric spike running up his ankle, into his leg. He fell forward and braced himself with his left hand and kept his head and his right hand up. He was not even ten feet away from the door. As the guard spun and tried to bring up the shotgun, Wells fired once, twice, three times, not caring whether the rounds went through the door itself or its center window. Against a 9-millimeter round at close range, a painted plywood door offered no more protection than a piece of cardboard. The wood burst and blood spattered through the sudden holes in the guard's white short-sleeved shirt. But he was still raising the shotgun.

Wells scrambled forward, toward the house, left of the door. The shotgun blast tore the door off its hinges and echoed off the concrete walls. For a second, Wells couldn't hear anything at all, and then sound came back bit by bit.

He was squatting with his weight on his right leg, his face pressed to the house's back wall, maybe two feet to the left of the doorway. His right hand, his gun hand, was closer to the doorway. He leaned over and fired twice for cover and peeked inside. The guard lay on the linoleum kitchen floor, three feet inside, almost close enough for Wells to touch, the shotgun beside him. Blood soaked his shirt from shoulder to waist.

Salome yelled in Hebrew from the front of the house and the guy coughed and tried to answer, but he could manage only a bubble of blood. No saving him. He would be dead in minutes.

Wells fired twice more and reached into the house and grabbed the shotgun by the barrel, its steel slick with blood. The guard's fingers were still wrapped around the stock, and Wells had to wrench it away. He looked up to see Frankel in the hallway, maybe thirty feet away. Frankel fired three times as Wells spun back to the safety of the wall. One shot smacked the door frame and the second was close enough for Wells to hear it whistle by. The shotgun was a pump-action Remington 870, a 12-gauge. Wells checked the tube magazine, found four shells. He wiped off the blood as best he could and racked a round, the *chk-chk* as unsubtle a warning as a sidewinder's rattle. He set the gun aside, hoping he'd bought a few seconds to figure out how badly he'd injured his leg. He turned, putting his back against the wall, and pushed himself up with his good leg, thankful for all the squats he'd forced on himself over the years. When he was standing, he put a feather of pressure on his left leg. The pain flared as he bore down. But Wells could handle pain. The deeper problem was that he couldn't put weight on the front half of his foot. He'd broken at least one bone, maybe torn the big ligament, too. He couldn't remember the name but it was the one that always bothered basketball players. Even the light pressure he'd applied caused his foot to rearrange itself in real time, and not for the better. Evolution in reverse.

He'd broken the foot in Afghanistan years before and banged it up again in Istanbul three weeks earlier, but he'd thought he was fully recovered.

Wrong.

He could stand. And he could hobble, if he used his heel and kept all the weight off the front of his foot. But he sure couldn't run. *What do you call a woman with one leg? Eileen.*

Lucky he wasn't in the middle of a gun-fight or anything.

Frankel fired twice more from inside the house. He seemed to be moving closer, coming down the hallway. Wells reached across his body, grabbed the shotgun, fired blindly through the door. One shot and one shot only. Even after grabbing the Remington, he was still far too close to black on ammunition for comfort. He had just three rounds in the shotgun, five in the Glock. The pistol had a seventeen-round magazine, but Wells had already fired eleven rounds, four in front and seven back here. He had a plastic bag with loose ammunition in his pocket, but he couldn't imagine Frankel would give him the time he needed to re-load.

Duto had better get inside before then.

Again Wells caught Salome wrong-footed. She was watching the yard, but the shots came from the back, the kitchen. Three. Then a shotgun blast. She turned and ran, trying for the hallway. But Wells stuck a pistol through the remains of the back door and fired twice more. She skidded into the back wall of the living room to stop herself.

She peeked down the corridor. Gil, the second of the bodyguards she'd brought, lay on the kitchen floor. She couldn't tell if he was still breathing. "Gil!" she yelled. He turned his head a fraction, but if he spoke she couldn't hear him.

"Adina," Frankel said from the bedroom halfway down the hall, just as Wells appeared again in the kitchen doorway.

"Amos, he's coming for the kitchen —"

Frankel spun out of the bedroom and into the hall and fired as Wells reached down and grabbed the shotgun from Gil's hands. But Frankel missed, and Wells vanished again. Now Wells had the shotgun and could keep Frankel out of the kitchen. But Frankel had an open shot at the hallway, so he could keep Wells from coming inside. A standoff.

They had to take him down while they knew where he was, before he disappeared again. And Salome saw how.

"We can pin him. You stay, keep shooting, make him think you're coming down the hall. I go through the window in there" — she nodded at Witwans's room — "come around the side of the house. The alley's not even ten meters. He won't have a chance. I'll blow his head off." And once Wells was dead, she and Frankel could grab Witwans and shoot their way out against whoever was outside without worrying that Wells was behind them.

"What if he turns that way?"

"Even better. He'll run right into me."

"Unless he figures out what you're doing and starts shooting around the corner. Then you'll be the one who's trapped."

Five seconds to get through the window, five to get down the alley. Ten in all. "Ten seconds," Salome said. "Keep him busy back there that long."

"Let me do it —"

She shook her head. She would kill Wells. No one else.

She fired twice down the hallway toward the kitchen. She pushed past Frankel into the bedroom where Witwans huddled in a corner, his hands over his ears, a seventy-five-year-old child.

"Please," Witwans yelled in English.

"Please."

She ignored him. A siren sounded somewhere in the distance. Salome pushed up the window, twisted her body into the alley. Ten seconds.

Wells heard Salome and Frankel in the hallway, a low conversation in Hebrew. Making a plan. He wondered if he should try to limp out the alley, but he couldn't possibly move silently or quickly enough. He was furious with himself, with his body for its betrayal. Would this be where the trip ended for him, boxed in behind this ugly yellow house?

He had come too far. Witwans was too close. He needed one more move. One more.

From inside the house Witwans yelled "Please" twice in English. Like Salome was planning to shoot him. But why would she?

Amos shot three times and Wells chanced a peek around the door. Frankel had crouched at the far end of the hall. He was almost taunting Wells, daring Wells to step in with the shotgun and try for him. Wells knew he wouldn't have a chance even on two good legs. He would have to expose himself for a decent shot. As soon as he moved, Frankel would light him up.

But where was Salome?

Frankel raised his pistol, fired twice more —

And everything clicked. The conversation. Why Witwans had yelled. Wells had used misdirection against Salome. Now she was doing the same to him. She was coming down the alley while he focused on the doorway.

He couldn't stay on the wall. She would use the corner for cover and he had no defense. And he couldn't go for the door. Frankel was waiting. To survive, he needed to give himself an angle to shoot her as she reached the corner.

With his foot wrecked, he had only one play.

He put his weight on his left heel, ignored the screaming in his foot, took one big stride with his right leg toward the rear right corner of the backyard. He planted on his right foot and spun right ninety degrees while his momentum still carried him forward. He pulled up the shotgun just as Salome reached the corner —

She took her last step down the alley, ready to flank him. She wasn't going to shoot him right away, she wanted him to know what she'd done, how she'd beaten him —

Then she saw him moving, he wasn't against the wall by the door like she expected, or coming flush around the corner of the house, instead he was lunging for the back corner of the yard, spinning toward her, she needed a moment to understand why, he wanted the *angle,* he was raising a shotgun to her —

And she swung the pistol around, knowing she was too late, no time to speak, to curse or beg, she screamed a half-note for her death to come —

Her chest exploded, but she felt no pain, and for a moment she thought he might have missed. But then, why was she lying on her back looking at the concrete walls and the clouded sky? Everyone was wrong about dying, the easiest thing in the world. She didn't even have to move, didn't fly anywhere, it was the other way, the world and all the sky raced away from her, faster and faster until a single point of light was left at the end of a million-mile tunnel, the tiniest pinprick —

With just one good leg Wells couldn't handle the Remington's recoil. It knocked him back and down and the shotgun came out of his hands. He looked up at the doorway to the kitchen and saw Frankel running toward him, raising his pistol, and Wells scrabbled for his own pistol, but he couldn't find it, he had tucked it in his waist, but the fall must have knocked it out —

And the shots came from the house, one-two-three —

But it was *Frankel* whose mouth opened in surprise, Frankel whose body arched forward and windmilled down —

Duto.

Wells forced himself to his feet, hobbled toward the corner of the house. The pain was intense, but if he kept the weight on the heel he could move. Salome was dead, a baseball-size hole in the center of her chest, her eyes open in death. Another second and she would have had him. Wells had never killed a woman before. Funny. And funny that he couldn't think of a better word, a more powerful word for his feelings. But it wasn't just his weapons that were low on ammunition. Wells was as exhausted as he had ever been. He supposed he ought to close her eyes, but he couldn't imagine touching her. He left her on her back staring at nothing as Duto appeared in the back door, his mouth open wide. *Grinning.*

"Thank you? Huh? Maestro?"

Wells wanted to shoot him right there, this

man who had just saved his life. Six weeks before, Duto had asked Wells to meet a man in Guatemala City. All this madness had started then. Wells hadn't wanted to go, but he'd owed Duto a favor, and he'd hated the idea of being in Duto's debt.

So what did he owe Duto *now*?

A second siren joined the first. The question would have to wait. "Thank you."

"The pleasure's mine. What happened to your leg?"

"Tell you later."

They found Witwans on the living room couch, staring at the television. His face was flushed, his cheeks swollen, his eyes wide and watery.

"You know why we're here, Rand?"

His head bobbed *yes* over his slumped shoulders. "Please don't hurt me. Please." Thinking about himself to the end. Nothing about anyone else in the house. Hard to believe that this pathetic specimen was their only chance to stop a war. But they didn't need him to be a hero. They just needed him to tell the truth about what he'd done to the President. Looking at him, Wells knew he would.

Rand Witwans didn't have the strength to lie.

"Lucky man," Duto said to Wells. "Going to the White House."

Without waiting for Witwans to answer, they pulled him off the couch to begin his trip.

EPILOGUE: ONE HOUR . . .

Donna Green trudged down the West Wing corridor that led to the Oval Office. The first fighters were about to take off from Incirlik. She ought to be running. But every step came harder than the one before.

What she wanted, more than anything, was to turn the other way. Walk to the Farragut West Metro stop, three blocks away at 17th and I. Step to the edge of the platform. She might have to wait a few minutes. But soon enough a train would come. And before it reached her, she would step off.

She wasn't a suicidal type. She'd never even considered the act before. But anything at all, even nothing, had to be better than the conversation she was about to have. She remembered the stupid threat Duto had made in the parking lot, *Bend you over so hard you won't sit for a month,* and how tonight on the tarmac at Dulles, Duto hadn't bothered to hide his smile as Witwans choked out the truth.

Suddenly, she couldn't move, not forward or back.

Elizabeth Hoyt, the President's chief speechwriter, strode past, nearly knocking her down. "Sorry, Donna."

"How's the speech?" *Might want to start a rewrite.*

"Not bad. Our brave troops. Protecting the homeland. Et cetera. I gotta —"

"Go, go."

Our brave troops. Tens of thousands of men and women were about to risk their lives for a lie she should have uncovered. Cowardice now would only compound her failure.

Too soon and too late, she came to the outer office.

"I need to see him."

"Liz just went in — he's working on his speech —"

"Now."

"Tell me you're joking," the President said three minutes later.

"I'm sorry, sir."

"Fuck you, Donna. *Fuck you.*"

He had never spoken that way to her before.

"You're sure?"

631

She squeezed her hands tight, made herself stay steady. "He's a mess, Witwans, an alcoholic, but not a liar. He showed me the bank transfers. We can trace that money. And I talked to Rudin — the Mossad guy — and he confirms that Witwans is the one who delivered the stuff to Israel."

What she didn't say, what she couldn't make herself say, was: *And it makes sense. It answers a lot of questions that we should have asked but didn't, because we were so sure that the uranium was from a government.*

The President spewed a stream of curses, picked up the five-page speech on his desk, tore it in half. He tore the halves in half again, balled up a piece as if to throw it across the room. Then put it down.

"Okay. Tantrum over. I'm asking for real, any way we go ahead?"

She didn't want him to rip her again, but the question had only one answer.

"No, sir. Even forgetting about morality, Duto destroys us."

"Then let's solve that problem first." The President reached for his phone. "I need Belk." The Secretary of Defense. "Roger. Call it off." A pause. "No. I am not. Call it off. We are not invading Iran —

"Ask me again if I'm joking, I'll fire you. Nothing's happened we can't undo, right?"

He listened.

"Then keep it that way. I promise I'll tell you why later, but for now just land the drones, unscramble the jets, whatever you do when you change your mind about a war. *Now now now.* Am I clear, Roger?"

He slammed down the phone without waiting for an answer, reached into his desk for the Zippo and the pack of Marlboro Lights she knew were inside. He lit up, offered her the pack. She shook her head.

"You just destroyed my presidency, Donna. My reputation for the next hundred years. You should at least join me in a cancer stick."

They smoked in silence, the President puffing viciously.

"That was the easy part," he said. "The hard part is, how do we explain?"

"The truth —"

"They will *impeach* me, Donna. It's not just that we got suckered. It's who did it. What did Duto say he wanted, Donna?"

"Nothing specific. He said he knew you would do the right thing."

"That's funny."

"Isn't it."

"He say he was going public?"

"He said it would depend. I didn't push. I

was mainly worried about getting back here."

The President stubbed out his cigarette, lit another.

"He goes public, there's nothing we can do. Let's assume he's keeping his mouth shut. Maybe he thinks I can help him get —" He wagged the cigarette around the room. "Seems to me my only play is to make it look like I blinked at the last minute. Lost faith in the lightfoot strategy."

"So we pack up the Marines and the Rangers and the Airborne?"

"Soon. For now. We leave them all, but announce a new deadline, a nice long one, six months. Everyone will know what that means. Congress will pummel me, the media. Say I got scared. But it's better than the truth. In a day or two, we start to leak concerns about the evidence. And in a week, you go to Tehran and you lick their boots and tell them we don't want a war —"

"What about the planes?"

"*We* started this, Donna. Two weeks ago. We bombed their capital with no warning, and I don't care if it was just the airport. You tell them we view the planes as a stand-alone act of terror and we will investigate that way. You make sure they understand that means we aren't invading them. In a month or so, I fire Hebley and all his boys, they don't resign, I fire them. We buy time, we pull back, and in a couple more months this becomes the war that wasn't."

The consequences would be devastating. The Iranians would be equal parts furious and triumphant. They wouldn't understand why the United States had picked a fight with them. But they would know that they'd won. They'd believe they had carte blanche all over the Middle East.

"What if we tell the truth, the real truth, the whole story, blame Duberman?"

The President shook his head.

"No. First of all we don't even have it yet. Second, at best I look like a dupe instead of a co-conspirator. Get impeached anyway. Third, it means admitting our intel on Iran is so terrible that we fell for this. And last, you want me to blame a Jewish billionaire for trying to start a war. The world already doesn't like Jews much. This takes it to Elders of Zion territory." The President paused. "I promise. Duberman will pay. The highest penalty. But not now. When the time is right."

If there was a better answer, she couldn't see it.

His phone rang.

He picked it up, listened briefly. "Thank

you, Roger. I'm sure you must have questions. We'll talk later." He hung up, pointed at the door. Like she was a secretary. "Go get Liz. Quickest speech ever written."

At the door, she stopped. "Who are we telling about this? The truth, I mean?"

"Only Hebley and Carcetti for now. By the way, Donna. I'll need a resignation letter from you."

We all fell for it. Not just me. And ten days ago, when I tried to warn you, you shooed me off.

Not fair.

But *not fair* hardly mattered at this moment. "What about my trip to Tehran?"

"Postdate it three months. Maybe I'll change my mind."

He smiled his liar's smile. She'd seen him use it on other people in this room. Never her. Didn't he know that she knew? If he did, he didn't care.

"Of course, sir."

"Thanks, Donna."

Wells and Duto sat in the library of Duto's house in Arlington, watching CNN on mute. It was past midnight now and the countdown clock was counting *up*. They'd have to fix that somehow.

Wells didn't even know why he had come

here. Probably because he had nowhere else to be. Shafer was in jail until the morning, and Wells didn't exactly have a lot of friends in Washington. Or anywhere else. For a moment, he'd considered calling Exley — *hey, babe, remember me?* — but reason had prevailed.

Duto's house was brick and big. New and built to look old. Full of dark wood and brown leather. A single silver-framed photo of him with two late-twenty-something men who shared his heavy features sat on a bookcase beside the television. The picture looked to have been taken at a wedding. All three men wore tuxedos. Duto offered a politician's grin. The younger men were hardly smiling.

"Those your sons?" Wells realized how little he knew about Duto's family.

"Yeah."

"You're divorced?"

"Long ago. My first posting was Mexico, she didn't mind that. But then they sent me to Nigeria and she said no. She kept the boys. I didn't argue."

Duto reached for the box of cigars on the table beside him and began the slow clubby ritual of lighting one, examining the band and putting the wrapper to his nose, cutting the cap and sparking a long wooden match, and finally touching flame to the cigar's tip while spinning and puffing it. Wells suspected Duto had put more thought into lighting the cigar than into his divorce.

"You good with them?"

"Nothing like you and Evan." Duto smirked. He set aside the cigar, went for the whiskey bottle he'd brought out from the kitchen. "High West. All these small batches now."

"We ought to send Jacob a case for his help." The South African had texted them with the news of his narrow escape.

"Please. Guy had the time of his life," Duto poured himself a slug. "Try some?"

Wells didn't answer.

"Back to being a good Muslim this month, John."

"Maybe I just don't want to end up like Witwans." Who was sleeping upstairs. Duto had given him an Ativan.

"You know what I told Shafer three weeks ago? After Mason kidnapped you in Istanbul. He had some dumb idea about going over and saving you. I said, 'You think you can do better than the best field guy ever.' You are, too. Man. Cutting Gideon's Achilles. Where did you come up with that?"

Duto sipped his whiskey. Wells waited. A *but* was coming, he was sure.

"But you want it both ways. Do it and feel bad about it. Like this boy of yours, trying to build a relationship with him, you can't see that all he wants is for you to leave him alone."

Wells grabbed Duto's cigar, stuffed it into his whiskey glass. It gave a satisfying hiss as it flamed out. "Save your advice, Vinny."

The count-up clock ticked forty-three seconds before Duto spoke again. "My mistake. I overstepped. Anyway, it's not about him. It's about you. Some part of you feels you have to apologize for what you do out there."

"Conscience, you mean."

"We stopped a *war* today. You want it to be clean, John? It's impossible. You don't stop beating yourself up, you'll crack for real. Or that conscience of yours will kick in at the wrong time. Either way, you get yourself killed."

"And you care because?"

Duto poured himself a new glass of whiskey.

"You'd be tough to replace."

"The cemeteries are full of indispensable men, Vinny."

"Not ones who owe me favors."

Wells had to laugh.

"How psychopaths give pep talks."

"Then retire, John. That chick cop in New Hampshire will take you back."

"And who would run your errands?"

"Exactly. You are who you are. Accept it." Duto sipped his glass. "At least admit the world would be a better place without Duberman. And him, he's not a Saudi royal, doesn't have a whole country protecting him. It'll take some doing, but he's gettable."

"I'll think about it."

"You do that."

They sat awhile more.

"Can I ask you something?" Wells said. "Ever been in love?"

Duto's silence told Wells all he needed.

"If I'm honest with myself, I don't think so," Duto said eventually. "I thought I loved Laura for a while, but I look back, it was just that we screwed pretty good and I wanted to get married. Now you're going to tell me that's what all this is about for me, power, filling a void, blah blah blah. Let me tell you, John. Maybe. But maybe I want it because I know I'll use it *right*. Maybe I love this country, the idea of it."

"Maybe you just love the idea of being President."

"And what do you love, John?"

Now Wells had nothing to say. Exley?

Anne? He'd left them both easily enough. His son? He would die to protect Evan. But he hadn't raised the boy, and Evan didn't even consider Wells his father.

CNN spared him from having to answer. The words *Breaking News: President About to Speak* appeared in massive letters. Duto turned up the sound just as the feed switched to the Oval Office, the President at his desk.

"I know what I am about to say will surprise you —"

ACKNOWLEDGMENTS

Some of the usual suspects this year, and some new ones. Neil Nyren and Ivan Held are the captain and first officer of the S.S. *John Wells* (I'll let them sort out who's who), overseeing Putnam's crack publicity, marketing, and sales teams. One word: airports. Bob Barnett and Deneen Howell keep 'em all honest. Everyone needs at least one tough outside first reader, and Deirdre Silver is mine. And thanks to Mike Whitty. He couldn't save Flight 49, but he did make sure its details were right.

A big group hug for Jackie and Lucy.

This year the emails and comments came faster than ever, but I — barely — kept my promise to read and respond to all of them. (Including the note from a guy named, wait for it, John Wells. He said he had no problems identifying with my characters. Best reader email ever.) Anyway, keep on writing, and I'll keep on writing back. If you'd like more frequent updates, follow me at facebook.com/alexberensonauthor or twitter .com/alexberenson.

That's all I got. Until next year, anyway . . .

ABOUT THE AUTHOR

As a reporter for the *New York Times*, **Alex Berenson** covered topics ranging from the occupation of Iraq to the crimes of Bernie Madoff. His eight previous John Wells novels include Edgar Award-winner *The Faithful Spy*, and most recently, *The Night Ranger* and *The Counterfeit Agent*. he lives with his family in Garrison, New York.

The employees of Thorndike Press hope
you have enjoyed this Large Print book. All
of our Thorndike, Wheeler, and Kennebec
Large Print titles are designed for easy reading, and all our books are made to last.
Other Thorndike Press Large Print books
are available at your library, through
selected bookstores, or directly from us.

For information about titles, please call:
(800) 223-1244

or visit our Web site at:
http://gale.cengage.com/thorndike

To share your comments, please write:
Publisher
Thorndike Press
10 Water St., Suite 310
Waterville, ME 04901